POLICING THE PLAINS

MOUNTED POLICE ROUNDING UP HORSE THIEVES.

*From painting by C. W. Russell, Montana.
Courtesy of the Osborne Coy., Toronto.*

R. G. MacBeth
Author of
"The Romance of Western Canada."

POLICING THE PLAINS

BEING THE REAL-LIFE RECORD
OF THE FAMOUS NORTH-WEST
MOUNTED POLICE

WITH ILLUSTRATIONS

Copyright © 2007 BiblioBazaar
All rights reserved

Original copyright: 1921

POLICING THE PLAINS

CONTENTS

I	A GREAT TRADITION	11
II	ENTER THE MOUNTED POLICE	29
III	MOBILIZING	38
IV	THE AMAZING MARCH	51
V	BUSINESS IN THE LAND OF INDIANS	61
VI	HANDLING AMERICAN INDIANS	80
VII	THE IRON HORSES	92
VIII	RIEL AGAIN	103
IX	RECONSTRUCTION	122
X	CHANGING SCENERY	136
XI	IN THE GOLD COUNTRY	147
XII	STIRRING DAYS ABROAD AND AT HOME	166
XIII	MODESTY AND EFFECTIVENESS	195
XIV	ON LAND AND SEA	220
XV	GLORY AND TRAGEDY IN THE NORTH	240
XVI	STRIKING INCIDENTS	250
XVII	THE GREAT WAR PERIOD	264
XVIII	GREAT TRADITIONS UPHELD	277

LIST OF ILLUSTRATIONS

Mounted Police Rounding Up Horse Thieves 2
Sir John A. Macdonald 20
Hon. Alexander Mackenzie 20
Hudson Bay: R.N.W.M. Police with Dogs 21
Major-General Sir A. C. Macdonnell, K.C.B., C.M.G., D.S.O. 36
Major-General Sir Samuel B. Steele, K.C.B., etc. 36
Superintendent A. H. Griesbach 37
Inspector J. M. Walsh 37
Commissioner A. G. Irvine 53
Commissioner George A. French 53
Commissioner James F. Macleod 54
Commissioner Lawrence W. Herchmer 54
Sitting Bull 68
Colonel James Walker 69
Colonel T. A. Wroughton 109
Lieut.-Col. Aylesworth Bowen Perry, C.M.G. 110
Colonel Cortlandt Starnes 111
R.N.W.M. Police Wood Camp, Churchill River 112
Indian Tepee 125
Dog-Train 125
Yukon Rush: Summit, Chilcoot Pass 139
Group of Indian Children on Prairie 140
Chilcoot Pass: R.N.W.M. Police and Custom House 154
Klondyke Rush: Squaw Rapids, between Canyon and
    White Horse Rapids, 1898 154
Supt. Constantine in Winter Uniform on the Yukon 168
Piegan Indians at Sun-Dance 169
Rev. R. G. Macbeth, M.A. 183

Group, R.N.W.M. Police, Tagish Post, Yukon 183
Fort Selkirk, Yukon 198
Esquimaux Family 198
Coronation Contingent, London, 1911 212
Indians Receiving Treaty Payment on Prairie 213
Fort Fitzgerald, Athabasca 213
Ice-bound Government Schooner 214
Herschell Island, Yukon Territory 227
Esquimaux Visiting R.N.W.M. Police Tent 227
Barracks at Fort Fitzgerald, Great Slave River 228
R.N.W.M. Police Shelter, Great Slave Lake 228
Cabin of Rev. Fathers Le Roux and Rouvier 229
R.N.W.M. Police Barracks, Churchill, Hudson Bay 242
Police with Dogs and Equipment on Split Lake, N.W.T. 242
Inspector Fitzgerald 256
Supt. Charles Constantine 256
Inspector La Nauze 257

* * * * *

CHAPTER I

A GREAT TRADITION

A few years ago I was away north of Edmonton on the trail of Alexander Mackenzie, fur trader and explorer, who a century and a quarter before had made the amazing journey from the prairies over the mountains to the Pacific Coast. We looked with something like awe and wonder at the site of the old fort near the famous Peace River Crossing, from which, after wintering there in 1792, he had started out on that unprecedented expedition, and we followed up the majestic Peace to Fort Dunvegan, past whose present location Mackenzie had gone his adventurous way. And during our trip we came across a little frontier encampment building itself into a primitive wooden town in view of the advent of a railway that was heading that way. It was a characteristic outfit with lax ideas in regard to laws which touched upon personal desires as to gambling, strong drink, Sunday trading and the rest. These men were out to make money as their type has been on most of the frontiers of civilization, and the unwary traveller or the lonely settler who ventured unduly was promptly fleeced of his possessions and turned out amidst a good deal of revelry in the hours of night. And then one day there rode into that shack-town a young athlete in a uniform of scarlet and gold, the rough-rider hat, the tunic of red, the wide gold stripe to the top of the riding boots and the shining spurs. He rode in alone from the nearest post some 60 miles away and, when he dismounted, threw off the heavy saddle and picketed his horse, a sudden air of orderliness settled on the locality. The young man, going around with that characteristic cavalry swing, issued a few warnings, tacked up a notice or two and then saddling his rested steed rode away at a canter over the plain. But the air of orderliness remained in that region after the horseman had disappeared over the horizon just as if he were still present. This was puzzling to a newcomer who was along, and he asked me what manner of man this young rider was that he was received with such deference and that his orders, so quietly given, were so instantly and so continuously obeyed.

The answer was made out of a life-long acquaintance with the history and the real life of Western Canada: "Well, it is not the young constable himself that counts so mightily, though he is a likely looking fellow enough who could be cool anywhere and who could give ample evidence of possessing those muscles of steel which count in a hand-to-hand encounter. But you see he is one of that widely known body of men called the Royal North-West Mounted Police. They have patrolled and guarded and guided this whole North-West Country for the last forty years and more. During that period they have built up a great tradition which rests on a solid foundation of achievement. Their reputation for courage is unchallenged, their record for giving every man of whatever race or colour a square deal is unique, their inflexible determination to see that law is enforced is well known and their refusal to count the odds against them when duty is to be done has been absolutely proven again and again. All these elements and others have created the Mounted Police tradition to such an extent that the one constable you saw is looked on as the embodiment of the Empire which plays no favourites but which at the same time will stand no nonsense from anyone. And perhaps most wonderful of all is that part of their record which shows that they have done all this and more without any violence or repression, except as a last resort. They were always more ready and anxious to save human life than to destroy it."

"All that is very interesting," said my friend; "I would like to hear more about these men, and would be glad if you would tell me something of their history." And out there under the open sky of the North Country, with the stars sparkling above us and the Aurora Borealis dancing and swishing over our heads in a wonderful panorama of colour and movement, we talked long into the night about the men in scarlet and gold. Their whole story could not be told in a night, but the eager interest of the listener and the creation of a new pride in things Canadian in his heart, led me to resolve that the history he was seeking should some day be published to the world. Many requests for the story have come since that night in the Peace River country, and now that one period of Police history is closing through the extension of the jurisdiction of the Force over the whole Dominion, East as well as West, accompanied by the word "Canadian" in their title instead of "North West," the time seems opportune for a real-life record of what these men throughout the years have meant to Canada. Such a record should cause every Royal Canadian Mounted Police recruit to realize that he has to be worthy of the tradition built up by the achievements of nearly half a century through valorous men, many of whom have now passed over the Great Divide. It will deepen in all men of sincerity a respect for authority in a restless age. And it will bring into the light facts hitherto unrevealed that will fill all men with pride in their country.

I know that the men of the Mounted Police have been averse to saying anything about themselves. They have the usual British characteristic of reticence intensified. But though I have been brigaded with them on active service, I have not been a member of the corps, and hence do not feel bound by their policy of silence. Let the plain truth, which is always stranger than fiction, be told about these gallant riders as an inspiration to young Canadians and to men of the blood everywhere. With this purpose in view I am now keeping the resolution made that night in the North, as I am in this book extending and telling to a larger audience the story then unfolded to an individual. My humble hope is that the larger audience may be equally interested.

The Wide Westland

In the year of Grace 1920, we, in the West, celebrated with enthusiasm the birthday anniversary of the Hudson's Bay Company, which has attained to the ripe old age of 250 years. Yet the eye of this ancient organization is not dimmed by time, nor does its power show signs of impairment. As it is around this old and honourable commercial and colonizing concern that the early history of Western Canada principally revolves, a few paragraphs on this subject seem to be necessary as we begin our story. We must have proper historical setting for the entrance of our famous police force on the stage of Western Canadian history.

About the end of the first decade of the seventeenth century, Henry Hudson, the intrepid navigator who was looking for a North-West Passage by water through the North-American Continent to the Western Sea, discovered the great Bay which bears his name to this day. Marooned by a mutinous crew, he paid for the discovery with his life, after the manner of many pathfinders, but he had unlocked a new Empire for the human family. Then for years there was silence around the Bay which Hudson had opened at such great cost to himself.

Away in the East, following the early explorations along the banks of the St. Lawrence in old Canada, adventurous hunters and trappers began to push their way westward and northward, past the Great Lakes to the prairie land beyond. This was about the middle of the seventeenth century, and at that period the New World was full of opportunity for the daring who saw visions beyond the sky-line.

And so it came to pass about half a century after Hudson's time that two French adventurers, Radisson and Groseilliers, reaching out from the St. Lawrence to the wide north-west, came into contact with Indian tribes who told about the great bay to the north and the vast riches of the region in furs and skins. These adventurers went to see for themselves and they found that the half had not been told. And because, despite many theories, no one has ever discovered a way to carry on a big enterprise without capital, these hardy pioneers returned to the East and endeavoured to organize a trading company from amongst their French compatriots. But the enthusiasm of the men who had seen could not awaken response in the men who had not seen. The faculty of faith was not very highly developed in these French habitants by the St. Lawrence. But the zeal of Radisson and Groseilliers was unquenchable. They tried Boston in vain, and then betook themselves to France, where they were not any more successful, except that they got a letter of introduction to some men of leading in England. The Englishman generally loves a sporting chance for exploration and discovery, and so Prince Rupert, more or less a soldier of fortune who had lent his name and his sword to almost anything that offered a possibility of adventure or substance, took up the matter of the fur trade and was instrumental in sending out vessels with Radisson and Groseilliers to prospect on the shores of Hudson Bay. Once again the men who went and saw came back, not only with tales of an El Dorado in fur, but with the furs themselves, and the dashing Prince forthwith secured from the easy-going Charles II a monopolistic charter to trade and generally to control the whole vast region drained by rivers that emptied into Hudson Bay. The territory thus granted, with more added later by licences, extended generally speaking from the Great Lakes to the Pacific and from mid-continent to the North Pole. It was as large as half a dozen European Kingdoms and has become one of the greatest adjuncts of the British Empire, but King Charles did not know nor care much more about it than the French king who later on gave up Canada with a light heart, saying it was only "a few hundred acres of snow."

It is not our duty in this book to follow the fortunes of "the Governor and Company of the Adventurers of England trading into Hudson Bay" as the Royal Charter described this little band of less than a score of men to whom had been handed over the control of half a continent. It is enough to say that the Hudson's Bay Company, as the popular habit of shortening long titles rendered it, held this vast region for two whole centuries. During that time the immense resources of the country tempted others to disregard the monopolistic provisions of the Royal Charter and to venture in upon forbidden ground. Companies such as the North-West Fur Company, formed by the Scottish merchants of Montreal, rushed to secure part of the rich harvest in trade that was being reaped by the English Company, whose employees, it may be said, were largely the hardy Scots from the Highlands and Islands. But the leaders of the Hudson's Bay Company, "stabbed broad awake" by this opposition and strengthened by the trustworthiness and endurance of their employees, held their ground and extended their operations till they by degrees absorbed all opponents and became in 1821 monarchs of all they surveyed.

Meanwhile in the Old Land many things of world-wide interest and influence had been transpiring. The years around the opening of the nineteenth century were made stormy by the Napoleonic effort to subjugate Europe and while their men of military age were away fighting for the liberty of Europe against "the little giant of Corsica," certain areas in the north of Scotland were "cleared" of their inhabitants by heartless landlords who felt that sheep were more profitable for the owner of estates than human tenants. To these evicted crofters in the Highlands came that noble altruist and philanthropic colonizer, the Earl of Selkirk, who, having obtained from the Hudson's Bay Company an immense district principally in what is now Manitoba, offered the outcasts of a tyrannous land system homes in the great free spaces of Rupert's Land, as the Hudson Bay territory was called. The offer was accepted thankfully, and in the years from 1812 to 1815 these Selkirk colonists came to the Red River of the North.

It is not part of this story to follow the fortunes of these famous colonists of whom I have written more particularly in *The Romance of Western Canada*. They encountered unaccustomed climatic obstacles, they were persecuted and hunted by the fur-trading opponents of their benefactor, they were tried by the disasters of floods and by plagues of devouring locusts, but with the dogged and stern determination of their race and creed they held on and demonstrated to the world the possibilities of a country which is now the granary of the Empire.

And the world got to hearing of this Arcadian Colony of Scots in the new North-West. So when the old Provinces of the East were brought together under the name of the Dominion of Canada in 1867, the men of light and leading at Ottawa lost no time in looking westward to secure the vast western domain for the new Confederation. Despite the difficulty of travel, settlers had already begun to percolate from Eastern Canada through the States or the wilderness spaces west of the Great Lakes, into the Red River country made famous by the Selkirk Colony. And it had been becoming more and more apparent to the Hudson's Bay Company itself as well as to others that the great fur-trading and mercantile organization could no longer adequately administer an area which was soon to overflow with the human sea of an incoming population. For many years previous to Confederation the Hudson's Bay monopoly in trade had been more or less of a figment of the imagination and no one knew that better than the Company itself. It still retained its monopoly nominally, but it made very little effort to restrain the half-breed and other "free traders" who opened up stores and bartered for furs with the Indians. In any case in one form or other all the trade of the country practically came, in the last analysis, through the Hudson's Bay Company, who controlled the money market by having their own bills in circulation. But the wise old Company saw what was coming and began to get ready to let go its monopolistic fur-trading charter and adjust itself to the new conditions.

Hence it was not a difficult matter to persuade the Company to give up its charter for a consideration. My father, who was a member of the Council of Assiniboia, a magistrate, and a close personal friend of Governor McTavish, who was in charge at Fort Garry on the Red River where settlement had begun, always used to say that the Hudson's Bay Company was glad to find a reasonable way of getting the responsibility for the government of the growing country off its hands.

Accordingly, when the Canadian Government deemed the time was ripe, two members of that Government, the Hon. Sir George E. Cartier and the Hon. William McDougall, were sent to London to negotiate with the Imperial authorities for the transfer of the North-West to Canada. In view of the attitude taken by the Hudson's Bay Company, as stated above, the matter was not difficult to arrange. And after a brief discussion in London, the famous old fur-trading organization, which had held charter rights since the days of Charles II, relinquished those rights to the Imperial Government for £300,000 sterling, certain reservations around their trading posts, along with one-twentieth of the land in the fertile belt. Then, as previously understood, the Imperial Government was to transfer the vast North-West to Canada, which in turn undertook to respect and conserve the rights of the people in the area thus added to the Dominion. This arrangement was concluded in the spring of 1869, and it was then expected that the purchase money would be paid on the 1st of October following, and that probably on the 1st of December the Queen's Proclamation would issue, setting forth these facts and fixing the date of the actual transfer to Canada.

So far all was well. The ideas leading up to the acquisition of this great domain were in every sense statesmanlike, and, if carefully carried out, were calculated to be of the greatest benefit to the people in the new territory and the Dominion as well. We should pay unstinted tribute to the men whose ideals were for an ever-widening horizon, and who felt that "no pent-up Utica should confine the powers" of the young nation just beginning to stretch out and exercise its potentially giant limbs. Once the older Provinces in the East were brought into Confederation it was wise to look forward to a Canada stretching from ocean to ocean, and to take the necessary legal steps to secure the broad acres of the West as part of the Dominion. But just when everything seemed to be going well a cog in the diplomatic equipment of the Canadian Government power-house slipped and taking advantage of the occasion, one Louis Riel, the son of the old hot-headed agitator on the Red River, threw a wrench into the machinery.

The Canadian authorities who wisely carried through the negotiations with the Hudson's Bay Company and the Imperial Government seem to have blundered by overlooking the fact that the new territory had within its borders some 10,000 people, apart from the Indians, who ought to have been informed in some official way of the bargain that was being made, and of the steps that were being taken to conserve the rights and privileges of these early settlers.

It is true that rumours of the transaction reached the Red River country through unauthoritative sources, but the main result was to produce a feeling of uneasiness amongst the people there. And especially was this the case when the rumours were given point by overt acts. Even before the transfer of the country had been legally completed men were sent out from the East to open roads from the Lakes into the settlements. Surveying parties entered the new territory and went hither and thither, driving their stakes and erecting their mounds, to the bewilderment of the people, and to cap all the indiscretions, a Governor, the Hon. William McDougall, was dispatched from Ottawa to the Red River before the Hudson's Bay regime was formally superseded and before a Queen's Proclamation, which would have been instantly recognized by all classes in the community, was issued.

The Selkirk Settlers and other people of that class, however perplexed at the procedure, had the utmost confidence that the Canadian authorities would ultimately do substantial justice to all, and hence they awaited patiently though somewhat anxiously the developments of time. But the French half-breeds, more fiery and more easily excited, more turbulent of spirit and warlike in disposition, accustomed to more or less fighting on the plains, and withal, as a class, less well informed than their white brethren, were not content to wait. They felt that the course being followed by the Canadian authorities might lead to the loss of their rights, and so they rose in a revolt, that while accomplishing some of the objects that could have been reached by constitutional means, left its red stream across that early page of our history. But in the midst of all our statements let it be remembered, in mitigation of the attitude of the Canadian authorities, that communication between Ottawa and the West at that period was very difficult. There were no railways nor telegraphs and the mails were few and far apart. Though, on the other hand, that condition of things should have made all parties more tolerant and cautious.

Strange that the two Louis Riels, father and son, should lead in agitations that were somewhat contradictory. The elder Riel was a famous antagonist of the Hudson's Bay Company regime with its apparent or alleged monopoly in trade, and the younger Riel, while no lover of the Company, opposed the Canadian Government which was to replace it. The truth seems that they were both temperamentally against authority and that they were both afflicted with a megalomania which led each to imagine that he was some great one.

SIR JOHN A. MACDONALD.
Who, while Premier, founded the Mounted Police.
(Photo, Pittaway Studios, Ottawa.)

HON. ALEXANDER MACKENZIE.
Who, while Premier, organized the Mounted Police.
(Photo, Pittaway Studios, Ottawa.)

HUDSON BAY: R.N.W.M. POLICE WITH DOGS.

The younger Riel had the "bad eminence" of leading two rebellions in Western history before winding up his tragic career on the scaffold at Regina. He it was who opposed the entrance of Governor McDougall to the Red River in 1869. He it was who, after having stopped the Governor, rode down and captured Fort Garry in which he and his men fared sumptuously all that winter out of the Hudson's Bay Company store. He it was who imprisoned those who opposed him and ordered the shooting of Thomas Scott, a young Canadian prisoner—an act which estranged from the rebel chief the sympathy of many who believed that he had some grounds for protest against the incoming of authority without any guarantee of the settler's rights.

But the reign of the rebel was not long. The Imperial authorities who have never forgotten the teaching of history in the loss of the American colonies, have more than once called the governments in free colonies to a sense of their duty and have followed up their advice with military backing if necessary. And both were forthcoming in this case. The hand of the good Queen Victoria is seen in the following dispatch from Earl Granville to Sir John Young, Governor-General of Canada:

> "The Queen has heard with surprise and regret that certain misguided persons have banded together to oppose by force the entry of our future Lieutenant-Governor into our territory in Red River. Her Majesty does not distrust the loyalty of her subjects in that settlement, and can only ascribe to misunderstanding and misrepresentation their opposition to a change planned for their advantage.
>
> "She relies on your Government to use every effort to explain whatever misunderstanding may have arisen— to ascertain the wants and conciliate the goodwill of the people of Red River Settlement. But in the meantime she authorizes you to signify to them the sorrow and displeasure with which she views the unreasonable and lawless proceedings which have taken place, and her expectation that if any parties have desires to express or complaints to make respecting their conditions and prospects, they will address themselves to the Governor-General of Canada.
>
> "The Queen expects from her representative that as he will be always ready to receive well-founded grievances, so will he exercise all the power and authority she entrusted to him in support of order and the suppression of unlawful disturbances."

The closing paragraph of this fine message indicates the traditional British Empire position, that though grievances will be heard and remedied, there will be no quarter given to any nonsense on the part of rebels. And it was in keeping with this position that Colonel (later Field Marshal Sir Garnet) Wolseley was dispatched to the Red River country with regular troops, who arrived at their destination only to find that Riel and his forces had decamped before their arrival. Two regiments from Eastern Canada came later and remained on duty at Fort Garry for some time after the regulars under Wolseley had returned home.

The Red River country was ushered into Confederation as the Province of Manitoba, and the Hon. Adams George Archibald, of Nova Scotia, was sent out from Ottawa in 1870 as Lieutenant-Governor. He took a rough census of the country and with the resultant crude voters' list the first regular Western Legislature was soon elected and at work.

But west and north of this little Province of Manitoba, itself sparsely settled, lay an immense hinterland stretching nearly a thousand miles to the Rocky mountains and northward to the pole itself. This enormous area, then commonly called "The Saskatchewan," was unpeopled except for thousands of Indians, many groups of nomadic buffalo-hunters mostly half-breeds, a few scattered missions of various churches, and a large number of Hudson's Bay Company trading posts. Manitoba was under the oversight of a regularly constituted Government and Legislature. But out in the vast north-west hinterland it was a sort of interregnum time, in view of the fact that the Hudson's Bay Company, which had controlled the country for two centuries, had given up its charter and authority to the Dominion of Canada which had legally but not yet visibly taken possession. Or, to change the figure, the period was, governmentally speaking, a sort of "No man's land" with one party technically out of possession and the other not yet recognized by the traders or Indians as being in control. Such a situation gave a great deal of opportunity for lawlessness by warring tribes, horse-thieves, whisky peddlers, boot-leggers and all the rest of that ilk. And the proximity to the American boundary line making escape easy was an additional temptation to the lawlessly inclined. That this class did not allow the opportunity to go by unused soon became apparent to men who were upon the ground. Mr. Lawrence Clark, a noted Hudson's Bay officer, whom I remember in his later years, handsome, eager, alert and well-informed, said that both traders and Indians were learning the dangerous lesson that the Queen's orders could be disregarded with impunity.

And it is now pretty well known that our good Queen and her advisers who had been shocked by the Riel outbreak in 1869 were concerned for the good government of the vast domain that had been recently handed over by the Imperial Government to Canada. It was not the British way to allow things to get out of hand, nor to permit wards of the nation, like the Indians, to become the victims of the lawless in trade and in morality. Hence the Governor-General of Canada received for himself and his responsible advisers more than one dispatch from the Headquarters of the Empire admonishing that steps should be taken to preserve peace in the vast new domain and to give all who would immigrate thither the proper British safeguards as to life and liberty and the pursuit of their lawful avocations. And, of course, the Canadian authorities, chagrined over the Riel outbreak and having some knowledge of the immense responsibilities they had assumed by taking over the North-West, were anxious to prevent anything that would make the new country unattractive to the people who were desirous of coming with their families to settle within its borders.

As a result of all this, Governor Archibald, of Manitoba, within a few weeks after his arrival in Fort Garry, took steps to secure a report on conditions on "The Saskatchewan," outside the Province where he was the representative of the Crown. The fact that he did this so soon after assuming office and when matters in his own Province required special attention, indicates strongly the pressure that had been brought to bear upon the Canadian authorities by headquarters. And when a man was required for the special mission out over the far North-West he was there on the spot in the person of Lieutenant W. F. Butler of the 69th Regiment, afterwards famous as Sir William Butler, of South Africa. On account of his splendid powers of endurance, his great faculty for observation and his remarkable literary genius, he was a man with unique qualifications for the task—the difficult and delicate task—to which Governor Archibald called him. A person has to be sadly destitute in the religious sense to believe that Butler was on hand by accident. It is exceedingly interesting to find that another man, who afterwards became noted in South Africa, namely the bluff and valiant fighter, Redvers Buller, was in the Red River expedition with Wolseley and had been mentioned in connection with the mission to the North-West hinterland. Years afterwards in the Boer War time this same Redvers Buller, then commanding the British forces on the veld, said to Colonel Sam B. Steele, of Strathcona's Horse, who also had served under Wolseley: "I know Lord Strathcona very well: when I was at Fort Garry on the Red River Expedition he spoke to me about going out over the plains to investigate conditions, but I was recalled to my regiment and Governor Archibald sent Butler out instead, a good thing too; for he wrote a very good book on his journey which I could not have done." And this big-hearted, manly, generous reference by Buller properly indicated that he not only recognized his own limitations, but was glad to pay tribute to the literary genius who wrote that Classic *The Great Lone Land* and the noble biography of General Gordon of Khartoum.

But Butler had more than literary gifts. He had, as already stated, great powers of observation and that remarkable faculty for forecasting, which was exemplified, then, on Canadian prairies as it was later on the South African veld.

In the book *The Great Lone Land*, to which allusion has been made, Butler tells us with manly frankness that in 1869 he had come to a standstill in his career as a soldier, because he had neither the means nor influence to secure any promotion in such a piping time of peace. And so, when news of the Riel Rebellion in the far West drifted to London, Butler cabled to Canada for an opportunity to serve in the Red River Expedition. He immediately followed his cablegram, but on his arrival found himself too late for a place. However he was given a special mission to go from Toronto to Fort Garry by way of the United States in order to find out how the people of that country along the boundary looked at matters on the Red River. Butler went on to Fort Garry, passed through the rebel zone, met Wolseley and with him entered Fort Garry, which had just been evacuated by Riel. As things quieted, Butler was going to leave for the East, when Governor Archibald got hold of him, as stated, and sent him out over the West to report on conditions and make recommendations. He left Fort Garry in October, 1870, treked 900 miles to the Rocky Mountains, then wheeled northward to Edmonton and down the Saskatchewan River to Lake Winnipeg, boxing the compass so far as the great hinterland of the plains was concerned. He heard much and saw more, witnessed the smallpox scourge lashing the Indian tribes, saw the general disquiet and disorder with no one in control. The steed of the far West was riderless, the reins had been thrown away and the country was running wild. Butler's report is graphic in the extreme and has many recommendations, but the one that mainly concerns us just now is that which advises the establishment of constituted authority with sufficient force to back it up, for it was that recommendation which led to the establishment, though delayed strangely for two years more, of the famous corps known originally to history as the North-West Mounted Police.

The particular wisdom of Butler's recommendation lies in the fact that he advocated along with the civil government a material force which would be located "not at fixed points or forts." For he said that any force so located "would afford little protection outside the immediate circle of these points and would hold out no inducements to the establishment of new settlements." Wise man was Butler who saw that settlers must be secured to pour into this vast country and make it the granary of the Empire, and that a force movable enough to be readily at the call of scattered settlements would be absolutely necessary. The sequel has proven how well Butler forecasted events because settlers by the thousand soon desired to come and it was the presence of the Mounted Police that gave to these settlers the sense of security that made it possible for them to turn the vast plains into waving fields of grain and cause the wide areas of pasture land to shake under the tread of domestic herds.

And the other special point in which Butler's wisdom in recommendation comes out in regard to the force to be established is where he states that such a force should be independent of any faction or party either in church or state. His wise hint in this regard was taken and followed, and hence all through their history the Mounted Police have gone their way, caring for nothing and for nobody in their intentness on doing their duty. It is quite well known to some of us that in many places on the plains, in the mountains and away in the land of the golden Yukon, the Police were often strongly urged to relax their vigilance in the interests of some political party or some business that was financially concerned. But all such temptations fell on deaf ears, and the scarlet-coated riders, looking on intimidation and efforts at bribery with contempt, pursued the even tenor of their way and gave every man a square deal according to his deserts no matter who he was or to what colour the sun and the wind had burned his skin. Such was the force which this wise recommendation of Butler called into existence.

That such a force would have no sinecure and would have no room for "misfits or failures," Butler tells us in 1870 in that clause of his report in which he says, "As matters at present rest, the region of the Saskatchewan is without law, order or security for life or property; robbery and murder for years have gone unpunished; Indian massacres are unchecked even in the close vicinity of the Hudson's Bay Company posts and all civil and legal institutions are entirely unknown." It was high time for government control with an adequate material force to give it power.

And because I have referred to Butler's foresightedness it would be unfair to his memory to close this section without quoting the magnificent paragraph with which he ended his report in March of 1871. It reads as follows:

> "Such, sir, are the views which I have formed upon the whole question of the existing state of affairs in the Saskatchewan country. They result from the thought and experience of many long days of travel through a large portion of the region to which they have reference. If I were asked from what point of view I have looked upon this question, I would answer—From that point which sees a vast country lying, as it were, silently awaiting the approach of the immense wave of human life which rolls unceasingly from Europe to America. Far off as lie the regions of the Saskatchewan from the Atlantic seaboard, on which that wave is thrown, remote as are the fertile glades which fringe the eastern slopes of the Rocky Mountains, still that wave of human life is destined to reach those beautiful solitudes, and to convert the wild luxuriance of their now useless vegetation into all the requirements of civilized existence. And if it be matter of desire that across this immense continent, resting on the two greatest oceans of the world, a powerful nation should arise with the strength and the manhood which race and climate and tradition would assign to it—a nation which would look with no evil eye upon the old motherland from whence it sprung; a nation which, having no bitter memories to recall, would have no idle prejudices to perpetuate—then surely it is worthy of all toil of hand and brain, on the part of those who to-day rule, that this great link in the chain of such a future nationality should no longer remain undeveloped, a prey to the conflict of savage races, at once the garden and the wilderness of the central continent."

These great words were written nearly half a century ago. What has taken place in Western History within that time shows how this remarkable man "had his ear to the ground," as the Indians used to express it and that he was in effect saying, with Whittier:

"I hear the tread of nations,
　　Of Empires yet to be;
The dull low wash of waves where yet
　　Shall roll a human sea."

　　　　　* * * * *

CHAPTER II

ENTER THE MOUNTED POLICE

Great bodies are proverbially slow in their movements, and in this regard all governments seem to be great bodies. It may be that a healthy difference of opinion within a cabinet tends to cautious procedure, but that type of caution is rather trying on people whose nerves tingle for action.

The first Government of Canada under that astute and tactful statesman, John A. Macdonald, was a sort of composite organization which needed careful handling to prevent explosions, and some vast new problems such as the construction of a transcontinental railway were in that day swinging into politics. So, despite Butler's urgent report in 1871 and the rumours more or less exaggerated of intertribal Indian fights with the accompaniments of massacre and scalping-knife torture, the Government took another year to think over it, and in 1872 sent Adjutant-General P. Robertson-Ross to make a general reconnaissance and bring back further expert opinion. And Colonel Ross, after many many months of travelling, brought in a quite pronounced series of suggestions pointing out the great need for such a force as Butler had suggested, and definitely advised the placing of detachments of "mounted riflemen" all the way from Manitoba to the Rockies, and for that matter from the boundary line to the Pole.

It is interesting to note in this report of Colonel Robertson-Ross a reference to the matter of the uniform of the proposed force in the following paragraph:

> "During my inspection in the North-West, I ascertained that some prejudice existed amongst the Indians

against the colour of the uniform worn by the men of the Rifles, for many of the Indians said, 'Who are these soldiers at Red River wearing dark clothes? Our old brothers who formerly lived there (meaning H.M.S. 6th Regiment) wore red coats,' adding, 'we know that the soldiers of our great mother wear red coats and are our friends.'"

The Indians like the bright colour, but they also in this case connected it with the regular regiment that had come to the Red River to keep the peace. Referring to this same subject of uniform, Mr. Charles Mair, noted author and frontiersman, recently said: "There is a moral in colour as in other things, and the blind man who compared scarlet to the sound of a trumpet was instinctively right. It does carry with it the loud voice of law and authority so much needed in this disjointed time. It disconcerts the ill-affected and has no small bearing in other ways."

The Hon. Frank Oliver, of Edmonton, who has known the West from the early days, wrote not long ago on this point:

> "For nearly half a century throughout Canada's great plains, the red coat of the Mounted Policeman was the visible and definite assurance that right was might. A red speck on the horizon was notice to both weak and strong, honest and dishonest, that the rule of law prevailed; while experience taught white men and red that 'Law' meant even-handed justice as between man and man without fear or favour."
>
> "The red coat was evidence that wherever the wearer was, he was there with authority. In any other colour he might have escaped hostile observation. Not so when clad in red."

Following Colonel Ross' report in 1872 the Government at Ottawa was subjected to a sort of fusillade on the question from the floor of the House of Commons. Hon. Alexander MacKenzie (afterwards Premier), Hon. Dr. John Schultz (later Sir John, Governor of Manitoba, who had been imprisoned by Louis Riel and had escaped with a price on his head), an ardent Canadian, Hon. William Cunningham, a newspaper man from Winnipeg,

Hon. Donald A. Smith, a Hudson's Bay Company man (who as Lord Strathcona was to have such a large share in the making of the West) and the Hon. Letellier de St. Just were some of the members who wanted to know what the Government was contemplating in view of all the reports received. Sir John A. Macdonald, who took special pride in the police in later years, and the Hon. Joseph Howe, whose office was to look after the West, said that the Government was fully alive to the situation and would act in due time. As a matter of fact the Government, especially Sir John, had been for some time in consultation with experienced service men, notably Major (later Colonel) Arthur Henry Griesbach, who was in Ottawa for many months advising in regard to the force of which he was afterwards to become one of the earliest and most honoured members. It also emerged later that Sir John and his associates had been making some study of such famous organizations as the Irish Constabulary, and that he had set his mind on having a force that would be distinguished for hardiness in service and readiness in response to calls of duty rather than for "fuss and feathers," as he expressed it in his favourite way.

Finally, on May 3, 1873, the Premier moved for leave to introduce a bill dealing with the administration of justice and for the establishment of a police force in the North-West Territories. It was adopted by the House on May 20, and so the organization of the now famous corps was definitely on its way. An interesting fact was that this was to be a civil force in uniform, not a military organization subject to the Queen's regulations, but dependent for discipline upon the personality of the officers, the esprit de corps that would be generated and the *noblesse oblige* idea that would emerge in the course of service. And all these things actually developed as we shall see in the process of this story.

Having finally passed the Act, the legislators rested on their laurels a few months more, for it was not until September that actual enrolment of the new force began to take place. The process of enlistment was then hurried somewhat and later on some sifting was done in order to throw out any culls. But in the main the men measured up well to the demands of that most interesting and important clause in the Act, which says:

> "No person shall be appointed to the police force unless he be of sound constitution, able to ride, active and able-bodied, and between the ages of eighteen and forty years, nor unless he be able to read and write either the English or the French language."

This was sane legislation, for these men were not going out on a picnic. They were going to patrol the widest and wildest frontier in the world. And that frontier has always said in the words of Robert Service:

> "Send not your foolish and feeble; send me your strong and your sane:
> Strong for the red rage of battle; sane, for I harry them sore.
> Send me men girt for the combat, men who are grit to the core.
> Them will I gild with my treasure; them will I feed with my meat;
> But the others—the misfits, the failures—I trample them under my feet."

And in order that readers may have other testimony than that of the author on the question of the need for strong men, let me quote words written by the Hon. N. W. Rowell, who, as President of the Council and Governmental head of the force, had specially studied the history of the Police:

> "When the Canadian West first saw the scarlet jacket the prairies were in a transition stage which contained grave possibilities of danger. The old era, in which the Hudson's Bay Company and the Indians had dealt peaceably together, was breaking up, and the private trader, irresponsible and often not too scrupulous, was laying the seeds of trouble in a land where the Indians still were numerous and powerful. Tribe waged war against tribe, and formidable hosts, fresh from fighting against the American army, surged across the forty-ninth parallel."

And the words also of the frontier statesman already mentioned, the Hon. Frank Oliver, of Edmonton:

> "Ordinarily speaking no more wildly impossible undertaking was ever staged than the establishment of Canadian authority and Canadian law throughout the Canadian prairies by a handful of Mounted Police. The population consisted chiefly of warring tribes of Indians, of whom the Blackfeet Confederacy was the most important, the most warlike and the most intractable. Next to the Indians in numbers were scattered settlements of half-breeds, who lived by the chase; no less warlike although more tractable than the Indian. Then a few white and half-breed traders and missionaries; and last and best, the commencement of white settlements at Prince Albert and Edmonton. An imaginary line separated Canada from the United States for a distance of 800 miles. South of that line, strategic points were garrisoned by thousands of United States soldiers; an almost continuous condition of Indian warfare prevailed; and the white population in large measure ran free of the restraints of established authority. There had been an overflow of 'bad men' from Montana into what is now Southern Alberta and South-Western Saskatchewan, who repeated in Canada the exploits by which they had made Montana infamous. In large measure, world opinion took for granted that lawlessness must accompany pioneer conditions. Canada's Mounted Police Force was the challenge to that idea."

And as evidence of the way in which the police backed Canada's challenge nothing finer is written than the following in a letter to me some time ago from Governor Dr. R. G. Brett of Alberta, who has been on the frontiers for nearly forty years:

> "The manner in which so small a force kept down the liquor traffic, controlled the savage tribes of Indians, protected the lives and property of the settlers, affords an illustration of paternal administration that is probably without parallel in the world's history."

These are tributes from men who know. And Governor Brett goes on to commend the idea of a history of the Police when he adds:

> "Every Canadian cannot but be a better citizen after reading the history of the lives of the modest heroes, whose devotion to duty and even-handed distribution of justice have commanded the admiration of the civilized world."

From the beginning the officers of the force have been almost invariably of outstanding strength who won the respect of the men under their command by their willingness to share all the perils of the service and by being always ready to be in front of the troop when there was danger ahead. Not long ago a veteran hospital Sergeant of the Force, Dr. Braithwaite, of Edmonton, said finely, "I know of no officer in the force who would order any man to do any work at all, that the officer would not do himself. A man would not be asked to ride a refractory horse that his officer would not or could not ride. This is what has given the Force its reputation—the absolute confidence of the men in their leaders, and the complete esprit de corps that was always there."

That the general spirit of the original legislation which insisted on good physique and respectable character in the men of the force was carried out in practice, those of us who have known these men in almost all circumstances and places can testify. To illustrate, I recall in Winnipeg seeing the men who were going over to form part of the Empire's tribute on the occasion of Queen Victoria's Diamond Jubilee. After a stop-over for a couple of hours they fell in to the bugle call on the railway platform. The men looked like models for the statue of Apollo, and with the clear eye, bronzed faces and alert movement born of their clean and healthful outdoor life on the plains, they were goodly to behold. And when I remarked to Major (now Commissioner) Perry, who was in command, that it was generally looked on as rather a dangerous thing to let a body of men loose amid the temptations of a strange city, Perry replied: "That has no bearing on these men, even though there was a saloon on every corner. Every man feels that the honour and good name of the force depend on his individual conduct, and so he can be trusted." And when in London, the Mounted Police won golden opinions, not only for their splendid appearance, but for their gentlemanly bearing.

Still another general remark may be made here. It will be remembered that Butler had recommended that the force to be organized in support of constituted authority be independent of any party or faction either in Church or State. And here also Butler's advice has been borne in mind. Governments have come and gone in regular cycle of years according as they were thought worthy or otherwise of the people's support. And partisan politics have played a considerable, and not always a creditable, part in Canadian history. But the Mounted Police force has never been in the game. Mounted Policemen have always been strictly non-partisan in politics and no interference with them by politicians of any party would be tolerated for a moment. These law-enforcers have always been absolutely independent of any local or other influences except the commands of their officers in the line of duty, and to this in large measure is due the remarkable reputation of the force for giving every man a square deal, regardless of race or creed or colour. Mounted Policemen have never been respecters of persons. They treat every one alike. Referring to political parties, for instance, it is recalled that the corps was scarcely organized when Sir John Macdonald was retired by the Canadian electorate and the Hon. Alexander Mackenzie was elevated to the premiership. But this made no change in the matter of the force which from the beginning has been the servant not of any political party but of the nation. It is historically correct to say that Sir John Macdonald started the organization, but it fell to Mr. Mackenzie's lot to perfect the organization, and start it definitely on its Western career. Governments may come and governments may go, but the Police have kept on the even tenor of their way throughout all the years.

MAJOR-GENERAL SIR A. C. MACDONNELL. K.C.B.,
C.M.G., D.S.O.
KNIGHTED FOR SERVICES TO THE EMPIRE.

MAJOR-GENERAL SIR SAMUEL B. STEELE, K.C.B., etc.,
KNIGHTED FOR SERVICES TO THE EMPIRE.
Photo. Elliott & Fry.

SUPERINTENDENT A. H. GRIESBACH.
The first man to enlist in the Mounted Police.
"The Father of the Force."

INSPECTOR J. M. WALSH.
Who handled the Sitting Bull situation.
Photo. Murray, Brockville.

* * * * *

CHAPTER III

MOBILIZING

Perhaps the startling story of "The Massacre Ground" at Cypress Hills, some 40 miles north of the boundary line, and kindred stories were the last straws which, added to the weight of evidence for the necessity of an armed force in the West, moved the Dominion Government to active organization work. This Cypress Hills event is a gruesome story enough, but it is part of the setting for the entrance of the Mounted Police on the stage of Western life.

It appears that a party of men—we call them men by courtesy as they were human beings of the male persuasion—crossed over from Montana on a trading expedition. They were white men, but perhaps of various races, for they were mostly adventurers who had served in the American Civil War and had not much regard for human life. These men deluged an Assiniboine Indian Camp with deadly whisky in return for every valuable thing the Indians had to trade. And when the Indian Camp was ablaze with the light of campfires and was a mad whirl of dancing drunkenness the miscreant traders from the South, in a spirit of utter wanton devilry, got under cover of a cut bank by the creek where the camp was, and proceeded to shoot the Indians who were defenceless in their orgy. A volley or two accounted for two score killed and many wounded, only a few escaping to the hills. And this carnival of bloodshed was witnessed by an American trader, Abe Farwell, who, being alone, was helpless to prevent, but who testified as to the frightful occurrence.

Nor was this very far from the general order of the day. Bloods, Piegans, Blackfeet, Crees, Assiniboines and the other tribes maddened with doped liquor from outlaw traders, fought each other whenever they met. And some cases were known where Blackfeet and Crees, implacable enemies, happening to meet at some trading post, struggled with fierce brutality, while the Hudson's Bay trader in the fort had to barricade his gate and let them fight it out amongst themselves. I have myself seen Indian braves with half a score of scalps dangling from their belts, and others with no end of nicks in their rifle stocks to indicate the number they had slain. Buffalo-hunters from the white and half-breed settlements by the Red and the Assiniboine Rivers only ventured westward in large companies heavily armed. Explorers ran great risks, and the famous Captain Palliser had to hunt one whole winter with Old Sun, the Chief of the Blackfeet, that he might become as one of that fighting tribe and get leave to draw his maps.

Communication was difficult, but the news of these events of frightfulness percolated through to Ottawa and the order went out in September, 1873, that officers already appointed should proceed to recruit in the Eastern Provinces and rush some part of the force to the far West, so as to be on the ground by the next spring. The principal recruiting officer seems to have been Inspector James Morrow Walsh, who became one of the noted men of the Force in later years. It is a somewhat remarkable coincidence and a decided testimony to the directness with which the Mounted Police when organized struck at the very heart of the lawlessness in the West, that Fort Walsh, called after this recruiting Inspector, was built as a Police post not many months later practically on "The Massacre Ground" in the Cypress Hills country. That Fort was a direct and visible challenge to every outlaw, white or red, who expected to have his own way in British territory.

We shall meet Walsh from time to time in this story and his name simply occurs here as one of the earliest recruiting officers. I knew him at different stages in his career, but most particularly when he had retired from the Force and entered the coal business in Winnipeg. Later on he was the Civil Governor of the Yukon Territory. Clean-cut in figure, athletic, wiry and always faultlessly dressed, Walsh was a good-looking type and bore in his carriage the unmistakable stamp of his cavalry training. In Winnipeg he was popularly known as the man who had tamed Sitting Bull, the redoubtable Sioux of Custer Massacre fame, but others of the Police also had a hand, as we shall see, in that extraordinary experience.

There was no difficulty in getting men to enlist in the Mounted Police. This was clearly not due to any mercenary motives on the part of men enlisting. The remuneration for both officers and men was small, as it remains comparatively speaking to this day, when we remember that the work has always called for an unusual degree of endurance, initiative, reliability and courage. But the Government no doubt placed considerable reliance on the fact that the spirit of adventure is strong in the hearts of young men and that the lure of a new land would draw them with compelling magnetism. In this the authorities were not disappointed. In fact, Colonel George A. French, a Royal Artillery Officer, then at the head of the School of Gunnery at Kingston (who died recently after much distinguished service to the Empire during which he rose to a Major-Generalship and a Knighthood with many decorations), and who was early given command of the Mounted Police with the title of Commissioner, saw the danger of a rush for places in the new Force and took steps to weed out undesirables. More than once in Toronto and again at Dufferin in Manitoba when the great venture of the march out into the unknown began, Colonel French put the matter before the men in a sort of forlorn-hope admonition. They were to be one of the few forces in the world constantly on active service and neither Garibaldi nor Bruce of Bannockburn ever warned men more distinctly of what possibly lay ahead of them. And the picture, as after events proved, was not overdrawn. These men were to face cold and hunger and the perils of drought in the various seasons of the year; they were to leave the comforts of civilization and live under the canopy of the sky amidst the storms of summer and the blizzards of winter; they were to be called to root out nests of outlaws who had no scruples about taking human life, and they, a mere handful of men, were to control and guide Indians whose brethren to the south of the boundary were engaging attention of thousands of soldiers in the endeavour to keep them in order. All this and more did French tell the new recruits. But only a very few dropped out and throughout the years the force has attracted a fine class of men both from Canada and the British Isles. Young men from the towns and farms of the old Provinces, University Graduates and younger sons of the nobility in the Mother Land, men of birth and breeding and social advantage have always been in the ranks. But once in the force there were no social distinctions sought or recognized. Genuine manhood was the only hall-mark allowed as a standard. The fine democracy of Robert Burns,—

> "The rank is but the guinea stamp;
> The man's the gold for a' that,—

has had right of way. There was an intangible but real atmosphere in the corps which in some quiet but quite definite fashion, eliminated any man who did not measure up to the mark which the members felt they ought to reach. Mr. Charles Mair, the author and frontiersman, already quoted, says finely, "The average Mounted Policeman was an idealist regarding the honour of his corps; and if, as sometimes happened, a hard character crept into it, physically fit, a good rider or a good shot, but coarse, cruel and immoral, he fared ill with his fellows, and speedily betook himself to other employment."

The men who first enlisted in the East, mainly in Ontario, in September, 1873, were sent away westward by the Great Lakes and the difficult Dawson Route to the Red River country in order to be on the ground and get down to work preparatory to the trek towards the setting sun. The Dawson Route, so-called after the designer of it, was a trail which utilized the water-stretches and on the whole was more suited to amphibious animals than human beings. Some of the men now coming over it with the police had travelled it with Wolseley a few years previously and would have vivid recollections of the flies and mud and portages and the need of manufacturing skidways over the bogs, but they would also recall the irrepressible and uproarious spirit in which they used to sing of their additional accomplishments in the rollicking "Jolly Boys" chorus:

> "'Twas only as a volunteer that I left my abode,
> I never thought of coming here to work upon the road."

The Police, however, were coming in the fall of the year and escaped some of the plagues of the earlier seasons. They duly landed at Lower Fort Garry, the old Hudson's Bay post still romantically standing on the banks of the Red River some 20 miles north of the present city of Winnipeg. They came in three troops or divisions, "A," "B," and "C," of fifty men each, which was the number of the Force which the law-makers at Ottawa thought would be sufficient to patrol 300,000 square miles of territory where lawlessness was beginning to be rampant. In the meantime it was not very pleasant for the Police to land at the Fort near the beginning of winter and to learn a few days afterwards that their winter clothing had been commandeered by the weather and frozen in somewhere on the Dawson Route. But this too was accepted with good grace by the men who had declined to be sifted out of the Force by the warnings given them as to hardships ahead.

These men at Lower Fort Garry had been on the pay-roll since their enlistment in September, but they were not actually on service till the 3rd of November, 1873, when they were sworn in by Lieut.-Colonel Osborne Smith, who was then in command of the Western Military District with headquarters at Winnipeg. It is not generally known that Colonel Osborne Smith, who had seen service in the Crimea and the Fenian Raid in 1866, was really appointed Commissioner of the Police so as to give him full authority until a successor was invested with the command. But I have before me as I write the elaborate parchment which so appointed Colonel Smith. It is dated September 25, 1873, and bears the signature of J. C. Aikins (afterwards Governor of Manitoba) as Secretary of State as well as that of Sir John A. Macdonald. Colonel Osborne Smith, whom I knew well in later days and under whom I served in the Winnipeg Light Infantry, brigaded in 1885 with some of the Police of this original troop, was an ardent Canadian Imperialist, and I imagine it was he who drew up the enlistment oath that was subscribed before him that day at the old Fort. In view of the fact that the word "Canadian" has been substituted in the name of the Force for the word "North-West" and that the jurisdiction of the corps has now been extended over the whole Dominion, it is suggestive of prophetic vision that the original oath should have borne the heading "Mounted Police of Canada."

It is also interesting to note in connection with this oath, which pledges faithful performance of duty and the protection and due care of their equipment and other public property, that the first signature is that of Arthur Henry Griesbach, who was then Regimental Sergeant-Major, but who later on became one of the ablest Superintendents. He has already been referred to as the special adviser of Sir John A. Macdonald in Ottawa for some months prior to the organization of the Police, and on this account shares with Sir John the designation of the "Father of the Force." Griesbach's signature was witnessed by Samuel B. Steele, who was then Troop Sergeant-Major, and who, after very notable service in the Police and the Militia, was promoted to a Major-Generalship and Knighted. Amongst other well-known signatures is that of John Henry McIllree, then a Sergeant who, with much excellent work in the Force to his credit, became Assistant Commissioner and is now retired with the rank of Colonel and the Imperial Service Order. The list of men on that first roll holds the signatures of many whose names became household words in Western Canada and whose contribution to the Empire was of far-reaching value. They were the real originals of a corps which was looked on by many as an experiment in the beginning. But their work set such a high standard for those who came after them that men who joined in later years felt the pressure of prestige to which they must live up if they were to hold their place in the organization. The result has been that the reputation of this remarkable corps has grown with the years and any writer of their history would be sadly lacking in the historical sense if he did not see how profoundly they have influenced for good the trend of life west of the Great Lakes.

It is worth while at this point to emphasize and illustrate this statement for the sake of readers who may not know the history of the West as some of us do who have lived in the country all our days and have witnessed the developments throughout the passing years. Nothing could be a greater mistake than to look upon the Mounted Police as a body separate from the elements that have gone to the making of the Canadian West. As a body, it is true, they were aloof from partisan political strife, from class struggles in the social order and from the activities of commercial endeavour, but their influence was felt constantly on the pulse of the growing country which, like a boisterous growing boy, needed restraint and guidance in reaching the fullness of its powers. They were not party men, politically or socially, but they saw that every person and every organization that was sane and law-abiding and constructive, got fair play without interference from anyone. The Police did not as a body engage in commercial activities themselves, but they made it possible for the settler and the miner and the railroad-builder and others in all lawful occupations to go about their work in peace and develop the country under the shield of police protection. In brief, the record of this famous corps is woven into Western history to such a degree that without the fibre of that record the present great fabric of a new land, strong, sound and unbreakable, would have been impossible.

Two things specifically might be said here in this regard. Butler, in the famous report already quoted, dwelt eloquently, it will be remembered, on the necessity for the organization of a force that would be a protector and guide to the settlers who would flow into the West. It is rather a curious coincidence that when the first of the Mounted Police contingent came over the Dawson Route they assisted families on the way to the Red River country who would probably never have got through without the help of these kindly giants. And that was just a prophecy of what was to be the rule. Settlers did not hesitate to go where there was Mounted Police protection and the occasional patrol to remote homesteaders to see whether there was anything required made the lot of many a lonely household much more carefree and happy than it would otherwise have been. There is absolutely no doubt that the tide of humanity flowed freely into the vast new frontier land by reason of the fact that the scarlet-coated riders had made the wilderness a safe abode and a place of opportunity for the law-abiding and the industrious. Thus did the Police fulfil the vision of Butler and make the settlement of the great areas not only possible but speedy.

Another impressive way in which the Mounted Police made history was their extraordinary handling of the Indian tribes who were the original possessors of the soil. History, both ancient and modern, is full of the bitter tragedies created by the way in which incoming people have treated original inhabitants of the lands they were coming to possess. In our own day just across the border, owing to mishandling by some unfaithful Government agents and other causes, there was war for decades between the Government and the Indians, who looked upon the cavalry and other military bodies in that country as their enemies. This was never the case with our Western Country. The first business our Mounted Police did was to stand between the Indians and the vile creatures who would give them drink and rob them of all they possessed. So that some two years after the scarlet tunic had made its appearance in the foothill country, Crowfoot, the famous Chief of the warlike Blackfeet, referring to the Police, said in his beautiful imagery, "They have protected us as the feathers protect the bird from the frosts of winter." The Indians knew that they could not commit crime and go unpunished any more than the white man, but the Indians also knew that the Police would see that every man, whether red or white, got fair play. Hence the Indians recognized the Police as their friends and not as their enemies. With thousands of Indians, accustomed to almost constant war, thrown upon their hands, the Police never had any real revolt on the part of the Indians to deal with save only when the mad Riel inveigled a few of them on the war-path by cunning guile. And with some personal knowledge of that whole affair we venture to say that had the warning given by Superintendent Crozier and other Policemen months before the outbreak been taken, and had the Police Force been doubled and given a free hand, there would have been no rebellion and no bloodshed. But when the outbreak did come we are also ready to affirm, as amongst those who took part in its suppression, that but for the missionaries and the Police the rebellion would have been far more widely spread. And equally are we ready to declare that the Police were the backbone of every brigade in which they served, and this we say without any desire to minimize the arms of the service to which we belonged.

It was the swearing in of the "originals" of the Mounted Police that led to the writing of these special reflections. For on looking back over the years of this West that I have known from childhood, it seems to me that the day of that first enlistment oath was a pivotal point around which much of the destiny of Western Canada would turn for the rest of recorded time. Hence it is at this stage of the story that the formative day at Lower Fort Garry should be noted.

That winter in the old stone-walled fort was a busy one for the new recruits. After they were sworn in by Colonel Osborne Smith, that officer returned to his duties at Upper Fort Garry. He had done a good day's work, and if he addressed the men in the crisp, incisive style I have often heard him use on patriotic occasions, then he had made additional contribution to the considerations that inspired the Police to determined endeavour. On his leaving

Superintendent W. D. Jarvis, who had seen service in Africa and became a very popular officer, took over the duties of Adjutant and Riding Master, Griesbach took charge of discipline and foot-drill, while S. B. Steele, popularly known in the West to the close of his days as Sam Steele, looked after the breaking of the broncos and gave instruction in riding, which latter proved to be highly necessary. There were no eight-hour days, the only limit being the daylight each way. Steele drilled five rides a day in the open, and the orders were that, unless the thermometer dropped beneath 36 degrees below zero, a rather cool temperature, the riding and breaking were to proceed. The broncos were of the usual exuberant type, given to every device to throw a rider, and falls on the frozen ground were not infrequent, but by spring the men knew how to handle broncos so as to become the pioneers of fine horsemanship amongst the riders of the plains.

Lieut.-Colonel French came in November, 1873, and assumed his command. It did not take him long to see that a handful of 150 men, however gallant, would be totally inadequate for the gigantic undertaking ahead of them. The Force has always been too small in numbers, but at the outset the proposed strength was absurdly below the mark. Fortunately the news of the lawlessness that was abroad in the far West made it possible for Colonel French to get the proposed number doubled and brought up to the 300 which Constable T. A. Boys made famous in his well-known poem "The Riders of the Plains," from which we quote the following verses:

> "We muster but three hundred
>   In all this Great Lone Land,
> Which stretches from Superior's shore
>   To where the Rockies stand;
> But not one heart doth falter,
>   No coward voice complains,
> Tho' all too few in numbers are
>   The Riders of the Plains.
>
> "Our mission is to raise the Flag
>   Of Britain's Empire here,
> Restrain the lawless savage,
>   And protect the Pioneer;

> And 'tis a proud and daring trust,
> To hold these vast Domains,
> With but three hundred Mounted Men,
> The Riders of the Plains.
>
> "And though we win no fame or praise
> But struggle on alone
> To carry out good British rule,
> And plant old England's throne;
> Yet when our task is ended,
> And Law and Order reigns,
> The peaceful settler long will bless
> The Riders of the Plains."

Meanwhile down in Eastern Canada the left wing of the Force was being recruited and, permission being obtained from the United States, three divisions, rather over strength, left Toronto on June 6, 1874, and came west via Chicago and St. Paul to the end of steel at Fargo in North Dakota. Colonel French had gone back East to come out with them. It was a motley outfit that dumped itself out of the train on that Dakota plain. The men were a carefully selected and fine appearing lot, and the horses were of the handsome Eastern type; but the wagons in pieces to be assembled, and the saddles shipped from England in parts, were strewn over the ground for acres. The Fargo people rather enjoyed the idea of these men with their interesting mission being amongst them for a week or so getting ready for the trail. But to the amazement of those townsfolk the Police starting at four o'clock in the morning and working in four-hour relays "hit the trail" within twenty-four hours and pulled out their cavalcade for the trip to Canadian Territory. It had taken two weeks from Toronto, including the rather testing experience for men of a day off in Chicago and St. Paul, so that we like Colonel French's note at this point saying, "I must say I felt a great load off my shoulders at again being on Canadian soil." But the Police had begun early to create a good impression, and he adds, "The conduct of the men had been most exemplary, their general appearance and conduct invariably attracting the favourable notice of the railway officials and others *en route*." In preparation for the march westward to the foothills of the Rockies the three divisions "A," "B," and "C" that had been quartered for the winter at Lower Fort Garry left that point on June 7, 1874, and were at the rendezvous at Dufferin near the boundary line to greet the Commissioner and the three divisions "D," "E," and "F," which had come through as related from Toronto.

Just before leaving Lower Fort Garry with the original divisions, Inspector James Farquharson McLeod had been appointed Assistant Commissioner of the Force. Thus one of the noted figures in the after history of Western Canada came upon the scene of his future work and triumphs. McLeod had served as Assistant Brigade Major in Wolseley's Red River expedition and for his services then received the brevet rank of Lieut.-Colonel and the C.M.G. He was originally from Calgarry in Scotland (hence the name of the city of Calgary in Alberta in his honour) and had all the judicial faculty of the Scot coupled with the ardour of his Highland ancestry. His absolute reliability and fearless fairness gave him an influence over the Indians in later days that can only be described as extraordinary, and the time came when that commanding power over the warlike Blackfeet stood Canada in good stead.

Commissioner French lost no time in getting his men into shape at the rendezvous. From the divisions he brought with him he drafted fifty men to bring the original divisions up to strength. He arranged the night camp with the Eastern horses inside the zariba of wagons, and the Western horses, mostly broncos, on the outside—an arrangement that turned out well in view of a stampede that took place. The occasion of the stampede (and there is nothing more fearful than a stampede of maddened animals) was a terrific thunderstorm, which transformed the prairie into a sea of electric flame and sent bolts crashing into the zariba amidst the horses that were tied to the wagons. Sergt.-Major Sam B. Steele (that was then his rank), who was riding near this enclosure, thus vividly described the scene: "A thunder-bolt fell in the midst of the horses. Terrified, they broke their fastenings, and made for the side of the corral. The six men on guard were trampled under foot as they tried to stop them. The maddened beasts overturned the huge wagons, dashed through a row of tents, scattered everything, and made for the gate of the large field in which we were encamped. In their mad efforts to pass they climbed over one another to the height of many feet. I had full view of the stampede, being not more than 50 yards from the horses as they rushed at the gate and attempted to pass it, scrambling and rolling over one another in one huge mass." Inspector (now Colonel) Walker leaped on a passing horse and went out with them into the night. He pursued the frightened animals for some 50 miles across the boundary, and helped to round them up and bring them back twenty-four hours after they had stampeded. Colonel Walker says: "The horses did not get over their fright all the summer, and had to be watched closely as any unusual noise would stampede them." This was truly an exciting introduction to prairie life.

Commissioner French, who had been sworn into his office on December 16, 1873, was handling the situation with the thoroughness and ability of a trained soldier. He believed in discipline and showed independence by declining to tolerate any outside interference with the work of the Force. Perhaps it was French who laid the foundations for the non-partisan character of the Police by resisting anything which bore the resemblance of using political pull to secure place and promotion in the corps. He stood strongly for merit as the basis for preferment. Evidence is not lacking to show that Ottawa was rather too much disposed to run the Force by long-range activity on behalf of some favourites. Dispatches came from the seat of Government, showing pronounced lack of knowledge of local circumstances and requirements. To some of these French replied so forcibly that interference with the internal management of the Force largely ceased in time. In one case, amongst French's books of letters, I found this recently: "Sub-Constable—has not as yet shown the necessary qualification to justify his promotion to the position of Acting Constable, much less to that of a Commissioned Officer." In another case he wrote: "I beg to point out that if the members of this Force are encouraged to communicate with the Department direct, thereby ignoring all those supposed to be placed in authority over them, it will be very difficult to maintain anything like proper discipline in the Force." Wise man, who saw a dangerous tendency, and courageous man to point it out with frankness. At another time some wise person suggested to pay by cheque, to which French replied, "Who will cash them in the wilderness?" Similarly, he objected to members of the Force being encouraged to write of their grievances to the newspapers.

That French looked carefully into details for the sake of the men's comfort is evidenced by letters in his book which protest against an inferior kind of tea being sent out for use in the Force, and that he was very watchful against the class of people who, on various pretexts, try to get some of the Government property, is attested by the following letter to a man whom I remember well to be of that shark type: "In answer to your letter of the 28th of August, I beg to say that I do not see the necessity of giving you a Government wagon, because, through some carelessness in your business arrangements, you have lost one of your own." There is wit as well as rebuke in that communication. On the whole we repeat that, though he had a task of unusual difficulty, French laid the foundation of the Force, and gave the superstructure a trend that affected for good the after history of the famous corps. It was this man who was now to lead his column on the longest march in history for a column carrying its own supplies. He was leading it "out into the unknown," but though many prophesied disaster, he was not to fail.

* * * * *

CHAPTER IV

THE AMAZING MARCH

That thunderstorm, with the resultant stampede at Dufferin, along with some blood-curdling prophecies of attacks by the scalp-gathering Sioux Indians, had the good effect of weeding out the few non-adventurous spirits who, up to now, had thought that the hardships and dangers of the expedition had been painted in too lurid a colour. This suited Colonel French, as he had no desire to venture into the wilderness with any but the very best of men. A very necessary part of Police equipment, namely their revolvers, did not arrive from England till early in July, but once they had come French, who was impatient of delay in beginning so tremendous a trek, gave orders on July 8 for a "pull out," or what the old traders used to call "a Hudson's Bay start." The idea of a "pull out" before the real journey began was to shake the line of the caravan into shape, take out any kinks that might need straightening, and generally see that everything was working satisfactorily. With field guns and mortars, seventy-three wagons, and 114 of the wooden prairie conveyances, known as Red River carts, new harness and other equipment that needed testing, the "pull out" in this case was highly desirable, but every care had been taken, and after a 2-mile test, camp was pitched for a day or so till the real trip, across the 1,000-mile plain, was commenced on July 10, 1874, a red-letter day in Western history.

The prairie had witnessed many a remarkable outfit striking out over the plains with dog-trains in winter and carts and buffalo-runners in summer, but it had never seen anything so business-like and highly picturesque as this Police marching-out state. The six divisions or troops of the mounted men, with the convenient alphabetical designation from "A" to "F," had been given horses of distinctive colour, so that in order there came for the start, dark bays, dark browns, light chestnuts with the guns, greys, blacks and light bays. After these came wagons, carts, cows and calves, beef cattle, and a general assortment of farming implements. Meat would be necessary when the buffalo were not available, and it would keep better "on the hoof." Posts would have to be supplied with food, and haying, ploughing and reaping would be necessary if men and horses were to live at some of the remote points. So they took the necessaries along as far as they could. Of course, the impressive order of march at the beginning could not be maintained throughout the gruelling expedition. A thousand miles across swamp and *coulées* and rivers, over areas of waste and desolate prairie, where fires had swept every vestige of grass away, through sections where flies and drought and excessive heat, turning into cold as the autumn approached, played the inevitable havoc. All these elements combined to throw that ordered line into confusion at times. Here and there cattle died, oxen gave out and quit, horses broke down through lack of food and water, men, hardy as they were, took ill sometimes, but none succumbed, and as Colonel French observed in concluding his first report to Ottawa: "The broad fact is apparent that a Canadian force, hastily raised, armed and equipped, and not under martial law, in a few months marched vast distances through a country for the most part as unknown as it proved bare of pasture and scanty in the supply of water. Of such a march, under such adverse circumstances, all true Canadians may well be proud." And so say we all.

COMMISSIONER A. G. IRVINE.

COMMISSIONER GEORGE A. FRENCH.

COMMISSIONER JAMES F. MACLEOD.

COMMISSIONER LAWRENCE W. HERCHMER.

It would be impossible to follow that amazing march in detail—that would take a whole volume, but the main outlines are within our reach. The officers who led in that remarkable episode in Canadian history deserve mention, for it has always been a Police tradition that officers would never ask men to go anywhere where they were not prepared to go themselves. Personally, or by reputation, at one time or another, I have known practically all of these officers, and they would all measure up to requirements, though some would excel others in initiative and activity. They were Lieut.-Colonel George A. French, Commissioner; Major James F. MacLeod, C.M.G., Assistant Commissioner; Staff-Dr. J. G. Kittson, Surgeon; Dr. R. B. Nevitt, Assistant Surgeon; W. G. Griffiths, Paymaster; G. Dalrymple Clark, Adjutant; John L. Poett, Veterinary Surgeon; Charles Nicolle, Quarter Master. Division "A": W. D. Jarvis, Inspector; Severe Gagnon, Sub-Inspector. Division "B": G. A. Brisebois, Inspector; J. B. Allan, Sub-Inspector. Division "C": W. Winder, Inspector; T. R. Jackson, Sub-Inspector. Division "D" (Staff Division): J. M. Walsh, Inspector; J. Walker and J. French, Sub-Inspectors. Division "E": J. Carvell, Inspector; J. H. McIllree and H. J. N. LeCaine, Sub-Inspectors. Division "F": L. F. N. Crozier, Inspector; V. Welsh and C. E. Denny, Sub-Inspectors. These were the originals amongst the officers, and the originals always attract our special notice. The Force has been as a whole, wonderfully fortunate in its officers. Here and there, as in the rank and file, there have been some throughout the years who were less strenuous and able than others, but their uniformly high character, and their incorruptibility at the hands of men who were ready to pay large sums if the Police would look the other way, have never been questioned. Many of these officers throughout the years might have become wealthy had they either neglected their duty to take business investments on the frontier, or had they been susceptible to anything like bribery. It stands to their credit that those of them who have passed on, died in comparative poverty, and that those who survive have nothing but their not too generous pay, or the still less generous pension allowance.

The original officers above named set a high standard in that famous march across the wilds in 1874, and they were supported by as gallant and hardy a body of men as ever crossed the plains. Most of them were young men from the Eastern Provinces, who had no experience in the life of the prairies, and hardly any conception of the difficulties to be met and overcome, but they faced situations as they arose, and with the same initiative, resource and courage that have characterized Canadians on other fields of service, they persevered and won.

Broadly speaking, the aim of the Police expedition was to strike at the lawlessness which was specially defiant and open in the foothills of the Rockies, where the proximity of the international boundary line made it easy for outlaws of all types to evade the consequences of their crimes and depredations on both sides in turn. Besides that it was proposed, by a sort of triangular distribution of the 300 Police, to cover the whole North-Western territory, and in that way give visibility to authority in all localities. To fulfil these aims and reach these objectives, the main body of the Police was to be sent on this march out to the Bow and Belly Rivers, near the Cypress Hills, made infamous by the massacre already described, and countless other criminalities. Another detachment, separating from the main body, was to go northward to Edmonton, by way of forts Ellice and Carlton, while a third, under the charge of the Commissioner, was to return to the proposed headquarters at Fort Pelly or Swan River, on the north-west boundary of Manitoba. These objectives were all reached after many serious hardships, the only modification in the places being in regard to the Swan River. On returning to that point in the beginning of winter, Colonel French found that the barracks were not ready for occupation, some wiseacre having started to build them amid granite boulders on a hill. Moreover, prairie fires had burned the hay intended for the Police, and the Hudson's Bay Company, having lost their supply also, could not assist. Consequently the Commissioner left only one division there, under that very competent officer, Inspector Carvell, and with the rest he pushed on to Winnipeg and the original starting-point at Dufferin, where he arrived in 30 degrees below zero, November weather, after a total march for his contingent of nearly 2,000 miles. We shall look at these three movements of the Force briefly.

The whole column kept together as far as La Roche Percée, or the pierced rock, on the banks of the Souris, a distance of nearly 300 miles from the starting-point at Dufferin. Near here the Commissioner established what he called Cripple Camp for the maimed and halt, both of man and beast, for already the hardship of the route had begun to take its toll. But there was no time to lose, and French throughout was insistent on getting forward, for the way was long, and it was necessary to get out to the Cypress Hills country, get some shelters erected for the men and horses, and lay in some stores of provisions. By the end of August they were pretty well to their destination. In the meantime, Colonel French had gone over the line to Fort Benton, Montana, the nearest telegraphic point in those days, secured some stores and learned from Ottawa that after arrival at the foot-hill points, he was to leave Assistant Commissioner MacLeod in charge and return himself with "E" and "D" Divisions to Fort Pelly or Swan River, as the headquarters of the Force. While Colonel French was in Montana for a few days several half-breed buffalo-hunters visited the Police camp and told some ferocious stories about the desperadoes who were entrenched out in the cattle-stealing and boot-legging belt waiting to dispute possession with the new-comers. The scarlet-coated men took in all they said and smiled. Forts "Whoop-Up," "Stand-off" and the rest, with some of the outlaws in garrison, would have been a welcome diversion after the hardships they had experienced.

Perhaps the leading incident of this particular part of the big trek was the discovery by the Commissioner of Jerry Potts, a short, heavy-set, taciturn man, half Scot and half Piegan, a wonderful plainsman, skilled in the language of the Indian tribes and a past-master in all the lore of the prairies. His father was an Edinburgh Scot, who was killed in Missouri by an Indian, and it is said that Jerry, though a mere boy, followed the Indian into camp and shot him. Anyway, Jerry Potts became a splendid help to the Police, a trainer of scouts, a matchless diplomat with the Indians, an incomparable interpreter, and a highly respected guide who, without consulting maps, seemed to know the way by instinct either in summer or winter. He began to be useful as soon as he took service with the Force in that fall of 1874. He guided them to the best feeding-places for the horses and cattle, and to the watering-places which were so constantly needed. And when, a few days after he came, the column struck herds of innumerable buffalo, it was Jerry Potts who warned against shooting at certain times, lest the bisons would stampede and trample the whole cavalcade under foot. Potts remained with the Police as interpreter till his death in 1906, making a long service of twenty-two years. We shall meet his name here and there in this story—a diamond in the rough, entitled to a niche in the hall of the men who helped to shape the early years of our history.

Shortly after this trip to Montana, Colonel French, with the divisions above named, left the foothill country, and, coming back by way of Qu'Appelle, Fort Pelly and Swan River, he reached Dufferin, as already mentioned, in the 30 degrees below zero weather, he and the men with him having travelled about 2,000 miles since leaving there in July.

The third party already mentioned as leaving La Roche Percée was a small detachment under Inspectors Jarvis and Gagnon. With sick and played-out horses, a lot of cattle, and not much general provision, and hardly enough men to keep up the rounds of duty, the lot of this detachment starting out on a march of 850 miles was not very enticing. The detachment left La Roche Percée on August 3, and reached Edmonton, by way of Fort Ellice and Carlton, on the 27th of October. Pasture was poor, water was scarce and, except where they struck Hudson's Bay posts or, as in one case, met a caravan of traders from whom some rations in the shape of pemmican were purchased, the outlook all the way was hazardous. When the weather began to get cold the weakened horses often had to be lifted in the morning and their joints rubbed, before they could proceed on the journey. During the last 25 miles it seemed as if the enterprise would collapse near the goal, as the cold had so stiffened the half-starved horses that they could not travel over the hard-frozen and icy ground. They had to be lifted and rubbed hour after hour. No wonder Inspector Jarvis said after reaching Edmonton, "Had these horses been my own property I should have killed them, as they were mere skeletons." However, the detachment got through finally, and were warmly welcomed by Mr. Hardisty, the Hudson's Bay factor, who, in addition to his own open-hearted nature, had joy in exercising to the full that generous hospitality for which the old Hudson's Bay men have been famous for two and a half centuries. They had ruled in a benevolently autocratic way throughout the years, and one would almost imagine that they would have looked askance at the scarlet-coated men who were representing the powers that were superseding them. But the Mounted Police had no more loyal friends and helpers than these grand men of the old Company, who were of enormous assistance to the Government and the Police in the critical days when there was a change of rulers taking place and the problem of the Indians had to be peaceably and satisfactorily settled.

Inspector Jarvis, who was a gallant and popular officer, has this notable paragraph in his report to Colonel French: "In conclusion, I may state, on looking back over our journey, I wonder how we ever accomplished it with weak horses, little or no pasture, and for the last 500 miles with no grain, and the latter part of it over roads impassable. We made them, that is to say, I kept a party of men ahead with axes and, when practicable, felled trees and made corduroy over mudholes, sometimes 100 yards long, and also made a number of bridges and repaired the old ones. We must have laid down several miles of corduroy between Fort Pitt and here. Streams which last year when I crossed them were mere rivulets, are now rivers difficult to ford. *And had it not been for the perfect conduct of the men and real hard work*, much of the property must have been destroyed." Loyal men were those splendid pathfinders, who would do their utmost to conserve the equipment which belonged to their Sovereign. They had a keen sense of honour and a fine appreciation of the trust reposed in them.

It is highly interesting to find emerging occasionally in these reports the names of men who afterwards became outstanding figures in the Force. Constable Labelle is especially singled out for mention by Inspector Jarvis, because of his special attention to the horses which were pulled through largely by his assiduous care. A man of that kind wins our respect and appreciation. A horse is perhaps the most sensitive animal in the world, and the West is full of stories of the positive attachment which grew up between the men on the frontier and the faithful animals to whose endurance and courage in storm and blizzard the troopers often owed their lives.

And Inspector Jarvis mentions another in his first report from Edmonton when he says, "Sergt.-Major Steele has been undeviating in his efforts to assist me, and he has also done the manual labour of at least two men."

That Steele, whom we shall meet more than once in this story, could do the manual labour of at least two men we can well believe. Years after the date on which this tribute was written by Jarvis I met Steele in the foothills of the Rockies, and in his tall, powerful figure, deep-chested proportions and massive shoulders, he suggested prodigious strength to the onlooker. And that Steele not only could but would do two men's work if it seemed his duty, goes without saying to those who knew him. Lieut.-Colonel J. B. Mitchell, of the 100th Grenadiers in Winnipeg, one of the original '73 men of the Mounted Police, tells us that when he went to Kingston to take an artillery course, before the Police Force was organized, he was told by Battery Sergt.-Major John Mortimer that some of the sergeants might try to take advantage of him, as he was new at the business but Mortimer added, "You can always rely on Sergeant Sam Steele." And the certificate of that grizzled old Sergt.-Major never had to be cancelled.

And thus we have seen the Mounted Police come upon the stage and take their positions at the end of extraordinary marches. It will be our place and privilege to follow them as they play their large and serious part in nation-building in Western Canada.

* * * * *

CHAPTER V

BUSINESS IN THE LAND OF INDIANS

Orders from Ottawa had disposed the Mounted Police into four different locations, although, as we have seen, the fourth had become only necessary at Dufferin, because there was neither shelter nor adequate provision for headquarters at Fort Pelly. But, when we look back into the situation, we can readily see that the Assistant Commissioner, Colonel MacLeod, had the most difficult and dangerous situation of all. They had all reached their destination after tremendous hardships, the Edmonton detachment perhaps most of all. But the three detachments, namely those at Edmonton under Jarvis, Fort Pelly under Garvell, and Dufferin under the Commissioner, had shelter and reasonable provision. But MacLeod was out in the open with the winter coming on and no shelter from the blizzards that blow at times even across that foothill country. He was hundreds of miles away from any possibility of help in men or substance from Canadian sources, and he had only three troops of fifty men each in the midst of a turbulent gang of outlaw whisky-peddlers and horse-thieves. He was completely surrounded by thousands of the most warlike of Western Indians, with some thousands still more warlike just over the line. Perhaps it was well that he hailed from the land where they say, "A stout heart to a stey brae," because, if a figure of speech from the sea is permissible on the prairie, he and his men knew that they had "burned their ship behind them," and that they must hold their ground or perish. They proved equal to their task, but a sketch or two from the reports of that period reveal the situation even to those who do not know the country. Colonel MacLeod decided that he could not hope to pull the horses and cattle through the winter in the locality where he was making his headquarters, so he dispatched Inspector Walsh and the weakest of the horses and cattle to Sun River, some 200 miles to the south. Walsh was evidently on the look out for service, for MacLeod says, "Walsh was anxious to be sent, and he deserves great credit for the way in which he is performing this service." In another place MacLeod says about November 1: "We had a severe snowstorm, with high wind and extreme cold, the thermometer going to 10 degrees below zero. When the storm broke I had all the horses driven into the shelter of the woods near by; every one blanketed and fed with oats and corn. Then I was extremely anxious about them, and glad they got through so well." The righteous man is merciful to his beast, even though the beast is Government property. And then we come across this fine human touch in which the emotional nature of the Highlander breaks through: "I hope soon to have ample accommodation for all if another storm breaks out. I have made up my mind that not a single log of men's quarters shall be laid until the horses are provided for, as well as a few sick men." If the dumb animals cannot speak for themselves, the Colonel speaks for them. If the men who are laid aside cannot plead their own cause they will not suffer, for the Colonel does not forget them. And MacLeod is early teaching his officers that he will have no "carpet knights," who claim immunity from hardship because of their rank, for he goes on to say, "Then the men's quarters will be proceeded with, and after that the officers'." We think the officers would all say amen to this, and that is why they always had the confidence of their men. By the time it was 20 degrees below zero they had got the men inside buildings with enough chimney to allow a fire to be kindled. But officers were still on the waiting list, for the report says in December, "Winder, Jackson and the doctor are in a tent in the woods."

With officers and men of that stamp we hear no whining about being unable to enforce the laws of the country. And it was no easy place to enforce laws of certain kinds. The whole region around Fort MacLeod, as the necessarily crude outpost was called, being conveniently near the boundary line, had been for years the favourite stamping ground of the whisky-peddler. There had been no one to interfere with his activities. The Hudson's Bay Company regime, never very active in that locality, had been out of commission for four years, and nothing had taken its place. For

Canadian authority, governing in a long-distance fashion, had not yet impressed itself visibly on the vast plains. Hence the outlaw trader had gone his riotous way, and as a result the poor Indian, who had an insatiable thirst for stimulant, had lived riotously to his own great detriment.

And so, busy as the Police were in trying to build some shelter for their horses and themselves, Colonel MacLeod lost no time striking a body blow at the liquor traffic. Hearing from an Indian named Three Bulls that a coloured man was doing business in firewater about 50 miles away, MacLeod sent Inspector Crozier and ten men, accompanied by the inimitable interpreter, Jerry Potts, to gather in the outfit. Two days afterwards Crozier returned, bringing in the coloured gentleman and four others with some wagon-loads of whisky, a small arsenal of rifles and revolvers, as well as many bales of buffalo robes, which the whisky-sellers had taken from the poor Indians in exchange for the drink that was so fatal to these children of the wild. The whisky was poured out in the snow, the robes were confiscated for the good of the country, and the culprits given the option of a fine or jail. This process revealed the headquarters of the traffic, for a sporting man, rejoicing in the sobriquet of "Wavey," came up from Fort Benton, in Montana, and paid the fines of the white men. There was an extra charge against the coloured man, whose name was Bond, and as "Wavey" would not intervene Mr. Bond had to go to jail. MacLeod would stand no nonsense. On one occasion, a gentleman from the same country as Bond, who was sent to jail without option, and who had in his own locality contracted the bad habit of talking back to judges, said to Colonel MacLeod, "When I get out of here, if you put me in, I will make them wires to Washington hum." "Let them hum," sad the Colonel; "in the meantime you go to jail, and if you say more you may have your sentence doubled."

This was a Daniel come to judgment with a vengeance. To be more modern, it reminds one of Begbie, the great frontier judge on the west coast, who tamed the outlaw miners who tried to start rough-house in the gold-rush days. The dishonest extortioners on the prairie could do nothing to frighten or flatter or tamper with men like Colonel MacLeod and his red-coated patrols. Hence, we read the sequel in the Colonel's report in December, 1874: "I am happy to be able to report" (happy is a choice word—there are some things that make a good man happy)—"to be able to report *the complete stoppage of the whisky trade throughout the whole of this section of the country*, and that the drunken riots, which in former years were almost a daily occurrence, are now entirely at an end; in fact, a more peaceable community than this, with a very large number of Indians camped along the river, could not be found anywhere. Every one united in saying how wonderful the change is. People never lock their doors at night and have no fear of anything being stolen which is left lying about outside; whereas, just before our arrival, gates and doors were all fastened at night, and nothing could be left out of one's sight." And then Colonel MacLeod adds a testimony from the Rev. John McDougall, of Morley, at the edge of the mountains. He and his father, the Rev. George McDougall, who had been frozen to death on the plains, were widely known old-time missionaries. In later years I knew John McDougall well, missionary, scout and frontiersman, tall, full-bearded, handsome and keenly alive to everything that affected the welfare of the West land. And this competent witness said, "I am delighted with the change that has been effected. It is like a miracle wrought before our eyes." The Police were fulfilling their high, benevolent and patriotic mission.

Colonel MacLeod felt that the first business of the Police was to thus protect the Indians who were the wards of the nation, and so it was that he had struck a decisive blow at the drink traffic, which was bidding fair to exterminate these children of the plains. Once that was done the Colonel set himself to get into touch with the various native tribes, which from the earliest days of the explorers and fur-traders had been looked upon as the most warlike and dangerous. It is well known that even the Hudson's Bay Company, despite the experience and the remarkable tact of their employees, had always found it difficult to establish satisfactory relations with the tribes, amongst which at this period Colonel MacLeod and his men were seeking a sphere of service for the good of all concerned.

Accordingly, we find MacLeod reporting before the end of 1874 that he had interviewed the chiefs of the practically confederated tribes of the Bloods, Piegans and Blackfeet. He found them very intelligent men, and he described in some detail the stately ceremony with which these chiefs had conducted themselves in these interviews. They shake hands with Colonel MacLeod, and then, receiving the pipe of peace from the interpreter, Jerry Potts, they each smoke a few seconds and pass it around. MacLeod then explains to them the friendly attitude of the Canadian Government towards them, that the Police had come not to take the country from the Indians, but to protect these Indians against men who would despoil them and destroy them by sowing amongst them evil practices. And he adds that the Government would send soon some of the great men of the country to deal with the Indians and make treaty agreements with them.

At these early interviews the chiefs gave unstinted praise to the Police, before whose coming there had been constant trouble. The Indians said they used to be robbed and ruined by the whisky-traders, that their horses, robes and women had been taken from them, that their young men were constantly engaged in drunken riots and many were killed, that their horses were stolen, so that they had no means of travelling or hunting. All this, the chiefs said, had been changed by the coming of the Police. One chief, in the graphic way by which they gesture in accord with what they are saying, crouched down and moved along with difficulty, and then stood up and walked. "Before you came," said this chief to the Colonel, "the Indian had to creep along, not knowing what would attack him, but now he is not afraid to walk erect."

And so that first winter wore on with steady work on the part of the Police, who, while seeing that the Indians had every protection afforded them, also helped them to understand that they also had to observe the laws of the land. In view of the general situation amongst the Indians and the proximity of part of the North-West Territory to the boundary line, on the other side of which there was almost continuous warfare between the Government and the Indians there, posts were established now at several points all over the vast area that the Mounted Police had to control and guide. In some respects perhaps the most notable event in the spring of 1875, was the sending of Inspector Walsh with "B" Division to the Cypress Hills country, where a fort was built, named after this active and venturous Inspector. And this Fort Walsh became the centre around which for several years the Indian problem, in its various phases, surged backwards and forwards in varying force, but sometimes within dangerous possibility of becoming a tidal wave of destruction and death. There is no finer chapter in Canadian history than the one in which a mere handful of officers and men of the Mounted Police, with endless patience, unflinching courage and consummate skill in open diplomacy, kept the peace in an area larger than several European kingdoms, and within whose precincts thousands of warlike and well-armed Indians composed the reckless, restless and roving population. Years afterwards, when the first Canadian railway had crossed the continent away to the north, and conditions were entirely changed after treaties had been made with the Indians and reserves allotted to them, Fort Walsh was abandoned and dismantled, as it had served its purpose. A peaceful ranch now occupies the site, but though the debris of the old fort is strewed on the plain, the record of the men who made their headquarters there and in similar places is an imperishable bulwark and citadel in the life of our Dominion. Other posts were established about this period, such as Fort Calgary, Fort Saskatchewan, Battleford, Carlton, in what is now Northern Saskatchewan, Qu'Appelle in Saskatchewan and Swan River, an early post, Shoal Lake and Beautiful Plains in the northern section of Manitoba. All of these had their influence on the progress of the West, but none had in the pathfinding days the halo of romance that centred around Fort Walsh.

In the year 1875 Major-General Sir E. Selby Smith, who commanded the Militia in Canada, made a tour of inspection throughout the Dominion and spent some months under escort of the Mounted Police travelling from Swan River to the far West. He was most favourably impressed by the physique and initiative of the men, commended the work that had been done, suggested the increase of the Force and the opening of some new posts, but there were many items in the report which revealed that a man cannot know the life and the needs of a country by making a trip through it. Perhaps the best thing in his report was where he said: "Too much value cannot be attached to the North-West Police, too much attention cannot be paid to their efficiency." The men on the ground knew the value of the Force and were taking good care that it would be efficient to the last degree.

It was at the time of this tour that a fort projected by Colonel MacLeod to be erected somewhere midway between Fort MacLeod and the Red Deer River was built by "F" troop of the Mounted

Police. It was erected near the Bow River and for a time was known as Fort Brisebois, after the officer commanding the division at the time. The name got into orders once or twice but without authority, and Colonel MacLeod put an end to any controversy over it by calling it Calgarry, after his birthplace in Scotland. Our Western mania for shortening names and thereby sometimes breaking with the historical past led to the cutting out of a letter and leaving the name in its present form. But the present city of Calgary, with its great buildings and its distinctive place within sight of the Rockies, has a definite background of early police history which has done much to shape her destiny.

In the seventies changes were taking place in the system of government in the North-West Territories that had pronounced influence on the future of the country in ways closely associated with police history. Heretofore the vast territory over which the Police had oversight had been governed from Manitoba by the Lieutenant-Governor of that Province, assisted by a small body of men called the North-West Council. But government at long range is not more successful than diplomacy of the same variety, and it was becoming evident that some visibility should be given to control in the North-West Territories that stretched from Manitoba to the Mountains and from the boundary to the Pole. Accordingly, in 1876 the Hon. David Laird was appointed Lieutenant-Governor, with a small Council to assist him consisting of Colonel MacLeod of the Police and Matthew Ryan and Hugh Richardson, Stipendiary Magistrates. Ryan was a man of considerable literary power, and Richardson became prominent as one of the trial judges in the cases of Riel and the other rebel leaders some years later.

SITTING BULL.
Famous Sioux Indian Chief.

COLONEL JAMES WALKER (CALGARY)
The oldest survivor of those who were commissioned
officers during the great march of 1874.

David Laird was a Prince Edward Islander of great stature and gentlemanly bearing. He was of imposing appearance, and had the grace of easy speech with a good voice. Fearless in his general attitude, he had withal a fine genius for diplomacy, and came to have a remarkable insight into the Indian mind. The Indians, who prefer giving men names that describe some outstanding characteristic, christened Laird as "the man who talks straight," or, in other words, the man who tells the truth and sticks to it. Few people, perhaps, nowadays know the obligation this country owes to men like Governor Alexander Morris, of Manitoba, and Governor David Laird, of the Territories, for the extraordinary success with which they and their faithful native interpreters, backed and flanked by the fair-minded Mounted Police, dealt with the Indians. The impressive scarlet uniform of the Police somehow or other came to be recognized by the Indians as a sign royal of friendship. Once when Inspector Walsh with several men was riding into a camp of American Indians who had crossed to this side in the winter time, with his dark blue overcoat lightly buttoned and the men in their great coats, the Indians, thinking they were American cavalry, met them with levelled rifles and angry faces. Walsh was not the kind of man to halt for that, and would probably have paid the penalty for his devotion to duty, had not one of the troopers, catching the situation, thrown his overcoat open and disclosed the scarlet tunic. In a flash the Indians lowered their rifles—they recognized their friends. Little wonder that Morris and Laird and the other treaty-makers were grateful for the high standing of these stalwart riders of the plains.

This matter of the Indian treaties deserved some special notice, because it is not well understood by people outside this country and because it is closely connected, as already intimated with the story of the Mounted Police. It is inevitable in the progress of human history that higher civilizations should supersede the lower. Wherever the contrary has been the case and a lower civilization overran the higher the movement of humanity was retrograde. Hence, if the Indian type of civilization in Western Canada was to be superseded by the British type and this change effected without injustice and hardship for the original dwellers in the country, the Government of the Dominion must proceed by process of treaty. By this we mean that the Government had at the same time to conserve the rights of the Indian and secure to them both a place of residence and means of subsistence by a system of reserves and money payments, and also had to so extinguish the Indian title to all lands outside their reserves as to enable incoming settlers to enter upon these lands and possess them on fulfilling certain conditions. That the Government of Canada, without regard to political party, has through all the years been more successful in these undertakings than the Government of any other country is generally conceded. This success has been due in part to the wise leadership of governors and commissioners and native interpreters. But we reiterate what every one knows who has studied the real history of this country at first hand, namely that this success was due in a very large degree to the presence of the Mounted Police who became from the first in the eyes of the Indians the embodiment of genuine friendship and British fair play.

The earliest Indian treaty in what is now Western Canada was made by Lord Selkirk, whom the Salteaux Indians in the Red River Country called "The Silver Chief," because for sterling gifts he obtained from the Indians for his colonists a strip of land extending back as far as one could see a white horse on the prairie in a clear day. That was a primitive method of measurement and depended somewhat on the individual's power of vision, but with a vast unpeopled land stretching a thousand miles to the setting sun no one raised questions about a few acres more or less. Later, when the country was beginning to fill up, greater care had to be exercised. Indians, though apparently stoical and unemotional, are in reality very sensitive and keenly susceptible to anything that looks like oversight or slight of them and their rights.

The year 1876 witnessed the retirement of Colonel French from the Commissionership of the Mounted Police. He had wrought hard in the critical tasks that fall to the lot of the foundation builder, but desired to return to his duty in the regular artillery service in England, where his eminent contributions to the Empire have been duly recognized. Colonel French, who retained to the end a warm interest in the Police, was succeeded in the Commissionership by Colonel James Farquharson MacLeod, who had already done such outstanding work during the long trek to the West and in getting to definite police duty at the key-position of the whole work in the foothill country. It was a tribute to MacLeod's work that he was appointed also to aid Governor Laird in the delicate work of making the treaty with the most difficult tribes in the North-West to handle. Treaties had been made with the Indians who had been most in contact with civilization in the more easterly districts of the Lake of the Woods, Lake Winnipeg and the Qu'Appelle Lakes. But the most imposing spectacles and the most difficult situation began to arise when the Governors, flanked by the brilliant scarlet of the Mounted Police, came to the farther North-West where the Indians retained much of their native dignity and barbaric splendour.

This point was reached when Commissioners Governor Morris, Hon. W. J. Christie and the Hon. James McKay came to

Fort Carlton to negotiate with Mistawasis, the great chief of the Crees, and his friend Ahtukahcoop. An interesting preface to this treaty was a threat made by a rascally Indian, Chief Beardy, of Duck Lake, who said that he would not allow the Commissioners to cross the south branch of the Saskatchewan River to come to Carlton. This information was imparted by Lawrence Clark, Hudson's Bay Factor at Carlton, to Inspector James Walker, who had arrived from Battleford with fifty Mounted Police the day before that on which the Commissioners were to arrive. Walker (now Colonel Walker, of Calgary), a man of commanding stature and strong determination, at once decided to take a hand in the proceedings. Initiative has always been characteristic of the Police. They were often miles away in distance from and worlds away in chance of communication with, any superior officer, and so they early developed the powers of resource which had to come into play in emergencies. Hence Walker, seeing the situation, swung out with his troop, in the small hours of next morning and hit the trail for Batoche. On the way he overtook the band of Indians with Chief Beardy. Walker paid no attention to them, but simply passed them and continued on the way. These Indians rarely indicate surprise, but this was the surprise of their lives, and they showed it in spite of themselves. They evidently did not calculate on the presence of the force in that part of the world, and to have these stalwart red-coated riders come up from the unexpected direction was too much even for their impassiveness. When Walker met the Commissioners farther on, he told Governor Morris of the situation and then, wheeling his men, formed a scarlet escort around the carriage. When they met Beardy he was in a repentant mood and shook hands with the Governor. But this disorderly Chief would only sign the treaty in his own camp. Not long afterwards Inspector Walker with two constables had to go to Duck Lake and face this same chief and a band of his insolent warriors and prevent them from looting a store at that point. Still later we shall find the incorrigible Beardy on the war-path with the rebels Riel and Gabriel Dumont.

The treaty, known generally as "Number Six," was duly made at Carlton by Governor Morris and the other Commissioners, with a noted half-breed, Peter Erasmus, as the capable interpreter. Those present who had not been accustomed to the plains witnessed a spectacle of wild splendour, as preceding the treaty, over a thousand

Indians, brilliantly and fantastically painted, chanting a weird song, firing rifles, exhibiting marvellous horsemanship, beating drums and giving strange yells, advanced in a semi-circle near to the Commissioner's tent. All this was preparatory to the famous dance of the stem, where the chiefs, councillors and medicine men seated themselves on buffalo robes and a beautifully decorated pipe with a long stem was produced. This was carried around the semi-circle, then raised towards the heavens and the stem pointed in turn north, south, east and west. With more stately motion the Indians moved towards the Council tent, where they were met by the Commissioners who took the pipe and one after the other stroked it gently to indicate that they reciprocated the peaceful approach of the Indians.

The Commissioners present with Governor Morris at this treaty and others deserve special notice. The Hon. W. J. Christie was a famous Hudson's Bay Company Factor. When in January, 1873, the Ottawa Government appointed a North-West Council to act with Governor Morris in governing the far hinterland towards the mountains, Mr. Christie, who had a very wide knowledge of conditions and who had education and judgment, was one of the men chosen. An interesting fact in that connection was that when the first meeting of that Council was held, on March 8 in that year, Mr. Christie travelled 2,000 miles by dog-train from Fort Simpson to Winnipeg to attend it. It was a good opportunity for collecting mileage and perquisites, but the probability is that this public-spirited man and the great Company he served made the contribution to the country. His usefulness was so apparent at the meeting that he was asked to help the Government in the great task of treaty-making which had baffled so many other countries.

The other Commissioner whose name is found to nearly all the treaties was the Hon. James McKay, one of the most picturesque figures the western plains, amid all their unique characters, ever saw. I remember him in his later years. His father was a Scot, who had been on one of the Arctic expeditions in search of Sir John Franklin and had married in the Saskatchewan country one of the tall, stately and handsome daughters of the land. Their sons were all of distinguished appearance. The following description given by the Earl of Southesk, who had come on a hunting tour and a search for health in the great out-of-doors of the North-West years ago, is true to the subject. He says: "James McKay met me in St. Paul. His appearance greatly interested me, both from his own personal advantages and because he was the first Red River man I had seen. Immensely broad-chested and muscular, though not tall, he weighed 18 stone: yet in spite of his stoutness, he was exceedingly hardy and active, and a wonderful horseman. His face is very handsome—short, aquiline, delicate nose; piercing dark grey eyes; skin tanned to red bronze by exposure to the weather. He was dressed in Red River style, a blue cloth capote (hooded frock coat) with brass buttons; red and black flannel shirt, which served for waistcoat; black belt around the waist; trousers of brown and white striped home-made stuff, buff leather moccasins on his feet. I had never come across a wearer of moccasins before, and it amused me to see this grand and massive man pacing the hotel corridors with noiseless footfall, while excitable little men in shiny boots creaked and stamped about like so many busy steam engines." It was this splendid man who was present to assist Governor Laird and Mr. Christie in making treaties with the Cree Indians at Carlton on August 23 and at Fort Pitt on September 9. The last time I saw James McKay was when a number of us schoolboys rode up to Silver Heights to see some western sports and buffalo running in honour of the Governor-General, Lord Dufferin. And as the magnificent frontiersman drove about with his famous cream horse and buckboard, the great Irish diplomat realized what such men had done to make the great North-West peacefully into being a part of Canada.

Soon after these treaties, the headquarters of the Mounted Police were moved from Swan River, which had never been satisfactory, to Fort MacLeod, where they arrived on October 22. Apart from Swan River being unsuitable, it was evident that the centre of interest was gravitating towards that part of the territories where the names of Forts MacLeod and Walsh, Wood Mountain and Cypress Hills and other points were being printed indelibly on the map of Western history. This portion of the territory was close up against the international boundary line across which might be heard the roar of fighting between the Sioux Indians and the United States soldiery. To discuss that is not part of our story, but the Indians there vehemently declared that they had been for years robbed by swindling government agents and driven off their land by unscrupulous gold-hunters and lawless speculators. And, as in many other cases, soldiers who were themselves innocent of these things had to be called on to fight the Indians who had grown savage under a sense of wrong and who, savage-like, had taken revenge by killing whenever they could. That very year, only a few months before the headquarters of the Police were moved to Fort MacLeod, occurred the tragedy of the "Custer Massacre," when that gallant soldier and his no less gallant men, attempting the impossible, were wiped out completely by superior numbers of Sioux under the redoubtable chiefs Sitting Bull and Spotted Eagle. "The Long Hair," as General Custer was called by the Indians who always admired his dash and courage, fought desperately to the end, and was said to be the last man to fall. Only the arrival later of General Terry, with whom Custer was to have co-operated, prevented still greater disaster to the balance of the American force.

All this had its effect on our side of the border. It made our Indians, Blackfeet, Bloods, Piegans and others, restless, and it became known that the Sioux on the south of the line were making overtures to the Indians on the Canadian side either to go over and fight the Americans or to join with the Indians in the United States to drive all the whites out of the country on both sides. Inspector Denny, who did much valuable work in those early days and who made an arrest in a Blackfoot camp, reported in August of 1876 that he had been consulted by the Blackfeet Council and told of the efforts made by the Sioux to get the Indians on this side with them. However, the Blackfeet remained loyal mainly because they had learned to trust the Mounted Police. But shortly afterwards, matters were complicated by bands of Sioux crossing over the line into Canadian territory. We shall deal with this Sioux invasion in the next chapter, but in the meantime, as this is a chapter on treaties, shall record how the Canadian Government, being fully aware of all these events, took special steps at once to make treaties with the warlike tribes which inhabited that vast area from the North Saskatchewan River towards the boundary line. For this purpose the Commissioners appointed were Governor David Laird and Colonel MacLeod, of the Mounted Police. No better men could be chosen to make this famous Treaty Number Seven with the Indians at a very critical hour.

Accordingly, on September 19, 1877, at the Blackfeet Crossing of the Bow River, less than a 100 miles from Fort MacLeod, the Chiefs of the Blackfeet, Blood, Piegan, Stony and Sarcee tribes and some 5,000 of their men, women and children met to hear the Great Mother's chiefs. Mr. Laird's address was full of dignity and impressiveness, and couched in the picturesque language which, interpreted by the inimitable Jerry Potts, found its way to the hearts of his audience. Mr. Laird opened by saying, "The Great Spirit has made all things, the sun, the moon, the stars, the earth, the forests and the swift-running rivers. It is by the Great Spirit that the Queen rules over this great country and other great countries. The Great Spirit has made the white man and the red man brothers, and we should take each other by the hand. The Great Mother loves all her children, white men and red men alike. She wishes to do them all good." Then Mr. Laird made special reference to the Police which was good diplomacy, for the Indians had known the Police for three years and the wise Governor saw the advantage of linking up the Police with the Queen's government. He said, "When bad white men brought you whisky, robbed you and made you poor, and through whisky made you quarrel amongst yourselves, she sent the Mounted Police to put an end to it. You know how they stopped this and punished the offenders, and how much good this has done. I have to tell you how much pleased the Queen is that you have taken the Mounted Police by the hand and helped them and obeyed her laws since their arrival. She hopes you will continue to do so and you will always find the Mounted Police on your side if you keep the Queen's laws." Then Mr. Laird explained the terms of the treaty and asked the Indians to go to their Council tents if they wished to consider the matter.

Next day the Commissioners again met the chiefs and made all the points clear, and on the third day the treaty was concluded amid great satisfaction on all sides. There were some remarkable tributes to the Police by the Chiefs. Crowfoot, the head chief, said, "The advice given to me and my people has proved to be good. If the Police had not come to this country where would we all be now? Bad men and whisky were indeed killing us so fast that very few of us indeed would have been left to-day. The Mounted Police have protected us as the feathers of the bird protect it from the frosts of winter. I wish them all good and trust that all our hearts will increase in goodness from this time forward. I am satisfied, I will sign the treaty." Red Crow, head chief of the Bloods, the most powerful tribe of the Blackfeet Confederacy, said, "Three years ago, when the Mounted Police came to this country, I met and shook hands with Stamix-oto-kan (Colonel MacLeod) at Belly River. Since that time he made me many promises, he kept them all; not one of them was broken. Everything that the Mounted Police have done has been good. I entirely trust Stamix-oto-kan (Colonel MacLeod) and will leave everything to him. I will sign with Crowfoot." Many others spoke in the same strain, and after this great treaty was signed, on September 21, 1877, there was a salute of guns and general jubilation. The point to be specially recalled in connection with this treaty is that it was practically accomplished upon the splendid record that Colonel MacLeod and his men had made amongst these powerful tribes in the most difficult part of the West.

The annual money payment to the Indians under the treaties required careful and honest handling. And at the conclusion of his report to the Government in regard to this most famous of all the treaties, Governor Laird made this remarkable witness-bearing recommendation: "I would urge that the officers of the Mounted Police be entrusted to make the annual payments to the Indians under this treaty. The chiefs themselves requested this, and I said I believed the Government would gladly consent to the arrangement. The Indians have confidence in the Police, and it might be some time before they would acquire the same respect for strangers." That this suggestion was carried out, is attested the next year by that well-known officer, Superintendent Winder, who in his report says: "Inspector Macdonnell and party arrived from Fort Walsh with money for the Indian payments. Inspector McIllree paid the Bloods at MacLeod, Inspector Dickens the Piegans on their reserve, Inspector Frechette the Stoneys at Morley-ville, and I accompanied the agent to the Blackfeet Crossing to assist in paying the Indians there." All this requires no comment further than to say that when the fighting Sioux across the line tried to inveigle these warlike tribes into a war of extermination against the whites, and later when the fiercely magnetic Louis Riel sought to get them to join his revolt, the great work in the consummation of Treaty Number Seven stood Canada in good stead.

One more great treaty had still to be made, and though it is anticipating a date twenty years after the famous Number Seven Treaty, we record it here before closing the chapter of treaties with the Indians of the North-West. A vast region away northward from Edmonton, known generally as the Athabasca, Peace River and Mackenzie River region, had so far not been brought under treaty conditions. This was mainly due to the fact that settlement had not been making its way into that region. It was considered the home of the fur-trader and the hunter more than that of the farmer or the stock-raiser. But the investigations brought about by the Senate Committee at Ottawa on the motion and under the leadership of Senator (Sir John) Schultz, had called so much attention to the great agricultural possibilities of the country that, despite the total absence of railways, settlers were percolating slowly into that great northern area. Then the gold-rush to the Klondike began midway in the nineties, and as some of this rush was either going through the Peace River country to the Yukon or scattering down the northern rivers, it became necessary, in the view of the Mounted Police, who made recommendations to the Government, to make a treaty as early as possible, in order to prevent trouble. Accordingly, the Hon. Clifford Sifton, then Superintendent-General of Indian affairs in the Laurier Government, began arrangements in 1898 which led to the appointment of a Commission and the making of Treaty Number Eight in 1899. Strangely enough, the Hon. David Laird, "the man who talked straight," who had as Governor of the Territories made the famous treaties with the Indians of the plains twenty years before, was called to head the new commission and make this final treaty with the Crees, Beavers, Chippewyans and other Indians of the far North. Mr. Laird, after the term of his office as Governor had expired, had retired to his home in Prince Edward Island, but later on was appointed to take charge of Indian affairs in the West, with headquarters in Winnipeg. Along with this Indian Treaty Commission was a half-breed commission, of which the frontiersman author, Mr. Charles Mair, was secretary. The expedition took months, and involved hard if picturesque travelling, all of which is graphically described in Mr. Mair's narrative *Through the Mackenzie Basin*. The treaty was made beginning first at Lesser Slave Lake, and continuing at other points. Mr. Mair, in his book, gives us the names of the party, describes the camp equipment and then makes the following fine reference to the Mounted Police: "Not the least important and effective constituent of the party was the detachment of the Royal North-West Mounted Police which joined us at Edmonton, minus their horses of course; picked men from a picked force; sterling fellows whose tenacity and hard work in the tracking harness did yeoman service in many a serious emergency. This detachment consisted of Inspector Snyder, Sergeant Anderson, Corporals Fitzgerald and McClelland, and Constables McLaren, Lett, Burman, Lelonde, Burke, Vernon and Kerr. The conduct of these men, it is needless to say, was the admiration of all, and assisted materially in the successful progress of the expedition."

Thus did these nation-building Police set their seal to the great treaties which provided for the future of the Indian tribes and at the same time extinguished the title of the tribes in order to open up a new empire for higher civilization.

* * * * *

CHAPTER VI

HANDLING AMERICAN INDIANS

Nothing in the history of Western Canada was more charged with dynamitic possibilities of serious trouble than the unexpected influx into our country of thousands of battle-scarred Indians from the other side of the boundary line. The whole period for five years, from 1876 onward, bristled with difficulties. These Indians themselves had to be more or less provided for while upon our soil—they had to be controlled according to British law, they had to be kept from interfering with the loyalty as well as the rights and reserves of our own Indians, and they had to be restrained from making this country the base of any operations against our friendly neighbour country south of the line. The whole situation was filled with dramatic incidents and dangerous possibilities of international complications. The honour of handling it with masterly, firm and yet conciliatory methods must be given not to Ottawa, which was too far away and which often misunderstood, but to the officers and men of the Mounted Police whose consummate skill, courage and initiative are the leading features of that serious period. And the amazing thing about it all is that in the midst of seething thousands of American and Canadian Indians on the wide and lonely frontier, we had a mere handful of these gallant red-coated guardians of the peace.

The influx of American Indians began in December, 1876, when some 3,000 Indians, with large droves of horses and mules, crossed over and camped at Wood Mountain. They told the officers of the Mounted Police who visited them at once that "they had been driven out by the American and had come to look for peace; that they had been told by their grandfathers that they would find peace in the land of the British; that their brothers, the Santees, had found it years ago and they had now followed them; that they had not slept sound for years and were anxious to find a place where they could lie down and feel safe." It was not the British way to turn a deaf ear to that pathetic appeal, and so Inspector Walsh, then in charge at Fort Walsh, took charge of the situation, began at once to regulate the possession of arms and ammunition to what was necessary for hunting for subsistence and generally to keep in close touch with the Indian encampments.

In the following May the famous and redoubtable Sitting Bull with quite a large force came over and joined the American Indian colony. They also were interviewed at once by the Mounted Police and promised to observe the laws of the Great Mother. In the following months bands of Nez Perces and others arrived in flight from the American soldiers. And so the situation became more involved. Efforts were made to persuade these Indians to return to their own country, but they declined to do so and of course no one would compel them. The Indians said they had been robbed and cheated by agents, and so they had lost faith in the American Government, for they assumed that the Government knew or ought to know of these things. It was matter of common knowledge throughout the Western country that some agents who were receiving a salary of $1500.00 a year retired with fortunes after a few years in office, and even the most unsuspecting and docile Indian would baulk at that after a while.

Colonel McLeod, a very cautious man, in a report to the Hon. David Mills at Ottawa, said, "I think the principal cause of the difficulties which are continually embroiling the American Government in trouble with the Indians, is the manner in which these Indians are treated by the swarms of adventurers who have scattered themselves all over the Indian country in search of minerals before any treaty is made giving up the title. These men always look upon the Indians as their natural enemies, and it is their rule to shoot at them if they approach after being warned off. I was actually asked the other day by an American who has settled here, if we had the same law here as on the other side, and if he was justified in shooting any Indian who approached his camp after being warned not to advance. I am satisfied that such a rule is not necessary in dealing with the worst of Indians, and that any necessity there might be for its adoption arose from the illegal intrusion and wrongdoings of the Whites." Happy country was ours to have a MacLeod on the spot through these troublous years!

Meanwhile the Police had occasional problems with our own Indians, not in relation to the Government, but in connection with ancient or modern feuds or ordinary quarrels between tribes. The Police generally got things early under control. Here is a case. On May 25, 1877, Little Child, a Salteaux Treaty Chief, came to Fort Walsh and reported that his people and a large number of Assiniboines under Chief Crow's Dance had been camped together. The Salteaux desired to leave, and so notified Crow's Dance. This individual for some reason refused permission to the Salteaux to leave camp. But Little Child, feeling that he and his people had a right to go where they pleased "so long as they kept the laws of the White Mother," ordered his people to move. Whereupon Crow's Dance, who had 250 warriors, set upon the Salteaux, killing not any of the people, but shooting nineteen valuable sled-dogs, cutting lodges, upsetting travois, knocking down men, and frightening the women and children by firing off guns and giving war-whoops. When warned by Little Child, who did not retaliate, that he would report the matter to the Police, Crow's Dance struck him and said, "When the Police come we will do the same." Crow's Dance, backed by several hundred warriors, talked boastfully, knowing that there was only a handful of Police at Fort Walsh.

But the Police came, all told fifteen constables and a guide, under Inspector Walsh. They had also the surgeon, Dr. Kittson, along, because it looked as if his services would be required badly. Walsh and his handful of men struck that camp at three o'clock in the morning, after getting the report. He halted his men and inspected their arms and had all pistols ready. Then they rode swiftly into camp, and before anyone knew how it happened, he had "Crow's Dance" and "Rolling Thunder" and "Spider" and "The one who bends the wood" and the other leaders under arrest and out of camp to a butte near by. There Walsh ordered his men to breakfast, and sent word to the Assiniboine Chiefs still in camp that he would talk to them after breakfast. And so he did, making it very clear that no one had any right to interfere with others who desired to leave camp peaceably, and that he intended to take "Crow's Dance" and the others to Fort Walsh for trial. And they were taken accordingly.

Some were sentenced to short terms, others were allowed to go, as they were not specially involved. In reporting this incident to Ottawa, Assistant-Commissioner A. G. Irvine said: "In conclusion I cannot too highly write of Inspector Walsh's prompt conduct in this matter, and it must be a matter of congratulation to feel that fifteen of our men can ride into an enormous camp of Indians and take out of it as prisoners thirteen of their head men. The action of this detachment will have great effect on all the Indians throughout the country." Right loyally spoken, Major Irvine!

And Walsh in his report speaks of his men: "In conclusion I wish to say a few words for the men of my detachment. Before entering the camp I explained to them there were 200 warriors in the camp who had set the Police at defiance; that I intended to arrest the leaders; to do so perhaps would put them in a dangerous position, but that they would have to pay strict attention to all orders given by me, no matter how severe they might appear. From the replies and the way they acted during the whole time, I am of opinion that every man of this detachment would have boldly stood his ground if the Indians had made any resistance." A good testimony this from a keen leader of gallant men. And because a note of appreciation is always an encouragement, we quote the able Comptroller Fred White, who wrote Major Irvine on behalf of the Secretary of State, then the governmental head of the department: "The Secretary of State desires that you will convey to Inspector Walsh his appreciation of the courage and determination shown by him and the officers and men under his command in carrying out their duty."

This incident occurred while the Sitting Bull invasion was still an unsolved problem, and so we take it up again. Inspector Walsh, as already recorded, met him on his arrival on Canadian soil, and Sitting Bull promised to obey the Queen's laws and report to the Police anything that happened. Not long afterwards three Americans, one a priest, the second General Miles' head scout, and an interpreter, arrived in Sitting Bull's camp to persuade him to go back south of the line. "The black-robe" would have been safe, but the other two would have been shot on sight but for Sitting Bull's promise to Walsh. The Chief sent word to the Police that three Americans were in his camp, and Assistant Commissioner Irvine, Inspector Walsh, Sub-Inspectors Clark and Allen went out to hold inquiry regarding the situation. Including the Yanktons, a branch of the Sioux, there were some 205 lodges. This was Irvine's first meeting with the famous Sioux Chief, and he gives us this pen picture: "I was particularly struck with Sitting Bull. He is a man of somewhat short stature, but with a pleasant face, a mouth showing great determination and a fine high forehead. When he smiled, which he often did, his face brightened up wonderfully. I should say he is a man of about forty-five years of age. The warriors who came with him were all of immense height and very muscular. When talking at the conference he spoke as a man who understands his subject well and who had thoroughly weighed it before speaking. He believes no one from the other side and said so. His speech showed him to be a man of wonderful capability."

The conference referred to was between the police officers above mentioned and Sitting Bull and other chiefs of the Sioux, Pretty Bear, Bear's Cap, The Eagle Sitting Down, Spotted Eagle and others. Later on the three Americans were present. But the Sioux flatly refused to return to the South, Sitting Bull closing the conference with the words, "Once I was rich, plenty of money, but the Americans stole it all in the Black Hills. What should I return for? To have my horse and my arms taken away? I have come to remain with the White Mother's children."

The next step taken by the American Government which seemed anxious to have the Indians return South and settle down on certain conditions, was to send special Commissioners in the persons of General Terry and General O'Neill, replaced by Lawrence, to visit Canada, hold conference with Sitting Bull and the other chiefs to that end. The Canadian Government adhered to its position of being willing to protect the Indians so long as they were on British soil. Hence no undue pressure to leave would be brought on those who had sought asylum under the British flag, but at the same time both the Ottawa authorities and the Police would have been glad to see them go voluntarily. Those who had knowledge of the situation and the outlook knew that Canada would not set aside land as reserves for American Indians, and they knew also that with the early disappearance of buffalo and other game in the presence of advancing civilization, the burden of feeding and caring for these aliens would be very heavy.

Word was wired from Ottawa to Colonel MacLeod to meet the American Commissioners with an escort at the boundary and if possible to get the Sioux leaders to come to Fort Walsh to meet them and thus save the Commissioners the necessity for a long journey. Accordingly, MacLeod met the Americans at the line and escorted them to Fort Walsh, to which point Inspector Walsh brought Sitting Bull and the other chiefs in due course. Walsh had great difficulty in getting the Indians to come, as they said they did not trust the Americans and feared that the latter might bring soldiers across to attack them. The fact that the day Walsh was in the camp on his errand of persuasion a band of Nez Perces men, women and children, wounded and bleeding, after a fight across the line, had come there for refuge, did not make the Inspector's task any easier. But because they had received the assurance of both MacLeod and Walsh that no one could cross the line after them, the chiefs came—Sitting Bull, Bear's Cap, Spotted Eagle, Flying Bird, Whirlwind Bear, Iron Dog, The Crow, Bear that Scatters, Little Knife, Yellow Dog and some others of less importance. The conference was held on October 17, 1877. It is customary for all parties to shake hands before beginning these "talks," but on this occasion Sitting Bull, representing the Chiefs, entered and shook hands warmly with Colonel MacLeod, but passed the American Commissioners with the utmost disdain.

General Terry delivered the message from the President of the United States. Terry was a distinguished soldier, hero of Fort Fisher in the Civil War, a man of magnificent appearance, standing some 6 ft. 6 in., built in proportion, a very gentlemanly officer with a kindly face and gracious manner. He made known the wishes of the President, told the Sioux that they were the only hostile band remaining out, offered them reserves and stock with farm implements and instructors, the only condition being that they would settle down on their reserves and surrender their arms and their horses. The General made appeal to them that, because too much blood had already been spilled, they should all henceforth live in peace, and the whole bearing and appearance of the distinguished speaker indicated his personal genuineness.

But Sitting Bull and his friends would not be appeased. They were embittered by a long course of harsh and unfair treatment by unscrupulous agents and frontier exploiters. One after the other the chiefs rose and declined the offer because, as they said, they had no confidence that these fair promises would be carried out. Sitting Bull said, "For sixty-four years you have treated my people bad. Over there we could go nowhere, so we have taken refuge here. I shake hands with these people (the Police), you can go back home, that part of the country we came from belonged to us and you took it from us, now we live here." Some of the other chiefs spoke even more bitterly and even a squaw, though it was a most unusual thing for a woman to take part in a conference, added her hot protest against accepting the proposals of the Commissioners from the States. The burden of the Indian speeches was all to the effect that they had been given no rest on the other side of the line, but had been driven about from place to place.

So the United States officers returned to their own country, having failed in their mission, to their own disappointment, and it may be added to the disappointment of the Canadian authorities who would have been glad to be relieved of the responsibility for the care of alien Indians, but who would not attempt in any way to drive out any who had sought refuge on our soil.

But as the time passed the position of the Sioux became more and more difficult. They were kept under strict surveillance by the Police. On account of their warlike disposition, and their association with the massacres south of the line, their presence was prejudicial to settlement by white people. Superintendent James Walker, who was in charge at Battleford and who, having jurisdiction over a large area, showed marked judgment as well as firmness in dealing with Indians, has some very accurate forecasts in a report written at the end of 1879. He suggests that Police be stationed at Duck Lake and Fort Pitt as well as Prince Albert. Duck Lake was the home of Chief Beardy, with whom Walker had already taken some firm measures and who joined with the Riel-Dumont rebellion later. Fort Pitt was the home of Chief Big Bear, concerning whom Walker writes in that report: "I look upon Big Bear as one of the most troublesome Cree Indians we have in the territories." And this same Big Bear also became a rebel in Riel's day and, after the Frog Lake massacre, burned Fort Pitt as an extra in his exploits, as I witnessed with my own eyes.

These items are quoted to show Walker's foresight as well as insight, for these give special weight to another sentence in that report concerning Indians of the Sitting Bull tribe. "The very name of Sioux," wrote Walker, "strikes terror into the hearts of many of the settlers." On this account the wanderings of Sitting Bull from Fort Walsh to Qu'Appelle and generally round about, was an unsettling influence. In a year or two, however, with the buffalo growing fewer and no land reserve in sight on the Canadian side, a good many of Sitting Bull's following began to drop away from him and go back over the line. One day, with about 1,200 or so of his people, he turned up at Fort Qu'Appelle and applied to Superintendent Sam B. Steele, who had come to that point from Fort Walsh, and asked that a reserve be given him and his band in Canada. Steele told him there was no chance, but sent a wire to Indian Commissioner (afterwards Governor) Dewdney that Sitting Bull was there. Mr. Dewdney came to Qu'Appelle and told Sitting Bull that the Canadian Government would not give him a reserve, as he had a reserve on the other side of the line which the United States would give him to occupy in peace if he would go there. Mr. Dewdney offered to ration Sitting Bull and his band as far as Wood Mountain, and Steele sent an escort with the Indians to ration them to that point. When they arrived there Sitting Bull was in a rather vicious temper and went to Inspector A. R. Macdonnell, the Mounted Police officer in charge there, with a few men. Sitting Bull asked for food and was refused by Macdonnell, who was widely known as a somewhat erratic but absolutely fearless and fair-minded man. The Sioux Chief then said he would take food by force, but he had mistaken his man. Macdonnell replied that he would ration the band with bullets if they tried that game. Then said Sitting Bull, "I am cast away." "No," said Macdonnell. "You are not cast away. I am speaking for your own good and the good of your people and giving you good advice. You have been promised pardon and food and land if you return to your own reservation in the United States. I advise you to go and I will help you and your people to travel if you accept the terms that have been offered you." Sitting Bull knew that Macdonnell would keep his word in either case, and so he concluded to take the Inspector's kindly meant advice.

Accordingly, the next day Macdonnell personally accompanied Sitting Bull to Poplar River, where the Chief handed over his rifle to Major Brotherton of the United States Army in token of submission. Macdonnell then arranged that the Sitting Bull band should be supplied with transportation and food by Mr. Louis Legarre, a trader, at the expense of the American Government, and thus they all crossed over the line. A few years later there was some row on Sitting Bull's reserve over there in connection with arrests, and in the confusion the famous old chief was shot, it is claimed by mistake and unnecessarily. Thus ended the stormy career of a man who seems to have been honest according to his light in fighting for the rights of his people as he understood them. His methods in war were no doubt barbaric and cruel enough, but some civilized nations cannot throw stones at pagans in that regard.

I have written Sitting Bull's story as far as it affected Canada in some detail, because it was in reality a series of events full of dangerous possibilities. Papers and persons in Eastern Canada were demanding that regiments should be raised and sent out to the West to cope with the situation that foreboded war with the Americans, who had thousands of picked soldiers on the border to keep the Indians down. But to the utter amazement of Eastern Canadians and to the more profound surprise of the Americans our handful of Mounted Police, with masterly diplomacy, endless patience and steady, cool courage were able to handle the whole situation and solve it without the loss of a single life on either side. There are few such chapters anywhere in the records of history.

It is in keeping with the general attitude of the Police towards the Indians, whom they considered the wards of the nation which the men in the scarlet tunic represented, that we find many fine incidents scattered up and down throughout the years. At Qu'Appelle, about the time above noted, an epidemic of smallpox threatened in the winter time, when its deadly effects are most in evidence in the Indian camps. The Police never proceeded on the wretched maxim of some that "the only good Indian is a dead Indian," and so, when these children of the wild were attacked by plague or pestilence or other destroyer, the Police fought for the lives of the afflicted people with all the tenacity and the courage of their corps. On the occasion mentioned in this paragraph there was no doctor, but Acting Hospital Steward Holmes, who had studied medicine, though he had no graduation standing, threw himself into the struggle against this dread disease. He vaccinated the Indians on all the reserves, many white people and all the half-breeds in the district. This meant travelling incessantly in the dead of winter and sleeping without tent in the snow-drifts with the thermometer down to 30 degrees below zero and more. He was only drawing the usual constable pay of 75 cents a day, and Steele, who was in command, recommended him for a small bonus allowance and a promotion. For it was not only vaccination and treatment of smallpox that had engaged Holmes' efforts, but constant attendance upon hundreds of Indians who had been so worn down that it was only by his devoted efforts that they were pulled through that hard winter. To Steele's amazement neither of his recommendations as to this toiler for others was acted upon. But I do not suppose Holmes cared. He had done his duty and was not working for reward. But the ways of men who could pigeon-hole a recommendation like that are difficult to understand.

A somewhat similar case was away in another direction, where one Corporal D. B. Smith held the post all alone at the famous old Hudson's Bay Fort at Norway House on Lake Winnipeg. Scarlet fever and diphtheria in the most deadly form broke out amongst the Indians and half-breeds, who were being mowed down like corn before the scythe. Corporal Smith, though stationed there for ordinary duty, did not hesitate a moment in facing the situation and going into a fight against these violent twin epidemics. He looked after the sick with the tenderness of a nurse, he comforted the dying, he buried the dead when even relatives shrank from the duty, and by strong disinfectants he sought to clean the huts and tents of the poisonous germs. There was no glamour of war to lure him on, no crashing of music, no cheers of comrades, for he was alone. It was just a grim, determined, silent fight, in which he knew he might fall at any moment himself, and there was no one to tell of deeds that were worthy of the Victoria Cross. But he fought the plagues to a finish. And it is good to know that when the story of it all leaked out and got to the ears of the authorities the Corporal got an additional stripe in recognition of his valorous work.

Or take a later case, where one Sergeant Field away in the bitter North at Fort Chippewyan received word that an Indian had gone insane and dangerous some 300 miles away at another post. Field had just returned from a hard patrol and his dogs were fagged. Field was an experienced man and knew the danger, as he was tired out himself. But he hired a fresh team of dogs and started out. The Indian madman was hard to handle, for he was violent and strong.

Field had to tie him on the sleigh, but of course had to release him at times for fear he would freeze. On these occasions the lunatic would fight like a wolf and make attempts to get away. It would have been easy to let him get away and be lost in some night blizzard in the wilderness. But that was not the Police way, and in due course the unfortunate creature was landed safely at Fort Saskatchewan and given a chance to recover under new conditions.

When occasion required, the red-coated men could be firm enough, as all law-breakers found to their sorrow, but there is something amazing in the way in which these policemen risked and lost their lives at times in making arrests rather than shoot the Indians they were sent to bring in. In a most marked degree the police kept to the faith that they were come to save human lives rather than destroy them. In this connection and throwing in some incidents as above to illustrate our points, we think of the case of Sergeant Wilde, of Pincher Creek, who trailed a murderous Indian generally known as Charcoal into the foothills. When the murderer was sighted, Wilde, whose horse was one of the best, spurred away ahead of his men. Charcoal was riding deliberately along with a rifle slung across in front of him in plain sight of Wilde, who, however, would not fire upon him, but pressed on to make the arrest and leave the disposal of him to the law of the land. When Wilde rode up to him, the Indian wheeled in his saddle and shot him, following this up a few minutes after by putting another bullet in the body of the policeman as he lay on the ground. Wilde was one of the finest men who had ever worn the uniform—one of the men who had built up the great tradition of the Force. He was greatly beloved at Pincher Creek, where the citizens erected a monument to his memory. A pathetic incident took place on the day of his funeral, when a faithful and favourite hound that had always kept guard over Wilde refused to allow the pallbearers to remove the body and had to be shot before the funeral cortège could proceed. It was a pity to have to do this drastic thing, but the loyal and devoted dog would no doubt have died in any case of a broken heart.

And then there was the case of that other gallant young man, Sergeant Colebrook, up in the Prince Albert district, who was killed while proceeding to arrest a notorious Indian called Almighty Voice. Colebrook knew the character of the Indian because he had arrested him once before for cattle-stealing. This time Colebrook was trailing him for killing cattle and for breaking jail, and in company with an interpreter guide caught up to him on the open prairie. The Indian unslung his gun and called to the guide to tell the policeman to halt or he would shoot. But halting was not the Police way, and Colebrook, with the warrant to arrest, not to kill, as he said to the guide, went steadily forward and received a fatal bullet through the heart. It was the price he paid for his devotion to orders, but it maintained the Police tradition. Almighty Voice, of course, was not allowed to escape. He and two other Indians took up a stand in a clump of bushes, where they fought like rats in a hole against the Police and civilians, of whom they killed several before the bush was shelled and the Indians found dead when Assistant Commissioner McIllree with several men rushed the position from the open plain.

It was the willingness of the Police, even at great risk to themselves, to allow the alleged wrong-doer to get the benefit of a fair British trial after his arrest, that gradually gave the Indians a new sense of obligation to the men of the scarlet tunic. This splendid part of the Police tradition won its way steadily till great war camps came to realize that the Police stood for the square deal, and that if men the Police wished to arrest were innocent, they would not be punished. And with that lesson came also into the heart of the Indian the conviction that if any of their number did wrong they should, as westerners used to say, take their medicine and reap the due reward of their deeds. In either case the Police approved themselves to the Indians as their friends, not their enemies, and thus the famous corps became a very great asset to Canada in the interests of law and order.

* * * * *

CHAPTER VII

THE IRON HORSES

For some ten stirring and formative years the Mounted Police had been riding their gallant steeds over the virgin sod of the untracked prairie before the iron horses, crossing the Red River, hit the steel trail for the mountains and the Western Sea. It is quite certain that the presence of the men in scarlet and gold on western plains was an element in the situation which encouraged the promoters of the Canadian Pacific Railway, our first transcontinental, to undertake their tremendous project with more assured confidence. For these shrewd students of human nature knew quite well that people would look in various ways upon the coming of the railway.

There would be some who, like Thoreau, the hermit sage of Walden, would resent, though perhaps for a less æsthetic reason, the intrusion of this noisy and energetic sign of a new era. It was he who cried, "We do not ride on the railway, it rides on us." For, while there were some in our West who actually did feel regret at the passing of the quiet day of their pioneer life, most of those who had the aggressive spirit of the white race in them, were glad to see the vision of the earliest colonists being fulfilled by the opening up of the country. But there were others who had lived on the frontiers, and had been a law unto themselves, who said, like a trader who saw three wooden shacks built where Calgary now stands, "I am going to move back—this is getting too civilized for me," and the man who said that represented a class that had to be made to realize the presence of government.

Then there were the Indians, who saw in the advent of the railway the necessary disappearance of big game from the plains, which would become the habitat of the settler. More than once there were Indians who would have blocked the way of the railway builders or would even have swooped down in the night and torn up the rails, but for the restraining presence of authority. And besides all these, there were some amongst the huge gangs of navvies and general track-makers who had alien tastes and habits, who required to be, on occasion, reminded that, while in a British country no law-abiding man should be coerced into working against his will if he was not satisfied with conditions, he must respect the rights of human life and must not destroy the property of others. All these cases and conditions became actualities in the West, and with all these the Mounted Police dealt as occasions arose, in such a way as to enable the march of civilization to proceed unchecked and unafraid.

For the settlers who made the continuance of the railway possible, the Mounted Policeman was a sort of guardian angel, and the well-known painting by Paul Wickson which hangs in the Premier's office at Ottawa shows how the patrol went about asking the homesteader if he had any complaints. Only those perhaps who have lived on these far-sundered homesteads know how much this meant to these lonely men and their isolated families. Fighting prairie fires, when the mad battalions of flame wheeled with the gale and charged at the humble dwelling or the precious hay or wheat-stacks of the settler, was the willingly assumed duty of many a rider of the plains. One recalls the case of Constable Conradi, who, while on patrol one fall day when the dry grass was as inflammable as tinder, asked a settler if there was any homesteader living in the direction where a fire was rushing. The settler said yes, that there was a man named Young, his wife and children, that way, but it would be impossible to reach them through the fiery wall that was so plainly visible. "Impossible or not," says the constable, "I am going to try," and putting spurs to his horse he was soon lost to sight in the rolling smoke. The horse was so badly burned that he had to be shot, but Conradi saved the family. He found Mr. Young, the settler, exhausted. They both fought the fierce blaze, and when hope of saving the home was gone, the constable, plunging through the fire, found Mrs. Young and the children standing in the water of a slough. He saw that they would be suffocated when the fire encircled it, and so he plunged and carried the children to the burnt ground, the mother following. From the settler's grateful letter to headquarters we make this extract: "His pluck and endurance I cannot praise too highly, fighting till he was nearly suffocated, his hat burned off his head, hair singed and vest on fire. My wife and family owe their lives to him, and I feel with them we shall never be able to repay him for his brave conduct." Thus did the Police make the settlers' work possible, that they in turn might make the railway a reasonably safe investment. Then, when the Indians became awkward and threatened to stop the progress of the transcontinental railway across the prairie, it was the Mounted Police that stepped in to see that the road was not blocked. Eastern contractors and workmen, who had not been used to seeing war-paint, were somewhat alarmed when a band of Indians would swoop down with the air of people who owned the earth, and in all such cases the Police were quickly called by wire or otherwise. Superintendent Shurtcliffe tells of a rather odd case in which an Indian chief with the appropriate name of "Front Man" stopped a railway contractor from getting out ties and caused the whole outfit to leave the bush in a good deal of panic. Shurtcliffe, a capable officer, immediately sent for "Front Man" and told him how dangerous a thing it was to interfere with the progress of work authorized by Canada. "Front Man" realized that he had rushed in where he had no business, and on his promising Shurtcliffe that he would behave himself, the contractor and his men went back to their peaceable but very important tie business.

Then there was the case of Pie-a-Pot, who from the earliest days of treaty-making was crochety and rather defiantly opposed to the incoming of anything or anybody that would interfere with his nomadic habits and general inclination to please himself. He showed a disagreeable tendency to leave his reserve and wander with his camp following and general entourage, much to the discomfort of others who were not desirous of his presence. One day this chief took it into his head that he would wander on to the right-of-way being mapped out for the Canadian Pacific, and by spreading his camp across it put a damper on the enterprise. And he succeeded up to a certain point. The engineers worked up to his camp and politely asked him to move, but he laughed at them, enjoyed their discomfiture, while his braves circled around with their ponies and kept up a rifle fire to indicate what they could do to the engineers in case of emergency. Of course, the engineers were glad to retire as gracefully as possible, but they wired the Lieutenant-Governor that they were at a standstill. The Governor sent word to Police headquarters, whence a telegram went to the nearest Police post: "Trouble on railway. Tell Indians to move on." There were only two men there, a sergeant and a constable. They rode off at once, and when they arrived at the camp of the Indians and delivered the order, Pie-a-Pot and his chief men, who had not been much in contact with the Police, only laughed, while the braves performed their usual firearm feats and the squaws jeered. Then the sergeant indicated by showing his watch that he would give fifteen minutes for them to start moving. At this the braves on signal circled closer, backed their ponies against the troop-horses and made every effort to get the Police to start trouble, the idea being to let them take the offensive and be wiped out. But the Police were never to be drawn that way. In this case the two scarlet tuniced men sat coolly on their horses, which stood at the door of Pie-a-Pot's tent. And when the time was up the sergeant, throwing the lines to the constable, sprang off his horse, leaped past the surly Chief, entered the tepee and kicked out the centre pole, thus bringing the wigwam down nearly on the head of the defiant Indian. Without waiting, the sergeant moved to the next tent and repeated the operation with great precision, and then said to the chief and his men, "Now move and move quick." The chief was very angry, but he was no fool, and so in a very short time he and his whole outfit were on the trek to their reserve. The engineers went on with the transcontinental, and the two athletes in scarlet and gold, whose names were not even given out, rode back to their post, having made one more unadvertised contribution from the Police to the making of the West.

Now let us instance a case in which the Police had to deal with turbulent navvies on the railway who went on strike and threatened to destroy the company's property. The Police have never acted in any sense as strike-breakers, nor have they interfered between the parties. They simply saw fair play, took care that the country's lawful business was carried on and provided against destruction of human life and property. This was the position for instance at the Beaver in the mountains while the Canadian Pacific was under construction. For the time being it was a terminus, and all manner of lawless, desperate and disorderly characters were there to prey upon the navvies, many of whom were foreigners and a good many of whom were just as reckless and offensive as could be imagined. To keep these rough men in order, and there were several hundreds of them mostly armed, there were only eight Mounted Police, but they were under the leadership of the redoubtable Superintendent, Sam B. Steele, who had as his non-commissioned assistant Sergeant Fury, a short, heavy set, bull-dog type of a man, whom I remember well, quiet, determined and undemonstrative, but who could, while keeping cool, at the same time be everything his name suggested if occasion required. When the strike was starting, Steele did not interfere, but warned the strikers that they must keep the peace and not commit any acts of violence or he would punish them to the full extent of the law. When the strike did start, Steele was in bed with mountain fever and Sergeant Fury had only six men. One of them, Constable Kerr, who had gone for a bottle of medicine for the Inspector, found on his way back a riotous crowd with a desperate character, well known to the Police, inciting the mob to violence and especially to an attack on the barracks. Kerr, who was not a man to stand nonsense, promptly arrested the man, but a score of men overpowered him and released the prisoner. Sergeant Fury at once reported to Steele, who said, "It will never do to let the gang think they can play with us." Then Fury and another man tried to make the arrest without resorting to using weapons, but in a little while returned, with their uniforms torn, to report that once again the rioters had taken the prisoner from them by force. Steele said, "This is too bad. Go back armed and shoot any man who interferes with the arrest." He started off again with Constables Fane, Craig and Walters, while the other four constables with their Winchesters stood ready to guard the barracks, which were slated for attack by the mob. Johnston, a magistrate, was there to read the Riot Act if necessary. In a few minutes there was a shot. Steele got up and went to the window. Craig and Walters were dragging the prisoner across the bridge, the desperado fighting like a demon, and a scarlet woman following them with cries and curses. Fury and Fane were in the rear trying to hold back the gang of some three hundred men. Steele called on Johnston to come with him to read the Riot Act and then rushed out, got a rifle from one of the guard, and ignoring his fevered condition ran across the bridge, covering the crowd with the rifle and saying he would shoot the first man who dared to cross. The crowd could hardly believe their eyes when they saw Steele and shouted, "Even his death-bed does not scare him."

In the meantime the desperate prisoner was struggling fiercely with the men who had him, but when on the bridge Walters raised his powerful fist and struck him over the temple, and with Craig trailed him like a rag into the barracks. As the woman passed screaming, "You red-coated devil," Steele shouted, "Take her along too." Then Johnston read the Riot Act and Steele made a straight statement that the Police, though few, would not flinch and that if he saw more than twelve rioters together he would open fire and mow them down. And the eight Mounted Police stood there under Sergeant Fury with magazines charged, ready to act when ordered. The riot collapsed right there, the ringleaders were sentenced next day and there was no more trouble. The roughs at the Beaver had tried the game of rioting with the wrong men.

And in order to show that the Police took no sides, but sought to hold the balance level in these matters, we might recall an instance related by Superintendent J. H. McIlree, where men had been hired by contractors on the understanding that when a section of the railway was finished to Calgary, these men would be paid off and sent back to their homes in the East. However, the contractors, when they came to that point, would not provide transportation to the East, but wished to send them farther West. The men refused, and after a few days took possession of a train of empty cars going eastward. The Police could not allow this commandeering of the property of the railway company for the failure of certain contractors, and so they caused the men to leave the train, but these same Police, once they discovered the real situation, made it so hot for those contractors that they were glad to yield and give the men what they had agreed. So all along the line, from the time it crossed the Red River in 1881 till it reached the Pacific five years later, the Mounted Police stood guard over the railway which was the first to link together with steel the scattered Provinces of the new Confederation and the construction of which within a given time was required to get British Columbia to become part of Canada. Thus were these red-coated men nation-builders, in that it was under their protection that the vast enterprise was carried forward to completion.

It is not unexpectedly then that we come across two special letters from the builders of the great railway expressing their warm appreciation of the work of the Police. The first is from that remarkable man, Mr. W. C. Van Horne, who was afterwards

President of the Railway, and who was knighted for his distinguished services to the Empire as a builder of railways. Van Horne was a somewhat extraordinary composite. I recall having the privilege of being under his guidance around the fine art gallery of Lord Strathcona in Montreal, and had evidence not only of his genial companionship, but of his being an art connoisseur as well as a skilled user of the brush himself. Socially and in his home he was full of comradeship and bright joviality, but as a railroader he was as inflexible and apparently unemotional as the material with which he worked. He was not given to gushing letters, so that the following from him from his office as General Manager of date January 1, 1883, is noteworthy:

> "DEAR SIR,—Our work of construction for the year 1882 has just closed, and I cannot permit the occasion to pass without acknowledging the obligations of the company to the North-West Mounted Police, whose zeal and industry in preventing traffic in liquor and preserving order along the line of construction have contributed so much to the successful prosecution of the work. Indeed, without the assistance of the officers and men of the splendid Force under your command it would have been impossible to have accomplished as much as we did. On no great work within my knowledge, where so many men have been employed, has such perfect order prevailed. On behalf of the company and of all their officers, I wish to return thanks and to acknowledge particularly our obligations to yourself and Major Walsh.
>
> "I am, sir,
> "Yours very truly,
> "W. C. VAN HORNE,
> "*General Manager.*"

"Lieutenant-Colonel A. G. IRVINE,
    "Commissioner,
        "North-West Mounted Police,
        "Regina."

And at the close of the year 1884 the General Superintendent of the Western Line, Mr. John M. Egan, who was even less than Van Horne given to incursions into the sentimental, wrote the following:

> "MY DEAR COLONEL,—Gratitude would be wanting did the present year close without my conveying, on behalf of the Canadian Pacific Railway, to you and those under your charge most sincere thanks for the manner in which their several duties in connection with the railway have been attended to during the past season.
>
> "Prompt obedience to your orders, faithful carrying out of your instructions, contribute in no small degree to the rapid construction of the line. The services of your men during recent troubles among a certain class of our employees prevented destruction to property and preserved obedience to law and order in a manner highly commendable. Justice has been meted out to them without fear or favour, and I have yet to hear any person, who respects same, say aught against your command.
>
> "Wishing you the season's compliments,
>
> > "I remain,
> > "Yours very truly,
> > "JNO. M. EGAN."

Taken together these letters, with tributes from two such men, more than substantiate the claims we have made for the part played by the Police in that critical era of Western Canadian history.

It is anticipating in order of time, but this is our railway chapter, and so we note here another service of enormous value rendered the railway by the men in scarlet and gold. The road was completed in 1886 from Montreal to the West Coast, and people used to wonder how this railway, traversing some 3,000 miles across lonely prairie and lonelier mountains, escaped having its trains held up by robbers, as was so frequently the case in other countries. The reason emerged in a report given by Superintendent Deane, of Calgary, and that reason was the preventive power of the presence and prestige of the Mounted Police. Deane, in his annual report for 1906, refers to the only effort that had ever been made to rob a train, and starts with the following revealing statement: "It has for years been an open secret that the train-robbing fraternity in the United States had seriously considered the propriety of trying conclusions with the Mounted Police, but had decided that the risks were too great and the game not worth the candle. After the object lesson they received last May, it may be reasonably hoped that railway passengers will be spared further anxiety during the life of the present generation at least." And Deane's hope has been justified.

The special event of May to which he refers was a train robbery at Kamloops in British Columbia by a notorious train-robbing expert, Bill Miner, *alias* Edwards, etc., assisted by two gunmen, William Dunn and Louis, *alias* "Shorty" Colquhoun. A robbery had been committed by the same parties before nearer the coast, but it had been dealt with by local authorities and no trace of the robbers was found. However, the railway authorities were now thoroughly alarmed and, though the Provincial Police, one of whom, Fernie of Kamloops, did good work, were on the trail, were not inclined to take any chances. Accordingly, a wire was sent by C.P.R. Superintendent Marpole to General Manager Mr. (later Sir) William Whyte, of Winnipeg, who in turn telegraphed to Commissioner Perry, of the Mounted Police, asking that a detachment of his men be put on the work of hunting the robbers who had escaped into the difficult country south of Kamloops. Perry wired Calgary for two detachments to be in readiness, and left to take charge of the arrangements. From Calgary Inspector Church, with Sergeant Fletcher and ten men left for Penticton, so as to cut off the escape of the robbers over the boundary line. The Commissioner left for Kamloops, accompanied by Staff-Sergeant J. J. Wilson, Sergeants Thomas and Shoebotham, Corporals Peters and Stewart, Constables Browing and Tabateau, Wilson being in charge of the detachment. The weather was bad, the horses they secured at Kamloops were poor, but despite these handicaps this posse came on the robbers within forty-eight hours. The outlaws were armed to the teeth, but when they were discovered off guard were in the bush at dinner. Wilson reported what happened as follows:

"We all dismounted, leaving the horses standing, went into the bush and found three men eating dinner. I asked them where they came from. The eldest man, who afterwards gave the name of Edwards, said, 'Across the river.' I asked them where they were before that. Edwards said, 'From over there' (pointing towards Campbell meadows). I asked how long since they had left there. Edwards said, 'Two days.' I then asked them what they were doing. The one who afterwards gave the name of Dunn, answered, 'Prospecting a little.' I then said, 'You answer the description given of the train-robbers and we arrest you for that crime.' Edwards said, 'We do not look much like train-robbers.' Just then Dunn rolled over and said, 'Look out, boys, it is all up,' and commenced to fire his revolver. I immediately covered Edwards. Corporal Peters was standing close to Colquhoun, who was reaching for his revolver, and he covered him and ordered him to put up his hands, at the same time snatching away Colquhoun's revolver. Sergeant Shoebotham, Corporal Stewart and Constable Browning ran after Dunn, firing as they went, he returning the fire as he ran. After some twenty shots had been exchanged Dunn fell into a ditch and threw up his hands, saying, 'I am shot.' The men ceased firing and took two revolvers from Dunn. On taking him out of the ditch it was found he had been shot in the calf of the leg, the bullet going right through."

The Mounted Men brought the whole gang into Kamloops, refusing to give them up to anyone till they landed these desperadoes in jail, whence they were taken to serve sentences in the penitentiary.

It is interesting to note that at that time Mr. Marpole, in a statement issued to the press, strongly advocated the extension of the Mounted Police Force to other parts of Canada in addition to the Middle West. In recent years that has been done, and the result has been enormously beneficial, as we shall later consider.

And so Deane's expectation, as we indicated, was fulfilled, for, except for the clumsy efforts of a couple of foreigners, the train-robbers have evidently concluded to give a wide berth to any region where the Mounted Police stand for British Law.

And it is not inappropriate at the close of this railway chapter to quote Steele's account of the ride given him out of compliment to his work and that of the Police generally, on the train which was the first to go through to the coast after Donald A. Smith had driven at Craigellachie in November, 1885, the spike which united the two oceans across Canada. Steele was back on duty in the mountains again and, as he knew some of the party, was invited to go through from Kamloops on a private car with Mr. Dickey, the government engineer, and the manager of construction on the coast end of the huge undertaking. And Steele writes in his most interesting book, *Forty Years in Canada*, "Dickey knew the Manager well, which was sufficient to ensure a warm welcome, and the train rushed along at the rate of 57 miles an hour, roaring in and out of the numerous tunnels, our short car whirling round the short curves like the tail of a kite, the sensation being such that when dinner was served Dickey, the manager and I were the only men in the car who were not suffering from train sickness. I think this was one of the wildest rides by train any of us ever took. Many years have passed since that memorable ride, and to-day one goes through the mountains in the most modern and palatial observation cars, but the recollection of that journey to the coast on the first train through is far sweeter to me than any trips taken since. It was the exultant moment of pioneer work, and we were all pioneers on that excursion." And we add again all due honour to the famous corps that had watched over the destinies of the long steel trail.

* * * * *

CHAPTER VIII

RIEL AGAIN

Some years ago a well-known Senator told me that he was at a dinner party in Sir John Macdonald's house in Ottawa, when a telegram was delivered to the Premier at the table. He read it and put it under his plate. Nothing could be gained by throwing that bombshell in the midst of his guests. But in a few minutes, as the friends were saying good-night, Sir John came to the door with the Senator and said, "Mac, there's the very mischief to pay in the North-West." The wire had communicated the news of the Duck Lake fight, by which the rebellion, under that mad egoist, Louis Riel, was publicly staged in its opening act. And the Senator told me he recalled for all the years that followed the look on the Premier's face as one of pained surprise and unexpected shock. If the Senator was a good reader of faces and read that expressive countenance aright, he could doubtless see indications of pain, for Sir John was a tender-hearted man. But, if he saw surprise on the face of the Premier, it is proof positive that official pigeon-holes in the West had not divulged their secrets to Ottawa, or that his subordinates were hoping to quell the discontent of the half-breeds on the Saskatchewan without worrying the "old chieftain" unduly.

And this we say because the outbreak of rebellion was a surprise to Western residents only in the sense that the resort to arms was considered unlikely. But every one knew something of the discontent. The Mounted Police saw it coming to a head, and Superintendent Crozier, who was in command at Fort Carleton, on the North Saskatchewan, has reported in July, 1884, some eight months before the outbreak, that Riel had been brought from Montana to champion the "rights" of the half-breeds.

Superintendent Gagnon, who understood their language well, reported as to Riel's presence and the discontent of the half-breeds more than once. The causes of the discontent were not far to seek. Many of the half-breeds on the South Saskatchewan were the same who had taken part in Riel's first rebellion on the Red River fifteen years before. They were not people of a settled temperament. They did not take naturally to the farm. There was enough of the Indian blood in them to make them nomadic hunters rather than settlers, and enough of the fiery volatility of French blood to make them susceptible to the appeals of aggressive agitation. And Riel, though not specially anxious to fight himself, was a past master in stirring others up to get into conflicts. And when Superintendent Crozier notified the Government that this hot-headed, vain but magnetic agitator had come amongst his old compatriots, steps should have been taken to deport him, or otherwise put him where he could do no harm.

Gagnon was quite right when he stated later that the main cause of the discontent amongst the half-breeds was the introduction by the Government of the rectangular survey of land on the prairie. Under this system settlers had to hold their farms in square blocks of 160 acres or more, and in consequence such settlers would be necessarily some distance apart. This was not to the mind of the half-breeds, who were more given to social gatherings than to agriculture, and who preferred the old survey that they knew on the Red River and the Assiniboine, where their holdings were in narrow strips fronting on the river and running two miles back. To introduce this on the prairie, the Government contended, would lead to confusion, and so it was easy for the agitator to stir up discontent amongst these inflammable people who had always been accustomed to the freedom of the plains. It was easy for the orator to say that the Government was trying to break up their old social customs, and when such a statement was followed up by saying that their patents giving them title to land were being long delayed, and that possibly they would never be granted at all, a live coal had fallen on material as combustible as the dry grass on the prairie. And once the half-breeds began to consider revolt it was not hard for them to stir up certain bad Indians with the proposal that by combining they could drive out the whites and have the country to themselves again.

In any case our main interest in this book is the story of the Mounted Police, and we repeat that they did their duty in warning the authorities a long distance ahead. When their warning was not heeded and the flame of rebellion broke out, they, as this story will show, did more than their share in putting out the fire where it had started, and in preventing it from spreading, as it might have done, over the whole country.

We have quoted Superintendent Crozier's warning. Let us notice also the testimony of another experienced officer, Superintendent Sam B. Steele. It appears that in 1884, when Steele was still in command at Calgary, Mr. Magnus Begg, Indian agent of the Blackfeet, reported that the former friendly attitude of those Indians seemed to be changing to one of sulkiness and hostility. Steele asked him about a certain half-breed who had been with Riel in Montana, and Begg, on being given the description, said he was in the camp with Chief Crowfoot. Steele sent and had this half-breed arrested, but he escaped by making a leap from the train. And when next day Colonel Irvine and Superintendent Herchmer came to Calgary to take over the command from Steele, who was under orders for duty in the mountains, he reported the facts to them with his conviction that the half-breed was one of Riel's runners trying to stir up the Indians. They asked Steele to stay over and arrest him in Crowfoot's camp, and taking two men with him, Walters and Kerr, well known for their strength and reliability, he went to the camp, and, through L'Hereux, the interpreter there, demanded the half-breed, whom he found in Crowfoot's tent. Crowfoot, with the half-breed beside him and his chief men around him, had evidently been imposed upon by sinister Riel propaganda, and seemed to be quite hostile. He sprang up and faced Steele threateningly as he entered the tent, but the giant policeman waved him back and told him it would be the worse for him if he started anything, because he had come for the half-breed and that he was going to take him, as the Police always did when they started after a man. Then Steele, suiting the action to the word, seized the half-breed by the back of the collar, whirled him round, and, dragging him out of the tent door, handed him over to the two stalwart constables, who lifted him into the buckboard and drove away. Steele remained behind for a while, and told Crowfoot that he had been misled by the half-breed, and addressing also the hostile-looking band of

Indians present, the Superintendent told them that the half-breed had spoken to them with a forked tongue, and that it would be sensible for them to remain friendly with the Government and the Police. Steele told Superintendent Herchmer, when he came back to Calgary, that he was sure Riel was going to make serious trouble, and that he had runners like this half-breed in other places amongst the Indians, and the sooner the Government knew it the better. So the Police were doing their part to forewarn the authorities, but the men at Regina and Ottawa either did not get all these warnings, or else they treated them too lightly.

And, accordingly, Riel, down at Batoche on the South Saskatchewan, kept up the agitation, and in the atmosphere of the adulation of his half-breed admirers his characteristic vanity asserted itself till, refusing to acknowledge the authority of either Church or State, he looked on himself as a sort of Divinely ordained leader. Rattle-brained as he was, he possessed elements of strength and magnetism enough to get a large following in a short time, and, assuming the name of "Louis 'David' Riel, Exovede," he took the aggressive by plundering some stores, arresting the Indian agent and others, and sending a flamboyant message to Superintendent Crozier to come with his men and surrender to the rebel chief. Crozier, who had done splendid service at Wood Mountain, Cypress Hills and elsewhere, was not the kind of man to surrender, but with the hope that he might avert trouble and incidentally give the Government time to mobilize the long-delayed reinforcements, he offered personally to meet Riel and discuss the whole matter with him. Riel, however, would not venture out, and so Crozier sent Mr. Thomas McKay, a well-known Prince Albert man and native of the country, to see him at his headquarters. When McKay reached Riel's council room at Batoche he found things at white heat. Riel told him excitedly that there was to be a war of extermination, during which the "two curses," the Government and the Hudson's Bay Company, and all who sympathized with them were to be driven out of the country. "You don't know what we are after," shouted Riel to McKay; "we want blood, blood—it's blood we want." McKay had a cool head and so sparred for time, till the rebel sobered down somewhat and then McKay left and returned to Carlton, where he reported to Crozier. Next day, in answer to a request from Riel, McKay and Mitchell, a merchant of Duck Lake, with Crozier's consent, met two of Riel's men, Nolin and Maxime Lepine (a brother of Riel's adjutant in the Red River revolt), who demanded again the surrender of Fort Carlton. This, of course, was refused, and in a few days rebellion was rampant, with this man, half-knave, half-madman at its head.

The first clash came on March 26, 1885, when Crozier sent out a small detachment of Police with a few civilian volunteers from Prince Albert, under the general direction of that experienced and fearless frontiersman, Thomas McKay, above named, to bring in to Fort Carlton some Government stores from Mitchell's trading place above mentioned. This little detachment, of some twenty all told, were met when near Duck Lake by that mischievous Indian, Chief Beardy, with his warriors and Riel's fighting Lieutenant, a famous half-breed plainsman, Gabriel Dumont, this rebel force being estimated by Duck Lake residents at between 300 and 400 men, all well armed, though all did not appear then on the field. A confab took place, Beardy and Dumont being very insolent, and endeavouring evidently to get Crozier's men to begin hostilities so that the rebels might wipe them out. But McKay, though boldly standing his ground, would not be drawn, and after a somewhat stormy interview, retired to Carlton, daring the rebels to follow.

In the meantime, the Commissioner, Colonel A. G. Irvine, a careful and conscientious officer, who had succeeded MacLeod in command of the Police in 1880, wired from Regina to Ottawa and got orders to take all available men, less than 100, and proceed to Prince Albert, as that whole section of country was exposed to the utmost danger. Irvine made a record march through slush and snow, outwitted Riel's forces at South Saskatchewan by going through their zone, and arriving at Prince Albert with horses so used up by the spring roads that a day had to be taken to get them able to go further. He had received word from Carlton that there was no immediate likelihood of trouble, but he lost no time in pressing on to that point, reaching there in the afternoon of March 26, only to find that Crozier had gone out that day to Duck Lake with his handful of police and civilian volunteers and had just returned after experiencing a reverse.

At that time, and later in his formal report, Irvine expressed keen regret that Crozier, knowing the Commissioner to be within 50 miles with reinforcements, had not waited. But Crozier had been true to the Police record of not counting odds when duty seemed clear. And so, when his first small detachment, under Thomas McKay, had come back, the Superintendent doubtless felt that unless he acted at once, the rebels would say that the Police could be bluffed, and would thus be able to call to the cause of the revolt hundreds of half-breeds and Indians, who would take courage from the apparent apathy or weakness of the Government forces. Besides this, it became known later that the volunteers from Prince Albert were anxious to settle the rebels, as their homes were menaced by the uprising.

So the Duck Lake fight took place between Crozier, Inspector Howe, with Surgeon Miller and fifty-three men of the Mounted Police, aided by forty-one civilian volunteers from Prince Albert, under Captains Moore and Morton, a total of ninety-nine on the one side against Gabriel Dumont, Chief Beardy and a force of nearly 400 half-breeds and Indians on the other. The rebels first used a flag of truce, and under cover of conference partially outflanked our men on the one side, while the rest of their forces were well concealed under cover of log buildings and brush. The thing was too unequal, and our men, after fighting in the open with the utmost coolness and courage against a practically hidden enemy, gathered up their nine dead and five wounded, who needed care, and retired in good order to Carlton. The loss of the rebels, who concealed their dead, was not known, but Gabriel Dumont was wounded by a bullet which plowed along his head and felled him to the ground. A few years later Mr. Roger Goulet, a famous loyalist French half-breed land-surveyor in Winnipeg, who was on the Commission to inquire into the question of half-breed rights, said to me: "The Duck Lake fight was worth while, because Gabriel Dumont's wound, which I saw later when he took off his hat to make an affidavit, cooled his ardour to such an extent that he was timid for the rest of the campaign, or the rebellion might have lasted much longer." Goulet's theory possibly accounts for the fact that Dumont, whose judgment was for a night attack on Middleton's camp at Fish Creek, gave up the idea rather swiftly when Riel did not seem to see its advisability. When Colonel Irvine reached Carlton, as related, and found out how things stood, the immediate thing to settle was as to whether he should hold that post or not. This was not hard to decide. Carlton was simply a Hudson's Bay post without population, while Prince Albert was the largest white community in the whole region. The people there must be protected as a first duty, and it was only fair to the Prince Albert volunteers, who had left their homes and came so splendidly to the aid of the little body of Police, that the latter in turn should not leave those homes exposed to the barbarities of the rebels now intoxicated by a certain success. Accordingly, Fort Carlton was abandoned. It took fire from a hospital mattress and an over-heated stove, just as the Police were leaving, and burned to the ground. Irvine and his men, with their wounded, arrived in due course at Prince Albert, which they found full of refugees from surrounding homesteads as well as the town. Most of these refugees were in the church there, which they had surrounded with a wall of cordwood in dread of attack. The women and children were wild with apprehension of possibly falling into the hands of Beardy's tribe. And there was a band of Sioux to the north that it was feared might at any moment assert their traditional love of the warpath.

COL. T. A. WROUGHTON.
Asst.-Commissioner in command at Vancouver, B.C.
Photo. Steffens-Colmer, Vancouver.

LIEUT.-COL. AYLESWORTH BOWEN PERRY, C.M.G.
Commissioner since 1900.
Photo. Rossie, Regina.

COL. CORTLANDT STARNES.
Senr. Asst.-Commissioner, Ottawa.
Photo. Topley, Ottawa.
HEADQUARTERS STAFF, 1921.

R.N.W.M.P. WOOD CAMP. CHURCHILL RIVER.

The Duck Lake fight, with its balance in favour of the rebels, encouraged Big Bear up near Fort Pitt to rebel and do all the damage he could, starting in with the massacre of nine white men, Government agents, etc., on the reserve and imprisoning the rest, including the Hudson's Bay factor and his family, who gave themselves up to the Indians at Fort Pitt. It stirred up the powerful Cree element under Poundmaker at Battleford, where depredations were committed, and where the white people barricaded behind stockades suffered siege and the imminent danger of famine and attack for many weeks. It sent its echoes down into the south-west part of the territories where the warlike Blackfeet confederacy had its centre. At each of these points, as at Prince Albert, the few Mounted Police that were on duty became a literal tower of strength. At Battleford, Inspector Morris, with his few men, organizing also a home guard, guarded nearly 400 women and children who sought refuge inside the stockade. And Constable Storer, riding out alone from that stockade, when all the wires were cut, though pursued for 60 miles, carried the dispatch to the relieving column at Swift Current. At Fort Pitt, in the Big Bear country, Inspector Francis Dickens, son of the famous novelist, with a mere handful of men, one of whom, young Cowan, was killed by the Indians, and another, Loasby, was wounded, held that Hudson's Bay post until the factor and his family and employees gave themselves up to the Indians, when Dickens, having no farther object in staying there, dropped down the river to Battleford and took part in the fight against Poundmaker. And away in the south-west, where the whole region was charged with the electricity of revolt, the masterly hand of Superintendent Cotton, a cool, courageous and diplomatic officer, ably assisted by Inspector Antrobus and Surgeon Kennedy, was able to restrain the most dangerous of the Indian tribes in the West. Superintendent McIllree commanded at Maple Creek and Medicine Hat, and kept a constant eye by scouting parties on the Cypress Hills region, and Inspector McDonnell's services at Wood Mountain were of much value. Superintendent Deane was in charge at headquarters in Regina, and did a great deal of important work in recruiting men and using his influence for peace amongst Indians, such as Chief Pie-a-Pot and others. Northward, in the Edmonton country, where there were great numbers of Indians, amongst whom Riel and Big Bear had runners, that experienced soldier, Inspector A. H. Griesbach, "the father of the Police Force," as he was often called, accomplished tasks of first importance by holding Fort Saskatchewan, where many settlers took refuge, and by assisting with the organization of the Edmonton Home Guards, as well as patrolling the whole region round about. No one who knew the situation as it really existed at that critical hour, could ever dream of apportioning honours differently to men who were actually in action and those who stood guard over helpless settlers, or prevented by determined diplomacy the uprising of the Indians in their localities.

Some who did not know the situation—arm-chair critics at a safe distance—levelled some darts of fault-finding at Colonel Irvine at Prince Albert, and I write a paragraph or two in reply, because I know whereof I speak. I have some reasons for claiming to know Prince Albert, which was founded as a mission and named by some of my relatives in 1866. At the time of the rebellion there were two brothers and a sister, as well as many other relations there whom I saw on my way down the Saskatchewan after the rebellion was over. They knew that some people in the East had raised the question as to Irvine remaining at Prince Albert during the rebellion. But they spoke with indignation in regard to all such critics, and said if these people who were talking in that way only knew what panic would have ensued if the Police had been withdrawn, and how likely it was that the whole settlement would have been pillaged and probably wiped out, the criticism would cease. If the British way is "women and children first," then the duty of protecting them against death or worse comes before the desire to save oneself from possible criticism. The Mounted Police, in over ten years' previous service on the plains, had established an unprecedented reputation for courage under all circumstances, and wherever in the rebellion time they had opportunity in the field, they shone out conspicuously as men who had no thought of self when fighting was the duty of the hour. In proportion to the numbers engaged, more men of the Mounted Police were killed or wounded than any other military body in the field. But when savages were on the warpath, and defenceless people, principally women and children, rushed for refuge to Prince Albert, Battleford or any other point, nothing could be so un-British, not to say inhuman, as to abandon them for the more exciting life on the field. Not only on Western plains, but in India and other such portions of the Empire, has this been exemplified. This much is said from the viewpoint of the ordinary sensible and chivalrous onlooker. But more can be stated.

When the rebellion started with the fight at Duck Lake, the Government dispatched General Middleton from Ottawa to the West. The plan of campaign outlined had three objectives. General Middleton was to attack Riel at Batoche, where the rebel headquarters were; Colonel Otter was to march from Swift Current to the relief of Battleford, where Poundmaker's band was in arms; and General Strange, a veteran of many years' service, was to mobilize at Calgary whatever forces he could muster and go northward into the Big Bear country, to relieve the Edmonton district, settle with Big Bear and release the prisoners he had taken at Frog Lake and Fort Pitt. Middleton, a good soldier and a brave man personally, was in the supreme command of all the forces in the field, including the Police, and it is not too much to say that he asserted that fact very strongly all through the campaign, partly because of natural disposition and partly because he under-estimated the value of the "raw soldiers" of Canada, as he called them in a famous dispatch. Withal, while he was totally unaccustomed to the kind of warfare he was facing, he was not given to receive counsel from those who did know, and from close personal contact with the situation at the time, as well as from careful study since, I feel that General

Middleton rather resented the dominant place of the Mounted Police in the mind of the West, and was more ready to make some slighting remarks about them than to take their counsel. And this I say without seeking to disparage the general quality or the personal valour of the officer in supreme command.

Hence it was that General Middleton never intimated in any way to Colonel Irvine that he or any of his men should leave Prince Albert and come to the seat of war at Batoche. On the contrary, Majors Bedson and Macdowell, who made their way to Prince Albert from Middleton's camp by way of Carrot River, told Irvine that the General wished the Police to stay where they were and look out for the scattered half-breeds. And one day, when things were quieted around Prince Albert and Irvine made a reconnaissance in force to the south as far as Scott's, some 14 miles out, he was met by one of Middleton's scouts with a message to return to Prince Albert.

That the above represents General Middleton's general attitude is further attested by the fact that when Riel's stronghold fell and Middleton was on his way by Prince Albert to close the campaign by proceeding against Chiefs Poundmaker and Big Bear, he declined Irvine's offer to go with him with his men, who knew the country and the Indians at first hand. Irvine offered to take his men, carrying their own rations, and go a day ahead of the General, or to go on the other side of the river, but was refused. Yet orders came back to Irvine a few hours later to go to Carlton, which he did, arriving there before Middleton, and sending out scouting parties in search of Big Bear's band that, as we shall see in a later page, had been scattered by Strange's column. It was not long before one of these Police scouting parties had captured Big Bear with some others and landed them in the jail at Prince Albert. And it is rather interesting to recall that it was big Tom Hourie, a Police interpreter, accompanied by two Police scouts, Armstrong and Diehl, who captured Riel and took him into Middleton's tent at Batoche. It is also interesting at this point to reproduce an overlooked extract from a letter written by the Earl of Minto, who, as Lord Melgund, was chief of General Middleton's staff, and who, therefore, wrote out of personal knowledge of the situation. After speaking of our three main columns, this fine soldier, who was wounded on duty, says:

"Besides these three columns there was another force in the field—the North-West Mounted Police detachment, under Colonel Irvine, the value of which has always seemed to me underrated. The fact of Colonel's Irvine's force being at Prince Albert afforded a safe refuge to many outlying settlers, and, if it had not been there, the task General Middleton had to solve would have been quite a different one. Hampered, as Colonel Irvine was, by the civilian population of the settlement and by a difficult country, the possibility of successful junction with Middleton must always have been doubtful, whilst the moral effect of the force at Prince Albert was certain."

I have gone ahead of the history in mentioning the capture of Big Bear, the pursuit of whom is the record of General Strange's column which, as already noted, mobilized at Calgary. In addition to the 65th Rifles of Montreal, the Winnipeg Light Infantry, with whom I served, and some irregular scouts under Major Hattin and Osborne, we had two Mounted Police detachments, one from the mountains under Inspector Sam B. Steele, and the other from Fort MacLeod under Inspector A. Bowen Perry, the present able Commissioner of the Force. Both these officers, coming at that time under the command of General Strange in the Militia, were given the Militia rank of Major. Steele enlisted a number of men, mostly ex-Mounted Policemen, as scouts, his whole corps, thus augmented, being generally called Steele's scouts. Perry, who was selected by Superintendent Cotton on account of special fitness, brought with him a nine-pounder gun, which did unique service in demoralizing and scattering Big Bear's murderous and pillaging band, to whose outrages we have already referred. These two Police detachments became the tentacles of our column and the mainspring of its ultimate success.

Of the two officers Steele was the senior in years and in length of service. He had been in the Red River Expedition, and was in the School of Gunnery at Kingston, when he enlisted in the Mounted Police at its organization and worked his way up from the ranks. Powerfully built, he had all the appearance and carriage of a frontier soldier, accustomed to unexpected situations and always ready for any action that might be necessary. Perry attracted me first by his stalwart appearance and fine horsemanship. Even in a country where riding was a fine art, Perry was a distinguished figure on a horse, and later on I discovered that he made a point of doing everything well. He was a graduate of the Royal Military College, and had served with the Royal Engineers before joining up with the Mounted Police, where his genius for thorough administration and his general popularity raised him to the highest position in the Force.

The news from the North coming to us at Calgary, indicated that the whole country north of the Red Deer River to Edmonton and beyond was full of rather surly and hostile Indians, who would rise at any moment if they thought there were any chances of success. Hence, General Strange, a thorough-going soldier greatly beloved by all of us, determined to push on to Edmonton with all speed accompanied by Steele. We of the Winnipeg Light Infantry waited a few days till Perry could reach us from MacLeod, and then we also started north under his guidance. We forded the Bow River, but when we got to the Red Deer we found it flooded by the spring freshets into what our Adjutant Constantine, who later did such splendid service with the Mounted Police, called, in warning the men, "a wide, swift-flowing and treacherous stream." Strange had crossed before the river rose, but how we were to get over was a problem. Our chances of getting on to the north looked slim. It was well that Perry, whose service with the Royal Engineers meant something, was along in command of the column. He decided to throw a rope across with the little skiff, which was the only thing in sight and then construct and cross by a swinging raft. The raft was constructed under his direction, and his own detachment of Police, with the gun and ammunition and harness put on board. Of course, he went himself, as he never asked his men to go anywhere without him. Things went fairly till near the other side, when the rope made out of the picketing lines of the horses broke by binding round the tree, from which it was being paid out, and the raft began to go down the raging current. At the risk of their lives Perry and Constable Diamond, grasping another rope, plunged into the torrent and managed to reach the shore and fasten it to a tree. But the current was too strong and this rope gave way. The boat went down a mile or so and, being caught in an eddy, was beached, and the stuff on board dragged up a steep cut bank. Then

Perry commandeered lumber from a primitive saw-mill down the river, and built a ferry on which, in a day or two, we crossed. In the meanwhile, as we were in the hostile Indian country, Perry had accomplished the difficult task of crossing the 65th Regiment in the little skiff, taking a whole dark night to do it. He kept our regiment on the south side till the ferry was built. He thus had both sides guarded against any attack. Once over the river, we made a quick march 100 miles to Edmonton, where General Strange paid a high compliment publicly to Major Perry for the splendid way in which he had overcome obstacles and got our relief column through in such good time. The people of Edmonton gave us a hearty welcome, as their position in the midst of a big Indian country was very serious for a time.

Big Bear, with the prisoners, was now treking away to the north, and it was our business to overtake him. The Infantry went down the river, while the Mounted Men went by trail near the river bank, or our clumsy, open flatboats might have come under fire. Forced marching, from Fort Victoria by Frog Lake to Fort Pitt, brought us to the scene of the Big Bear's atrocities, as we saw from the Sun-dance Lodge, the mutilated body of Constable Cowan and the charred remains of the nine white people who had been massacred at Frog Lake reserve. Fort Pitt was burning, but we saved two buildings. Big Bear and his marauding band in large force had kept up their retreat and vanished, but whether it was on the north side of the river, or the south side where they would effect a junction with Poundmaker could only be ascertained by scouting parties. Accordingly, General Strange at this point detailed Major Perry and seventeen men of his detachment (keeping the rest for the nine-pounder gun) to cross the river to the south side and move towards Battleford. It was not an enviable duty, and as the men crossed the river in the darkness and started their ride through a region that was supposed to be infested with hundreds on the warpath, it looked rather like a last patrol. However, after a hard ride they made Battleford to find that Poundmaker had surrendered, Middleton having just then arrived. Perry reported to Middleton with the information that Big Bear must be on the north side, arranged for a steamer to go up with supplies, which we needed very badly, and got on the steamer to return with his men. When part of the way back he got word that we were engaged with

Big Bear, and so he landed his men and sent the steamer back to Battleford for reinforcements. After one of the most severe and risky rides of the campaign, Perry and his men rejoined us to find that his gunners under Sergeant O'Connor, and the nine-pounder, had made fine gun practice, and had been mainly instrumental in demoralizing the forces of Big Bear, with whom we had been in contact for two hot days. General Strange was much pleased with the way in which Major Perry had carried out the difficult reconnaissance with a handful of men.

Meanwhile, after our fight with Big Bear and his flight from Frenchman's Butte, where he had a strong and well-fortified position, Major Steele, with his mounted detachment, had made a rush to Loon Lake, where, in a rattling encounter during which Sergeant Fury was severely wounded, he completed the defeat of Big Bear. Two days or so afterwards our scouts crossed Gold Lake in birch canoes and secured the release of the remaining prisoners of Big Bear, the others having come in to our lines after the fight at Frenchman's Butte, where Constable Donald McRae, still happily surviving, was wounded, but refused to leave the field till he had exhausted his ammunition.

On the disbanding of the Alberta Field Force General Strange, who had served ever since the Mutiny, warmly commended the Infantry, and expressed the opinion that he had never commanded better soldiers than were in the Mounted Police detachments, ready for all kinds of duty.

Preceding the surrender of Poundmaker, already mentioned, at Battleford, the fight at Cut Knife Hill had occurred. Colonel Otter had made a swift march from Swift Current to Battleford and relieved the beleaguered garrison and civilians there. With Otter came Superintendents W. M. Herchmer and Neale with a few Mounted Police. And when Otter decided to go out and attack Poundmaker these, with the few who had been at Battleford, and those who had come from Fort Pitt under Inspector Dickens, made up seventy-five Police, who went on that errand with Otter, and some 200 of his infantry and artillery. Just why Otter went out has never been very clear, except that he possibly wished to punish the band of Indians and prevent a possible junction of Poundmaker and Big Bear. Anyway, the Police were under his command, and they went in obedience to orders, as was their fashion. And the

Police, being the advance guard to Cutknife, and both the advance and rear guard on the return, as well as in the hottest part of the fight for seven hours, where they behaved with great gallantry, lost heavily in killed and wounded in proportion to their numbers. It is not any reflection on the gallantry of the other corps, who were totally unused to Indian warfare, to say that it was the masterly tactics of the Police which extricated the column from the ravine after Colonel Otter saw that it was not advisable to continue the conflict against the large force of Indians who had every advantage in position. A few days after this Poundmaker, who was a very splendid-looking Indian, and who had given the order to cease fire when Otter was retiring, came in and surrendered to General Middleton, and the rebellion was practically over, though it was still a few days before Big Bear was captured, as already related.

Perhaps there is no finer summing up of the services of the Mounted Police during the rebellion than that given by Dr. A. Jukes, Senior Surgeon of the Force, in his report at the end of that year. He says, "While I must leave to those whose duty as combatant officers it more especially becomes to record with sorrow, not unmingled with pride, the names and services of the gallant men who have fallen unflinchingly in the path of duty, I cannot withhold my humble tribute to the courage and fortitude of the mere handful of Mounted Police who, fewer in numbers than any battalion engaged in active operations, and generally far overmatched by enemies wherever it was their privilege to meet them, have left beneath the bosom of the prairie of their dead, 'killed in action,' a number greater than that of any battalion in the field, save one whose record, at least, they have equalled."

And one cannot close this chapter without emphasizing what has often been overlooked by those who do not know Western affairs at first hand. Looking back now over the years, one is not surprised to have to see that the collapse of the rebellion, instead of leaving the Mounted Police Force carefree, actually added to their burdens and ushered them into a period of pronounced and continuous strain. The Militia, which was made up of several thousands of men—infantry, artillery, cavalry—all were withdrawn and scattered to their homes in various parts of Canada. The Mounted Police stayed at their posts or moved from place to place, as required in a readjustment period. The defeated rebels and many of the Indians were in a sullen mood, the year had been wasted from the standpoint of producing anything for food, the Indians were off their reservations in some cases, in others the reservations had been laid waste, and the buildings that had been erected for their comfort had been burned or wrecked by themselves when the spirit of destruction arose as they went on the warpath. Yet the officers and men of this remarkable corps, without any cessation or furlough, took up the ravelled skein of human life around them, and with great patience, skill and tact, soon had things running smoothly again. It was a wonderful piece of reconstructive statesman-like work and, as it proceeded, both the half-breeds and Indians who had been disaffected began to regret deeply the action they had been misled by agitators into taking contrary to the advice of the men in the scarlet tunic, who had always been their friends, and who always had stood for the square deal for every one. It was not only not the fault of the Mounted Police, but largely through ignoring their long-repeated warnings to the Government that the rebellion had taken place. While it lasted these Police did their duty like men at great cost without ever saying, "We told you so." And when it was over they so comported themselves in the midst of a distracted population that it could never occur again.

* * * * *

CHAPTER IX

RECONSTRUCTION

In writing these chapters it is necessary to throw in a story or incident here and there out of the regular sequence in time, so as to relate cognate subjects to each other. Hence, as their names have all been already mentioned, it may be well here to indicate the terms of office occupied by the several Commissioners who have directed the destinies of the famous corps. With all of these, except Colonel French, who was the first in order, I have had some personal contact. The office of Commissioner has been held by Colonel G. A. (later Sir George) French from 1873 to 1876, by Colonel James F. McLeod from 1876 to 1880, by Lieut.-Colonel A. G. Irvine from 1880 to 1886, by Colonel Lawrence W. Herchmer from 1886 to 1900, and from 1900 up to date by the present Officer Commanding in the person of Colonel A. Bowen Perry, C.M.G. These all had their distinctive traits of character and each had his own speciality—foundation building, discipline, organization and so on—but they all meet on a common plane as soldiers and gentlemen without fear and without reproach. Of Colonel French we have already written—he was the layer of the corner-stone—and the after-history of the Police as a spirit level proves that it was well and truly laid. Colonel McLeod came into the command when the Indians, under changing conditions at home and amidst perplexing problems born of the Indian situation south of the boundary, had to be handled with unusual discreetness and care. And MacLeod was distinctly the man for such a period, of wide human sympathies, absolutely impartial and even-handed in his magisterial decisions and inflexibly courageous, he became to

Indian and white man alike a sort of embodiment of the highest ideals of British administration.

Colonel Irvine had served with credit under Wolseley and was highly esteemed by his men. His commissionership fell within the stormy time of the second Riel rebellion, and despite the fact that he was not generously treated by the Commander of the Militia forces during that period, he emerged from it with an enhanced reputation and with the respect not only of his own men, but of all who knew how difficult and important his task had been.

Colonel Lawrence W. Herchmer, besides some service with Imperial forces, had been through some especially important work in connection with the Frontier Boundary Commission. This experience proved of much value to the Force and the country when he became Commissioner. Coming in the restless period succeeding the rebellion, Colonel Herchmer's contribution to Police history was his extension of the patrol system all over the vast territory under his oversight. A man of fine appearance and courteous bearing he was well liked and popular with the men and the community during his term of office.

Colonel Perry, the present Commissioner, has had the longest term of service in the supreme command. As his name will come up frequently in the remaining chapters of this story, we need not make special note of his work here. But it is not too much to say that owing to his outstanding ability and his wide range of general knowledge, as well as his keen perception, he has during his long term of office practically recreated the Force in many particulars. He has unusual power for getting to the heart of a situation by a sort of intuitive insight. He has the reputation of being able to grasp and analyse the contents of documents almost at a glance and seize their salient points for action. His decisions are thus made after rapid assimilation of the facts, and he expects his orders to be carried out with exactness and dispatch. In this he is not disappointed, as the officers and men under his command have such confidence in his judgment that they work out his plans with enthusiasm. He is fair to all classes, but will not tolerate movements that make for the subversion of the constitution or the wanton disturbance of law and order. Intensely Canadian, he is not insular, for few men in his line have read more extensively in the fields of history. Having made these notes on the men who have guided the Force, we can take up the story again where we ended the last chapter with the close of the second Riel rebellion.

As intimated at that point, the Militia Forces were withdrawn and the Mounted Police were left alone to deal with the problems of reconstruction and peace. Certain of the rebels who had been specially seditious and murderous had to be rounded up and dealt with by process of law in order that such unseemly doings should not again menace the safety of the settler and the march of civilization. It fell to the lot of the Police to gather the evidence, to secure the presence of witnesses, to furnish guards, and at headquarters in Regina the duties were very heavy. But these trained men worked with steady precision, for the lesson had to be taught that insurrection and murder were not to be tolerated under our flag. The men in the scarlet would see that whatever had been true of other frontiers, Canada was not to have a wild west or a wild north either. So the rebels suffered the due reward of their deeds. Louis Riel was tried and, despite the efforts of his lawyers, Lemieux and Fitzpatrick, brilliant men who came from Quebec to defend him and whose conflict with the Crown lawyers, B. B. Osler and Christopher Robinson, afforded a consummate spectacle of dialectic sword-play, this leader of two rebellions was executed at Regina. Several Indians, notably Wandering Spirit, who was the evil genius of the Big Bear revolt, were also visited with capital punishment. Big Bear himself, who had become decrepit, and the lordly Poundmaker, who sturdily maintained that he had only defended himself when attacked at Cutknife, were confined to the Stony Mountain penitentiary for a time, but released when a medical board decided that the change from out of doors would soon end their lives. Poundmaker was a splendid-looking man, stately and grave in manner, and his chivalry at Cutknife, where he ordered the "cease firing" when Otter was withdrawing, entitled him to consideration. I recall his pride in the long pleats of glossy black hair that adorned his handsome head. It was a graceful recognition of his gallantry that the authorities at the penitentiary, at the instance of the Department, left the fine locks of their captive unshorn during his prison term. At the suggestion of the Mounted Police officers many of the chiefs who had remained loyal were taken on a tour of the east, where they received many tokens of the kindly attitude of Canadians towards them.

INDIAN TEPEE.

DOG-TRAIN.

I recall a story in that connection—a missionary story. It is in place here because no one knew so well as the Police what a large part in preserving peace in the rebellion time was played by missionaries like John McKay, of the Mistawasis Reserve near Carlton, John McDougall, of Morley, George McKay, of Prince Albert, Père Lacombe and others. In the partnership of the Police and the missionaries the law and the gospel wrought together for good ends. The story was told a group of us by John McKay, to whose influence over Chief Mistawasis was largely due the fact that that powerful Cree chief, whose reserve was almost within sound of the guns of Duck Lake, did not join in with Chief Beardy and Dumont. After the rebellion, Mistawasis was one of the chiefs taken east as a reward for his loyalty. I recall seeing some of them being driven around eastern cities in cabs to see the sights. They preserved the usual stoical silence and evinced no surprise, but they missed nothing and when they got back home their tongues were loosed and for many a day they recited their experiences and told the story of the white man's great cities and manifest power.

Mistawasis, on his way home, met John McKay on the plains, and they sat around the camp fire late that night as the chief poured out his recollections of what he had seen. One thing had puzzled the Indian, though he had thought much over it. "The strangest thing that happened," said Mistawasis, "was in Ottawa, where some good people had a missionary meeting at a house, and they were singing songs, and a lady played on the singing machine (piano). At last they asked me and Star Blanket to sing. We both were ashamed, because we could not sing much. But I told Star Blanket I would sing what the missionary taught us out on the plains and I began, and all of a sudden the lady ran to the singing machine and began to play and then they all joined in and I was leading the whole band." "Now," continued the Chief, "how did they know in Ottawa the same thing you taught us out at the reserve in Saskatchewan?" And then John McKay told him the tune was "Old Hundred," which all good people knew, and that the company sang it in English words while he sang in Cree, but that they were singing the same thing. This delighted Mistawasis, who felt that he and the white people there were really one in the deep experiences of life. And that meant brotherhood to him.

But all the Indians were not like "Big Child," as this chief's name meant, and so the Mounted Police had strenuous work for some years after the rebellion, when scarcely a thousand of them had to patrol and guard a territory twenty times as large as some European kingdoms.

From the ably written and graphic Police reports for the years following the rebellion, one can visualize the changing conditions of the country. The outbreak had undesignedly advertised the wide

West. The thousands of men who had come out on military duty, having spied out the wondrous fatness of the land, had gone back to the east to become unofficial immigration agents by telling what they had beheld. And so the tide of humanity began to flow over the plains towards the setting sun. This means that the buffalo were gone for all time and that game generally would become a precarious means of existence, that the ranch and the farm would supersede the open plain, that settlers would need much guidance as well as protection, that the Indians would have to be taught to stay on their reserves and make a living there, and that the half-breeds, who were no lovers of agriculture, would have to be weaned from their nomadic inclinations. In some parts of the vast country, as at Prince Albert, Superintendent A. B. Perry, who took charge there after the rebellion, states, "The general attitude of the half-breeds and Indians was one of regret for what had happened." All was going well, but in some other quarters there was a sort of sullenly defiant spirit abroad which took all the tact and the courage of the Police to overcome. It was fortunate that the officers and men of the Police had from the beginning so commended themselves to the Indians and half-breeds as exponents of fair play that these natives of the country never seemed to hold the Police responsible for the errors, delays or mistakes of any government.

In speaking of Police reports I would like the reader to bear in mind that, in addition to the reports furnished by the combatant officers generally so classified, commissioners, superintendents, inspectors and others, some of the most remarkable and important documents sent forward to the proper authorities, through the usual channels, were written by the surgeons and their assistants, and also by the veterinary surgeons. Men and their troop horses were companions on the long trails, and they both had to be cared for by sympathetic experts in each line. It was vastly important that both should be kept fit if the work was to be done, and of the two the men themselves were always more anxious about their horses than about their own comfort. Hence these health-preserving specialists were of peculiar value for the efficiency of the corps. And as they were men of education as well as keen observers, their reports bore the evidences of research, which made them treasuries of information.

As an indication of the way in which the Police showed that they were in the country not only to preserve law and order but to guide settlers in the interests of the country's development as well as for their own welfare, I quote from one of Commissioner Lawrence Herchmer's annual reports this valuable statement in 1886: "As a rule too little fall ploughing is done in the North-West, and there is consequently too much hurry amongst the farmers in the spring and large tracts of land are sown, but not sufficiently worked—nearly all the farmers work too much land for their strength. Very few of them made any use of the manure from their farmyards, and although at nearly all Police posts, farms are quite close, I am not aware that any manure is drawn from our stables by any farmers." This statement was amply justified and very much needed, as those of us who knew the country then can affirm. Many had rushed west with the idea of getting rich "quick." They spread themselves over too much land, they neglected fall ploughing and ran the risk of getting caught with frost next season, and they thought they could save themselves time and money by doing without a fertilizer and taking all they could get out of the land. No doubt Herchmer and his thousand men preached the gospel of good farming with effect, for not many years passed before the flagrant mistakes he pointed out were remedied, to the great benefit of the country which has become in large measure the granary of the Empire.

In patrol work the following from Superintendent Neale throws a little side-light on some of the frequent experiences of the Force in that period. The reference is to the "Old Man's River" in the foothill country in December. Neale says: "I had gone ahead to try the ice and found it unsafe. The saddle horses were then crossed, followed by the wagons, one of which, the hospital spring wagon, came to grief by the horses refusing to face the wind, trying to get on the ice and breaking the pole. Both men and horses were covered with ice, as the wind was very strong and bitterly cold. The stopping place at Kipp being only in course of erection, there was no place to go into, and the raising of a tent was an impossibility. However, the horses were placed in the shelter afforded by some haystacks, and after being dried and fed the men managed to get a cup of tea and then turned in with their horses." There is not much detail here, but one who knows that country at that season reads between the lines and shivers. And that the conditions might crop up at other dates is evident by a line in the same report which says that "Inspector Sanders travelled the whole distance from Lethbridge to Bull's Head *coulée* in a driving snowstorm." That would be a dangerous outing.

That others of the Police were taking note of new conditions for the benefit of the country, as Lawrence Herchmer did in his remarks on farming above quoted, is evidenced by a recommendation by Superintendent Steele, who says in 1886: "I wish to call your attention to the quality of wood used last winter for fuel, causing large fatigues, much waste and consequently great expense. This could be avoided by entering into coal contracts with people residing near the coal beds on the North Saskatchewan, who would be able to supply at low rates." Thus were these guardians of the peace keeping their eyes open and urging forward the proper industrial development of the country.

There is a striking and characteristic passage in a later report from Superintendent Perry, the general truth of which is just as vital to the well-being of the State to-day as it was when written not long after the rebellion. It appears that Perry and his men had traced and brought for trial a good many cattle-killers, mail-robbers and others, but found much difficulty in getting convictions in local court where jurymen and others seemed to have more sympathy with the accused than necessary. Perry sees the far-reaching danger of this attitude, and refers to it as follows: "I regret that convictions for the serious crimes were not secured against the guilty parties. Evidence was produced for the defence which could well be doubted. Not only has this case produced sympathy for crime, but in other cases, it has been plainly manifested. Petitions have been forwarded to lessen the penalties where laws of the country have wilfully and knowingly been broken. So notorious has this become, that it has disheartened us in attempting to secure criminal convictions. There seems to be an absurd idea that the dismissal of a charge means a snub to the Mounted Police, whereas it strikes home at the root of society and threatens the lives and property of the very men who jeer and flaunt." The frontier was fortunate in having men who saw and pointed out this tendency in time. There is the ring of a statesman in that declaration.

But Perry and his men were by no means deterred, even if feeling disheartened by that state of apparent sympathy with law-breakers. This is attested by the fact that when the first stage robbery ever accomplished in the territories took place by the holding up of the Prince Albert mail near Humboldt, Perry and his detachments under Inspectors Begin and Guthbert so combed the whole country in search of the perpetrators that this attempt to introduce the Jesse-James programme into Canadian territory was effectually discouraged. It took some time to land the robber, a man named Garnett, in the north country, who was given a long term sentence in the penitentiary.

The Police were always on active service, but the service was very varied in character. It is interesting to find this note in one of the reports of that period written by Superintendent Deane, then in command of the Headquarters District at Regina. "On the 15th of August it was reported to me that a child about two and a half years old, the daughter of Mr. and Mrs. Pringle, of Regina, had strayed from her mother, who was on a visit to Pense. A Police party was dispatched to search the neighbourhood. The child was lost on the evening of the 15th, but the loss was not reported to me till the following afternoon. The child was found on the evening of the 17th in some bushes a mile or two away from the house from which it had strayed, and beyond being somewhat frightened, was little the worse for the exposure." One can quite imagine the concern of these red-coated knights of the saddle for the lost child. They would not say much, but thoughts of food and sleep would be put aside till the child was found. What plan they employed is not stated, but I have seen men under similar conditions, mounted or dismounted, holding hands and swinging in compass circles on the plain so as not to leave a foot of ground unsearched. Deane's report is as above, but again those who know the country and the men will read between the lines and see these uniformed athletes quieting the fears of the little one and then going away to some other duty glad with the remembrance of the child and the rejoicing parents.

For a few years after the Riel outbreak there was a lot of unrest amongst the Blood Indians down to the south, where the proximity of the boundary line gave much opportunity to horse-thieves, cattle-killers and smugglers of whisky, but the watchfulness of Superintendents Neale and MacDonnell, Inspectors Howe, Sanders, Wattam, Sergt.-Major Lake and others checkmated every effort at lawlessness. Inspector Sanders made a clever capture of two Bloods, "The Dog" and "Big Rib," who were tried and sentenced, but who escaped to the other side of the line from the sheriff. This escape led some of the Bloods to think they could get ahead of the Police. In fact one of the chiefs, "Calf Shirt," brought in liquor from Montana and said he would defy the Police, while another Indian, "Good Rider," tried cattle-killing on the Cochrane Ranch. But the Police took a hand at this point. Superintendent Neale wired Superintendent MacDonnell for a detachment of officers and men, and MacDonnell sent Inspector Howe with twenty men to meet Neale with a like number at Stand Off. The result was that both "Calf Shirt" and "Good Rider" were arrested at two different camps, and each was duly tried and sentenced to a term with hard labour. This nipped the law-breaking in the bud. That was the Mounted Police way.

After this experience it is not surprising to read in Commissioner Herchmer's report for 1888, "There has been a remarkable absence of crime during the past year and, outside arrests of criminals from the United States, we have made no important arrests in our territory." This was the gratifying result of the thoroughness of the Police patrol system, and the natural sequence to the fact that there was not much use or profit in trying to thwart the law when these red-coated guardians of the peace were around, and as the Indians found that law-breaking did not pay, they turned to more profitable pursuits, in which they were encouraged and helped by the Government and the Police. Hence this observant Commissioner is able to say that "in all quarters of the territories the Indians are making rapid strides towards self-support." The day was coming when, under the same paternal encouragement, the Indians would be the prize-winners at the fairs on the plains where they had once hunted buffalo—a very remarkable transformation.

In the same year Herchmer calls attention to the highly pleasing fact that the introduction of the telephone would lead to an enormous saving of men and horses, and notes the able and diplomatic way in which Superintendent Steele, assisted by Inspectors Wood, Huot and Surgeon Powell, had quieted matters in the Kootenay country where Chief Isadore's attitude had discouraged settlement. With his usual social insight, Herchmer indicates that the Mormon settlement in southern Alberta, with its possible polygamy, will be the better of some oversight in the interests of British law. This latter was a wise decision, and led at least to the practical abandonment of a doctrine that had brought much odium upon that sect.

It is interesting to find in that period of the late eighties a letter to Superintendent Deane, at Lethbridge, from the Montana Stock Growers' Association conveying a resolution of "thanks to the officers and men of the North-West Mounted Police and also to the Canadian authorities generally for assistance given to many of the citizens of Montana in recovering horses stolen from our territory." And that the Police were just as ready and willing to see the Indians got their dues either way is evidenced by another entry in which Deane pithily says, "A Blood Indian named 'Mike' laid an information against a Blackfoot for stealing his horse. 'Mike' recovered his horse and the Blackfoot is now serving three months' imprisonment here." Touching on the question of smuggling near the boundary, Deane tells of a patrol consisting of Constables Campbell and Chapman who, between Pendant d'Oreille (evidently a place where people should step lively, for the Superintendent says it "bristles with rattlesnakes") and Writing-on-Stone. These constables came across a man named Berube with five horses and a wagon. His story did not sound well to them, and so they asked him to come to camp. He agreed with evident reluctance, and when he said he was hungry and his team tired, the Police told him to unhitch the team, mount one of them and come along to camp for breakfast. Then Berube wished to get his pocket-book out of the wagon, but instead he fished out a revolver and galloped away saying he would riddle them if they followed. Of course they followed. With the usual Police restraint they forbore to shoot. Campbell overtook the smuggler, but just as he ranged alongside the policeman's horse stumbled and fell, Campbell, leaping off as the horse fell and grabbing at the halter of Berube's horse, but failing to hold him owing to the speed. Berube again threatened the riddling process, but the constables chased him to a slough, where the smuggler's horse got mired, but Berube tried to lead him out. Campbell fired in the air, but Berube kept going, whereupon Campbell shot the smuggler's horse, and the patrol took Berube and his four horses into camp. Deane says that as the horses appeared to be glandered, he wired for Veterinary Surgeon Wroughton (now the able Assistant Commissioner), who declared the case virulent, and ordered everything destroyed. This was done, and Deane adds, "The slaughter and destruction were carried out by the Police, some of whose clothes suffered destruction in the process for which they, not unreasonably, look for some compensation." And we hope they got it. Handling glanders was almost as dangerous as either the bullets or the rattlesnakes.

Superintendent Perry, who with the good assistance of Inspector Cuthbert commanded in the Prince Albert district in 1888, made some specially valuable recommendations as to the future care of the Indians, and praised the work of the missionaries amongst them. He said, "The hope of improvement in the Indian lies in the training of the rising generation, and it is to be hoped that before long the children will be taken in hand." And Perry's recommendation then made as to Industrial Schools bore fruit not many years later to the great advantage of the Indian and the country as well. Thus were the Police doing social service work as their duties proceeded.

An interesting side-light is thrown on the changing conditions of the West by our finding that in the late eighties a detachment of Police was sent by request from that Province into southern Manitoba. This detachment, under Inspector J. A. McGibbon (recently Assistant Commissioner at Regina, now retired), who had done important work at Moose Mountain and other far western points, had headquarters at Morden. The business of this detachment was to patrol the whole country near the boundary line, to grant special "Let Passes" to people who were entitled to cross backwards and forwards, to prevent wood being taken from the Canadian side by Dakota settlers, and generally to stand for law and order. In connection with other work I was up and down that region a good deal in those days, and recall the sense of general security the scattered settlers had because of the presence of McGibbon and his men.

After five years in command of the Prince Albert district, which had been the critical storm centre around which the winds of the Riel rebellion had beaten fiercely, Inspector A. B. Perry, before changing to another command, makes another valuable contribution to the development of Western history when he writes some special paragraphs in regard to the future of the half-breeds. Game was disappearing and the occupation of freighting on the prairie was being rendered useless by the incoming of railways. Perry says, "The mass of the half-breed population must therefore turn their attention to other methods of making a living. They have no alternative: farming must become their occupation in earnest. The English and Scotch half-breeds have already done this successfully; but very few of French descent have yet made any real attempt at it." Perry was right. These people had the blood of the nomad and the volatile in their veins. Perry continues, "As farming is the inevitable pursuit of the French half-breeds, all who are friendly to them should agree in urging and encouraging them to remain on their present holdings, so that they may at once face their destiny and ultimately obtain the position of a self-supporting people. They should be treated with patience and aided generously, remembering that it is not easy for white men possessing all the advantages of education and civilization to change their occupation. Can the half-breed hunter or freighter be expected to be more apt in adapting himself to change? It would be an astonishing thing if they quietly and quickly adapted themselves to the work of a farm on which success is only obtained by hard, patient and continuous labour." And Perry goes on to advise special instruction for these people. And he concludes, "There is a tendency on the part of some to regard the problem of the future of these people as insolvable. Knowing their many sterling qualities I cannot despair, but believe their descendants will be prosperous and desirable citizens of our North-West Territory." Words like these could not be written by a man who contented himself with the routine duty of a policeman, but by a wide-awake Canadian who was anxious for the future of his country and his fellow-citizens, and it is because there were so many in the Force who saw these questions in the light of Canada's future that we have always placed the Mounted Police amongst the real nation-builders of this new Dominion.

And the decade which ended with 1890 finds one of the new pages in the story of the Police in the patrol by Inspector J. V. Begin across the stormy waters of Lake Winnipeg up to the bleak shores of Hudson Bay at the famous old post of York Factory. This patrol involved much hardship and danger, but it stabilized conditions in that remote Keewatin area. In this regard Inspector Begin's trip was successful, but during his absence in the north there occurred the wreck of the Police boat on Lake Winnipeg, taking down with it Corporal Morphy and Constable Beaujeu, to both of whom the Inspector was warmly attached. They were splendid young men, full of gallantry and courage, but they answered the last roll-call while in the discharge of duty in a Force that has always been on active service.

* * * * *

CHAPTER X

CHANGING SCENERY

The decade from 1890 to 1900 witnessed changes and incidents that were fully up to the Police history record for matters of thrilling importance. In 1891 Sir John A. Macdonald, who was the originator of the Force, and who had always taken great pride in its splendid efficiency, passed away after a brief illness at the historic homestead, Earnscliffe, in Ottawa. Not even Sir John's most rabidly partisan friends had ever claimed perfection for their political idol, but I did hear one man say that he was so devoted to "The old Chieftain," that he was quite prepared to support him whether he was right or wrong. This was probably an extreme case, but it illustrates the extraordinary magnetism of the remarkable man who had been the chief pilot in taking the country through the shoals and rocks that threatened to wreck Confederation at its launching. Sir John's Canadianism was intense and so was his Imperialism, for was it not he who said, "A British subject I was born and a British subject I will die"? The undoubted political lapses in his career seemed to proceed from his being possessed with the idea that his presence at the head of affairs was so necessary for the well-being of the country that he should get there and stay there at any cost. His two great achievements in connection with Western Canada were his inauguration of the Canadian Pacific Railway, and his organization of the Mounted Police. This does not mean that in these two projects he had not the aid of others, for in some measure he had the support of even his political opponents, who differed from him in considerable degree on the railway policy, but who supported him in his proposal to organize the Mounted Police.

When I last heard this Disraeli-looking man speak, it was in Winnipeg, when he was making his first and last trip across Canada on the railway for which he had done and ventured so much. In his semi-humorous and semi-serious way he said, "I used to state that I never expected to live long enough to see the road completed, but that when my friends would be crossing the continent upon it, I would be looking down upon them from another and better sphere; my opponents said I would be looking up, but in reality to the surprise of both, I am doing it on the horizontal." On that same trip the veteran took great delight in seeing the scarlet and gold uniforms of his favourite corps on their "native heath" in the great prairie land of the West. Such was Sir John's interest in the Force that, despite his heavy duties, he retained the headship of the corps to the end of his days. In later years Sir Wilfred Laurier, Sir Robert Bordon, and the Hon. N. W. Rowell were outstanding also in their high opinion of, and their great interest in, the riders of the plains. In fact all public men who really understood the Western situation and the wide-reaching influence of the Police on Western history have always been ready to estimate highly the great services rendered by these remarkable men. During that same decade which rounded out the century Colonel MacLeod, who had been appointed to the Bench and whose fine character had endeared him to the Police and the country, crossed the Great Divide amid the grief of all who knew him. The Assistant Commissioner, W. M. Herchmer, who had throughout nearly thirty years served with distinction in the Militia and the Police, died much regretted, and was succeeded by Superintendent John H. McIlree, who retired in 1911 after thirty-eight years of most valuable service.

It was in that decade also that the gold-rush into the Yukon took place, as we shall see, and furnished a new occasion for one of the most remarkable periods in the history of the Police, replete with incidents of adventure and tales of endurance along with a devotion to duty and a triumphant enforcement of law which added immensely to the already great prestige of the Force, and made a record that not only astonished but won the admiration of the world. We will, however, review some notable events of that decade before coming to the Yukon.

Tragic but glorious was the fate of a young constable near Pendant d'Oreille, who was out on special duty when a blinding snow-storm gathered to the height of a blizzard across his path. Losing the way, the troop-horse stumbled into a ravine and broke his neck. But the athletic young policeman, who had developed muscle as well as mind in his university, extricated himself and struggled on in his determination to carry out his commission. The odds of blizzard and cold were too heavy, and the gallant lad succumbed in the unequal contest. But he would bring no discredit on the Police tradition, and when his body was discovered by a search party the following words, scribbled with freezing fingers, were found on a paper in his dispatch bag, "Lost. Horse dead. Am trying to push on. Have done my best." In the long roll of honour there are few more remarkable incidents than this of the young policeman battling with the relentless elements which some of us have witnessed raging on these Western plains. But he did not fail. From his numbing hands he had passed on to others the supreme duty of upholding the great tradition.

And then we can swing to another and lighter, but still very important phase of Police life. In the nineties Superintendent Steele, who was at Fort MacLeod, gives us some vivid and interesting pictures of social evenings in the winter, and out-door sports in the summer. The Police were leaders in these gatherings, but all the country-side turned out, and the barrack hall was thrown open on occasion for winter gatherings. There was wisdom in all this, for to teach people to enjoy proper recreation and play is to make them better citizens and more cordial one to the other. In the summer the Bloods and Piegans with their ponies and dogs attended the sports, and took active part under the general oversight of that incomparable scout and interpreter Jerry Potts.

In the roping of the huge wild steers there was much opportunity for the display of skill and nerve. When these big steers had been run out and had passed the line the cowboy on his trained pony followed at racing speed. His pony seemed dowered with full knowledge of the methods, and so watched the lasso thrown over the steer's head, when the wary pony, with all four feet braced to meet the strain, came to a sudden halt. This swift stop caused the steer to go heels over head and fall on his back, the pony holding the rope tight till the rider dismounted and tied the steer up in orthodox fashion, the pony watching every movement till the task was finished.

Bronco-breaking was a regular industry, and every meet of the kind just described had its bucking contents, but not after the manner of circuses with a few dispirited animals that go through a programme without springing any surprises on the rider. A real prairie bronco five or six years old, that had never been ridden or even handled since he was branded when a foal had no set programme. The rider never could tell what that bronco would do next. The animal might start away quietly, as if he was wondering what had gotten on his back when he was blindfolded. Then suddenly he would leap right up into the air, "swap ends," so the cowboys said, and come down facing the opposite way Then he might rear up and fall backwards, or throw himself down and roll over, but the rider was always on the bronco's back before he could get going again. This went on for some time, varied by a swift race out over the plain, from which the return would be made with the froth down over the hooves of the horse. Then the cowboys pronounced the bronco broken, but woe betide the unsuspecting tenderfoot who was tempted to get on the hurricane deck of what these men called a broken horse.

YUKON RUSH: SUMMIT. CHILCOOT PASS

GROUP OF INDIAN CHILDREN ON PRAIRIE.

The Police were good riders and each Division had several constables who made a speciality of breaking refractory broncos. And the work was necessary because for months after the horse was first broken he would break out again on occasion. One day on our line of march to the north from Calgary, a constable after the noon hour stop found on mounting his horse that the bronco spirit was still existent, and that bucking was evidently the order of the day. But the policeman was ready. He banged the horse over the head with his hat and used the spur till the unruly animal made a few kangaroo-like leaps and came to a sudden halt at the edge of the hole where the camp fire had left a bed of hot coals. The rider was not disturbed by the shock, but the buckle of his cartridge belt gave way under the strain and the whole thing dropped over the horse's head into the fire. Those of us who were looking on lost no time in taking cover when the fire got at those cartridges.

Steele tells us in this same connection of an extraordinary feat of horsemanship he witnessed by Mr. Charles Sharples, of the Winder Ranch. Sharples had brought some horses to MacLeod to sell to the Mounted Police, and had them in a stable near the Old Man's River, where there was a perpendicular bank about 30 feet high. He started out to show one of the horses to the Commissioner at the Fort, but the brute bucked fiercely towards the cut-bank, sidling and fighting against its rider until at last there seemed to be nothing for it but to go over the bank side-on. That did not suit Sharples. He turned the brute sharply towards the precipice, gave it the spur and went out into space. Everybody rushed to the top to see what had become of this bold horseman, and were amazed to see him still firm in the saddle with the horse swimming towards the opposite bank, none the worse for his wild leap. Steele does not tell us whether Sharples made a sale of that horse, but he deserved to succeed in so doing. A horse like that would come in handy.

Perhaps the races and other sports inaugurated by the Police had their effect in discouraging the Indians from the barbaric Sun-dance which the Government sought to end as soon as possible, although not desiring to repress them by force. The Sun-dance was a semi-religious, semi-tribal festival for the purpose of enabling young braves to prove that they had courage and stamina enough to go on the war-path. While we were engaged in the Riel rebellion campaign we saw several Sun-dance lodges along the line of our march after Big Bear, these lodges being left standing with a view to frightening our men from pursuing braves who could demonstrate their courage in the way the lodge indicated.

The Sun-dance lodge was a circular wooden structure of poles with rafters coming together to a point above. From these rafters hooks were suspended by thongs of tough leather. The prospective braves danced around furiously within the structure in a frenzy of excitement, fastening the hooks in their skin and thus lacerating themselves till they sometimes fainted away. This performance was an annual affair on the general principle that they should be always ready for war. There was nothing in the festival that would justify a forcible suppression of it, which would offend the Indians by interference with an ancient custom. But the Mounted Police used their persuasive influence against it and showed the younger Indians how foolish and useless it was. Accordingly, we find Superintendent Steele, who was in command at Fort MacLeod, saying in 1891, "This year both Bloods and Piegans indulged in the time-honoured Sun-dance. From personal observation and careful inquiry I am convinced that this festival has almost entirely ceased to have any significance except to the old people. The vanity of the ancient warrior is no doubt gratified when he recounts his scalps, but there seemed very little interest and no enthusiasm on the part of his audience. The young Indians of both sides seem to look on the whole thing as an excuse for a picnic. Many Indians on the reserves did not take sufficient interest in the festival to attend it. Two braves were made at the Blood dance and none at the Piegans'." So this pagan custom was vanishing. It is now a thing of the past, but we must credit the Police with gradually ending it. About this period there were still some rumblings of discontent amongst the Sioux Indians south of the boundary line in the region of Manitoba. There were recurrent "scares" and many rumours of "Ghost dances" on our side of the line, in expectation, it was said, of an incursion by the Sioux, who were reported to be stirring up our Indians to commit depredations on the settlers. But the presence and the constant patrols of Inspector J. A. McGibbon and his men in the scarlet tunic soon restored the equilibrium of things and calmed the fears of the settlers so that they went peacefully on with their work. A literary outcome of the situation was the widely quoted and beneficially humorous utterance of a punster on the staff of the Winnipeg Free Press, who asserted that the Sioux (sue) scare was seizing a lot of fellows who owed money.

The relations existing between the Mounted Police and the American soldiery south of the line were always of the most cordial and fraternal type. Superintendent A. W. Jarvis, who was in charge at Lethbridge in the nineties, refers to this in one of his reports. He says, "Several deserters from the American army arrived here in the spring, but only one of them brought a horse. This was taken from him and was sent back to the officer commanding at Fort Assiniboine. This was the only opportunity I had to reciprocate the courtesy so freely extended to us under similar circumstances by the American officers at that post. These gentlemen have always shown themselves ready and willing to assist the Mounted Police by any means in their power." Speaking of desertions it was generally felt that a man who would desert was not really worth a search. So far as the Mounted Police were concerned, there were not many desertions, but there was probably more relief than otherwise when some unworthy man took French leave and escaped. Such a man was not wanted. The standing of the Force was to be maintained, and so the statement once made by Commissioner Lawrence Herchmer became a classic: "I want to see the Mounted Police Force to be the hardest to get into and the easiest to get out of in the world."

There is a fine human picture in another clause of Superintendent A. W. Jarvis' report already mentioned. He says: "On November 20 two boys, aged 16 and 10 years respectively, sons of leading citizens of Medicine Hat, were caught in a blizzard a few miles south of that town and frozen to death. Two days later the Police Patrol from Bull's Head found the bodies. Sergeant Mathewson remained alone all night on the open prairie to watch them and protect them from the cayotes, till the Police team came next day to take them to town." Mathewson had a lonely and dangerous vigil on the blizzard-swept plain, but it was characteristic of these big men to stand guard in such pathetic cases.

The same fine touch comes out in a brief medical import in 1892 from that able man Senior Surgeon Jukes at the Regina headquarters. It had been a time of stress in the hospital work, and Dr. Haultain, the assistant surgeon, had been laid completely aside by illness. So Dr. Jukes cut out the office work and let reports go in order to devote himself to the sick. Then Assistant Surgeon Fraser arrived from Calgary to help, and Dr. Jukes has time to send in a brief note before the time for having reports in the printer's hands expires. And he says at the end of it, "I am assured by the comptroller that in consideration of the enormous amount of work which has been thrown on me for the last three months, no censure can possibly be passed on me for having devoted the whole of my time to the sick under my charge and other professional duties, in preference to the writing of an annual report." Well spoken, Dr. Jukes, and the authorities saw the point at once. Reports could wait, but the sick had to be looked after at once. That, too, is a police tradition. Take care of the casualties now and report later.

That the Mounted Police Force was continuously progressive to ever higher efficiency was due in no small measure to the fact that officers and men were encouraged to be on the look out for improved methods and to feel free to suggest these to those in command. Superintendent Perry had been the means of bringing about a system of districts and sub-districts with constables scattered over many points rather than concentrated at headquarters, qualified only by the suggestion that changes be often made so as to keep all in touch with regimental duties. And I find that Inspector Constantine, a man of quite unusual gifts and powers, as we shall see later, makes a striking recommendation in his report from Moosomin in 1893. He says that the farther division of districts into groups in charge of a non-commissioned officer has increased the self-respect of these men and developed their interest and initiative. He says men are more to be trusted than regulations. "Get good men forward, give more power to individuals, create a confidence through all ranks one with the other and things will work harmoniously in maintaining the peace of the country." And because all the men cannot be experienced from the outset Constantine suggests that a special instruction book should be issued to every recruit, a necessary part of his equipment, and to be produced at kit inspection or whenever called for by the officer commanding. And this keen Inspector adds that young men who had this book would be in a better position to carry out their duty "besides having the confidence inspired by a knowledge that they were right and not being in an agony of indecision caused by being advised by parties having different interests." Happy the Force that had leaders able and free to suggest new departures to greater efficiency. That the officers were always careful about minor details with a view to the comfort of the men and economy at the same time as far as possible is evidenced by some suggestions from Inspector A. C. Macdonnell, who was in charge at Wood Mountain in 1893. Macdonnell (now Sir Archibald, Commandant at Kingston Military College and the wearer of many war decorations) says that he had the old mud-roofs removed and replaced by shingles and painted, and makes the recommendation which those who know the country will understand, "that next year all the log-buildings be chinked with mortar. It would last five years and be much cleaner and neater in appearance than mud, and save the cost of the annual mudding." These officers kept their eyes on everything. It is in keeping with what was said above as to deserters that Macdonnell reports a desertion and adds, "As this constable was the possessor of an exceedingly bad defaulter's sheet, the Force sustains no loss." Let the Force be made easy for undesirables to leave, as Herchmer said some years before.

In 1893 Superintendent Perry, in referring to the reports he was transmitting from Superintendent F. Norman, of Wood Mountain, Inspectors McGibbon, of Saltcoats, J. O. Wilson, of Estevan, C. Constantine, of Moosomin, and W. H. Routledge, in Manitoba, says these reports show "how varied and multifarious are the duties which are demanded of us—at Wood Mountain our men are found acting as cowboys, rounding up and driving back across the boundary vast herds of wild American ranch cattle which again and again wander northward in search of better feed and more water. At Estevan and Gretna they are seen in charge of large herds of quarantined cattle, attending sick animals, milch cows, and at the expiration of their term in quarantine driving them long distances by trail, loading on trains and conveying them to their different destinations; in Manitoba they are engaged in enforcing the customs laws, aiding the regular customs officials, whose duties they at times perform, and executing the Crown Timber and Dominion Land regulations; and, in addition to this work of a special nature, everywhere carrying out their regular duties of detecting crime, aiding the administration of justice, acting as prairie fire and game guardians, and maintaining a patrol system which covers weekly some 1,200 miles." No wonder Perry adds, "Such extended duties test the capacities of the Force and their successful performance illustrates the diversity of attainments in the personnel of the North-West Mounted Police." And those of us who have seen them under many circumstances can vouch for their being not stereotyped officials, but all-round adaptable men. There are flashes of humour all through the reports of Police Officers. Sometimes they may have been unintentional, but humour is a saving grace and men who were facing tragedies almost every day would have given way under the strain if they had not put a little comedy into life even in their reports. Here, for instance, is an item from a report by Inspector Z. T. Wood, who later on did such splendid work in the Yukon. Writing from Calgary in 1894 he reports a case by saying, "On the night of July 5 a man named Wilson took his effects from a C.P. Railway car and started north without going through the usual form of paying the freight thereon. He was caught, brought back and committed for trial." Superintendent Deane exposes one of the peculiar technicalities of law when he says, "On the 15th of August a traveller had a pair of field glasses stolen from his buckboard at a ranch about 12 miles from Lethbridge. We know who took them, but the one witness who could convict the thief had disappeared." The same officer elsewhere observes, "On the 15th of September last, in the Pot Hole country, a saddle was stolen from the back of a piqueted horse whose rider had dismounted to shoot some ducks. We know who is responsible for this piece of impudence, but shall be lucky if we succeed in recovering the saddle." Deane saw humour in the situation, but was evidently rather sceptical about the ways of law. These examples of wit could be multiplied readily from what to the casual student seem to be dry annual reports. In reality these same reports pulsate with life. But it is often only found between the lines by the reader who knows the history of the land.

Nearly midway in that last decade of the last century the golden Yukon swung out of solitude into the vision of the world and there as elsewhere in the vast north-land the Mounted Police were to play a large and brilliantly useful part. To some study of that part we shall come in succeeding pages.

* * * * *

CHAPTER XI

IN THE GOLD COUNTRY

Away on the banks of the Red River hard by where the City of Winnipeg with its aggressive business marts and its surging polyglot population now stands, there is the old Kildonan Church, which the original Selkirk Settlers, pioneers of the West, built for themselves and their children. These early colonists, unmindful of worldly gain, had the traditional hospitality of the Highland race to which they belonged, and the proverbial absence of class distinction which always obtains on a frontier:

> "No bolts had they to their doors
> Nor bars to their windows,
> But their houses were open as day
> And the hearts of the owners."

It was natural that to such a place should come on frequent visits the Hudson's Bay men, the explorers and pathfinders, most of whom were of the same race and creed as the pioneers. And it was natural too, that when these pathfinders came to the end of the long trail their bodies should be brought back to rest in the God's acre around that old church, the famous cemetery where

> "Each in his narrow cell forever laid,
> The rude forefathers of the hamlet sleep."

There were other lines of Gray's immortal poem that could be applied with great appropriateness to that churchyard that lay in the midst of a settlement in which were men of undoubted talent and power had their lot been cast in other surroundings. Such lines, for instance, as these:

> "Some village Hampden, who, with dauntless breast,
>   The little tyrant of his fields withstood:
> Some mute, inglorious Milton here may rest:
>   Some Cromwell guiltless of his country's blood."

But there are many resting there who became known far beyond their early circle. Most of them are not connected with our present story, but one monument in that ancient churchyard bears the name of a man whose record shines out with splendour in the history of the Yukon, which region was afterwards the scene of one of the most brilliant, successful and grandly tragic chapters in the record of the Mounted Police. The name is that of Robert Campbell, the famous Hudson's Bay Company explorer, who threescore years before the famous gold-rush which required the guardian presence of the Police had discovered the Yukon River, and had travelled for years in the regions which later on became known as one of the great gold-fields of the world. Campbell was not looking for gold or caring for it. He was opening out a new Empire for trade with the usual self-forgetful devotion of its employees to the interests of the great Fur Company.

I remember Campbell, guest often in my father's house on the Red River in my boyhood, and later, for he lived to a great age. A Highlander too was he, from Glenlyon in Perthshire, tall, stately, handsome, with black hair and beard, his whole bearing suggestive of power. A modest man withal, for he refused to call after himself the great river he had discovered, and he left no material out of which a real biography could be written. But it was because he had blazed the way and because another Hudson's Bay man, Hunter Murray, had built Fort Yukon, that others throughout the years began to penetrate into the wild until, in the nineties, there came the discovery of acres of gold which attracted the wildest rush in the history of mining. There have been many wild rushes in different parts of the world, but those who went on the Yukon rush faced climatic conditions in blizzards, bottomless snow drifts and desperate cold, as well as on torrential streams and treacherous rapids, which, from the standpoint of hardship and privation, dwarf all other mining expeditions into insignificance. Of all this burden and exposure and hardship the Mounted Police, in the simple discharge of their duties, bore the lion's share, and that without any financial compensation such as others expected who were drawn to the north by the lure of gold. The Police had nothing beyond their small pay, and they kept themselves strictly and sternly aloof from opportunities to enrich themselves either in the way of business or in the way of allowing any offers to be made them as a price for shielding law-breakers. They did not make any money, though it was being made by thousands all around them. But they did their duty so valiantly and so uncompromisingly that they added to their already great prestige and showed the world a new record in keeping potentially dangerous frontier camps almost entirely free from crime. There was hardly any gun play. There were only two or three homicides, and there were no failures in justice and no lynchings.

When in 1894 the first rumours of a probable rush into the region came to the outside, the Dominion Government felt that it was imperative that, in order to prevent lawlessness as well as to protect the interests of Canada in respect to the area within her boundary, the famous corps that had policed all the western frontiers should be represented immediately in the gold regions of the far north. And it was vitally important that a man should be sent in as officer commanding who would be specially fitted for such an unprecedented and extraordinary task. That man was found in the person of Inspector Charles Constantine, and he, taking with him other picked men in Inspector D. A. E. Strickland, Assistant Surgeon A. E. Wells, Staff-Sergeant Brown and twenty non-commissioned officers and constables, left for their distant field of action in the month of June. Strickland, who had done fine service on the plains, was to be of great value in the north on account of his knowledge of woodcraft logging, building and such like, in addition to his regular police duties. Wells was to have his hands full, since for some time he was, as some one said, the only doctor in a region as large as France and had, with sometimes inadequate means, to fight scourges of scurvy and the other diseases incident to food and climate. The men in the detachments were experienced and hardy enough to face anything that might turn up either in the shape of man or beast or difficult atmospheric conditions.

Constantine had served in the Red River expedition, and then, on account of special qualifications, had been made chief of the Provincial Police in Manitoba, where he was a terror to evil-doers. When the second Riel rebellion broke out and a volunteer regiment was being hurriedly raised in Winnipeg for service in the Big Bear country, Constantine, to the great delight of all of us who joined up with that regiment, became Adjutant. During that campaign he was always to the fore in every crisis and showed particular skill in rooting out men who were inciting the Indians to revolt. One morning of dense fog away beyond Fort Pitt our outside picket was fired on when I had charge of the guard. Calling out the guard and getting them under arms I went over to notify the officer commanding in the camp, but met Constantine with his forty-five ready for action. He had scented the alarm and did not wait for notice before getting out to see what was doing. A less keen-sighted or an excitable man would probably have shot anyone looming up through the fog, as I did from the direction of the shooting, but Constantine, though as quick as a flash, always had himself in hand. After the rebellion he became an Inspector in the Mounted Police, and had so approved himself as a wide-awake, intelligent and courageous officer that when the Yukon sprang up with its special demand he was appointed to be the pioneer in that far region of the north. Of medium height but very compactly built, Constantine was immensely strong, quick in his movements and capable of enduring tremendous strain. If it came to a rough and tumble he was as hard a man to handle as anyone would care to find. These qualities, along with his mental alertness and judicial training, made him a good man to send to a region where he had to exercise many functions until fuller government could be established. Constantine first of all made an investigating and exploratory trip accompanied by Staff-Sergeant Charles Brown. Leaving Moosomin in May in obedience to orders to report in Ottawa for special duty, Constantine received instructions to proceed to the Yukon and make recommendations as to general administration. He accordingly left for the north and by crossing over by the Lewes-Yukon he reached Fort Cudahy on August 7, where he remained about a month before returning by St. Michaels and arriving at Victoria in October. He reported elaborately on the resources, climate and possibilities of the whole country. This was in 1894, and in consequence of Constantine's grasp of the situation and his talent for organization he was sent back next year with the officers and men above indicated, arriving at Fort Cudahy on July 24.

It was well that Strickland was a practical logger and builder, for quarters had to be provided. It was a land of extremes, with intense cold in the winter and equally intense heat in the summer. Constantine speaks of an occasional 75 degrees below zero in the winter and the heat as high as 120 degrees. In another report he writes, "The miners have a simple method of determining when it is too cold to work by hanging a bottle containing mercury outside the house. When it freezes it is time to remain inside." We should rather think so. Albeit, the climate is dry and healthy when people are prepared for it and are not found fasting after prolonged exposure.

It was in the hot weather that Strickland and his picked men went up the Yukon amid the heat and flies, cut down the logs and floated them to where Fort Constantine was built before the extreme cold struck the region. The men who stayed with Constantine had cleared the ground of moss and brush with great effort. The moss varied from one to three feet in depth. Below it was ice, so that the report says the men worked a good part of the time up to their knees in water. "If it was not 90 degrees in the shade it was pouring rain." Up the river Strickland and his men were getting out the logs as stated, but without any appliances except their own physical strength and energy. Only men of the finest type could have stood it, and the Inspector gives them unstinted praise.

The buildings were rushed up as stated before the winter. They were chinked with moss and the roof covered with earth, there being no time to saw boards to cover. All this was not so bad for the winter, but when the spring came the men who had fought the intense cold were subjected to another kind of hardship. Constantine says in a later report, "During the heavy rains the roofs leaked so badly that oil sheets and tarpaulins had to be put up over all the beds to keep them dry. The earth roofs of this country will only absorb a certain amount of moisture and when the limit is reached, a deluge of very dirty water is the result." Evidently the men were not having a picnic.

However, Constantine and his detachment keep the country in order, administer justice, collect customs due to the Dominion and generally make conditions civilized and British. There was a time when it was generally believed that most of the gold-bearing creeks were on the American side of the line, but a survey made under direction of the Police revealed the opposite to be the case and Constantine notified the miners on Miller, Glacier and other creeks that they were on Canadian territory, subject to British law and amenable to regulations as to mining fees, Constantine's modesty and determination are illustrated in one quiet paragraph, which some of us who knew him will find luminous between the lines. He says, "A few miners denied Canada's jurisdiction and right to collect fees on the ground that there was a possibility of error in the survey. However, I went up to Miller and Glacier Creeks and all dues were paid without any trouble except that of a hard trip, but as all trips in this country are of that nature, it was part of the bargain. On Glacier Creek a number of miners undertook to run matters in accordance with their own ideas of justice and set themselves up as the law of the land. The trouble ended, however, by the Canadian law being carried out." Constantine was clearly serving notice on all and sundry that the Mounted Police were on hand to live up to their reputation of seeing justice done and playing no favourites. The authorities had made no mistake when they sent him in as the pioneer.

Then he speaks in 1896 of new discoveries which began to cause the mad rush from all parts of the world as the news percolated through to the outside. "In August of this year a rich discovery of coarse gravel was made by one George Carmack on Bonanza Creek, a tributary to the Klondike. His prospect showed $3.00 to the pan." Not bad picking for George, who became wealthy. But George's shovel and pick and pan, clattering as he worked, awakened echoes to far distances and the wild stampede of all kinds of people, prominently the adventurous and the get-rich-quick class, began with a vengeance.

Constantine got ready for it, strongly recommending the establishment of civil courts, the appointment of an administrator and law-officer and the reinforcing of the Police so that they could be scattered up and down the new mining areas as required. A post called Fort Herchmer, after the Commissioner, was built at Dawson which was to become the big centre shortly, and the Police Force was augmented by the arrival of two small detachments under command respectively of two well-known officers, Inspectors Scarth and Harper. And not any too soon were these precautions taken, for Constantine lets light in on the kind of people who began to head for the diggings when he says in his graphic way, "A considerable number of people coming in from the Sound cities appear to be the sweepings of the slums and the result of a general jail delivery. Heretofore goods could be cached on the side of the trails and they would be perfectly safe, now a man has to sit on his cache with a shotgun to ensure the safety of his goods. Cabins in out-of-the-way places are broken into and everything cleaned out." That was before the newcomers realized that the Mounted Police were to the fore. Constantine and his men kept on their track and perpetrators of ordinary offences were astonished when they were run out of the country in order to save food for the decent people who were willing to work without preying on others. And the Inspector gives parting salute to the deported individuals by saying, "Many of them could well be spared in any community, for the rush had brought in toughs, gamblers, lewd women and criminals of almost every type, from the petty thief to the murderer."

But Constantine gave them no quarter, and so it was that by the time the big stampede took place into Dawson and the Creeks it had become known far and wide that the Mounted Police would stand no nonsense. So the way was made simpler, though not at any time a sinecure, for those who followed the intrepid pioneers in the scarlet tunic. But coming at the summit of an active and strenuous life, the exposure, responsibility and general wear and tear of his Yukon years undermined the once rugged strength of Constantine. He was transferred to the prairie after nearly four years in the Yukon, but never fully recovered his vigour. His leaving the Yukon had a very human side. The miners showed their appreciation of his manly, straightforward character by crowding in and presenting him and his wife and boy with nuggets of gold and indicating in their diffident but genuine way that if ever any of them needed help they could count on their Yukon friends for anything required. Which reminds us that tribute should be paid to the wives of these policemen who braved the wilderness places of the west and north to be helpers to their husbands and to make their homes centres of social refining influence where such influences were of untold value.

CHILCOOT PASS: N.W.M. POLICE AND CUSTOM HOUSE.

KLONDYKE RUSH: SQUAW RAPIDS, BETWEEN CANYON AND WHITE HORSE RAPIDS. 1898

Inspector Cortlandt Starnes, the present efficient Assistant-Commissioner at Ottawa Headquarters and who has done valuable service all the way across the country from Hudson Bay to the Yukon as well as on the plains, took over the command from Constantine and remained in charge till the arrival of Superintendent Steele, a period extending from June to September, 1898. Starnes, who is a short, heavily built and powerful man, capable of enduring much hardship, had come through in the previous winter, staying some months at Lake LaBarge and Little Salmon, accumulating stores of goods from the coast to be taken through in the spring to Dawson, where a shortage was impending. He had no easy time getting over the route, he and his men only saving themselves from wreck on Lake Bennett by throwing overboard some of their freight. With forty below zero and everything frozen up, Starnes had to build winter quarters at Little Salmon, and with the true democracy of the frontier we find the officials he was escorting into the Yukon giving a hand—Judge McGuire, Mr. F. O. Wade, Crown Prosecutor, Dr. Bonnar and others. But early in the spring Starnes moved on to Dawson. The rush was setting in and with Inspector F. Harper and a few men he had to hold the place for law and order during a sort of interregnum period. No civil courts were established till Judge McGuire came, and to administer the law under such conditions was always trying. But it was done. Offenders were given no rest. "Gunmen" were made impossible and gamblers found no city of refuge in the gold country. In three months Starnes and Harper, principally the former, tried 215 cases, these being all the way from dog-stealing (dogs were dogs in the north), drunkenness, keeping or frequenting disorderly houses to vagrancy, using vile language and refusing to work. If men would not work when free they were sentenced to jail with hard labour, because these experienced men knew that idleness is the prolific progenitor of crime. In consequence crime never got a start in the most quickly crowded mining camp in the world. It had been held down from the beginning. The place had its saloons and dance hall and fools were fleeced there as they are in older centres, but the superb strength and incorruptibility of the Mounted Police proved too much for the lawless element, and the whole period makes one of the proudest records in the history of this wonderful force.

The big stampede for Dawson started in 1897-98, and to cope with the incidentals and probably accompaniments of it, there was a whirlwind series of movements by the Mounted Police which seemed to anticipate every contingency, head off all manner of calamities, make provision for protecting the boundary line against infractions of the customs regulations, and generally see that law and order should prevail all over the wide area that was soon teeming with a nondescript heterogeneous population of excited gold-hunters. Two of the big men of the Force, Superintendents A. B. Perry, a masterly organizer, and S. B. Steele, a determined enforcer of law, were called on to go up to the north and meet the unprecedented situation. That these two superior officers did not shirk any of the hardships could be demonstrated from many an instance like the following related casually by Steele as to an incident at the outset. "At Dyea I met Perry and together we returned to Skagway in a small sailing boat. The weather was very cold and as the tide was out we were obliged to wade through the pools in our moccasins. When we embarked we were soaked to the hip and our clothes were frozen like boards." And they came that way the whole distance to Skagway, where they got no time to change as Perry had to leave for Vancouver that night in regard to further arrangements.

With these two from the beginning, indeed some were in the country ahead of them, was a group of very able officers, Superintendent Z. T. Wood, Inspectors P. C. H. Primrose, C. Starnes, F. Harper, W. H. Scarth, A. E. Strickland, R. Belcher, A. M. Jarvis, F. L. Cartwright, Surgeons W. E. Thompson and S. M. Fraser. Non-commissioned officers like Tucker, Macdonnell, Barker, Bates, Graham, Hyles, Corneil and Raven were amongst those in charge of early detachments or attached to hospital bases in the first year of the big rush, and these with the help of as able and resolute a body of men as ever wore uniform led the way to a new world record for policing a country in a paternal method of oversight which guided and controlled but never resorted to shooting. The use of the word paternal calls to mind the way they threw a cordon around the country to prevent at the threshold the entrance of men who were unprepared for the hardships with either clothing or supplies or physique. And the manner in which the Police interposed against the madness of inexpert men who were anxious to run the White Horse Rapids and the Miles Canyon in crazy boats on the way to Dawson was admirable in its quiet forcefulness. A good many of these people were men and women from offices and stores in American cities who knew boats only by hearsay. So when Steele arrived at the Rapids he gathered the stampeders together and said:

> "There are many of your countrymen who have said that the Mounted Police make the laws as they go along, and I am going to do so now for your own good, therefore the directions that I give shall be carried out strictly and they are these: Corporal Dixon, who thoroughly understands this work, will be in charge here and be responsible to me for the proper management of the passage of the Canyon and White Horse Rapids. No women or children will be taken in the boats. If they are strong enough to come to the Klondike they can walk the five miles of the bank to the foot of the White Horse and there is no danger for them here. No boat will be permitted to go through the Canyon until the corporal is satisfied that it has sufficient free board to enable it to ride the waves in safety. No boat will be allowed to pass with human beings in it unless it is steered by competent men, and of that the corporal will be the judge. There will be a number of pilots selected, whose names will be on the roll in the Mounted Police Barracks here, and when a crew needs a man to steer them through the Canyon to the foot of the rapids, pilots will be taken in turn from that list. In the event of the men not being able to pay, the Corporal will be permitted to arrange that the boats are run without charge."

Some of the impetuous who were willing to risk everything for the glitter of gold rather demurred at this strong paternalism, but when it was all over they thanked their stars that the Mounted Police had been on hand to head off the folly of fools.

We have anticipated in the last paragraph in order to illustrate how the Mounted Police guided the wild stampede. But let us get back and find Superintendent Perry on the ground just as the rush was starting for the passes. He made a swift trip and placed detachments of police on the Chilcoot and White Passes, putting those reliable officers Inspectors Belcher and Strickland in command. Up to a certain date it had almost been taken for granted that the whole country was on the American side as the names of Miles, the Indian fighter, and Gordon Bennett had been given by enthusiasts to the Canyon and the lake. But when Perry put Belcher on the Chilcoot and Strickland on the White Pass to hoist the British flag and collect customs levies, intimation was given that the great gold country was on the Canadian side of the line and that all who wished to pass that way must contribute to the Dominion exchequer and thus swell the revenue of Canada. Weather conditions were nothing less than awful. Steele, who, with Constable Skirving, went up the Chilcoot from Dyea where they had come on a craft which was covered from stem to stern with six inches of ice, says, "As we proceeded up the pass we faced a wind so cutting that we had often to make a rush for the shelter of a tree or walk in a crouching position behind the tailboard of a sleigh for a few minutes' respite. We overtook some on the trail next day out of a notorious tent town known as Sheep Camp. Many of them were staggering blindly along, with heavy loads on their backs, some of them off the trail and groping for it with their feet. These we assisted or they would have fallen by the way."

The same writer goes sympathetically into the following vivid description: "It would be difficult to describe the hardships gone through by the Mounted Police stationed at the passes. The camp at the Chilcoot under Inspector Belcher was pitched on the summit, where it is bounded by high mountains. A wooden cabin was erected in a couple of days. The place where it was in the pass was only about 100 yards wide. Below the summit, on the Canadian side, was Crater Lake, named after an extinct volcano. On its icy surface the men were forced to camp when they arrived. In the night of February 18 the water rose to the depth of six inches. Blankets and bedding were wet, the temperature being below zero with a blizzard. The tents could not be moved and the sleds had to be taken into them to enable the men to keep above the water at night. The storm blew for days with great violence, but on the 21st abated sufficiently to admit of the tents being moved to the top of the hill, where, although the cold was intense, it was better than in the water-covered ice of Crater Lake."

"The nearest firewood was seven miles away and the men who went after it often returned badly frost-bitten.

"Belcher, collecting customs, performing military as well as police duty on the summit, lived in the shack, which had all the discomforts of a shower-bath. Snow fell so thickly and so constantly that everything was damp and paper became mildewed. For some weeks the weather was very cold without storm, but on the 3rd of March there was a terrific day when the snow buried the cabin and the tents on the summit, the snowfall for the day being six feet on the level." The occupants had to shovel constantly to keep from being suffocated.

On the White Pass Inspector Strickland and his men had to pitch tents on the ice at first, no timber for cabins or firewood being nearer than 12 miles. Logs were cut and hauled in by horses. There were raging blizzards and great danger constantly threatened the men, who had to be on the alert to avoid being lost or frozen. However, on February 27 the Union Jack flew to the breeze and collection of customs began. A strong guard kept the trail and men were told off to examine the goods of the stampeders. There was a tremendous rush, and Strickland, overworked and suffering from severe bronchitis, struggled along, ably assisted by his splendid men. An enormous amount was gathered from those who were rushing in by thousands from the other side of the line bringing their supplies with them.

About this time Inspector Cartwright arrived from Regina with twenty men, and Steele, going up the White Pass with him, put him in charge, sending Strickland to Tagish, where the dry air soon restored him to health. It is an illuminating comment on Steele's disposition to look after others and forget himself that he was also, as Dr. Grant said, suffering from bronchitis which he had contracted weeks before when wading through icy waters to a boat. But as there was no one around to order him off duty he just kept right on, trusting that his strong constitution would see him through.

If physical conditions were bad with storm and cold, moral conditions from the coast to the summits were worse. The authorities on the American side seemed to accept as a sort of axiom the statement that a frontier had to be lawless. Anyway "Soapy Smith," a notorious gunman and gambler, who was eventually killed by a United States Marshal who was going to arrest him and who was killed by "Soapy" at the same time, both firing at one moment, had, with a big gang like himself, terrorized Skagway and the trails for months. Murders, robberies, shell games and the rest were practised without cessation up to the Mounted Police line on the summits, where they suddenly ceased because things of that sort would not be tolerated for a moment. At that point the incomers put their "guns" away and went quietly about their business. One finds it difficult to account for this difference unless by the assumption that immigrants into the American Republic had taken advantage of her wide proclamation of the ideal of liberty and had abused the ideal by turning it into licence. In this way nests of law-breakers and anarchists were allowed too much opportunity by local officials, where in a similar case a compact force like our Mounted Police with no local strings on them and with intense sentiment for the honour of the whole force, never permitted a situation to get out of hand in any locality however remote from the centre of government.

In a preceding paragraph I mentioned the name of Dr. Grant. He is the Rev. Dr. A. S. Grant, a Presbyterian Missionary who went in over that White Pass trail with a pack on his back. He could stand it better than most men, for he was a broad-shouldered and powerfully built man. Going as a missionary he was a man of peace, but he would not allow anyone to be imposed on in the difficult road. Hence one day when a bully elbowed a grey-haired man roughly into the snow, Grant interposed and receiving only insult, taught that bully a lesson he did not forget. To the credit of the bully be it recorded he took his medicine and shook hands with the man of peace who believed in protecting the weak.

Grant had taken a course in medicine which proved of immense value on the trail and during the early days in Dawson. Steele says of him, "Dr. Grant, a clergyman as well as physician, treats hundreds of sick without remuneration. Our force owes him a heavy debt of gratitude for the way he saved our men. More than half of those at the summit and Lake Bennett had pneumonia but were so well treated that we lost none. I have never seen men in such a dangerous state and it seemed impossible that they should recover, but they were pulled through."

This same Grant when he got into Dawson started the Good Samaritan Hospital with his own funds and became a large factor for the physical and moral well-being of the place. And his tribute to the Mounted Police is unstinted, for once he wrote me saying, "Canada owes to these men a debt of lasting gratitude. A true history of the West will say much about the self-sacrifice and heroism of this body of men. Many of their noblest deeds will remain unknown but they will be registered in a higher type of civilization expressed in a truer type of citizenship. Many of these deeds will find register only in the writing of the recording angel."

The official reports of the officers of that period as of others are full of self-suppression. For instance, that able and unassuming officer Superintendent Z. T. Wood, says in one place, "I received orders to take the money of the Government in customs, licences, fees, etc., to be deposited in the bank at Victoria. I accordingly left Bennett going out by the Chilcoot and Dyea and took $150,000 in gold and bills. I reached Victoria in due course and handed over the money." That is all, but in fact it was a very dangerous journey. He had the stuff in police kitbags, but those were the days of "Soapy Smith's" gang of ruffians. Going from Dyea to Skagway, Wood had to threaten to fire on a boat that was following. Soapy Smith and his toughs were on the wharf at Skagway, but the determined bearing of Wood and his few men, together with the presence of the crew of the C.P.R. boat *Tartar*, got them through. It was a ticklish situation.

A word should be added here as to the famous gold escorts. The practice was to turn the gold into ingots and send these to the coast under care of the Mounted Police in small detachments of from two to six men. The amounts thus carried often ran into tens of thousands and the care of these valuable loads of gold could only be given to men of the highest trustworthiness such as these guardians of law and order had always proven themselves to be. Not a mite ever went missing. It is a fine thing to quote this as a testimony that strengthens our faith in humanity. And this splendid incorruptibility was shown by men serving amidst difficult conditions in trails and rivers in all sorts of weather for a mere pittance a day.

Inspector A. M. Jarvis speaks about the "continuous roar of the snow-slides" which one would imagine to be rather disturbing music. He relates that when he started to collect customs at Dalton cache the first man to pay was a doctor from St. Thomas, Ontario, who had been living in the Western States for over twenty years. "The doctor came over, saluted the flag by taking off his hat, and said it was the first time he had seen it on British soil in that period." Of a trip taken with Constables Shook and Cameron on snow-shoes Jarvis says, "The snow was soft, and despite the snow-shoes we sank deep at every step. The following afternoon we returned to camp, having been travelling forty-six hours without blankets and only one meal."

Inspector Cartwright, who relieved Strickland at the White Pass, gives us a little insight into the problem of keeping warm in rather porous canvas tents by remarking that wood cost as high as $110.00 a cord. It was a case of supply and demand. And so in the manner recorded in this chapter did these pioneer policemen in the Yukon possess the land in gallantry under the Union Jack.

Meanwhile back on the prairie, the Mounted Police were alive to every movement and much was done to save people from their own overweening desire to get into the gold country by any route that might show possibility of success. Thousands had gone in by the front door of the coast and then over the passes, but a good many tried to enter by the back door, going by Edmonton and then over the routes that had been trodden years before by great explorers like Alexander Mackenzie and Robert Campbell. Hence Commissioner Herchmer thought it wise to send patrols out over this vast region of the Peace, Athabasca and Mackenzie rivers in order to prevent the loss of any of these more or less inexperienced gold-seekers.

The big patrol of that period was made by Inspector J. D. Moodie, who was sent out from Edmonton on September 4, 1897, to discover the best route for those who intended to get to the Yukon by the way of the Peace River and then over the Mountains. Moodie was accompanied by Constable F. J. Fitzgerald, Lafferty, Tobin and a French half-breed guide Pepin. They went part of the way with horses, part with dogs and part with boats. There was endless hardship through difficulty as to supplies and transportation and this long patrol to Fort Yukon took a year and two months. Moodie made a detailed report and his complete diary was published. Some idea of what the patrol involved may be gathered from the following paragraph in the report: "We arrived at Fort Graham on January 18, and were then entirely out of supplies for men and dogs. There was no dog-feed here and very limited supplies in the Hudson's Bay Store. Hearing that fish could be secured from some lakes about 25 miles away I next day sent out some of the men to fish with nets through the ice while others tried their luck after moose. Neither, however, were successful. I sent out in different directions to find Indian camps which were supposed to be somewhere within 50 miles of the post. These, however, could not be located. The dogs were almost starving, the snow was five feet deep in the bush and no guides to be had. I had therefore reluctantly to give up all idea of going farther till spring." In spring a start was again made and Fort Yukon reached as stated in about fourteen months after leaving Edmonton. Moodie's description of the route and the difficulties was not such as to encourage anyone else to try it. In that way the patrol did good service. For the rest of it, the collapse of the gold rush after 1898 made it practically unnecessary. But it demonstrated again the endurance, judgment and reliability of the police in carrying out any duty assigned to them.

To show the thoroughness with which the country was covered by the police in order to prevent danger and catastrophe to the rather improvident gold-seekers, a patrol was made by Inspector (later Assistant Commissioner) W. H. Routledge a distance of 1,100 miles or so from Fort Saskatchewan away north to Fort Simpson. This patrol was of value in getting into touch with many groups of "Klondikers," taking in their mail and bringing it out and also in making known at remote points the laws that were specially applicable to their situation. And there was also a patrol under Inspector A. E. Snyder undertaken with a view to seeing whether Inspector Moodie had been successful in getting forward towards the Yukon. This patrol under Snyder went as far as Fort St. John up near the sources of the Peace River and returned to report that Inspector Moodie and his men had gone on to Fort Graham, whence their way would be clear in the spring for the last lap of the long patrol as above related.

While the Yukon was being opened up the members of the Force on the plains and in the mountains were steadily doing their duty. They were perhaps less in the limelight for the time being since the attention of a good part of the world was centred on the gold country, but their presence was equally necessary as a terror to evil-doers and an encouragement to those that did well.

The construction of the Crows Nest Branch of the Canadian Pacific Railway entailed a very heavy amount of work on the Mounted Police. This came under the oversight of Inspector G. E. Sanders, who in turn was under the nominal direction of Superintendent Deane, then in command at Fort MacLeod. Deane had a busy time, as he had to cover about 400 miles of front with less than 200 men, of whom as many as fifty at a time had to be at certain construction points in British Columbia. Referring especially to the railway part of the work Deane says, "Inspector Sanders' report which I enclose will give a good idea of the amount of duty devolving upon him and his men, and I beg leave to record my opinion that it was well done. The effect of even a single mounted policeman's personality upon a lawless mob requires to be seen to be fully appreciated, and there were countless occasions where the qualities of tact and readiness of resource were required to supplement the prestige which is begotten of discipline alone."

"It would be impossible to estimate the thousands of men that have passed hither and thither along the line during its construction. A considerable proportion of them were entirely unsuited to the work. The construction authorities claim that by the operation of the Alien Labour Act they were deprived of the services of the professional railroader, the man who travels with his outfit all over the continent from railway to railway, and who would have made light of the difficulties of which so much has been said. It is undeniable that many men have suffered great hardships, but it is equally true that many of them should never have turned their attention to railway construction. Some have never done a day's work on the railway in their lives, and some have never done it at all."

There was a good deal of wage dispute on the line, but Inspector Sanders says, "As to the amount of wages received by the men and their not having any money to send to their families in the east, it was very noticeable to me that the men who complained most drank most." This needs no comment.

It is interesting to note here the outside opinion of the "Fort Steele Prospecter" as contained in an editorial in that paper in February, 1898. After giving a general description of the mixed class of men on the road it says, "The crimes along the road, however, are surprisingly small, considering the vicious element which comprises the contingent of camp followers" in the way of whisky sellers, gamblers and disorderly characters. "This happy state of affairs is due to the innate fear of Canadian justice and the scrupulous surveillance of the efficient corps of the North-West Mounted Police into whose hands the enforcement of law is committed. No one can travel over the line without a feeling of admiration for the system which can produce such excellent results, the absolute security of life and property in a region infested by rogues and adventurers from every clime." Sanders agrees that hosts of men had taken up work to which they were wholly unaccustomed. A lot of men were happy when handling an axe, but the pick and shovel had a saddening effect on them. And Sanders is in keeping with the general habit of the Police when he says, "We tried our utmost to have the real grievances of the men settled, and my representations to the general manager of construction always met with prompt attention." So they should, for they would be fair and just.

Inspector Howe, who was in charge in 1898 at Regina, had a wire from Boston about a man who had robbed the merchants of that æsthetic city of large sums of money. The man was supposed then on the train heading towards Regina. Howe sent a sergeant to Qu'Appelle, who boarded the suspected train and located his quarry in a Pullman compartment, which was locked. The man within, who was accompanied by a lady, would not open the door. At next station a Mounted Police constable got on board and the two men in scarlet uniform smashed the door. The woman threatened to blow their brains out, but failed. The runaway couple had the money and bonds, and after due process went back to Boston to serve a term.

Inspector Howe tells rather a rich story of a Police Inspector in Montana who apologized profusely to Howe for not answering by wire a telegram in which Howe had notified the said Montana Inspector of the whereabouts of a man much desired by the Police in that State. The Montana Inspector writes, "I handed my deputy a telegram and told him to send it off to you at once. He went out to send it but was shot dead, and this morning the coroner handed the telegram to me. It had never been sent, so you will see I am not altogether to blame." Howe considered the excuse valid, but the estimate of the value of human life in Montana it disclosed did not suit the ideas of a Mounted Policeman.

* * * * *

CHAPTER XII

STIRRING DAYS ABROAD AND AT HOME

In the report of Superintendent Cotton for the year of the big Yukon stampede there is related one of the many incidents which indicated that on the plains the Mounted Police were keeping up to their record for initiative and daring, even though their work was less in the limelight than the spectacular world rush to the Yukon furnished. It seems that some months before the date of the report a prisoner named Nelson, sentenced to a term of imprisonment for a serious offence, escaped by jumping from a train on the way to the Manitoba Penitentiary from Regina. Constable Clisby, who was on duty at Saskatoon, was notified by wire from Dundurn station, and at once took up the recapture. The Saskatoon ferry was out of order, so he could not use it. But he was not to be deterred from the pursuit of a criminal by a trifle like that, or he would not have been up to the Mounted Police standard in resource and inventive capacity. So, as the river was impassable in the ordinary way, Clisby commandeered a railway hand-car, and possibly nailed an extra plank or two upon it. Then he got his troop-horse to climb up and stand upon it, while this strong-armed constable took hold of the "pump-handle" and worked his way across the trestle railway bridge many feet above the surging river. One can easily see what a desperate risk this was to take in cold blood. The big bronco had been broken enough for use on the solid earth by an expert. But to venture into the air with a semi-wild horse, which by any movement of fright at the unusual experience might upset the whole outfit into the river, was about as daring an experiment as anyone could try. But the strange transport got safely over, and Clisby, shaking out that bronco into a long gallop, found his man in the home of a settler, engaged in filing off the leg-iron in order to be able to get away more swiftly. Of course the prisoner was gathered in, as was also the settler who had loaned the file and was standing by watching the interesting process. The peculiar thing was that when the settler, who had given the escaping prisoner the file and stood by to see him use it to make his escape more certain, was brought up before two magistrates for helping a prisoner to elude his sentence, these sapient administrators of law dismissed the charge. This miscarriage of justice so disgusted both the constable and his superintendent that in, contemplation of it they seemed to forget the astonishing feat with the hand-car. But we dig it up proudly from the old report. It is in keeping with this desire on the part of the Mounted Police to see justice meted out to the guilty for the protection of society that we find them impatient with legal technicalities which freed the guilty, or the views of any legally constituted body which headed off further investigation into what was possibly serious crime. And this remark is made at this point, because I come across a report in which a Mounted Police Superintendent, while not openly complaining, thinks it worth while to call attention to a Coroner's jury which, after inquest in the case of a man who had been found dead with his neck broken, brings in the unexpected verdict that the man died by the visitation of God. The fact that the Superintendent simply states the matter without note or comment indicates pretty clearly his opinion of the intelligence of that jury. It recalls the case of the famous frontier judge, Sir Mathew Begbie, of British Columbia, who is said to have been much disgusted and amazed when a jury acquitted a prisoner whom the evidence clearly indicated had sand-bagged an innocent citizen. The judge had no option but to discharge the notorious character whom the jury of his peers had exonerated. "You may go," said the indignant judge, "but it seems to me that you would be doing good service to this country if you sand-bagged every man on that jury."

SUPT. CONSTANTINE IN WINTER UNIFORM ON THE YUKON.

PIEGAN INDIANS AT SUN-DANCE.

While the gold-rush of which we have been writing was at its height in the Yukon there were rumblings of conflict on the dark continent where Paul Kruger, the grim old President of the Boer Republic, was getting ready to launch a war which he said would "stagger humanity." The trouble had been brewing for some years. Many thousands of British men were in the Transvaal, developing its resources, adding to its wealth and doing everything for its upbuilding but without the privileges of citizenship. And these British men were agitating for representation in addition to the taxation they already enjoyed for the benefit of the Boers. It is doubtful whether Canadians generally took much trouble to investigate these questions of franchise and suzerainty, which have always had two sides up for discussion. Canada was willing to trust the judgment of British statesmen on the subject, and when Britain is at war Canada is not disposed to stand back. Conan Doyle probably sensed the situation when he wrote the stirring lines:

> "Who's that calling?
> The old sea-mother calls
> In her pride at the children that she bore
> 'Oh, noble hearts and true
> There is work for us to do,

> And we'll do it as we've done it oft before
> > Under the flag,
> > Under the flag our fathers bore.'"

There had been a swift sting, too, in a certain telegram sent by the Kaiser of Germany congratulating Kruger on the failure of the raid under Doctor Jamieson, for "Doctor Jim" was a popular idol. And the rather crude but strong lines of a music-hall song had percolated to the outposts of Empire:

> "Hands off, Germany; hands off, all.
> Kruger boasts and Kaiser brags.
> Britons, hear the call.
> It's back to back around the world
> And answer with a will;
> It's England for her own, my boys,
> And Rule Britannia still."

So the "sons of the Blood" began to foregather from the ends of the earth.

And when cavalry units were desired from Canada the Mounted Police got a certain degree of opportunity. We put it in that way because for reasons known to the Dominion Government there was always necessity for keeping the larger part of the corps in Canada. They could not be allowed to enlist in a body for any war, and men who had special grasp of the problems at home could not be spared to go abroad. Nothing can be gained for the Empire through losing ground at home in efforts to gain it abroad. And this applied to both the Boer War and the recent Great War, in so far as the Mounted Police were concerned. At the Boer War period, we had the Yukon rush, which meant an extraordinary mob of desperate characters to deal with, in addition to the problems ensuing from large immigration into the Middle West. And at the period of the Great War, there was a singularly elusive but definitely pronounced tendency to destructive revolution in various parts of Canada, which only a corps with the great prestige of the Mounted Police could successfully meet with firmness and tact. The undisciplined violence which raw forces might use in such a restless, mutinous period, would work positive harm to the whole

Dominion. Hence we could not on either occasion let the whole Force go abroad.

But on both occasions some opportunity was given to a certain number of officers and men, the main difficulty being, as the Commissioner said, "not who would go, but who *must* stay at home." However, in the Boer War the Mounted Police furnished, most being on the active roll, but some ex-members, nearly 300 officers and men to the Canadian Mounted Rifles, Strathcona's Horse, South African Constabulary, and other corps. Their identity was lost by merging them with various units, but, nevertheless, they did conspicuous and distinctive service. It is no reflection on those with whom they were merged to say that the special qualities which came from years of discipline and esprit de corps, as well as the decided initiative which their training on the frontier always developed, gave the Police a place of peculiar influence and prominence on the veld. And this was true of ex-members of the Force who served in various corps. There was "Charlie" Ross, for instance, whom I recall meeting at Battleford in Riel's day as the Mounted Police scout who seemed to bear a charmed life, and who did much to save the situation in the fight with Poundmaker at Cutknife Hill. Ross went to South Africa as a sort of free lance, but he joined up with a scout body, and so distinguished himself that he was permitted to form a corps of his own which, as Ross's Scouts, did some dashing service. All the Western Canadians gave a good account of themselves. They were not strong on the fine points of military etiquette, and sometimes offended by failing to recognize and salute officers in strange uniforms. They were rather restive in barracks, and did not take kindly to the life in Cape Town, but they were at home when in the saddle on really active duty, and got their full share of it before the war was over. Their presence on the veld and their effective work won high praise from such high-class officers as Sir Redvers Buller, Lord Dundonald, Lord Kitchener and, later on, in London, "the first gentleman of Europe," King Edward himself.

A thoroughly characteristic story is told by several writers about a C.M.R. man who had been a cowboy and "bronco-buster" in Alberta. An Imperial Regiment, under General Hutton, was bewailing the fact that they had a magnificent black Australian horse, a regular outlaw so vicious and powerful that none of their men could handle, much less ride him, and they were quite sure that no one else could, so that the animal might as well be shot. One of the C.M.R. officers who was present said some men in his troop could ride, and he would ask them about it. He went over and several of them volunteered, but they settled amongst themselves that Billy should tackle the situation. Next morning was the time fixed, and Billy, in cowboy costume, carrying his own trusty saddle and a quirt, sauntered over to the spot careless-like, and not knowing the insignia of rank very well, walked up to an Imperial officer in gold lace, and prodding him jocularly with the quirt, said, "Where is the black son of a gun that you say can't be rid?" The officer looked amazed at being so accosted, but, like a good sport, laughed and ordered the horse to be turned loose. Billy's friends promptly lassoed the "waler," hogtied and saddled him in a hurry. Billy was in the saddle when the snorting animal was on his feet. The horse put up a game fight, bucking, kicking, biting, "swapping ends," and doing everything else that a thinking bronco can indulge in to get rid of his rider. But Billy enjoyed it. He banged the horse over the head with his big hat, smote him with the quirt, and used the spurs, till the mad animal raced in fury a mile or two, only to come back with froth down to the hooves. But Billy had him under thorough control, quiet enough to eat out of his hand. And when Billy pulled off the saddle he remarked casually to the astonished officers who had expected an inquest over him, "Out in my country that hoss would cut no figure, for out there we can ride anything with legs under it, even if it is a consarned centipede." The Canadian Mounted Rifles 1st, 2nd and 5th, had some 220 officers and men of the Mounted Police, while Strathcona's Horse had only some forty or so, though the rest were men accustomed to the kind of irregular warfare they found on the veld. The fact that Strathcona's Horse was raised, equipped and wholly paid for out of the private purse of Lord Strathcona, the only case in the Empire during the war, gave that corps a unique place in the public eye. Lord Strathcona, who was a member of the House of Lords and High Commissioner for Canada, placed it in command of Superintendent Sam B. Steele, a widely known officer, entertained the corps lavishly both before and after the war, fitted it out as no other regiment was equipped, brought the officers and men into contact with Royalty, kept it more or less in touch with the Associated Press—and all of this tended to put this regiment more in the limelight than others from Canada. This, of course, did not make their task any easier, but rather the contrary, since any failure on their part would have been quickly known. As a matter of history they did their part in such a way as to bring the utmost credit to all concerned. The corps was officered by highly capable men. The Mounted Police officers, serving in Strathcona's Horse were: Superintendent S. B. Steele (in command), Inspectors R. Belcher, A. E. Snyder, A. M. Jarvis, D. M. Howard, F. L. Cartwright and F. Harper: included also were, Ex-Inspector M. H. White-Fraser, Sergt.-Major W. Parker and Staff-Sergt. H. D. B. Ketchen. The two last named were granted commissions in the Army and Colonial Forces. The commissions of the other officers of this corps were all in the Imperial service. Strathcona's Horse took part in many major engagements, did much scout and patrol work, and one of the Mounted Police serving in it, Sergeant A. H. L. Richardson, on July 5, 1900, won the highest of all the decorations for valour, the Victoria Cross. At a hot engagement in the village of Wolvespruit the odds were so heavy against our men that they were given the order to retire. One of our dismounted men, wounded in two places, lay on the field, and Sergeant Richardson, seeing his plight, rode back and brought him in, although exposed to a warm cross-fire at close range, and despite the fact that Richardson's horse was so badly wounded that he could only go at a slow pace. It was a very gallant action.

When at the close of the main part of the war the South African Constabulary was formed, Steele, of the Strathcona's, was appointed its Colonel, and much "mopping up" was done in the pursuit of irregular Boer bands. Inspector Scarth, Constables C. P. Ermatinger, and J. G. French were given commissions. For their service with the 2nd and 5th C.M.R., Inspectors John Taylor, Demers, Sergt.-Major J. Richards, Sergt.-Major F. Church, Sergeant Hillian, Sergeant H. R. Skirving, Constables A. N. Bredin and J. A. Ballantyne were also granted commissions.

I have mentioned certain circumstances which set Strathcona's Horse more in the public eye than the Canadian Mounted Rifles, in which the majority of the North-West Mounted Police served, but the latter took a part in the war which involved much hard fighting, and did much to enhance the prestige of Canadian soldiers, whose service abroad up to that time had not been in military units. The North-West Mounted Police officers who joined the various units of the C.M.R. and received commissions in the Militia were: (2nd C.M.R.) Lieut.-Colonel L. W. Herchmer (the then Commissioner of the Police, who commanded the battalion), Superintendent J. Howe, Inspector A. G. Macdonnell (afterwards in command of 5th C.M.R.), Inspector J. D. Moodie, Inspector J. V. Begin, Inspector T. A. Wroughton, Superintendent G. E. Sanders, Inspector A. E. R. Cuthbert, Inspector H. J. A. Davidson, Inspector F. L. Cosby (Adjutant), Inspector M. Baker (Quartermaster), Inspector J. B. Allan, and Veterinary Officer Lieut. R. Riddell. These officers and the men they commanded were intent upon their duties, and such able soldiers as General Hutton, General Lord Methuen, and others, gave them unstinted praise for their work in the Orange Free State and their advance guard work on the march to Pretoria, under Lord Roberts, who was greatly impressed by their ability in scouting and patrol work.

It fell to the lot of that able and popular officer, Superintendent (Major) G. E. Sanders, to show on two special occasions, with small detachments against large odds, the mettle of the North-West Mounted Police. Near Middleburg, when Sanders with 125 men was guarding the railway, he was attacked by a considerable force of the enemy with artillery. A hurry call for reinforcements was issued, but before they came the Canadians had beaten the Boers back, Major Sanders and Lieutenant Moodie, as well as some of their men, being wounded in the determined resistant fight. Two months later, Sanders, with a handful of sixty men, formed the advance guard for General Smith-Dorien's column, but his guide missed the way and all of a sudden Sanders and his men, completely out of touch with the General's column, came in contact with a larger force of the enemy. The rifle fire of the enemy was very heavy, but the handful of Canadians held on till orders came from the General to retire. While they were retiring Corporal Schell's horse was killed, and the corporal was hurt by the horse falling on him. Sergeant Tryon most gallantly gave his own horse to Schell and himself continued on foot. And then Major Sanders, taking in the situation at a glance, galloped to the assistance of Tryon, whom he endeavoured to take before him on the saddle. It was a splendid effort, but, as Sanders endeavoured to lift Tryon, the saddle cinch slipped, the saddle turned to the side of the horse, and both men fell heavily to the ground. Sanders was stunned somewhat by the fall, but pulling himself together ordered the Sergeant to make for cover and he would follow. But a Boer sharpshooter dropped Sanders wounded in his tracks. Then another fine thing took place. Lieutenant Chalmers, a former Mounted Policeman also, who had led one wing of the advance guard, wheeled his horse and spurred to the help of Sanders, but he was unable to move him alone, and started for the firing line. The Boer sharpshooter was still abroad and, turning his attention to Chalmers, shot that brave officer, who fell mortally wounded from his horse. Major Sanders and Tryon were both rescued by a rush of reinforcements, and the Major is still doing effective service for the country as Magistrate in Calgary. It would seem to an onlooker that the decoration "for valour" should have been awarded to Sanders for his gallant and dangerous endeavour to rescue Tryon, and in a posthumous way to Chalmers, who sacrificed his life in the effort he made to save his superior officer. One recalls in this connection the similar action of former Inspector Jack French, whom I recall well as a stranger to fear, who at Batoche rushed in on foot and carried the wounded body of Constable Cook in his powerful arms from the fire zone to a place of safety. Many of the sacrificial deeds of men are unheralded.

Officially, the officers and men of the North-West Mounted Police who served in the Boer War, were noted as on leave from their own corps, and therefore their services to the Empire are not recorded in the Police reports. But Commissioner Perry, in this particular case, gives in his annual report an extract from Militia orders, in which Lord Roberts wires the War Office: "Smith-Dorien stated Major Sanders, Captain Chalmers, behaved with great gallantry rear-guard action, November 2." To this the Commissioner adds: "I greatly lament the untimely but glorious death of the gallant Chalmers, with whom I had not only served as an officer in this corps, but also as a cadet in the Royal Military College."

And then the Commissioner expresses this well-grounded opinion: "I regret much that the identity of the Force was lost in South Africa. The North-West Mounted Police are well known beyond the bounds of Canada. And I would like that it had been known to the world as one of the corps which had taken part in the

South African War. With but few exceptions all ranks were willing to go, and it was not a question of who would go, but who must stay at home." This is well and wisely expressed. If ever there should be another war, which we hope not, unless absolutely unavoidable, Canada should strive to have her units kept intact. Destruction of identity leads to destruction of great traditions to which men should be true, and to the loss of the esprit de corps and *noblesse oblige* elements, which go so far to creating unconquerable regiments.

At the end of the war, in addition to the Victoria Cross won by Sergeant Richardson, as already related, the following honours, gained by members of the North-West Mounted Police while on service in South Africa, were announced in general orders:

To be Companion of the Bath and Member of the Victoria Order, 4th Class:

Superintendent S. B. Steele, Lieut.-Colonel commanding Lord Strathcona's Horse.

To be Companions of the Order of St. Michael and St. George:

Inspector R. Belcher, Major 2nd in command, Canadian Mounted Rifles.

Inspector A. C. Macdonnell, Captain Canadian Mounted Rifles.

Inspector F. L. Cartwright, Captain Lord Strathcona's Horse.

Awarded the Distinguished Conduct Medal:

Sergeant J. Hynes, Sergt.-Major Lord Strathcona's Horse.

Sergt.-Major Richards, Sqd. Sergt.-Major Lord Strathcona's Horse.

Constable A. S. Waite, Private Canadian Mounted Rifles.

The conclusion of the Boer War, with the additional service in the South African Constabulary, marked the transference of Colonel Sam B. Steele from the North-West Mounted Police to the Militia service of Canada, as he was appointed to the command of Military District No. 13, with headquarters at Calgary, though later he took over Military District No. 10, with headquarters at Winnipeg. He was one of the "originals" of the Police, joining up in 1873, and became one of the distinctive and picturesque figures in the famous Frontier Force. Capable of an enormous amount of work in a given time, he had never spared himself in efforts for the country and for the Force. He had large gifts as an administrator, as well as a fighter and enforcer of law, and these he placed unstintedly at the disposal of his generation. When he left the Police Force and accepted service in the Canadian Militia, he did much to recognize existing work and establish new units. When the Great War broke out he offered his services at once, and while waiting for overseas service he was intent on recruiting all over Canada. He went over in command of the Second Contingent from Canada, but the tremendous strain of his forty years of service began to tell on his once powerful physique, and to his deep disappointment he was prevented from leading his men in the field. In recognition of his services to the Empire he received Knighthood and a Major-Generalship, which represented a long and strenuous road travelled up from the ranks. He died in England while the war was still raging, and a funeral service in London was attended by a great number of people prominent in the world of affairs. But his body was brought back to Canada, the land he loved so well, and was buried with full military honours in Winnipeg, the city to which he had come long years before as a soldier under Wolseley.

It is not generally known that, though he had not been in the Force for nearly twenty years, one of his last acts was the writing of an earnestly worded and, under the circumstances, a pathetic letter, to Sir Robert Borden, Premier of Canada, then in London, pleading for the full recognition of the military standing of the Mounted Police in Canada. In that letter he recounts out of his own recollection the history of the corps in which he had served from the outset for some thirty years. He recalls the work they had done as a military force on what was really active service all through the years, points out the high military qualifications of the men who were officers in the corps, as well as the uniformly high type of men in all ranks, to the large contributions the Mounted Police had made to the Empire in wars abroad, and spoke of the heavy responsibility resting upon the Force in the Dominion. He said: "I question whether the present command of Canadians overseas in England is equal to the great responsibility held by the Commissioner of the Mounted Police and his Assistant in Canada." The letter asks the Premier to do certain things for the officers and men, the effect of which would be to give them equal rights with members of the permanent Militia Force in respect of titles, decorations and general standing. And the result of the requests, if granted, would be to place the Mounted Police in the same position as the Militia in regard to medals, pensions and land grants, a matter of great interest and importance to the members of the Force. There is something very fine in this personal endeavour of "Sam" Steele, who, with many anxieties and responsibilities of his own at the time, made a serious appeal to obtain what he considered the rights of the comrades with whom he had shared hardships and dangers all over the vast North-West of Canada. A copy of this letter of Steele's, which was occasioned by changes then taking place in the Police organization, came into my possession from a private source, but it is not a confidential document, and is published here in recognition of the enduring loyalty of this sturdy old soldier to his companions, the veteran riders of the plains. They richly deserve the recognition for which he pleaded.

And we cannot turn over the page of the Boer War and leave it in history without recalling that a few pages above reference was made to the fact that Canada had gone into the war more because she had faith in the judgment of the statesmen of Britain, whose life-long training and world-vision inspire confidence in their decisions, than because she had studied out the situation at first hand. British statesmen have made mistakes here and there, but since the tragic day when through ignorance of the situation they failed to recognize the rights of British colonists on the American continent to have a voice in the government of the country, they have not erred by refusing their Dominions overseas the privilege of governing themselves where they have proved their capacity for so doing. But there was a bold and world-startling faith manifested when they granted self-government to the Boers within a short time after the war ended. True, these same statesmen had led up to it by the ministry of reconciliation exercised by the high-souled Kitchener with a Canadian Mounted Policeman, Colonel Steele, a noted administrator, as Chief of the South African Constabulary. And these and others who worked with them to remove bitterness and misunderstanding from the minds of the conquered Boers had supporting evidence of good-will on the part of the conquerors in the fact that our soldiers had acted chivalrously in the enemy's country during the years of war, so that no woman or child in all that region was ever knowingly hurt or molested. All this with the gift of responsibility transformed our gallant enemies into loyal friends who stood by us splendidly in the recent war, and who contributed to the councils of the Empire in a critical hour the magnificent ability and statesmanship of Botha, Smuts and others.

Meanwhile, in the homeland here in Canada, the steadfast, unflinching and imperturbable Mounted Police were doing their duty just as pronouncedly as their comrades on the veld. They had practically all wanted to go if required, but the Government had interposed and, as we have already quoted, it was not a question of who should go, but who *must* stay at home. And they were greatly needed here, for nothing is gained by consolidating the Empire abroad if we allow it to disintegrate right under our eyes and around our own threshold. The Pax Britannica—the orderliness of British rule—had to be preserved in the vast spaces of the North and West of Canada. Thousands of potentially lawless men were surging through our mining country in the Yukon, challenging Canadian administration with the dictum that huge frontier mining camps had necessarily to be outlaw regions where every man did that which was right in his own eyes. And it became the duty of the Mounted Police to back the administration of law, to answer the challenge of lawless men, and to prove to them and to the world that the dictum above quoted was a lie in so far as Canada was concerned. And these intrepid men in the scarlet tunic did their duty so well that the world learned a new lesson by seeing policemen preserving order without killing anyone where it could be avoided, even at the cost of their own lives. The Mounted Police know how to use their "guns," but they never in all their history degenerated into "gun-men."

And, in addition to policing the Yukon mining country, these few hundred men had to guard human life and property in the immense stretches of the Middle West where, into a country larger than several European kingdoms, tens of thousands were pouring in a tidal wave of immigration. From the ends of the earth these immigrants were coming, hosts of them, alien in race and tongue, as well as in religion and morals—people who had lax ideas as to the sacredness of human life and the sanctity of home. They, too, must be taught to keep the peace, and to become loyal to the institutions of the free land where they had sought asylum from despotism and oppression. And nothing but consummate tact, endless patience along with unvarying coolness and courage, enabled the men of the old corps successfully to meet this unprecedented situation.

Besides, all that great north country had to be patrolled hither and thither into the circle under the shadow of the Pole itself. Wherever the flag flew, Indians and Esquimaux, as wards of the nation, had to be protected against the dangers of famine, the inroads of sickness, as well as from the exploitation of unscrupulous men. And they, too, had to be taught the sacredness of human life, as well as the rights of private ownership, in order that no loose ideas about property should prevail in the land. Few things, if any, in the history of the Empire equal the hardiness, the courage and endurance manifested in the great patrols of the Police into the ice-bound regions of the Arctic and sub-Arctic areas of Canada. For years the explorers who have searched for the Poles have been the heroes of many a story of thrilling influence on the minds of readers. One would not detract an iota from the achievements of these gallant adventurers. But for the most part they were equipped and outfitted abundantly with everything that money could buy in order that all requirements and emergencies could be met as they arose, and their expeditions were few throughout the years. The Mounted Police, on the other hand, were incessantly at this work, not in parties and highly equipped, but in twos and threes and sometimes singly, with nothing beyond their winter and summer uniforms and dependent largely on their own efforts for food, as they were not possessed of the means of carrying any large quantity. Many of these men probably said, as Inspector F. H. French recorded in his diary during the famous Bathurst Inlet patrol, of which we shall read later: "Have had no solid food for two days, and every one is getting weak; dogs are dropping in their harness from weakness. This looks like our last patrol." Only a brave man could write down words like that, and it detracts nothing from the splendid courage of him and his men that the words were not long written when providentially some deer were sent across their path and saved these men for future work. These men who went out on patrol only gave the barest outline of their experience in the reports which they had to make to their superior officers, and through them to Ottawa, but those who know the country could read between the lines and feel the thrill of admiration and wonder.

And these same officers, when not on the particular patrol they were commenting upon, paid unstinted praise to their men in their own reports, but even these reports were buried in the mass of material in the Department, so that the public did not see them. But once in a while we get hold of some comment, as when Superintendent Perry referred to one patrol and said "nothing greater had been done in the annals of Arctic exploration." Or when Inspector Sanders referred to the leader of another patrol and said his action "was in keeping with his brave and manly character." And I like the way in which Superintendent A. E. C. Macdonnell, with some manifest diffidence, introduced into a report from Athabasca Landing the following quotation from the *Toronto Star*:

> "The world takes a lively interest in Polar expeditions, but Canada supports a Northern Police patrol of which very little is heard, and the journeyings of some of these men is quite as daring as anything connected with searches for the North or South Pole. They contend with the same conditions, are inexpensively equipped, and, as a rule, succeed in all that they undertake. A sheet or two of foolscap, giving to the Department at Ottawa an official report of their travels and observations, is the only record that survives. And very few ever read these records, although they sometimes thrill those who do read them."

One other important duty fell to the lot of these Policemen in the home country, and reference has been made to it in the earlier pages, namely, the self-imposed duty of becoming builders of the country by making known the resources of all its various parts. And when they made known the resources of the country they, without any gain therefrom themselves, protected those who came in to develop them. Sometimes they had to protect these people against themselves. In the Yukon gold rush the Police threw a cordon around the entrances to the mining country and prevented foolhardy, unfit and unequipped men and women, crazed with the gold lust, from venturing a journey which would have meant their falling frozen by the wayside or being lost in the angry rapids, which even the inexperienced were ready in their ignorance to essay. These gold-seekers were allowed to go in when they were prepared or when they were under the care of men of experience. Similarly, at the time of this writing, the Police in the Athabasca, Peace and Mackenzie areas are guarding the ways to the reported oil fields of the North, so that the unfit in their wild desire for reaching oilfields may not perish in the midwinter, whose rigours they do not understand.

Yes, the Mounted Police, few and scattered in detachments, from the Great Lakes to the Yukon, and from the boundary line to the Pole, had enormous responsibilities at home, while many of their fellow-citizens were abroad in the Boer War. And the man who was Commissioner of the Police during that period had a burden to carry which only those who knew the situation can estimate. That man was Superintendent A. Bowen Perry, who succeeded Colonel Lawrence Herchmer in August, 1900, but who, from the time of the big gold stampede into the Yukon, had largely the direction of things there, and had taken over the command personally at Dawson City when Steele left there in the fall of 1899. Colonel Herchmer, who had been Commissioner from 1886, was an able and conscientious officer. He had gone over to the Boer War in command of the 2nd Canadian Mounted Rifles, but had to come back on sick leave, when he retired also from the Commissionership. From the date of Herchmer's appointment to the Canadian Mounted Rifles to Perry's accession to the Commissionership of the Police, the command of the latter body had been ably held and administered by Assistant Commissioner McIlree. Colonel McIlree, who retired from the Force a few years ago, and whose services won the recognition of the Imperial Service Order, was one of the original men of the corps, having joined at the outset in 1873. He had, therefore, a long record of highly important and creditable service when he retired in 1911, after thirty-seven years on the frontier.

REV. R.G. MACBETH, M.A.

GROUP, N.W.M.P., TAGISH POST. YUKON.

When Perry returned from the Yukon (where he was succeeded by that fine officer, Superintendent, later Assistant Commissioner, Z. T. Wood) and assumed the Commissionership he faced an exceedingly difficult situation. The Force was seriously depleted both in men and horses by the inroads made upon it by the war. And at the same time the work, as above outlined, was growing by leaps and bounds. True, recruits were being obtained and new horses were being purchased, but every one knows that it takes time and training to get a depleted force up to proper strength again. But the new Commissioner had a genius for organizing and handling men, and, as he had been away in the Yukon for a period, one of the first things he now did was to visit the prairie detachments, study the whole and map out a policy for the future. Conditions in the country with rapidly changing development as well as in the Force, owing to demands upon it, required a sort of re-creating of the famous corps, as well as a new disposition of it to meet the new times. And Commissioner Perry, with a great faculty for swift, decisive action, and a gift for attracting the cooperative efforts of his officers and men, was the type to undertake the task and succeed. Now, for a score of years he has directed the movements of the Force, meeting the extraordinary and unexpected situations which arise in a country that is a sort of melting-pot of the nations. A polyglot population, a babel not only of tongues but of ideals, the rise of new social conditions, the presence of agitators and mischief-makers who are experts in setting men against each other in opposing classes, the coming of destructive agents whose theories have made some old world countries into ramshackle wrecks, the persistence of the elements of lawlessness with outbreaks here and there—all these and much more have marked the unprecedented history of these years in this last new country in the world. And Canada, perhaps, will never fully realize the debt she owes to this quiet, gentlemanly, resolute man, who is a student as well as a soldier, and whose strong hand has been in constant evidence in controlling, guiding and guarding the interests of a country larger than half a dozen European kingdoms.

When Perry took charge, the Force, outside those at the war, numbered some 750 men. These were distributed so as to give about 500 to the oversight of the vast Middle West and the balance to the Yukon. The men in the Middle West prairie section were scattered in over seventy detachments all the way from Southern Manitoba to Fort Chipewyan in the far North, a distance of over 2,000 miles, while in the Yukon the distance between the most southerly outposts and the farthest North was over 500 miles.

Anyone who knows the country can realize the task of men who had to look after such an enormous area, when their number meant that one or two men would sometimes have to exercise control over districts many miles in extent. These men had to be constantly in the saddle or on the trail with dog-train. Verily Captain Butler's early suggestion as to organization of the Police, that the men sent out should be a "mobile force," was being amply vindicated as a good one to meet the necessities of a new land. And that the new Commissioner was looking ahead is evidenced by such clauses in his first report as "The great countries of the Peace, Mackenzie and Athabasca Rivers are constantly requiring more men. I am sending an officer to Fort Saskatchewan to take command of that portion of the territory." Later he says: "The operation of foreign whalers at the mouth of the Mackenzie will ere long require a detachment to control their improper dealings with the natives and control the revenue." And in due course they were there.

In that first report Perry indicates that "the Force should be entirely re-armed." A lot of the men had obsolete arms, and the Commissioner insists that "if the corps is to be armed it ought to be well armed." He suggests a change from the heavy stock saddle and accoutrements thereof, claiming that with some 46 lbs. on his back before the rider mounted, the horse had a right to ask: "Why this heavy burden?" And he speaks of necessary changes in harness, transports and uniforms. He discusses the question of the kind of horses required, even to the colour, and indicates ranges of country where horses can be bred that are "strong in the hindquarters." Quite evidently the new Commissioner had his eye on everything, and intended to have the corps equipped up to the limit of efficiency and comfort. He was going to speak out in the interests of his men and horses, too. For a mounted corps must have regard to both if the maximum of usefulness is to be attained.

The reports of officers in the Middle West for that year, Superintendents Deane of MacLeod, Griesbach of Fort Saskatchewan, Moffatt of Maple Creek, Inspector Wilson of Calgary, Strickland of Prince Albert, and Demers of Battleford, all indicate a good deal of cattle-stealing, the most of which, of course, was near the American boundary line, where outlaws from both sides dodged backwards and forwards in efforts to escape the authorities on either side, who co-operated and generally got these robbers in hold, But Deane felt that the ranchers themselves should exercise a little more intelligent interest, instead of leaving everything to the Police, who were few in numbers, and none of whom could be in more than one place at a time. Referring to the case of a man who had bought some cattle and had left them unbranded and unwatched in the pasture whence they disappeared in the night, Deane says, "Daly became very indignant, and has talked freely about bringing an action against the Mounted Police, but whether for allowing him to lose his beasts or for failing to find them I know not." However, Mr. Daly evidently concluded that he had no case against the Police, for he is not heard from again.

Up in the Yukon that year, as already mentioned, Superintendent Z. T. Wood was in command of the territory, with Inspector Courtlandt Starnes in charge at Dawson, and Superintendent P. C. H. Primrose at White Horse, and Assistant Surgeon Fraser on Dalton Trail. Besides these officers there were Inspectors J. A. McGibbon, W. H. Routledge, W. H. Scarth, A. E. C. McDonnell, as well as Assistant Surgeons Pare, Madore and Hurdman.

It was a time of general and reasonably stable prosperity, as evidenced by the fact that the men in Starnes' Division collected well up to a million dollars in royalties in the mining areas, the banner section being Grand Forks, including Eldorado, Bonanza and tributaries where Staff-Sergeant (later Inspector) Raven gathered nearly $520,000. The Government was spending freely for the oversight of the Yukon, but was getting back big dividends.

It is interesting to note in Starnes' report this significant clause: "To the early resident of Dawson the present sanitary condition of the town must be a source of congratulation and a matter of satisfaction." For thereby hangs a tale redolent with a record of hard work. In the spring of 1899 a Board of Health had been formed, under the general oversight of the Mounted Police, for Superintendent Steele (later succeeded by Superintendent Perry) was chairman, Corporal Wilson (though not on the Board) Sanitary Inspector, H. Grotchie and Dr. J. W. Good succeeding Dr. Thompson, who was the first medical officer, but had gone on leave. The year 1898 had been fever-scourged and haunted by a plague of scurvy, due largely to the lack of vegetables and fruit it was said. Dr. Good determined that this condition, resulting from the rush of thousands of people to camp on a frozen swamp, would not recur, and when Dr. Good made his mind up and contracted those heavy black brows of his something had to be done or he would know the reason why.

Dr. Good was a noted specialist in Winnipeg from the early days—a man of powerful physique, wide general education, and a grim kind of manner, which was redeemed from dourness by the constant bubbling up of the irrepressible humour which made him a most entertaining companion. He went into Dawson over the passes in the big trek principally from sheer love of the adventure, as most would say (and he had the adventurous spirit), but largely, I imagine, to be of service in what, to his practised understanding, might become a death camp. He had no need of seeking wealth, as his practice had always brought large revenue from the well-to-do, though a lot of poor people got no bills for his services. Dr. Good was and is (for he is still happily with us) a distinct type, and I say this out of personal acquaintance through many years. His battle for the health of the people of Dawson and districts was great and successful. He gives a semi-humorous report of it in a formal report to the Mounted Police Department. From it we make an extract: The Doctor says, "The duties of the Medical Health Officer were somewhat varied. I will give you a summary of them. Firstly, to inspect hospitals from time to time; secondly, to see indigents at his office or their homes, if necessary, and to examine them and see if they could be admitted to hospital. Thirdly, to inspect the water supply. Fourthly, to inspect the food and aid in the prosecution of those selling food unfit for use. Fifthly, to visit all vessels arriving, and when fish, cattle or food were on board, inspect everything before it can be landed. Sixthly, to inspect all cattle, sheep and hogs before they could be slaughtered to see if they were healthy, from which it must be inferred that the Medical Health Officer had studied veterinary medicine as well. I regret to say this was not the case." (This was the Doctor's modesty, but Steele says the knowledge of veterinary science he displayed was remarkable.) And then the Doctor adds in his humorous way: "Now, from the above, it must be plain that the Medical Health Officer led an exceedingly active and useful life." And we agree with him. And the Doctor goes on to give us a vivid picture of conditions in Dawson City when he took hold: "We found practically one vast swamp, which is usually navigable in the early spring, still in almost a primitive condition, or even worse, cesspools and filth of all kinds occupying irregular positions, typhoid fever and scurvy rife in the land. We immediately went to work to put the house in order, getting out all the garbage and refuse on the ice in the early spring, so that it might be carried down the river at the break up. We then specified places at which garbage, etc., should be dumped. We had the streets cleaned, by prison and other labour, had offensive material removed and rubbish burnt, while the Governor, with great vigour, inaugurated a system of drainage, so that in a short time the change excited the wonder and admiration of the people." The doctor is evidently fond of Scriptural phrases, for above he has spoken about "putting the house in order," and now he adds: "We had, of course, some difficulties to contend with, the fact that people to a large extent were 'strangers and pilgrims,' and unaccustomed to any restrictions unless those of a primitive order." But the Doctor, with the aid of the Mounted Police officers already named, as well as Corporals Wilson, McPhail and the men generally, triumphed and made the place healthy. Perhaps there is nothing more remarkable in the record of the Police than the way in which, wherever they were stationed, they always fought epidemics and disease amongst Indians or whites or Esquimaux to the utter disregard of their own safety, though it was not necessarily part of their ordinary duty.

How close an oversight was kept by the Mounted Police as to the movements of people in that wild country is evidenced by the fact that men could not "disappear" between the Police posts or elsewhere without their case giving rise to swift inquiry. If they left one point for another and did not arrive in a reasonable time the fact was in the knowledge of the Police, and they immediately started to trace the missing parties to see whether they had gone lost through missing the trail or had vanished off the earth by the hands of murderous characters. All this comes out in the famous case of one O'Brien who was tried and executed at Dawson for one of the most cold-blooded crimes imaginable. As I was writing, at this point a letter came from Mr. H. P. Hansen, of Winnipeg, who said he had stayed at Fossal's road-house in the Upper Yukon about two weeks before O'Brien committed his triple murder. He and O'Brien were the only guests and had started out on the trail together. Hansen says, "No doubt this man had murder in his heart at the time," but as he had no knowledge of the fact that Hansen carried money carefully concealed, O'Brien, probably with some disgust, did nothing. That O'Brien "had murder in his heart" is more than likely, because when his trial came off a "Bowery tough" who had been in prison with him in Dawson for some other offence testified that O'Brien had proposed that they should, when freed, go along the river and find a lonely spot. Here they should camp, shoot men who were coming out from Dawson with money, put their bodies under the ice, and thus cover their tracks. This was too much of a programme for even the "Bowery tough," but it shows O'Brien's disposition. O'Brien, however, seems to have decided to haunt that trail till he could make a killing, and so he seems to have doubled back after leaving Hansen and landed at Fossal's road-house again, whence he started out with three men on Christmas Day of 1899. The three men were Olsen, a Swede, who was a telegraph line repairer, and two men from Dawson, F. Clayson, of Seattle, and L. Relphe, who had been a "caller-off" in a Dawson dance-hall. Clayson was known to have a large sum of money on him, and he became the particular object of O'Brien's attention, but because "dead men tell no tales" the others had to share in the disaster, and O'Brien, at an opportune time in a camping-place, as afterwards transpired, shot all three men first through the body and then through the head to make sure. There was no human witness to the event. But when these men did not turn up at the next point on the trail, and O'Brien did, the Police began rapid investigation. If there were no eye-witnesses in the case a web of circumstantial evidence would have to be woven around the figure of the fourth man of the party if the facts that would emerge justified it. This was done with consummate skill but with absolute fairness by the Mounted Police, Inspector Scarth, officer commanding at Fort Selkirk, being the directing hand, Corporal Ryan doing some important parts and Constable Pennycuick being the "Sherlock Holmes" genius whose keen detective instincts and arduous persistent work won high praise from the judge at the trial, being those mainly instrumental in bringing this cold-blooded and cruel murderer to justice. The Police have always had a free hand as to expense in the enforcement of law, and the O'Brien case ran up a bill of over $100,000. But the reputation built up throughout the years by these guardians of public safety, that they would get a criminal if they had to follow him to the ends of the earth, saved the Dominions uncounted expenditure in other ways, and established Canada in the opinion of the world as a country where desirable citizens could come, build homes, rear their families and pursue their avocations freer from molestation than in any other similarly situated place on the face of earth. And that was an enormous gain for a new land which needed immigrants to populate its vast territory and develop its immense latent resources.

Somewhat briefly, the way the Police got O'Brien was in this fashion. The Police, as above mentioned, kept close "tab" on travellers by trail or river for the sake of their safety, and a few days after Olsen, Relphe, Clayson and O'Brien left Fossal's road-house at Minto, Sergeant Barker, who was in charge at Five Fingers, and who had been notified of their departure, wired to White Horse that the party had not been heard of since. And the wires were kept hot in all directions, while patrols also were sent out to locate the men who had not turned up at the usual points. At that time murder was not necessarily a theory connected with their disappearance. Nearly ten days after Christmas the alert Police at Tagish post saw a man with horse and sleigh making a detour of the trail on passing their quarters. This aroused their suspicion, and they gathered in the man and his outfit, after pulling them out of a hole in the ice to which the detour had brought them. The man said his name was O'Brien, but he was sullen and would say no more. They took no chances, but brought him before the commanding officer, who sentenced him to "six months" for vagrancy. Several big bank notes were found on his person, also packed in crevices on the sleigh, and also a strange nugget of gold, shaped like a human hand holding a smaller nugget. It was found out that O'Brien had displayed this nugget as a curiosity at a road-house a few nights before, and later on it was found that Relphe, one of the men who had vanished, had a penchant for curios, and amongst them had this nugget and a specially odd coin. Things were beginning to look interesting and, as Inspector Scarth wanted a man who answered O'Brien's description for robbing the cache of Mr. Hansen at Wolf's Island, O'Brien was sent up to Fort Selkirk and held on that charge. Then Sergeant Holmes (rather a curious coincidence in detective names) was sent on detachment to Fossal's road-house with Constable Pennecuick to see if there were any traces of the lost men. Pennecuick proved himself a veritable sleuth. In a short time he discovered a place on the river bank where some one had climbed, although snow had fallen plentifully since. He also found to his surprise a clear view of the river up and down for miles. This was unusual in such a place, and on investigation he found that trees had been cut down so that a look-out could be kept. He examined the tree stumps closely, and found they had all been cut with an axe which had three flaws in it, one at one end and two near together. He kept portions of the wood, and later on discovered that when O'Brien had been released from jail in Dawson, some months before, he had been given his stuff back, and the police-sergeant testified at the trial that he had furnished O'Brien with an axe (a very necessary thing for travellers on the northern trails) in place of one that had been lost. The sergeant said, "It was a spare axe and I sharpened it for him, and gave it to him with a sort of apology because it still had three rather large nicks in it, one at the top and two close together at the bottom." Of course, Pennecuick did not know about this axe when he found the trees chopped down, but his examination of the stumps shows that he omitted nothing in his scrutiny.

When Pennecuick noted that, he hunted for traces of a trail, and found such traces leading to the river. He got a broom and swept the whole way down. Klondikers recall Christmas '98 as soft in the morning and freezing at night. So marks made that morning would stay, and Pennecuick found that some heavy body or bodies had been dragged down to a place in the ice where, though now frozen over, these bodies had been put in the river. Pennecuick reasoned that if O'Brien was going to kill these men he would not do it on the river where he might be seen. So the sleuth went back up into the bush and swept away till he came to some evidences of blood, then he found three .32 revolver bullets, and one in the earth from a .45 rifle.

Next day, as Pennecuick came back to work he met a dog on the river. Dogs crop up all over the Northern history, and many times they were important links in the chains of evidence. Pennecuick recognized the dog as O'Brien's, which had been kept in barracks at Dawson by the Police and fed and petted when O'Brien was in jail there before. The dog recognized the uniform, fawned on the wearer of it, and when Pennecuick said "Go home, sir, go home," the dog turned and trotted up the bank and then turned aside where some slight trail showed. Pennecuick, of course, followed, and came to a tent cabin in which he found the .45-calibre rifle. Raking in the snow, he discovered that clothing had been burned, for he found some buttons with the name of a Seattle firm. Then he went in and searched the stove and found more relics. But he felt that probably O'Brien had emptied the pockets of his victims' clothes before he burned them, and likely had thrown the things away from the fire that might lead to his identification with the murder if he kept them. So Pennecuick did the same thing with articles out of his own pocket, watching where they fell. Then he carefully swept again, and found not only his own things, but a key that fitted Clayson's safe in Seattle and the strange coin that Relphe had carried. When the spring came the bodies were found on sand-bars and were easily identified, even by the fitting of some fragments of teeth that Pennecuick had found where the men had been shot in the head by the revolver after they had fallen before the rifle. And at the trial also the large bills that had been found in possession of O'Brien were identified as having been the property of Clayson, as the nugget and coin were shown to have been Relphe's.

There were other items of evidence, the exhibits nearly exhausted the alphabet, and there was a very long list of witnesses brought from many quarters. The Crown Prosecutor was Mr. Fred O. Wade, K.C. (now Agent-General for British Columbia in London), and he handled the case with consummate ability. His address to the jury was a marvel of logical, irresistible emphasis on every point of evidence. Inspector Scarth gave Mr. Wade most valuable assistance during the long trial. The prisoner O'Brien was ably defended, but there is no evidence so strong as circumstantial evidence when it is compactly pieced together, and the jury took only half an hour to reach the verdict of "Guilty." O'Brien received the death sentence, and spent a lot of time before his execution in cursing the Mounted Police who, as another outlaw once said, "would give a gunman no chance in this blamed Canada country." It was a long and costly effort on their part, extending nearly two years in the case of O'Brien, but it gave notice to the world that Canadians would not tolerate lax views on the sacredness of human life.

It seems appropriate that in that same year, 1900, an injustice to the Mounted Police should be at length removed by the granting of medals to the men of the Force who had served in the North-West Rebellion of 1885. At the conclusion of that rebellion, medals had been granted to all others who had been on military duty against Louis Riel's revolt, but they were only given to the Mounted Police who had been actually under fire in an engagement. We do not care to know who was responsible for this extraordinary piece of invidious distinction. The Mounted Police have practically always been on active service and always liable to be under fire at any moment. Those who know the history know that all the members of the Force rendered service of enormous value to Canada and the Empire during that war time, whether in an engagement or not. They policed the vast plains and, with endless patience and cool courage, held at peace the thousands of Indians who might have swept the defenceless settlements with destruction. These men deserved the medal and should have had it at the outset, but better late than never.

It is anticipating a little in one respect, but in another it is looking backwards. During the years since their organization the Mounted Police had furnished escorts and convoys for the successive Governors-General in their official tours over the vast North-West. Before the railway era this involved long journeys and much extra duty, cheerfully undertaken and chivalrously as well as skilfully carried out for the comfort of these distinguished travellers, amongst whom were our present good King and his much-loved son, the Prince of Wales. In recognition of these services the Commissioner has received for himself and his men warm thanks, as well as expressions of high admiration for the courtesies and services rendered by the Police, as well as for their fine bearing as soldierly men.

And all these find fitting climax in the fact that His Majesty King Edward, "First Gentleman of Europe," gave his personal recognition of all the splendid services rendered to the Empire by the Police by conferring on the Force the title "Royal." This intimation was made in the Canada Gazette in 1904 in this manner:

"His Majesty the King has been graciously pleased to confer the title of 'Royal' upon the North-West Mounted Police Force."

Referring to this honour, Commissioner Perry said in his report of that year:

"The force is deeply sensible of the high honour conferred upon it, and I trust it will continue by loyalty, integrity and devotion to duty to merit the great distinction which His Majesty has been so graciously pleased to bestow upon it."

The Commissioner has always trusted and believed in his men, and he has not been disappointed.

* * * * *

CHAPTER XIII

MODESTY AND EFFECTIVENESS

"The population of the Territories has doubled in ten years and the strength of the Force has been reduced by half. Our detachments have increased from 49 to 79." This was one of the striking and illuminating statements made by Commissioner Perry in his Annual Report for 1901. The Commissioner was looking around and ahead and did not intend that the Government should be left ignorant of the rapid changes which were taking place. The reduction of the Force was a tribute to the extraordinary efficiency of its members in establishing peace and order throughout a vast domain. But it is not fair or human "to ride a willing horse to death," and with increased population and widening areas to oversee, the strain being put upon the men in the corps was too great. In even the organized portions of the Territories there was only an average of one constable to every 500 square miles. It was highly important that with half the population foreign born, alien to our laws, unacquainted with our institutions and disposed to bring with them a sort of a hatred of authority born of experience under old-world despotisms, there should be present the educative and restraining influence of an adequate number of the riders in scarlet and gold. Without that influence the newly-found liberty of these European immigrants would soon degenerate into licence. Those of us who recall those critical formative days agree with the statement that the constables took a large view of their duties and that their tact and discretion led these strange people not only to obey the laws but to look upon the Police as friends willing to aid and assist them in every way.

The Commissioner therefore strongly urged not only the maintenance of a sufficiently large force to meet the situation, but pressed for the adoption of his particular policy to have a reserve of at least fifty men always in training at headquarters who would be qualified for detachment duty whenever occasion arose. He gives adequate reason for this policy when he says, "The men on detached duty are in responsible positions; they have to act on their own initiative, often on matters of considerable public concern; their advice is sought by new settlers. To carry out their important duties satisfactorily they must be well trained, have experience, and be of good character. It is therefore unwise, contrary to the interests of the public and the good reputation of the force, to send on detached duty men who have not the proper qualifications, necessary experience, and who have not yet established a reputation for reliability and sobriety; in other words who have not been tested and proved."

There was an old song, written perhaps in the days of the Peninsular War, to attract men to sign up for service in the possible hope that some one of them might be instrumental in putting the tyrant out of commission:

> "A raw recruit
> Might chance to shoot
> Great General Buonaparte."

But the Mounted Police Force was not built on those lines. Their business was to keep avoidable shooting off the programme altogether either by themselves or others, and to effect that desirable end they must be self-controlled, disciplined and tactful men. In order to be of that type every man must get thorough groundwork training in the depôt division before he goes out with the possibility of being on detached duty at any moment. Successful insistence on these points of policy was one of Commissioner Perry's early achievements. It was in the best interests of the country and the Force that such things should be recognized by the authorities.

How necessary it was that the Police should be wise and at the same time firm is evidenced that very year when Superintendent Charles Constantine was in command at Fort Saskatchewan. Amongst the Rutherian or Galician people there arose a religious controversy, and a religious controversy is a hard thing for civil authority to tackle. But Constantine was a very discreet officer. He saw how easily a serious conflict on the subject might be precipitated amongst an excitable people. "Religion," writes Constantine, "is a very real thing to the Galician and on this matter he feels very strongly." Constantine made special study of the situation. There were three different branches of the church amongst these people, the Roman and Greek Catholic and the Orthodox Russian or Uniate Church, which was in creed and ritual a sort of half-way between the other two. The Russian church people had put up a church building near Star, but having no pastor of their own, they divided on which of the two others, the Roman Catholic or the Greek Catholic priest, should conduct services. The discussion became quite warm and threats of violence were common. Constantine would not interfere as between the controversialists, but he kept his eye on the situation and gave special direction to certain of his men. Matters came to a climax on Easter Sunday, when the two rival priests, each accompanied by some 200 followers, came to hold service in the church. Constantine knew of the situation beforehand, and he had sent a sergeant and two constables, prudent men, to see that there was no breach of the peace. Both parties claimed the right to hold services in the church and neither would yield nor would they hold a joint service. So the Police held the balance level by locking the door and then asking the parties to go one to each side of the church outside and hold their own services. This was done and there was no ill-will. After the services they dispersed to their homes and the danger passed. Constantine thought well of people who could be earnest about religion and law-abiding. And he makes this general remark about them: "On the whole my observation leads me to believe that the Galician immigration has brought a very desirable class of settler to the North-West and one which will in a short time be of material assistance to the productiveness and prosperity of the Dominion." And the record of these people during the years since this wise officer wrote these words has amply borne out his opinion. In the earlier years the excitable character of the Galicians, and the absence of instruction in their old haunts as to rights of life and property, led them into the commission of a good many offences against our laws, but no alien race has been more anxious to become Canadian and especially, amongst the young people who have grown up in this country, we have met many who are a large asset to the Dominion. As a rule they are industrious, and Constantine's vision of their future has become a reality.

FORT SELKIRK, YUKON.

ESQUIMAUX FAMILY.

Up in the Yukon that year there were continued echoes of the famous O'Brien murder case detailed in our preceding chapter, the leading note being that the capture and execution of this desperate criminal had attracted world-wide attention to the efficiency of the Police and had made the Klondike country safer for everybody. For instance, Superintendent A. E. Snyder, who took over the command at White Horse from Superintendent Primrose, says, "I am very pleased to be able to state that there were no very serious cases of crime during the year. I am satisfied that it was not for want of material that we were indebted for such a happy state of affairs, as among the class of people continually on the move coming in and going out there are quite a few that would be capable of attempting anything if they were certain of escaping detection. I can only attribute the lack or comparative utter absence of serious crime to the extreme watchfulness of our men which renders it well nigh impossible for loose characters to engage in doubtful enterprises and stay in the country. The (under the circumstances) speedy and condign punishment meted out to O'Brien elicited favourable comment from citizens generally irrespective of nationality, the Americans especially commenting favourably on it and contrasting it with their experience of similar incidents in mining regions of the Western States." Referring to the same case Inspector Starnes, then in charge at Dawson, says, "This case has cost the Government a great deal of money, but I am sure it had a very salutary effect on the bad element, as it has shown them that nothing will be left undone and no expense will be spared to prevent crime and bring the guilty ones to justice." Starnes has a reference to the verdict of a coroner's jury in the case of one Dr. Bettinger which indicates that he thinks the jury "played safe." It appears that the doctor had started from Dawson for the coast on foot and that he was not clad well enough for such a trek. When he did not turn up at points he ought to have reached, Inspector McDonnell was put on the trail and all the detachment men along the river took up the search. In a few days the body of the unfortunate man was found seven miles off the Yukon trail up the White River. Inspector Wroughton, who was out on an inspection trip, held an inquest in order to have the body properly identified, so that any matters connected with the estate might not be confused. And this jury concluded that the body was that of Dr. Joseph Bettinger and that the said Bettinger "came to his death from some cause or causes unknown to the jury, but are of the opinion that death was caused by exposure during extreme cold weather." The opinion of the jury was no doubt correct, though they expressed it with proverbial caution.

Starnes refers with proper sarcasm to the cases in which people imagine the Police ought to save them from the results of their own carelessness. He says, "There have been a number of sluice box robberies on some of the creeks, and we have been fortunate in securing one or two convictions, but in many instances it was impossible to find the thieves. This class of crime is one of the hardest to detect, owing to a great number of miners leaving their sluice boxes unprotected when there is a lot of gold in them, and another reason being that it is impossible to identify gold dust. We may have our suspicions in many cases, and in some feel sure of our man to a moral certainty, but it is almost impossible to prove the guilt unless we catch the man in the act. The distances being so great, it is out of the question for us to place guards on every claim, and the miners who wish to keep their gold must take proper precautions. It would be just as well for a farmer in the East to leave ten dollar bank notes in his stable yard with no one to watch them, as to leave gold in the sluice boxes the way some of the miners do." Starnes here hits at the all too common assumption of people who, with sense enough to be responsible for their acts, think that some one else is under obligation in matters of health and property to save them from the consequences of their own practices. And he delicately suggests to the careless miners that they have missed the fact of contributory negligence when they have thus led others into temptation.

These policemen were making a constant study of the unveneered humanity on the frontier and developed a keen perception of right and wrong, and had a rugged conviction that every one should get a square deal, but should realize that he must bear his own burden of responsibility. A fine instance of the Police opinion that men should get fair play is found in the report of Inspector A. M. Jarvis, who in 1901 was in command of the Dalton trail post in the Yukon country. He says, "The Dalton trail, which is the pioneer route to the 'inside,' is much in need of repairs. A vast area is tributary to this trail. From the Yukon River to the 141st parallel and as far north as the White River the Dalton trail is the main artery. Three years before the Klondike was heard of, Mr. Dalton blazed his route into the interior, acting as guide to the explorers into the country where he had done important work or trading in furs. When the rush into the gold-fields took place, he spent large sums in bridges and corduroy, especially between Dalton House and Five Fingers, which, now that the Yukon has the monopoly in freight and passengers, brings him no return. While the construction of this trail was a business venture, yet it remains a benefit to the country, and is of great value to the prospector. I should like to see Mr. Dalton recompensed for his unprofitable outlay." What came of this suggestion history does not record. The world is under immense obligation to adventurers who have blazed new trails to hidden natural resources. But the world is not always as fair as this Police Inspector in recognizing its obligation.

In his report in 1902 Commissioner Perry, in view perhaps of comments made by some who were ignorant of conditions, and such are occasionally found in public bodies, frankly says that the expenditure on the Mounted Police is large, but that when it is looked upon as a factor in the peaceful settlement of a vast territory, such expenditure is a splendid investment which will pay big dividends to the country for generations in the form of a contented, happy and prosperous population. The Commissioner's words are that "the benefits will be reaped by posterity when the Force has disappeared and its work is forgotten." It is hard to get these policemen to estimate their work highly enough. They have the usual British reticence intensified by definite practise of it, and that is why no man who has been a member of the Force will ever give a true history of its achievements. He is afraid to give the Force its due lest he should seem to be boastful when he records deeds that are stranger than fiction. And so when the Commissioner speaks of the Force disappearing and its work being forgotten we must enter a protest against this being read except in the light of the well-known habit of these men to keep religiously far away from the braggart spirit. The Force has undergone changes and may ultimately disappear in so far as the present form of organization is concerned, but those of us who have known the country and the men all through the years affirm without reservation that it can never be forgotten. The work of the corps has been so indelibly stamped upon the history of Canada that the record can never be erased as long as this country endures.

How, for instance, can any country forget a Force concerning one of whose members this same Commissioner Perry, proud always of his men, writes in the very next paragraph, "To one who is unacquainted with the country it is difficult to convey any adequate idea of the labour involved in policing such a vast region and carrying out the multifarious duties imposed on us. As an instance of this I may mention the work done by Corporal Field last winter. He is stationed at Fort Chippewyan, Athabasca. He was informed that a man had gone violently insane at Hay River, 350 miles from his post. He proceeded there with dog train, accompanied by the interpreter only and brought the unfortunate man, who was a raving maniac, back to Fort Chippewyan, and thence escorted him to Fort Saskatchewan, travelling a distance of 1,300 miles with dogs and occupying forty-four days on the journey. This is not an isolated instance. It represents the work of Inspector West and his men in the Northern Country."

All this is written by the Commissioner with the most admirable and characteristic police restraint. He gives the facts in outline and leaves the rest to the imagination of those who know the country. He says nothing about Corporal (later Inspector) Field having just come in from a long patrol, tired and entitled to a rest, albeit he was a noted trail-maker. Nor does he relate any details of the trip after the insane unfortunate. But those who have travelled the broken plain can see much between the lines of the simply worded report. We can see the vast white expanse of snow and ice wind swept at times by the fierce blizzards out of the north. We can see the return journey when the violent man would have to be watched day and night and yet given liberty enough at times to keep him from being chloroformed with the cold. A fine humane act was this and one that could only be done by a man who embodied in himself the coolness, courage and gentleness that form so splendid a combination. This and countless deeds of a like kind ensure the Mounted Police an enduring place in our Canadian temple of Fame.

It appears that there were always some people who believed that all they had to do when any mishap occurred in their experience was to sit back and get the Police to put things right. This was a tribute to the way in which the Force had exercised paternal oversight in their districts. But it was carrying things rather too far and forgetting that the best help comes to those who help themselves. There was a good deal of horse-stealing and horse-straying in progress in 1902 and when their horse got out of sight some settlers imagined they were stolen when in reality they had only strayed. These people thought the Police should assume the task of securing the return of their herds and droves. This calls a mild protest from Inspector J. O. Wilson, when at Regina. Wilson says, "Settlers are still prone to report a horse stolen when it is missing without making any special effort to find it themselves. There is a case on record where a settler named Hansen, who for the past seven years has lost horses, now expects the Police to find them for him. Much time has been spent in fully investigating his complaints, but this gentleman is not yet satisfied and has written to say that he considers it the duty of the Police to hunt up lost horses." And then the Inspector indicates the lines along which the efforts of the Force are properly directed. "In connection with this," he says, "I beg to state that when horses are reported lost, descriptions are forwarded to all detachments and instructions issued that should they be seen or heard the owners are to be notified. A large number of horses have been returned to their owners in this way." But to leave their police duties and hunt the stray horses of careless settlers was a little too much to ask.

Up in the Yukon that year there were contrasting pictures of events in a country that could always be counted on for happenings of interest. There is a fine touch in a report from that tender-hearted officer, the late Inspector Horrigan. Two gallant Police Constables, Campbell and Heathcote, were drowned at the mouth of the Stickine River, where they were crossing in an old boat as no other was at hand. Campbell's body was not found, but Heathcote's was recovered and brought to the nearest point, Wrangel, in the United States, for interment. "I am informed that the funeral was one of the largest and most impressive ever held in Wrangel. The service was conducted by the Rev. Mr. Reirdon, of the Presbyterian Church, with a full choir. The edifice was crowded to the doors, and the majority followed the remains to the last resting place. I chanced to be in Wrangel on June 30, Memorial Day, and noticing a procession of children clothed in white, several veterans of the Civil War and a number of citizens, I followed them to the cemetery and witnessed a very touching sight. To my surprise I noticed that Constable Heathcote's was the first grave decorated with bouquets and sweet-smelling flowers by kind and loving hands. It mattered not to them what altar he knelt at or what flag he had served under. They knew him in life as a policeman, proud of his uniform and his country. In death they honoured his memory." This is well put by Horrigan, and the whole incident indicated the deep-seated attachment existing between the two great branches of the English-speaking race. Incidents like this go far to destroy the "ancient grudge" which some Americans have against Britain because a century and a half ago a foolish British King and a still more foolish set of advisers treated British subjects overseas in an absolutely un-British way.

And then in the same northern area we have in the report of that exact and capable Inspector, W. H. Routledge, another side of life in the account of a murder case which, in cold-blooded deliberateness and treachery, perhaps puts the O'Brien case into the shade. O'Brien was a very inhuman and brutal murderer, but he, though on the look-out for prey, seems to have somewhat accidentally fallen in at Fossal's road-house with the three men he murdered a few miles farther along the way. But there is no particular evidence that he had made special efforts to be their ostensibly friendly companion beyond the usual comradeship of mutual helpfulness on the trail. But in the case Routledge reports two men, La Belle and Fournier, seem to have gone to White Horse with the deliberate intention of ingratiating themselves with some of their fellow-countrymen by the use of their French mother tongue, joining them on the way down to Dawson, and then murdering them when they arrived at a convenient place. And so these two creatures found at White Horse, Leon Bouthilette, Guy Beaudien, and Alphonse Constantin from Beauce County, Quebec, who had recently come from the East, going to Dawson. La Belle and Fournier got passage with these men on a small boat, travelled with them, camped, ate, and slept with them till one night in camp on an island near Stewart River they murdered their three hosts, probably in sleep, and after rifling their pockets, and to hide their crime, they tied the bodies up, weighted with stones, and threw them in the river. Then they burned up all evidences of their crime, got in the boat and went to Dawson, from which place they proceeded farther, found another compatriot named Guilbault and murdered him on the way to Circle City, Alaska. Once again it was a case where the murderers left no possible witness to testify and considered they were safe. But they forgot they were in the Mounted Police country—in the land of the men in scarlet and gold who never let go till justice is done.

The Police at White Horse had the number of the boat, 3744, and the names of all the men in it. Other boats, starting from White Horse about the same time, arrived in Dawson. But boat 3744 and its occupants, though seen by several on the way, dropped out of sight at Stewart River and was not seen again till Constable Egan discovered it empty at Klondike city.

The body of a man who had been killed by bullets was found in the river, and there was a small key tag with the name "Bouthilette, Beauce, P.Q." on it. This gave the Police a clue, and it was followed with characteristic energy and skill. A web of circumstantial evidence had again to be woven. Later on another body was found and Surgeons Madore and Thompson were satisfied that another death by violence had occurred. The body corresponded with the description given of Guy Beaudien. Constable Burns, of the Dawson Division, who could speak French like a native, haunted the mines and creeks in plain clothes, unearthed Fournier, who was identified by one Mack, who had seen him at White Horse, as one of the men in boat 3744. Detective Constable Welsh, Sergeant Smith, Corporal Piper, Constables Burke and Falconer with others were on the scent. Welsh went to Skagway and found the sailing list of the boat *Amur* on which the murdered men had come from Seattle. To that point and others he went, and then acting on information from Constable Burns, who had combed the French Colony for evidence, Welsh went on through six different States and finally caught and arrested La Belle in Nevada. La Belle said enough to indicate the whereabouts of the murder event and Welsh wired this information. Corporal Piper and Constable Woodill and the Dawson photographer went, located the "Murder Island," gathered some incriminating articles and took photographs from every angle. Then the work went on and the Police accumulated such an unbreakable chain-mail web of evidence starting with a man who had come with the murdered men from Montreal to White Horse, continuing with others who had seen all the parties on boat 3744 and then with men who had seen articles and money on La Belle and Fournier which they knew to have been the property of the murdered parties, that these cold-blooded monsters practically confessed, each throwing the blame on the other. They were committed for trial, found guilty by judge and jury, and paid the extreme penalty for their horrible crime.

Down on the prairie the Police were equally intent on duty and equally successful in serving notice on all and sundry that tampering with human life and prosperity would not be tolerated. And every one who came into the Canadian West was wise if he governed himself accordingly. An accomplished young forger and potentially worse, by the name of Ernest Cashel, barely twenty-two, drifted up to Calgary from the State of Wyoming and proceeded to test the calibre of Canadian authority. He was arrested, but escaped from the city authorities. Then the Mounted Police, whose officer commanding at Calgary was Superintendent Sanders, D.S.O., were called upon and discovered that Cashel had stolen a pony at Lacombe to help in his escape. Shortly afterwards D. A. Thomas, north of Red Deer, notified the Police that a relative, J. R. Belt, had disappeared from the latter's ranch east of Lacombe. Constable McLeod investigated and discovered that when Belt was last seen a young man, who gave himself the name of Elseworth, was staying with him. The description indicated that Elseworth and Cashel were one and the same. Belt's horse, saddle, shot gun, clothes and money, including a $50.00 gold bill, had vanished. It looked like a murder case, and so Superintendent Sanders put our old friend Constable Pennycuick, who had unearthed O'Brien in the Yukon, on the trail of Cashel. Every detachment of the Police was put on the scent. In a while a man, answering Cashel's description, stole a diamond ring up in the edge of the mountains and, despite great cunning, was arrested by Constable Blyth at Anthracite. He was wearing some clothes like Belt's and had the diamond ring. Then Constable Pennycuick, hearing that Cashel had been staying at a half-breed camp near Calgary, went there and got some clothing Cashel had left there. Part of it was the rest of Belt's corduroy suit. Pennycuick also got track of the $50.00 gold bill which had been seen by some of the half-breeds with Cashel. Pennycuick traced Cashel's route from Belt's to near Calgary with Belt's clothes, horse, saddle and the aforesaid $50.00 gold certificate. But thus far there was no evidence that Belt was not alive somewhere, and so Cashel was tried for stealing and sentenced to the penitentiary. Two months later the river gave up its dead, and the body was identified by certain marks and by an iron clamp on the heel of the boot. Bullet holes in the body of the same calibre as the revolver and rifle carried by Cashel completed the evidence. He was brought back from the penitentiary, charged with murder, and after a trial in which he was brilliantly defended by Mr. Nolan of Calgary, was sentenced to be hanged.

But the end was not yet. John Cashel, a brother from Wyoming, had come up and was given permission to see Ernest in the cell. As he entered the chaplain was leaving and the guard being relieved. Taking advantage of the situation, John Cashel slipped his brother two loaded revolvers with which that evening Ernest held up the unarmed Constables and made his escape. It was a dark night, with heavy snow falling, and this clever and daring criminal well armed got clear away. Then the alarm was sent out, detachments were notified and Commissioner Perry, accompanied by Inspector Knight, went up to Calgary to take personal direction of the search. Evidently, as happens in such cases this outlaw had friends, who, supplied him with information, telling him what was being done and to add to the confusion, people all over the country became nervously excited and began "seeing things," so that several supposed Cashels were reported from a dozen directions. A drunken half-breed in Calgary caused excitement by telling that he had Cashel tied up in his camp, but the cool-headed Sanders saw through his yarn and locked up the half-breed for being drunk and disorderly. Superintendents Primrose and Begin, on the Commissioner's orders, sent patrols out through the ranches. Here they came across ranchers who had been held up for food and money by a man whose description tallied with that of Cashel. As the Police could not cover the whole country, some civilian volunteers were called for and these were placed along with police detachments. Finally Sanders mapped out the country, got detachments together to the number of five under Major Barwis, Inspector Knight, Inspector Duffus, Sergeant-Major Belcher and himself, and the order was to search every building, cellar, root house and haystack with instructions that if they found Cashel they were, if human life was to be saved thereby, to set fire to the building or stack where he was and smoke him out. The detachment under Inspector Duffus, consisting of Constables Rogers, Peters, Biggs, Stark and McConnell, while searching

Pittman's ranch 6 miles from Calgary, came across Cashel in the cellar. He was found by Constable Biggs, who was fired at by Cashel out of the dark hole. Biggs returned the fire and backed up the steps to tell the rest. Constable Rogers then ordered the men to surround the house and sent word to Inspector Duffus, who came and called on Cashel to surrender. But he would not answer and the building, a mere shack, was set on fire. When the smoke started, Cashel agreed to come out and was arrested. This was the close of an arduous hunt, a great many of the Police having been almost continuously in the saddle day and night in cold weather for weeks. They were determined that no one should boast of eluding the Police by making a clear "get away."

This time there was no escape, and the daring murderer was hanged in Calgary, first confessing his crime to the Rev. Dr. Kirby, his spiritual adviser. Once more the unbreakable net of the famous riders of the plains had been thrown out to show that the whole country became a prison for anyone who offended against its laws.

It was perhaps the recurrence of cases of this kind where the Police were proving the enormous value of the Force to the country that caused Superintendent Primrose in 1903 to make a plea for some increased recognition of his men. In his report he says, "In nearly every walk of life in the past twenty years wages have gone on increasing, but, I regret to state, the same scale of wages still obtains in the Police Force. For instance, I am at present employing a constable on detective work whose pay is seventy-five cents a day for which we have to pay a Pinkerton man eight dollars a day." And it is no disparagement to the Pinkertons to say that the Police could give them some "pointers" when it came to work on the frontiers.

The question of pay for their men was a constant anxiety for the officers, who were themselves receiving a mere pittance in comparison with the salaries paid to men of equal education and experience in other departments of the civil service. So we find, in 1904, that fine officer, Superintendent Wood, in the Yukon making reference to the fact that though an increase of pay had been granted to others the pay of the Police had remained practically the same since their organization. Wood feels that it is humiliating for the men. "A constable's life," he writes, "is not altogether an enviable one. He is liable to be exposed to the inclemencies of the weather at all seasons of the year, and is at times called upon to risk his life in the performance of his duty. He is under much closer and severer restraint than private individuals." This is putting it all very mildly, as was the manner of the Police when they were speaking of themselves. Then Wood goes on to say, "It is of importance that a member of the Force should be made to feel that his position is an honourable one, and that he is entitled by virtue of his office or calling to the respect of the community at large. This state of things could be arrived at if he felt that his position was equal to those in other walks of life, and that his services were rated equally as high. But the mere fact of his receiving 50 cents to 75 cents a day with his food and clothes while carpenters, blacksmiths and labourers on the outside receive five times as much and in the Yukon ten times as much, is enough to instill a feeling of inferiority so far as his calling is concerned." This is an important view. And Wood in the same report emphasizes his argument, though he does not refer to it in that connection, that the Police are expected to do work as mail-carriers, postmasters and such like, outside proper police duty, because the country could not get civilians to do it at the remuneration offered. The whole thing troubles Wood, who was of a sensitive temperament and very anxious to retain high-class men in the Force. And so he refers to it again in the following year and says that a constable who was a skilled mechanic and was saving the country great expense by looking after the manufacture of stove pipes, tinware, etc., had been offered as much an hour by town merchants as he was getting in a day in the corps on the scale allowed by the Police Act. And Wood, who feels keenly for the men, says, "Our poor circumstances are so generally known that it has become usual to send members of the Force complimentary tickets for entertainments and reduce the fees in clubs and societies for them." Probably what was in the minds of those who sent tickets and reduced fees was that it was an honour to have with them the men in scarlet and gold who made human life and property safe on the frontier and whose standards of manners and education made them most desirable company. But the comparative poverty was there amidst abounding chances to be rich in the gold country and elsewhere in a new land. Men who served through the dangerous formative periods of Western history died poor in worldly goods.

It is a fine thing to know that all through the years these men out of the sheer love of adventure and their high ideals of devotion to duty did such service, but the facts should not be lost sight of when the pensions of the "old guard" survivors are being considered from time to time.

The quality of the non-commissioned officers and men is often brought out in their detachment reports. These reports reveal not only men of ability and insight, but throw light on the kind of people these Police in the north had to guide. Sergeant Frank Thorne, for instance, was in charge at a place called Tantalus. The man who gave that name to the elusive mining prospects of the region had a sense of humour and the fitness of things. Thorne says, "Hundreds of people landed at Tantalus en route to the new White Horse diggings. Most of these people had been misinformed as to the best place to start from. I informed some of them, but found that a person with gold fever is very unreasonable and stubborn. Those that returned this way wore a very dilapidated and sorry appearance." But the Police, I suppose, helped them out of their troubles, for these red-coated giants did not lose their humanitarian disposition even amidst the follies of the foolish. And the Police knew well the strain under which these deluded and disappointed people often found themselves, for Wood tells us of the Police at Dawson and White Horse having as many as forty lunatics committed to their care in a single year. This involved heavy and anxious work, and the Superintendent shows the spirit in which it was done when he laments the lack of suitable accommodation and fears lest some of these unfortunates may hurt themselves in the unsuitable quarters provided.

Speaking of the humanitarian disposition of the Police, one finds many incidents to show how they resented offences against the helpless, and how relentlessly they brought the perpetrators of such offences to book. In the same year, 1904, of which we have been writing, Sergeant Field, of Fort Chippewyan, to whose rescue of a lunatic we have already referred, got word that an Indian had, at Black Lake, 250 miles away from the Fort, deserted two little children, two and three years of age and that these two children according to the testimony of other Indians had been devoured by wolves. Part of the clothing had been found and all around the blood-stained ground was trampled by wolves. The Indian was at Fond-du-Lac, but could not be advantageously arrested unless Field could get some evidence from others who were not there. So Field bided his time till all the Indians were at Fond-du-Lac in the summer. Some eight months had gone by, but Field did not forget. Fond-du-Lac was several hundred miles from Fort Chippewyan, but Field got there at the proper moment, arrested the Indian, took the witnesses along and started for Edmonton, where the Indian was tried and given a term in the penitentiary. It had cost Sergeant Field a strenuous trip by trail, river and train of nearly eighteen hundred miles, but he had by his action told the Indians of the whole region to deal properly with their children and their old people.

A very remarkable case in 1904 was that in which after an extraordinary display of mastery over difficulties, the Police under Staff-Sergeant K. F. Anderson (now Inspector) brought one Charles King to justice for the murder of his partner Edward Hayward, near Lesser Slave Lake in Northern Alberta. The case was not only a portrayal of the persistent methods of the Police, but it threw a fine sidelight on the way in which the Police had won the friendship of the Indians through guarding the Indians against exploitation by white men. It moreover gave a good exposition of the Indians' unique powers of observation.

CORONATION CONTINGENT. LONDON. 1911.

INDIANS RECEIVING TREATY PAYMENT ON PRAIRIE.

FORT FITZGERALD, ATHABASCA.

ICE-BOUND GOVERNMENT SCHOONER.

In October, Moos Toos, the headman of the Indian Reserve at Sucker Creek, came to Sergeant Anderson and told him that white men were cutting rails on his Reserve. Anderson immediately went over with the Chief and found men employed by a very prominent firm of contractors cutting rails. The Sergeant stopped them at once and made them pay the Indian for what they had already cut. This, of course, was pleasing to Moos Toos, who, on returning home with Anderson told the Sergeant that some days before, two white men with four pack-horses had come from Edmonton and camped on the Reserve near a slough. They had stayed there some three days or so and then one of them left, but there was no sign of the other. An Indian boy had noticed that the dog that had come with the white men would not follow the one that left. This was observation number one. Then some Indian women, as their custom is, went over to the place where the men had camped to see if anything was left that might be of service. One Indian woman noticed that the camp fire-place was much larger than required for ordinary use. Another Indian woman stood at the edge of the fire-place and looking up noticed, on the underside of the leaves of a poplar tree, globules of fat where the thick smoke had struck the cool leaves and the evaporating fat had condensed. She said, "He was burning flesh in this fire." These two things, added to the fact that a shot had been heard by other Indians in the direction of the white men's camp, made them suspicious. They told Moos

Toos, their headman, and he, in recognition of the goodness of the Police to him, told Anderson about it, and added that he thought something was wrong. Anderson thought so too, and with Constable Lowe went down to the place. They raked in the ashes and found fragments of bone and other substances which they carefully sealed up and kept for analysis. Moos Toos, who was on hand with some of his Indians to help, found a large needle with the eye broken, then by going barefooted into the slough where the water was four feet deep, discovered a camp-kettle which some of the Indians had seen with the white men. Later on Moos Toos and Lowe found in the slough a pair of boots in one of which was stuffed a rag with various articles, including the other part of the broken needle. In the meantime, Anderson had got into touch with the surviving white man at the home of a trader some distance away and asked for his story. This man, who gave his name as King, said that his companion was a man he had overtaken on the trail over the Swan Hills. His name, he said, was Lyman, and he had been on the way on foot. King said Lyman had left the camp on foot for Sturgeon Lake and that he supposed he was on the way there. Anderson sent out in that direction, but there was no trace of such a man at any point, and a Hudson's Bay employee who had just come from Sturgeon Lake met no one on foot and there was no trace on the trail of anyone so travelling. Anderson and Lowe then arrested King on suspicion and held him while they pursued further investigations. Anderson was convinced that the bed of that slough, if uncovered, could unfold a tale. And so he hired the Indians to divert it by digging a ditch that would drain it into Sucker Creek a half-mile away. It was quite an undertaking, but the Indians, who have lots of time on their hands in the summer and fall, offered to do the work for a hundred dollars. The work was well done and Anderson's expectations were not disappointed. He found amongst some minor articles a sovereign-case which was fairly conclusive evidence that the man who had vanished from the earth was probably an Englishman. The sovereign-case was traced back to the manufacturer in England and to the man who had sold that number to a certain Mr. Hayward, a man up in years, then deceased. The clue was followed up and a son of Mr. Hayward was found who recalled that his father had presented a sovereign-case to another son when that son left for Canada. The son who had gone to Canada was known to be in the Edmonton and Northern country, but the people at home had not heard from him for some time. Regardless of expense and without delay, the Police brought Hayward all the way from England to Edmonton for the trial. He identified the sovereign-case as the one given by his father to the missing man Edward Hayward. A specialist in analysing had been brought from Eastern Canada who pronounced the blood, brains and bones found in the ashes of the camp fire to be human elements. There were some twenty witnesses in the case, those outside the Police being Messrs. J. K. Cornwall, George Moran and the rest half-breeds and Indians. Once more the police had the chain of circumstantial evidence welded solidly link by link. King was declared guilty, but on a legal technicality a new trial was ordered. By this time the witnesses were all back home. But they were brought back, including the brother of the missing man from England. The verdict again was guilty and King paid on the scaffold the penalty for his mean and cold-blooded murder of a travelling companion. A very curious thing in this trial was the sworn statement of Hayward, the witness from England, that his sister had told him there, the morning after the shot was heard by the Indians near the Lesser Slave Lake, that she had dreamed that their brother Edward had died by violence in Canada. This was not offered or accepted as evidence, but was mentioned incidentally as at least an extraordinary coincidence.

The Mounted Police were evidently determined not to allow crime to make any headway because if the impression ever got abroad that men could play fast and loose with law and go unrebuked, there would be no end to it. So we find Superintendent Sanders saying again that the Force should have more men to cope with the demands of the immigration movement. "It is only natural," he says, "to expect that a percentage of criminals should accompany a large migration into a new country. A malefactor who finds it necessary to lose his identity for a while cannot choose a more convenient location than a country just filling with new settlers and where one stranger more or less is not likely to be noticed." This is sound reasoning, and Sanders is looking into the future when he is asking for men enough to deal with the new order of things so as to prevent trouble in the future. "Once," says he, "get the new-comers within our gates imbued with the proper respect for British law and British justice, and prevent the criminal element getting a foothold, and a work will be accomplished of inestimable value hereafter."

And up in the Yukon, Assistant-Commissioner Wood, out of wide experience, says, "It is a well-known saying that prevention is better than cure, and any innovation in our system tending to the prevention of crime in Canada, and more particularly in the North-West and the Yukon Territories, is to be welcomed." And then Wood goes on to advocate the adoption of certain methods for the detection of criminals which for that period showed that these men were keeping a little more than abreast of their times though they were on duty in the wilderness places of the earth. He advises the establishment of a Criminal Identification Bureau at Ottawa with branches in all the cities and at the headquarters of each division of the Mounted Police Force. He goes on to define methods by photographs of every one arrested, measurements under the Bertillon system and the use of the finger-print method, which he quite properly declares, as we now know, to be the most infallible means of identification. That Wood had made a special study of the subject is evidenced by the fact that he backs his argument by appeal to history. He says the finger-print system had been in use in Korea for 1,200 years as a means of identifying slaves and was adopted in India in 1897 as a way of preventing impersonation amongst the natives. The Scotland Yard authorities accepted the system in 1898, which was the year of the Yukon Gold Rush, and it is very interesting to find the Officer-Commanding on that frontier being so forehanded as to be amongst the first in Canada to advocate the use of methods now generally adopted. These men of the Mounted Police were wide awake and were determined, we repeat, to prevent the criminal class from getting a foothold in this country.

It is interesting to find in the same period that the Police never seemed to forget. As related above, Fournier and LaBelle had been executed in January, 1903, for the murder of Beaudien and Bouthilette. A third man of the same party had vanished at the same time, but no body had been found. Two years afterwards a body was found in the river, taken to Dawson, the clothes removed and washed by Sergeant Smith and the body identified by these clothes and a paper dried out, as the body of the third man,

Alphonse Constantin. Thus was the fact of his death established in the interests of relatives and estate—a matter of vital importance for the satisfaction of all concerned. And thus did the curtain fall on the final act in a dark tragedy of the North.

But all these incidents were making for the future peace of the country. It was the establishment of the "Pax Britannica," as Commissioner Perry said with justifiable pride in the record the Police had made throughout the years. He quotes the words of a famous Indian Chief to which we have already called attention in the chapter on Indian treaties when that Chief, referring to the Police, said, "Before you came the Indian crept along. Now he is not afraid to walk erect." "For thirty-one years," said Perry in 1905, "neither white man nor Indian has been afraid to walk erect, whether in the great plains, the far North or the distant Yukon."

And even at the time he was writing those words Corporal Mapley was on patrol over an unknown route from Dawson to the Peel River, Inspector Genereux of Prince Albert was away on a 1,750-mile trip North, of 132 days by canoe and dog-train to investigate a case of alleged murder, Sergeant Fitzgerald was on patrol to the mouth of the Mackenzie River and Inspector Moodie was establishing new posts around the Hudson Bay—all having a reassuring and stabilizing effect on the vast uncivilized North land.

And again turning to another side of their work there were many cases that were charged full of a Victoria Cross type of valour which went unnoticed except as things done in the ordinary course of duty unless some tragic element intervened to call special attention to it. Constable Pedley, of Fort Chippewyan, for instance, a noted trailmaker, had made many a trip (as others did) fraught with tremendous hardship. But it was not till one day when he broke for a while under the tremendous strain that his extraordinary efforts got into the light of public notice. Here is part of his modest report when he was detailed to escort a lunatic from Fort Chippewyan to Fort Saskatchewan: "I left Chippewyan in charge of the lunatic on December 17, 1904, with the interpreter and two dog-trains. After travelling for five days through slush and water up to our knees, we arrived at Fort McKay on December 22. Owing to the extreme cold, the prisoner's feet were frost-bitten. I did all I could to relieve him, and purchased some large moccasins to allow more wrappings for his feet. I travelled without accident until the 27th, reaching Weechume Lake. Here I had to lay off a day to procure a guide as there was no trail." This is put with great suppression of anything like telling what a difficult time he was having, but again we read between the lines. The trip is "without accident" but there was "extreme cold." Pedley was nurse and doctor as well as guard over the unfortunate madman who raved as they travelled along almost impossible roads. Then Pedley goes on: "I arrived at Lake La Biche on the 31st, and secured a team of horses to carry me to Fort Saskatchewan. I arrived on January 7, 1905, and handed over my prisoner." Pedley had spent his Christmas and New Year not in a happy social circle, but in the company of the unhappy victim of insanity. And he ends his report by saying, "During the earlier part of the trip the prisoner was very weak and refused to eat, but during the latter part of the trip he developed a good appetite and got stronger." Pedley's care was improving the madman's condition, but it was taking it out of himself. The unfortunate was transferred to Calgary guardroom, and that Pedley's nursing had worked a change is evident because Assistant-Surgeon Rouleau reports that it was "a remarkable case." He was taken to hospital and discharged in February. Says Rouleau, "His mind and speech were as good as ever. His life was saved." But the sequel is told in Commissioner Perry's report, "Constable Pedley began his return trip to Fort Chippewyan. When he left Fort Saskatchewan he was apparently in good health, but at Lake La Biche he went violently insane as a result of the hardships of his trip and *his anxiety* for the safety of his charge. He was brought back to Fort Saskatchewan and then transferred to Brandon Asylum." But we rejoice that this is not the end. Perry goes on, "I am glad to say that after spending six months there he recovered his mind and returned to headquarters. He was granted three months' leave and is now at duty as well as ever." And that this gallant man who was not conquered by cold and danger was not going to be conquered by the recollection of the breaking of a cord that had been subjected to too great a tension is attested by Perry's closing reference: "In spite of all, he has recently engaged for a further term of service." Comment on this is unnecessary. It is like a flash which dispels the night in a prairie thunderstorm.

* * * * *

CHAPTER XIV

ON LAND AND SEA

Reference has been made several times to the studied and determined reticence of Mounted Policemen concerning their own achievements. That characteristic is stamped on all their reports and probably accounts for the fact that no member of the corps would ever attempt writing a full record of its work as a nation-builder. And any outsider who knows the country's history, the manner of life on the frontier and who has also been in contact with these scarlet-coated riders, not only finds it necessary to read between the lines for the facts but will enjoy the ingenious efforts of these men to avoid anything savouring of egoism. Without being so intended some of these reports are positively humorous on account of this determination to keep "display" in the background. Here is a gem of that type. It is a report written by Corporal C. Hogg, who was stationed at North Portal on the Soo Line near the international boundary. Such localities are often a sort of "No Man's Land" where would-be desperadoes think they can set law to defiance. Corporal Hogg's report of an evening's proceeding in that region, with a foot-note by his superior officer who had received it, makes interesting reading. We quote them in regular order as follows:

> "On the 17th instant I, Corporal Hogg, was called to the hotel to quiet a disturbance." Hogg put the state of disorder mildly. He proceeds: "I found the room full of cowboys and one, Monaghan or 'Cowboy Jack,' was carrying a gun and pointed it at me, against sections 105 and 109 of the Criminal Code." It was taking long chances, but the Mounted Police generally waited for the other man

to start things. In this case they were started right there and then. For the Corporal goes on to say, "We struggled." This is terse, but it involved much more than was said, as will later appear. "Finally," proceeds the Corporal, "I got him handcuffed behind and put him inside. His head being in bad shape I had to engage the services of a doctor who dressed his wound and pronounced it as nothing serious. To the doctor Monaghan said that if I hadn't grabbed his gun there would have been another death in Canadian history. All of which I have the honour to report.

"(S.) C. HOGG, Corporal."

The Officer who received this report puts on the finishing touch by a memorandum upon it to this effect: "During the arrest of Monaghan the following property was damaged: Door broken, screen smashed up, chair broken, field jacket belonging to Corporal Hogg damaged, wall bespattered." It looks as if Monaghan's ancestors may have hailed from Donnybrook, and it must be admitted that he lived up to the traditions of Fair day in that region. But he had never met a North-West Mounted Policeman before and would probably be wiser in the future in regard to raising a "disturbance" when one of them was at hand.

Another evening a "bad man" from Idaho "blew in" to Weyburn. He was a sort of travelling arsenal and got very bold when he got into an unarmed Canadian town. He began shooting holes in verandahs, and if any one went to look out of a window the Idaho desperado threatened to "make him into a sieve." A prominent citizen was made to hold out his hat as a target for this pistol artist. This citizen remonstrated and warned the Idaho man that there was a Mounted Policeman not many miles away who would probably hear of the situation and come over. This enraged the "gun-man," who offered to bet that no Mounted Policeman could arrest him, adding, "if he comes to butt in to my game I will eat his liver cold." A telephone message was sent to Corporal Lett. It took some time to ride in, but Lett located the Idaho citizen terrorizing a bar-room. Lett walked in and the Idaho man had his gun up in a second. No one knew just how it happened, but Lett sprang at the desperado. There was a grapple and a fall, but when they got up Lett had the Idaho "gun" in his hand. The rest was simple. The gun-man had to hold out his hands for the "bracelets." Whether he paid the bet or not no one has recorded, but Lett got an extra stripe for his daring.

This recalls another real incident which my friend, Robert Stead, the well-known writer, has put into verse under the title, "A Squad of One," though he gives fictitious names. A certain Sergeant Blue of the Mounted Police who was alone at a prairie post got a letter from a United States Marshal asking him to find and arrest two men who had committed murder and escaped to our side of the line. There was always cordial reciprocity between the police officials along the boundary, and so the Marshal warns the Sergeant to send out his strongest squad of men to make the arrest of these fellows, for he said:

"They's as full of sin as a barrel of booze and as quick as a
    cat, with a gun,
So if you happen to hit their trail be sure to start the fun."

The Sergeant was alone, but started out next morning clad as a farm labourer, called at the farm suspected, found the men with shooting-irons, but got them talking and then got them separated and bagged them both at "the nose of a forty-four." And when he got back to his lonely post he wrote and mailed the following note:

"To U.S. Marshal of County Blank, Greetings I give to you:
My squad has just brought in your men and the squad was,

                              Sergeant Blue."

Of a different variety but with the same brand of cool courage is an old friend Donald McRae, still speaking with the Gaelic accent and now living in Vancouver, who when I saw him first wore the scarlet and gold in Steele's command. We were in action and McRae was shot rather severely in the advanced skirmish line. The ambulance men were on hand in a few minutes, but McRae refused to leave his position. He said he had half his cartridges left and would not budge till he used them. He stayed there till he used them, and years afterwards our gallant old Commander, General

Strange, grizzled soldier of the Mutiny, met McRae on the coast and said jocularly to some in the company, that he had seen lots of service but that this Mounted Policeman was "the stubbornest man he had ever met." General Strange had Scottish ancestors and while quite stern about it at the time of the incident probably rejoiced in secret at McRae's tenacity.

These stories have been thrown in to indicate that all over the country the Police in their determination not to allow lawlessness of any kind to get a hold on the country, were doing remarkable exploits without advertising. But we exhume them from old documents to show how these things were done. And so as we resume our story we find Superintendent Wood in 1905 up in Dawson busy with the finger-print system in which he, as before mentioned, was a pioneer believer. Thus when a cabin had been robbed of a gold watch and other valuables, Wood was satisfied, without any other clue to the thief, when he found a finger-print on a lamp-chimney which the man had to light in order to see what he could annex. Then Wood proceeded to hunt for a criminal of the thief class, for he says, "It is well known that the criminal class at large are segregated into groups according to the line to which their abilities are applied." By following this idea he settled on a group of five who would likely do that sort of thing. Four of them did not answer to the finger-print test, but the fifth showed a facsimile of the print on the lamp-chimney. He was the man. So the Police were making it daily more impossible for criminals to ply their trade even in the remotest points.

In those days in quite another direction and with the purpose of inquiring into the possibilities of the Hudson Bay and Arctic regions, Inspector J. D. Moodie was engaging in his explorations, and his reports, with those of Starnes, Beyts, Pelletier, Howard, French, Sellers, Rowley and others, are being consulted anew in view of the project of railways to the great bays of the North. Some of these famous patrols we shall discuss later.

But speaking of railways it is interesting to find statements from that observant officer, Superintendent Constantine, who despite the fact that his health had been undermined by the hardships of the Yukon was still on duty in the Peace and Athabasca regions. In 1907 he discusses the development of the Peace River country from an agricultural standpoint. He covers very carefully the great areas that include the Grande Prairie, Spirit River, Fort Vermilion and the rest and makes careful analysis of their agricultural capabilities. He sees great possibilities, but places forcibly in his report the absolute need of railway communication with the eastern centres before much can be expected. His forecast has proven correct in every particular. These regions now have railway and river transportation and are prospering accordingly. One wonders now why extracts from the reports of these men on the ground were not put before the people in general instead of being allowed to suffer from being buried alive in the departments of Government. All through these official reports from the Mounted Police officers and men, we find statements and suggestions that might have influenced the progress of the country greatly had they been given wider publicity throughout the years.

The Yukon country was undergoing a good many changes. The mad rush of miners into the Mining areas had dwindled away and big companies with new hydraulic processes were crowding out the individual miners and causing them to seek new fields for exploitation. But the vultures and vampires of human society were slow in letting go their victims, and the Mounted Police had to be constantly on the watch to prevent the unwary and the foolish from being caught in their dens. That reliable officer, Inspector Wroughton, who was in command at Dawson City in 1907, says, "Dance-halls and their accompanying evils have been more or less accountable for a good deal of the existing crime. But for these institutions the wanton and the sneak-thief and the confidence man and woman would find their opportunities seriously curtailed. During the last session of the Yukon Council, I am glad to state, the ordinance licensing these places was repealed after a hard and bitter struggle. This does not mean that the evils are entirely eradicated. Our great difficulty is to get evidence. It is, however, more difficult now to carry on evil businesses." The law in the Yukon as elsewhere was fulfilling the function assigned to it in the famous words of Gladstone, "A good law is intended to make it easier for people to do right and harder for them to do wrong."

That great mining frontier, with its money-mad and heterogeneous population (albeit there were many splendid people there), was at the same time the problem and the glory of the men in scarlet and gold. It was their problem because the criminal class which always makes a dead set on a frontier was determined from the outset to make the Klondike country a sort of hell on earth, and it was their glory because they prevented the thug and the outlaw from getting a foothold where the old flag flew. There also the lawless individual sought to get away to some other clime, for he said there as he said in the mountains, "These blamed Mounted Police won't give a man a chance." That was one of the biggest testimonials ever given to guardians of the law in any country.

It is not at all generally known that a real "red" revolution that aimed at seizing the banks and mines with the hope of dividing the spoil amongst the "revolutionists" was planned in the Yukon a decade or more before the Bolshevistic terror was let loose in Europe. "Soapy Smith" the unsavoury but reckless gunman of Skagway, had developed a school of imitators. There were probably a couple of thousand or so of these tough characters scattered all through the north country camps, and the idea was to rally them to a centre, overpower the few policemen, establish a sort of "liberty" government, seize the money and anything else that could be carried, divide it up and then scatter to the outside before any reinforcements could come to the aid of the Mounted Police from the East. It was an ambitious programme and the "revolutionists" had gone some distance in their preparations. They had arms stored in certain localities, they had a seal for the temporary government (which seal I have personally seen), they had maps prepared indicating the centres to be attacked as well as a record of the Mounted Police posts with the number of men in each.

But these same Mounted Police were not asleep. They never hunted after publicity for themselves. They never thought of the grandstand. It would have been often more spectacular to have allowed things to come out into the open and then fight them in a dramatic way. But the preventive power was what they preferred to exercise. It brought them less advertisement and public notice, but it was best for the country and that was the main thing with the scarlet and gold men.

So Superintendent A. E. Snyder, who was in command at White Horse, where the principal leaders of the plot had, unfortunately for themselves, located, discovered the half-hatched conspiracy. A knock-about kind of fellow who had a wholesome fear of the police gave Snyder a hint about some meetings in a stable loft. Snyder got his men to search the stables and they discovered some incriminating literature as well as the White Horse seal of the "republic," which latter Snyder still has in his possession. Then he wired to Superintendent Primrose at Dawson and to Comptroller Fred Whyte in Ottawa, at the same time dispatching Inspector Horrigan to Skagway to put the matter before the American officials. This energetic type of action frightened the conspirators. They scattered to the four winds and most of them rushed out of the country. It was "good riddance of bad rubbish" and the Canadian authorities decided to let it drop at that point. But the incident, which hardly anyone outside the police officers above mentioned knew anything about till some years had passed, is another proof of the statement that the Mounted Police have headed off more crime without killing than any other body of men in the world.

In his report for 1908 Commissioner Perry quotes with justifiable pride from a judgment given in an extradition case by Mr. Justice Hunt of the United States Federal Court. Counsel for one Johnson who was fighting extradition put up the plea that Johnson would not get a fair trial in Canada and the Judge answers that plea very squarely in his pronouncement. He felt that a strong case had been made out against Johnson, and he practically ridiculed the suggestion that Johnson would not get fair play north of the line. The Judge said in part, "The fact that the officer (Mounted Police) who made the arrest of this defendant promptly notified him that whatever he said would be used against him, is a powerful bit of testimony, tending to show the care with which officers of the law proceed under British systems of government. Extraditing a prisoner for trial in Canada is not like returning him to a country where the institutions and laws are so at variance with our own that the courts might be apprehensive that he might not be protected, but in ordering that he be returned to Canada, certainly the courts in the United States will proceed on the well-founded belief, justified by the light of experience, that he will be afforded ample protection and that no injustice will be done him. The testimony of the defendant regarding a conspiracy against him, and his statement that he cannot get a fair trial, do not appeal a particle to a Judge sitting in a proceeding of this kind. He will get a fair trial up there."

HERSCHELL ISLAND. YUKON TERRITORY.

ESQUIMAUX VISITING R.N.W.M. POLICE TENT.

BARRACKS AT FORT FITZGERALD,
GREAT SLAVE RIVER.

R.N.W.M. POLICE SHELTER, GREAT SLAVE LAKE.

CABIN OF REV. FATHERS LE ROUX AND ROUVIER.
Murdered by Esquimaux, as found by Mounted Police,
September, 1915.

And it is very interesting to find in the same year Superintendent Wood, who was in command of the Yukon country with headquarters at Dawson, standing up against reports in Eastern papers which stated that the enforcement of law is lax in that country and morals at a low ebb. Wood heaps up testimony to the contrary. He quotes from two Judges, Dugas and Craig, both widely known and respected, who affirm that law is enforced there as well as anywhere else, and that there are few cities where men and women can go about at any hour as freely and safely as in Dawson. The minister of a prominent church wrote to the London *Times* and said, "Regarding Dawson, our city is most orderly and seldom is a drunken man seen on the streets. The Mounted Police rule with a firm hand, and life and property are safer in Dawson than in London." A gentleman who spent eleven years in Dawson, interviewed in 1907 in an Eastern city said, "I have seen more trouble and immorality here in a week than I saw all the years I was in Dawson." And Wood winds up by the strong admonition of a man who will not allow his corps to be slandered for laxity in law enforcement: "Let those who are so anxious to redeem the people of this Territory commence their crusade in their own city or town. Judging from the outside Press there are few if any places in Canada that can presume to give Dawson a lecture on morals."

But the Yukon service where the Police were at the beck and call of every case of need or distress or danger, no matter how much hardship and exposure they involved, was taking its toll. The men of the corps were paying the price for the proud privilege of preserving the Pax Britannica in a remote region inhabited by a mixed population and showing a record for justice and law-enforcement such as no area of a similar character in any part of the world had ever seen. For in that year 1908 Inspector D'Arcy Strickland, an officer of kindly generous nature, who had gone into the Yukon with Constantine at the very beginning, died at Fort Saskatchewan, the report stating that he had never recovered from the effects of that pioneer service in the North. In the same year Inspector Robert Belcher, C.M.G., who had won that decoration in the Boer War, retired after thirty-four years' strenuous service. It was Belcher and Strickland who had first flown the flag and established custom-houses amid the snow and blizzards and tremendous cold of those deadly summits of the White and the Chilcoot passes in the days of the gold rush. Wood himself, and Constantine the pathfinder, never threw off the effects of the Yukon days, though the former moved back as Assistant Commissioner to the prairie and the latter did much strenuous work in the Athabasca district where conditions were almost as severe as in the Klondike country. Many others there were, gallant officers, and no less gallant men, who bore the mark of their northern vigils and patrols to the end of their days. And this applies not only to the men of the Yukon but to those who in the Hudson Bay, Peace, Mackenzie and Athabasca areas were abroad in polar seas or on land that for months was hidden deep by snow and ice.

The year 1908 witnessed some notable trips and patrols. In order to wind up all matters connected with the Peace-Yukon trail Inspector A. E. C. Macdonnell was instructed by the Commissioner to proceed from Fort MacLeod via Calgary, Vancouver and the Skeena River to Hazelton in British Columbia to dispose of stores that were there and bring the horses back to Fort Saskatchewan. The Peace-Yukon trail was begun in order to have a road to the Yukon mines over British territory, and during its construction a great deal of valuable information as to the country was acquired and given out in reports by the Mounted Police. But the dwindling down of the rush to the mines rendered the trail practically unnecessary.

The British Columbia Government did not desire to assist and police detachments could not be spared, hence Macdonnell's trip. It involved a route by saddle horse and pack train of over 1,200 miles, but it was carried out in perfect order.

Inspector J. D. Moodie, a noted sea and land patrolling officer, was asserting the jurisdiction of Canada in the regions of the Hudson Bay where there was much trading by people from the outside. Sergeant McArthur, who held a lonely post at Cape Fullerton, receiving word that the natives were being urged by traders to kill musk-ox contrary to law, undertook on his own initiative, in the Arctic midwinter, a patrol which lasted fifty days. Sergeant Donaldson, soldier and sailor too, who was to meet a tragic death the next year, made a dangerous voyage from Fort Churchill to Fullerton and return. A patrol with mail went from Regina to Churchill, Assistant Surgeon LeCroix being sent with this patrol. Staff-Sergeant Fitzgerald, hero of many trails, and who also was to find a tragic end in the "white death" frosts of the Yukon, made that 1908 winter a patrol in a whaling ship to Baillie for the purpose of ascertaining the condition of the natives and asserting Canadian jurisdiction. Superintendent Routledge, going from Regina to Smith's Landing, some 1,100 miles, looked into the matter of wild buffalo herds, as did Sergeant Field and Sergeant McLeod, who went from Fort Vermilion to Hay River on a similar errand.

The most extensive patrol of that year was the one undertaken by Inspector E. A. Pelletier, who, accompanied by Corporal Joyce, Constable Walker and Constable Conway and at a later stage by Sergeant McArthur, Corporal Reeves and Constables Travers, McMillan, Walker, McDiarmid and Special Constable Ford, left Fort Saskatchewan on the 1st of June for Athabasca Landing on the way to Hudson Bay via Great Slave Lake, which latter point they left on the 1st of July. They in due time reached Chesterfield Inlet on the Hudson Bay. They were met at that point by Superintendent J. D. Moodie with the Hudson's Bay steamer *MacTavish* (called after a famous Hudson's Bay Company family). By this boat Pelletier and his men started for Churchill, but the *MacTavish* in a storm was driven on a reef and totally wrecked. The men all escaped and went to Corporal Joyce's lonely post at Fullerton. Pelletier was anxious to go on to Churchill, but had difficulty in persuading even the natives to go, for they said, "No one travels in December and January—the days are too cold." But the Inspector was thinking of others and writes in his report: "I knew what a lot of anxiety the delay of this patrol would cause and we hurried preparations." The trip was fraught with constant danger from cold and privation, but they made Churchill on January 11. Pelletier modestly says they did not suffer and shows how well off they were when he can state that their dogs were never without food for more than four days at a time! The men ran out of sugar and coffee, but he makes light of that, though both are a great help on a cold journey. They met no natives from whom their stocks of deer and other skins could be replenished, and so when they were stormbound for a day here and there they darned and patched so as to prolong the life of their shoes.

The Inspector lets in some light on the general situation when he writes: "The worst feature of a long journey like this in a country where no fuel is to be procured, is the absolute impossibility of drying clothing, bedding, etc. The moisture from the body accumulates and there are no means to dry clothing to get rid of it in any way, and every day sees it harder to put on in the morning and the beds harder to get into at night, until both clothing and bedding become as stiff as a board from the ice. It is a very uninviting task and disagreeable procedure getting into an icy bed at night and in the morning getting into icy clothes." When both clothes and food were frozen and even the prospect of getting an occasional piece of driftwood was dim, one can imagine the situation and wonder at the endurance as well as the daring of these men.

And when this state of affairs is realized one can appreciate the action of Constable Ford as related by Corporal Reeves and forwarded in the usual way by Superintendent J. D. Moodie, from Fort Churchill. Some driftwood had been secured, and clothes dried when the party, consisting of Sergeant Donaldson (in charge), Constables Reeves and Ford with two natives, were off Marble Island and anchoring their boat, the *MacTavish* (which was wrecked later, as mentioned). Ford went over to another island in a small boat to get some walrus meat, as they sighted some walrus there. He came back and reported having killed some, and the three constables went over to cut off their heads and bring these over. As they were engaged in this task it began to get dark, so Donaldson and Reeves left for the *MacTavish* with some heads, leaving Ford on the island to cut up the rest of the meat and one of the natives would come back for him later. On the way to the *MacTavish* a walrus struck the boat and Donaldson was drowned, but Reeves, who had done his best to help Donaldson, managed to swim back to the island where Ford had been left. Reeves was completely numb with cold and weak with his struggles. There was no means of getting a fire on that island, but gathering all his strength he shouted in the darkness and Ford, who had not seen the wreck, came to his help. Reeves writes vividly of an act of sacrifice on the part of his companion: "By this time I was very numb and helpless through being in the water so long and getting into the night air, which was very cold. My clothing being soaked through, I would certainly have perished had it not been for Constable Ford, who took off my wet clothes and gave me his dry ones—wringing out as much water from my clothes as he could he put them on himself." Then, in this icy suit, Ford searched all night for Donaldson in vain. It was running a most desperate risk of losing his own life, and if done under the eyes of others would have been declared as valorous as the deed of any man who ever rode back to rescue a wounded comrade under fire of the enemy.

Inspector Pelletier's patrol returned to Regina after nearly a year's absence, during which they travelled by trail and water about 3,500 miles, a most extraordinary feat. The report of the patrol decided some important points as to the nature of the country, the conditions of the natives and the places where detachments of Police should be located.

Up in the sub-Arctic regions in the other directions, the Mounted Police were keeping their lonely vigils and making their hazardous journeys. Staff-Sergeant (later Inspector) Fitzgerald, who after several years in charge at Herschell Island was relieved in 1909 by Inspector Jennings, gives a little pen-picture of the place when he says, "Herschell Island is one of the most lonely places when there are no whaling ships. There is no place one can go except to visit a few hungry natives, and there is no white man to visit nearer than 180 miles." After speaking highly of his comrades, Constables Carter and Kinny, he refers to one journey incidentally and says, "The heavy ice between Kay and King points formed large pools of water and we struggled with the large sleds all day, sometimes up to our waists in water." One wonders how these men stood it. The Commissioner was right when he indicated that service in the north required men of robust health and hopeful temperament. Inspector A. M. Jarvis says the sailors regard Herschell Island as a "blowhole." The wind blows one way or the other constantly, and he quotes the captains as saying that "a nor'-easter never dies in debt to a sou'-wester." But Jarvis introduces a fine human touch when he says of the inhabitants, "They are quite religious, holding services on Sunday and doing no work on that day. They neither beg nor steal, and slander is unknown amongst them. They are as near 'God's chosen people' as any I have ever seen. After my experience of this world I could almost wish that I had been born an Esquimaux. They are very fond of their children and take the greatest care of them. The children never require to be chastised and are very obedient. One never sees any quarrelling or bickering amongst them. They show the true sport in their games of football and baseball. The other day I noticed a crowd of little tots, in their skin clothes, playing on the snow for several hours as though they were in a bed of roses." This is a delightful picture and in rather painful contrast to our more artificial life, so that one can understand Jarvis' wish.

These policemen had a fine regard to the human side of the world's work, and often indicate their keen desire for the things that they deem in the highest moral interest of their districts. In the year we have been discussing, Inspector Horrigan went from Dawson to the Upper Pelly River to look into the matter of a supposed murder and to bring about a reconciliation between two groups of Indians that had fallen out about something. He found that the Blind Creek Indians were in the wrong and effected a better understanding all around. Of the Indians on the Upper Pelly, he writes in his report, "The Pelly Indians are sober, honest and provident. Morally their standard is very high. It seems too bad that so far no provision has been made for a school for the children, as they are a very bright, clever-looking crowd. I see a great field here for good, active Christian work." This is finely spoken—a good admonition both to Church and State—but incidentally also a rebuke to certain phases of a so-called higher civilization which often gives to the unspoiled children of nature its worst rather than its best features. And up in the Mackenzie River district where we left Inspector Jennings in charge we find that able officer also engaged in prescribing certain rules regarding the conduct of visiting ships which tend to ward off from the unsuspecting natives some practices which would not be for the good of these innocent people.

Down in the Middle West the Mounted Police were having difficulty with people whose type of religion, being unmixed with intelligence, led them into fanatical excesses. The Doukhobors, or "Spirit Wrestlers" as their name means, were a body of people who had come from Southern Russia, where they had not enjoyed anything like liberty. When they arrived in Winnipeg, where I recall speaking to the first band through an interpreter, they sent back a cablegram to their friends, which was shown me at the time by Mr. McCreary, Commissioner of Immigration at that point. The cable read, "Arrived Canada safe are free." The change was a little too much for them, and they did not realize that they were not free to become nuisances to others. They were ignorant, illiterate, but had the merit of being conscientious and being willing to suffer for conscience' sake. This latter characteristic always prevented me from condemning them wholly. Once their ignorance was removed they would become industrious and orderly citizens.

But in the early stages they were fanatics and used to go on pilgrimages, they said in search of Christ. Inspector Junget, Sergeant (now Inspector) Spalding and others of the Police had a lot of trouble in rounding them up, giving them food and preventing them from shocking communities by their parades. The Police used great tact and in the end succeeded in impressing these strange people with some sense of responsibility. In the midst of the difficulty a half-crazed man named Sharpe crossed from the States with some others. He said he was "Christ" going to "God's people, the Doukhobors," but as he was heavily armed and threatened to shoot anyone who tried to stop him, his claim was naturally rejected. Inspector Tucker and a detachment went to see Sharpe and reported that an arrest could not be made without shooting, so it was decided to wait and watch. Sharpe sent the following letter to Tucker: "To save bloodshed use some judgment. I will not give up alive, so some of us would be shot. If I have to continue amongst sinful men I had rather die. No one can say that Jesus is the Christ only by the Holy Ghost. The spirit came to Christ in the form of a dove. It came to me in the form of a lion. When the Doukhobors receive me, then the Lord will prove me and your eyes can open wide." But the Doukhobors were getting their eyes open and the Police, rather than kill anyone, pursued a waiting policy with close supervision. Finally Peter Veregen, the czaristic leader of the Doukhobors, warned the Doukhobors not to receive Sharpe. This nonplussed the fanatic, who had come possibly with an eye to business. He expressed disgust at the way the Doukhobors were in subjection to Veregen, "But they must be the people of God," he said, "or they would not be in such subservience. Veregen has a fine graft and I would like to run the spiritual side of the business for him." However, the redoubtable Peter wanted no partner, so Sharpe and his following crossed back to the States, informing Constable King, who saw them safely across, that "they would be back next spring." However, they came not. The Doukhobors, particularly the new generation, have made much progress and have prospered in establishing some useful industries. But for several years they were a source of a good deal of anxiety to the red-coated riders, who wished to guide them to better conditions without harshness. Events have justified the attitude of the Police.

Of course, these law-enforcers still had the ordinary class of offenders to deal with, for crimes like horse-stealing and "cattle-rustling" die hard. For instance, a man named Marker, then south of the line in North Dakota, who, having been allowed out on bail by the Canadian authorities, when he was under a charge of horse-stealing, lost no time in going across beyond the reach of the Mounted Police. Corporal Church, on detachment work, kept his eye on the border for a sight of Marker, who might come over to replenish his stock of horses. Church got word of his intention at a given time, and taking a man named Kelly with him he rode all night, and finding a companion of Marker's, he got the information that the horse-stealer would likely cross over some 20 miles westward. Their horses were pretty tired, but Church and his men kept on, and concealed themselves near a trail crossing the boundary about that distance away. In a few hours Marker and another man rode over and Corporal Church, galloping up to him, ordered him to halt. Marker wheeled, drew his revolver and made for the line. Kelly headed him off and Marker shot at him, but missed. Kelly then charged, knocking both Marker and his horse over. He quickly remounted and rode on, but Church intercepted him, telling him he would shoot if he did not stop. Marker attempted to shoot the constable, but his revolver missed fire. Church then shot Marker's horse and captured the horse-stealer before he got to the line. Church then hired a team to take the prisoner to the detachment headquarters. But when the wagon on a winding road seemed to be on the American side of the line, Marker threw himself from the conveyance and reaching a house at the spot, rushed in and slammed the door. Church reports: "I forced the door open and was met by a blow in the eye from Marker, who had taken his spurs off and used same as a weapon. I grappled with him and threw him on the floor, and with assistance tied his hands and feet after a good rough and tumble scrap." Church had done his duty surely, but whether lawyers and surveyors would prove that the arrest was made a few feet over the line or not we cannot say. The lads of the scarlet tunic always got their man, but the courts sometimes let him go again.

In support of the position taken by Superintendent Wood, already quoted in regard to the orderliness of the Yukon, it is interesting to quote from Inspector Wroughton, who was in command of the Dawson Division. He says, looking back over 1908, "I am pleased to report that there has been very little crime in this district during the last eleven months and, I might say, none of a serious nature." In the list of cases for gambling and such like one can gather from the names that the Mounted Police did not confine their efforts to suppressing gambling amongst aliens as some have done elsewhere. The majority of names mentioned are of our own race. The Mounted Police played no favourites.

In his report for 1910, Commissioner Perry makes the almost incredible statement that twenty-five new detachments have been established during the past year without any increase in the strength of the Force. The corps seems to have had all through the years an extraordinary elasticity. It seemed to be able to stretch itself over constantly growing areas of settlement and to meet the situation created by the increasing tide of immigration that was flowing over the great new West. That could only be effected because of the superior quality of the individual men, their ability to act separately and upon individual initiative. They did not require to have mass formation to keep their courage up to the necessary pitch. And still better they had the training that would make them reliable in judgment when sudden and unexpected conditions arose. Perry's policy to have a goodly number of men always in training at headquarters so that unready recruits should not have to go out to face emergencies, was being approved by events as highly statesman-like. But he was right in constantly keeping before the Government the need for increasing the numbers of the Force, because, although the men were wonderfully efficient and could be trusted even in "detachments of one," the fact was that burdens were laid upon one man that should have been borne by two or three. To many a man the increase in the number of detachments meant doubling his hours in the saddle and lessening his hours for recuperation. One wonders that more men did not break down under the strain. But for their invariable high calibre this would have been the result. An indication of the way in which the arduous labours of the Police were appreciated is found in the 1909 report of the Commissioner of Agriculture in Saskatchewan, who speaks of the "invaluable assistance given by the officers and men in enforcing the various ordinances of the department. In particular I refer to the Horse-breeders Ordinance, the Fire and Game Ordinances and the Public Health Act, the latter calling for vigilant work in patrolling foreign settlements quarantined for outbreaks of infectious and contagious diseases. Had it not been for the excellent service rendered to the department by this hard-working and highly-trained force of men, the spread of disease would probably have reached epidemic proportions."

Speaking of the kind of men required to keep up the reputation of the Force, Commissioner Perry has this illuminating statement: "We require sober, trustworthy men; those who are not, only remain in the Force until they are found out."

During the year 1910, there were some notable changes in the Force. Wood, who had served for thirteen years in the Yukon, ten of which as the highly efficient Officer Commanding, was promoted to be Assistant Commissioner; Starnes, who had done difficult work in many places, latterly in the Hudson's Bay district, was promoted to the rank of Superintendent; Sergeants Sweetapple, Raven, Fitzgerald and Hertzog became Inspectors; while two excellent officers, Inspector John Taylor, son of Sir Thomas Taylor, Chief Justice of Manitoba, and Inspector Church, the famous riding master, were called by death.

Superintendent Cortlandt Starnes gives a rather chilling picture of the Mounted Police surroundings at Fort Churchill where the weather indicator was for months hitting the bottom of the thermometer bulb, and where there was a general monotony in surroundings. He says, "The place is a dreary one, and there is nothing in the way of recreation for the men except reading and no place to go except the Hudson's Bay post and the English Church mission on a Sunday." This is a good tribute to the self-sacrifice of the missionary. Starnes goes on to say, "There was a gramophone, but it is broken and out of order. The mess-room is a cold and forbidding place." Starnes has a good appreciation of the value of some cheerful environment for his men, for he says, "I have had some chairs put up instead of the long benches, and I have requisitioned for a few pictures to put on the walls. I would also like to have the tin plates and cups replaced by the ordinary white crockery, or crockery of a cheap standard pattern." Starnes is not extravagant in his requisition. Canada is a rich country, and these men holding her lonely outposts deserve consideration, but some picayune arm-chair censor may cut things out, and so the Superintendent goes warily, but he will not desist altogether because he knows the place better than the censor, and he knows that his men should have some reasonable comforts. "A small billiard table," he says, "and some additional books and magazines would be acceptable. The library is well patronized, but in a year's time the most of its books will have been read." A year is quite a while to wait for a mail. It was at a post something like this one that one early Hudson's Bay Company official heard of the Battle of Waterloo a year after it happened. But he held a celebration even then, for were not these grim old traders men of British stock who were holding a new Empire for the British Crown? Of course, things were improving since the advent of the Mounted Police, for they had instituted what Inspector Jennings facetiously called a "rural mail delivery" through regions near the Pole. Jennings himself and his men had patrolled through snow and ice very extensively that year, and the sense of humour that could speak of this white wilderness as a "rural route" would be a saving make-believe in the midst of Arctic blizzards. And the thought of bearing a loving missive to solitary men from friends thousands of miles distant, might well thrill the imagination of these knights of the modern day.

* * * * *

CHAPTER XV

GLORY AND TRAGEDY IN THE NORTH

In the recent Great War a somewhat casual visitor was present when a vagrant shell smashed the refreshment dug-out where a young Red Cross man was handling some comforts for the khaki-clad boys near the front line. And when the alarmed visitor explained to the dispenser of refreshments, "I would not stay here for a hundred dollars a day," the answer came back swiftly but kindly, "Neither would I." He was not there for the hope of gain, but out of a sense of duty and adventure so strong that both danger and remuneration were forgotten.

There was a good deal of this spirit manifest in Mounted Police history from the beginning. Not the pittance in the way of pay drew men to the corps, but the love of the adventurous and the desire to do work in the out-of-the-way places, where new trails had to be blazed beyond the accustomed sky-line. This was especially true of the men who served and volunteered to serve again in the vast spaces of the white and frozen North. Not for a hundred a day would they have so risked their lives, as others risk them still in that region. It was because the jurisdiction of their country's flag had to be asserted, and because lonely outposts and scattered groups of sometimes starving natives challenged the best that was in them, that these uniformed crusaders went out again and again on their hazardous patrols.

And so, when in 1911 Inspector Fitzgerald, Constables Kinney, Taylor and Special Constable Carter, four men of the finest type and the most thorough experience in those desperate, trackless and frozen areas, men cast in so fine a mould that some of them were to be selected for the King's Coronation, perished on a patrol from Herschell Island to Fort Macpherson and Dawson City, Canada was stabbed broad awake to what the men of the Force had been doing for their country in those Arctic lands. It seems as if such catastrophes are periodically required to make a selfish world aware of what some men are enduring in order that others may live in comfort and ease. But the world does not always receive such lessons in the right spirit. The tendency is rather to raise a protest against the authorities who permit men so to sacrifice themselves. Thus, when those four gallant men fell in the Northern wilderness, the first note from the press seemed to indicate that this patrol was an exceptional occurrence, and that it should not have been allowed to take place in view of the possible sacrifice it might involve. This gave Commissioner Perry, than whom no one was more deeply distressed and grieved at the tragic event, an opportunity to remind the country that such patrols had been for years a common and every-day event in the work of his men in the North. From year to year, under the Polar sky, in scores of different directions, the Police had carried on this work, performing definite duties, carrying mails, visiting camps of Indians and Esquimaux who were the wards of the nation, maintaining law and order beyond the confines of civilization and generally exercising a wholesome oversight in the loneliest spaces in the world. "This is dangerous work," wrote the Commissioner; "in our rigorous winter climate and in spite of every precaution, a tragedy may occur at any time. It does not deter our men from seeking service there, and it is to the North many prefer to go." The spirit of adventure was in the blood of these men, and the tragic possibilities which no one foresaw as well as they did themselves erected no barrier which could discourage them in their endeavours. If there was the constant looming up of danger through the "white death" fog, there was also the glory of adventure under the flashing splendour of the aurora borealis.

R.N.W.M.P. BARRACKS, CHURCHILL, HUDSON BAY.

POLICE WITH DOGS AND EQUIPMENT ON SPLIT LAKE. N.W.T.

And when Commissioner Perry wrote in his report as above quoted, he was able to support his statement by actual facts from that very same year. He said: "All over the North-land members of this Force are carrying out these difficult journeys. Attached to this report you will find many reports of equally dangerous patrols. Sergeant Hayter, 700 miles return journey from Fullerton along the West Coast of Hudson Bay to Rankin Inlet, to meet Sergeant Borden, who went up from Fort Churchill, carrying mail and taking a census of the Esquimaux; Sergeant Walker from Fort Churchill to York Factory and return; Sergeant Nicholls from Norway House to Fort Churchill and return to Gimli; Sergeant Edgenton from Split Lake to Fort Churchill, arriving with dogs abandoned by the way, and three days without food; Sergeant Munday from the Pas to Lac de Brochet and return, 900 miles in fifty-one days; and Sergeant MacLeod from Fort Vermilion across the Caribou Mountains to Great Slave Lake." This is a most formidable list, and to anyone who knows the country and the climate it affords the imagination a moving panorama, in which constant danger and almost incredible endurance are portrayed. All this forcibly reminded Canada of the devotion of her sons in the Northern hinterland, and that was the purpose of it being definitely stated. And it gives us a sort of veneration for the memory of the four men of the Fitzgerald patrol whose magnificent strength, after having been tried and proven on many similar journeys for years, succumbed before a combination of intolerable cold, blizzard-swept trails, unfamiliar river passes, shortage of provisions and starving train-dogs. For it was the death of these men that brought home to the people the astonishing achievements and heroisms of Canadian chivalry on the frontiers.

Fitzgerald himself, as we have already seen, had been famous for years as an intrepid patrol man, and had been promoted to the rank of Inspector for his services. All the others, Kinney, Taylor and ex-Constable Carter, had been more than once mentioned in dispatches. This is a legitimate expression, because in reality the Mounted Police were always on active service, and their merits were made known in the reports of their superior officers.

Strangely enough, from the human viewpoint, it was at Fitzgerald's own request that he was selected by the Commissioner in 1910 to take command of the Mackenzie River district. It was only the year before that he, then a staff-sergeant, had handed over that district to Inspector Jennings, but after receiving his promotion, Fitzgerald heard the insistent call of the great familiar North so overwhelmingly that he asked to be sent back into the white wastes again. And further, to vindicate some divine purpose running through it all, he suggested the patrol in that direction himself. The patrol had always been from "Dawson to Fort Macpherson and Herschell," but Fitzgerald asked to have its order reversed, and offered to go from Herschell Island to Macpherson and Dawson, from which latter point he could get into touch by wire with headquarters at Regina and report on his district. To this the Commissioner agreed, and so notified the Comptroller at Ottawa, as well as the officer commanding at Dawson, who was told to expect the patrol from Macpherson about the end of January.

When the patrol started from Fort Macpherson everything seemed favourable for a mid-winter trip. The men were all in fit condition, thoroughly acquainted with conditions of winter travel, and so keen to make a record journey that they did not burden themselves with more food than necessary for themselves and their dogs, of which they had fifteen for their three trains. The sequel proved that had they been able to keep the route they would have made Dawson in good shape. The trouble came upon them when neither map nor compass or any previous knowledge availed them in the maze of rivers and mountains that lay in their way. Taylor and Kinney had never been over the route, Fitzgerald had been over it once on another trail from the Dawson end. Carter had been over the new trail once a few years previously, but he, too, had come over it from Dawson to Macpherson, and a route with its piloting marks of bluffs and trees or banks by the way-side looks quite different when traversed the opposite way. Carter was a powerful, experienced and thoroughly reliable man, who had seen much service in the Force. Though not in the corps at the time of the patrol, he had been confident of his ability to guide the party to Dawson, and Fitzgerald had taken him on in that capacity.

The weather was intensely cold, and the going heavy, with here and there the rivers bursting up through the broken ice and creating very difficult trails. But they were all used to that, and did not mind it. Over a portage at a certain point they secured the services of an Indian, named Esau, to break trail and guide them to a certain point from which Carter was sure he knew the way. There the Indian was discharged and returned to his camp, Fitzgerald probably feeling that extra expenditure of Government funds for a guide was not justified when Carter was along.

The scene changes to Dawson. The patrol did not arrive when expected, and Superintendent A. E. Snyder, an experienced officer, who was in command there, began to get anxious, and when some

Indians arrived from the Fort Macpherson direction he got in touch with them at once. From them he learned that Esau, who had been discharged at a certain point, expected the patrol to be in Dawson many days before the day of Snyder's inquiry. Snyder, fearing the worst, became alarmed. He wired the Commissioner as to the situation, and at the same time called Corporal Dempster from Forty Mile and instructed him to get ready a party to go in search of the lost patrol. The Commissioner flashed back instructions to send out a search party, and it went without delay. It is evident from his telegram that the Commissioner, who knew the perils of the trail and had his hand on every part of the country, thought the trouble was with the failure of the guide, because he asks why the Indian, who was mentioned by Snyder, was discharged, and in order that no undue risks be taken he says, "Send a well-outfitted party."

The party sent out was fully up to requirements. Corporal Dempster was a noted traveller of those Yukon trails, and at the date of this writing is out on the same difficult route, his strength unbroken by the intervening years. For his party in search of Fitzgerald he chose Constable Fyfe, ex-Constable Turner, and an Indian, Charles Stewart. They had all been over the country again and again, and so knew it well. They were all eager to go in the hope of reaching their missing comrades. The broad outline of their duty was given them by Superintendent Snyder, with the Spartan simplicity and directness characteristic of the Mounted Police. It ran thus: "Corporal Dempster. You will leave to-morrow for a patrol over the Fort Macpherson trail to locate the whereabouts of Inspector Fitzgerald's party. Indians from Macpherson reported him on New Year's Day at Mountain Creek. Fair travelling from Mountain Creek is about twenty days to Dawson. I understand that at Hart, no matter which route he took, he would have to cross the divide. I think it would be advisable to make for this point and take up his trail from there. I cannot give you any specific instructions; you will have to be guided by circumstances and your own judgment, *bearing in mind that nothing is to stand in your way until you have got into touch with this party.*"

Dempster and his men made a record trip, both going to Macpherson and coming back. And this they did despite the fact that they had to face high winds, blinding snowstorms and flooded ice, besides searching the rivers that branched off the main route. They arrived back in Dawson on April 17, 1911, gaunt and haggard. "It's the hardest patrol I ever made," said Dempster, and that not by the perils of the way, which he was well able to meet, but because, as had already been told to the world, he had found the dead bodies of his four gallant comrades, where they had perished of cold and hunger on the way.

The first two bodies, those of Kinney and Taylor, were found some 35 miles from Macpherson, and those of Carter and Fitzgerald within a score of miles of that place. Only a short day's run from Macpherson. If those who were there had only known, how speedily they would have gone to the rescue! It appears clear from what Fitzgerald had written in his diary, the first date in which was December 21, 1910, and the last February 5, 1911, that not many days after Indian Esau had left, it became apparent that Carter had over-estimated his ability to remember the route which he had only passed over once a few years before, and that the reverse way. Many landmarks may have been removed by fire and otherwise since that time. Poor Carter! I sometimes feel he suffered more than any of them when he found that he could not find the way he thought he knew. How hard he tried day after day, leaving camp with one or other of his companions and going up one river after the other, only to find that they ended as "blind alleys," along which they could proceed no farther. And so Fitzgerald has to write on January 17: "Carter is hopelessly lost and does not know one river from another. We have only 10 lbs. of flour, 8 lbs. of bacon and some dried fish. My last hope is gone, and the only thing I can do is to return and kill some of the dogs to feed the others and ourselves. We have now been a week looking for a river to take us over the divide, but there are dozens of rivers and I am at a loss."

One asks why they had not turned back days before, and as soon as they found the route uncertain. The answer is that it was not the Police way to turn back when they were out on a definite errand. These men were of the same calibre as the young constable in the foothill country who was caught in a blizzard while out on duty, and on whose body, as already quoted, was found a paper with the words: "Lost. Horse dead. Am trying to push ahead. Have done my best."

But Fitzgerald was not alone, and had to save his men if he could. Kinney and Taylor, less strong than the others, suffered from cold and severe pains, the results perhaps of the dog meat and dog liver diet. The dogs would not eat this food, and so the men gave them the fish they had for their own use. So, in a last effort to save his men, Fitzgerald ordered the return, in the hope of making Fort Macpherson, from which they had travelled over 300 miles. He and Carter could have made it had they not been hampered by the other two, who were sick. But they would not leave them, as shown by the fact that Dempster found the camps each night were only a few miles apart. Finally, it appears that in the hope of reaching Macpherson and getting help Fitzgerald and Carter gave all the food, such as it was, and all the warm sleeping-bags to their comrades, and tried to reach Macpherson, which was only 35 miles away. They made 10 miles and then gave out and fell. Carter was evidently the first to go, for his body was laid out, his hands crossed, and a handkerchief put over his face. Then the gallant Fitzgerald succumbed, first having written with a charred stick on a paper found in his pocket his will in the fine words: "All money in dispatch bag and bank, clothes, etc., I leave to my dearly beloved Mother, Mrs. John Fitzgerald, of Halifax. God bless all. F. J. Fitzgerald, R.N.W.M.P." Many times have the initials of the old corps been written in important and honourable connections, but never with greater honour to the Force than when they were thus set down with the thought of his mother and a benediction for all by the numbed fingers of the heroic Inspector who was faithful unto death.

When Dempster and his men found the emaciated bodies and the mail which the dead men had carefully guarded they covered the bodies over reverently with brush, for their dogs were too far spent by the hard, swift trip to draw them, and went on to Fort Macpherson with the sad news. Those at Macpherson never dreamed but that the four strong, splendid men who had left them weeks before had long ere the date of Dempster's arrival reached Dawson City. The news that now came blanched all faces and cast a great gloom over that little company in the far North. Next morning, March 23, Corporal Somers and Constable Blake got together three fresh dog-teams with which, accompanied by two Indians, Somers started out at noon and returned on the 25th with the bodies of the men who had given up their lives in the line of their duty. A grave was prepared, the only one of its kind in the Northland, where the four bodies were buried side by side, in coffins made and covered with black by Somers and Dempster. The funeral was held in the Anglican Church, that devoted missionary, Rev. C. E. Whittaker, conducting the service in the presence of Mrs. Whittaker, nine white men and the native residents. Dempster says finely here: "Even though the funeral was held in the most northerly part of the Empire, away in the Arctic Circle, hundreds of miles from civilization, I am glad to be able to assure you that everything was done in connection with the last sad rites that could possibly be done under the circumstances, and I am sure that the relatives and friends of the deceased will be glad to know that it was possible to have Christian burial services read by an ordained minister of the Gospel over the bodies of their loved ones." The honours were duly paid also by their comrades, for there was a firing party of five, Somers, Blake, Dempster, Fyfe and Turner, to give the farewell salute at the graveside. In the solitude of the vast Northland the rattle of that musketry would not carry far in one sense, but it awaked echoes in hearts that understood in far places of the Empire.

When Commissioner Perry sent his final report on the matter he voiced the feelings of all when he wrote: "Their loss has been felt most keenly by every member of the Force, but we cannot but feel a thrill of pride at the endeavour they made to carry out their duty. I cannot express it better than in the following extract from a letter addressed to me by His Honour the Lieutenant-Governor of Saskatchewan: 'While the occurrence brings deepest sadness to all, we feel that such an event gives greater lustre and enduring remembrance to the splendid Force.'" And Inspector Sanders, then at Athabasca Landing, who knew the men well and had received a report from Corporal Somers, wrote a statement to the Commissioner, in which these fine sentences occur: "It would appear that Inspector Fitzgerald was the last to succumb, and that he and Carter would probably have made Fort Macpherson had they not heroically stood by their stricken and weary companions. The pathetic attention evidently paid by Inspector Fitzgerald to his dead companions was in keeping with his brave and manly character."

Memorial services were held in Dawson and other places, and at the service in Dawson Governor Alexander Henderson said: "They did not fall in the shock of battle, but, none the less, they all died nobly in the discharge of their duty and in the service of their country."

The members of the Mounted Police Force raised a large amount for the purpose of a memorial tablet, but perhaps the most eloquent, if humble, testimonies were in the wide North, where the men and their achievements were so well known for years. Corporal Somers, at Fort Macpherson, cut a copper camp kettle into strips and engraved upon them the names of the brave departed, while more recently the famous old name of Smith's Landing at the end of the Athabasca River navigation was changed to Fitzgerald as a tribute to the memory of the gallant Policeman whose name was a household word in all that country.

The fatal ending of the Fitzgerald patrol remains as the most tragic happening in the long and remarkable history of the Mounted Police. But, as already suggested, it startled our people into a fuller realization of what the men of the Force were and are doing so unobtrusively for the country at such constant risk to themselves. The passing of Fitzgerald and his companions on that frozen way will not have been in vain if our Canadian lads learn new lessons from the men whose silent tents are, at the end of the trail, pitched on the eternal camping ground of Fame. If these lessons of heroism and devotion to duty are learned and practised by the young men of to-day, then that lonely fourfold grave under the Arctic sky will prove to be one of the bulwarks of the nation.

* * * * *

CHAPTER XVI

STRIKING INCIDENTS

The White North was taking its toll of the men who were at the outposts of Empire as exponents of British administration. When Fitzgerald left Herschell Island on his last patrol, Sergeant Selig and Constable Wissenden remained in charge of that remote and lonely point, but in January, despite the efforts of his solitary white companion Wissenden, Selig, after much suffering, passed over the Great Divide. Wissenden, with the help of the natives, made a coffin and placed the body in a storehouse to await Fitzgerald's expected return. Corporal Somers and Constable Blake at Fort Macpherson heard through Hudson's Bay Company men that Selig had died in January, and before they could take any steps to go to Herschell Island, Dempster came from Dawson with the news of the death of Fitzgerald and his comrades. One can imagine the strain upon these men Somers and Blake at Macpherson, and Wissenden alone on Herschell Island, where, besides suffering loss by the death of his companion, he was so isolated from the civilized world that he did not see the face of a white man from November, 1910, till March, 1911.

But as soon as Dempster's patrol left Macpherson for Dawson, Somers, who throughout acted with a thorough sense of what was necessary and fitting, left Macpherson for Herschell Island, where he arrived in April. The body of Selig, as above stated, was awaiting the expected return of Inspector Fitzgerald. Instead of that Wissenden received now the news of the death of the members of that patrol, and not only he but the natives of the Island were greatly shocked and grieved. Then the funeral of Selig was held, Somers bringing Mr. Fry, of the Church of England Mission, from Escape Reef for the service. The mourners were the two Policemen and every Esquimaux on the Island, all following behind the dog sled which carried the coffin to the bleak burial ground. "Sergeant Selig," said Superintendent Sanders in his report of the district, "was one of the best N.C.O.'s in the Force." And Fitzgerald, who knew men in that country at first hand, said in his previous year's report: "Sergeant Selig, S.E.A., is a most efficient N.C.O., and has done excellent work in the North. Since he has been in this country he has been on every patrol, both summer and winter. He is a most capable man for any kind of work in the Northern country." He, too, fell like a good soldier, dying at his post, in the swift illness brought on by the terrific exposure of years in the Arctic. The passing of Selig at Herschell Island and in Dawson of Sergeant E. Smith, who had done notable work in the Yukon, as well as the Fitzgerald patrol, showed a heavy casualty list in 1911 as the price of holding the North and protecting its inhabitants. In some other ways that 1910-11 period was quite notable. The years were beginning to tell upon the Force, which was always popularly considered as a corps of young men. But in reality it had travelled through time for wellnigh two score of years, and men who had joined up while scarcely out of their teens had given a long day's work and were entitled to go on the pension list. Most prominent of these was Assistant Commissioner John H. McIlree, who was one of the original group. He joined up when organization was first mooted in the autumn of 1873, coming West over the difficult mud-and-water Dawson Route to the historic Lower Fort Garry, where these pioneers who were to lay the foundation of a famous corps were sworn in by Lieut.-Colonel Osborne Smith, as already related. McIlree was then Sergeant, but in the coming years, by reliable and distinguished service, worked his way up to the Assistant-Commissionership. Before his retirement he received the decoration of the Imperial Service Order in recognition of the contribution he had made to the welfare of the country. Surgeon Pare, Inspector Camies and Inspector A. M. Jarvis, who had won his C.M.G. in the South African War, also retired to pension, as did a number of well-known non-commissioned officers and men, Flintoff, McClelland, Haslett, Nicholson, Butler, Smith, Thompson, Aylesworth and Carter. On the other hand, several non-commissioned officers moved up to the Inspectorship rank; Shoebotham, Telford and Newson, who had done good service on the plains and the Northland; and Beyts, Field and French, whose remarkable patrols on the Hudson's Bay, Athabasca and Mackenzie River areas had attracted wide attention. In that period, also, a detachment consisting of seven officers and seventy-five non-commissioned officers and men, selected from all the divisions of the Force, including the Hudson's Bay and Yukon areas, went over to the King's Coronation. Commissioner Perry accompanied them, and was given a very prominent place in connection with the Coronation ceremonies. The whole contingent formed a special guard of honour on different occasions, and won high appreciation for their splendid bearing and gentlemanly character. For this highly creditable bearing and reputation which reflected honour on Canada they were specially thanked in London by Sir Wilfrid Laurier, who took great pride in the corps all through his public life.

And all the time, at the far-flung outposts of the King's Empire, the Mounted Police at home in Canada were keeping the British peace and looking after the administration of British law where the banner of Britain flew. That versatile officer, Superintendent Deane, then in command at Calgary, tells us of a peculiar case which arose out of the disappearance of an eccentric old-time rancher, named Tucker Peach. He had been known for years as "Old Tucker," and it is said that only the postmaster at Gladys, where he got his mail, and an implement agent and rancher, named Jack Fisk, knew the Peach part of it. But Peach had a big roll of money, which had been seen by one or two when he was making purchases, and this old recluse kept it about the shack he occupied, as in his eccentricity he had no use for banks. No kith or kin had he in the country, and he had mentioned to a neighbour that he was going to sell his ranch and go back to England. One day he was absent from his accustomed haunts, but as no one expected that he would say good-bye to anyone his disappearance was not considered in any way odd, and it was not reported to the Police. Some young fellow came to live on the ranch, and he was supposed to be the purchaser or his agent. And as no one on the frontier in those days cared whether his neighbour was a "duke's son or a cook's son," as long as he "played fair," nothing unusual was suspected and things resumed the even tenor of their way. The young man on the ranch later said he was tenant in charge of the place for Mitchell Robertson, who owned it, but who was then working on the train as a brakesman out of Calgary. Robertson had left word with the postmaster at Gladys that any mail coming for Peach should be forwarded to Robertson's address in Calgary.

Some months later a body, headless, was found in the river, but it was so decomposed that the Coroner, Dr. Revell, finding no trace of foul play, ordered it buried. It might have been a drowning. Later still, a skull was found near by with a hole in the centre, batting in one ear and a dent on the forehead to one side of the centre. Then Dr. Revell had the body exhumed and called an inquest. The Mounted Police took a hand and Inspector Duffus watched the case. In the meantime, Robertson vanished suddenly off the train, but was caught at MacLeod by the Mounted Police there and brought back to the inquest at Okatoks. Meanwhile, Inspector Duffus got hold of some strong evidence. Ranchers had expressed the opinion that the skull was "Old Tucker's" by its shape and by the batting, and one "old-timer" was found who said the dent in the skull near the side was from a kick by a horse years before, and that he knew it because he had helped "Old Tucker" bind up the wound at the time.

Robertson was called to give evidence, and became so mixed in his testimony that Inspector Duffus called his attention to the discrepancies. Robertson would say nothing more and Duffus, with the Coroner's permission, took him into another room, and after warning him asked him if he had anything to say. The result was a full confession of the murder. It appears that Fisk, who was disposed to terrorize people, had told Robertson that he was going to do away with "Old Tucker," and that Robertson must come with him. After it was over Robertson was to have the land and Fisk the horses in the place. They went to Tucker's shack early one morning and, knocking at the door, Robertson told who he was. The old rancher got up and admitted them, and as he was dressing Fisk shot him through the forehead, and putting the revolver into Robertson's hand said, "Now you shoot also," which Robertson did. Then they got the money, hitched up the team and drove to the river, where they dumped the body. But the river again gave up its dead.

When the confession got this far word was wired to Calgary, from where three Mounted Police went out in a motor in the night and arrested Fisk, who was taken off guard or he might have made a fight. Both Fisk and Robertson were convicted. Fisk was hanged, but Robertson, who had turned "King's evidence," was given imprisonment for life. The community breathed easier when Fisk was out of the way.

A curious and interesting sequel was furnished by a handsome dog, which had belonged to Fisk, and was with him when he murdered Peach. When Fisk was arrested the human-hearted men of the scarlet tunic, who had pursued the inhuman murderer, adopted his innocent dog and called him "Fisk." The dog attached himself to Constable Davis, and was with him when he was shot by "Running Wolf," a desperate Indian whom he was arresting. Then the dog became attached to Corporal Watts, accompanied him for four years on special duty, and was with him at Exshaw, when Watts narrowly escaped death at the hands of a desperado there. Finally, when Watts (now Sergeant, and a man who has seen much service) was moving to Vancouver with the Division, "Fisk," who had become infirm and old, was run over by a street car in Calgary. This star-witness of many crimes, concerning which he could not speak, thus closed an exciting and adventurous career.

Back further in the years another case of a somewhat similar type occurred, and all these cases indicate not only the certain and deadly precision of the Mounted Police methods in relation to the capture of criminals, but they also suggest to the imagination what the lonely prairie would have been to settlers without the presence of this watchful corps. The case to which I now refer was one in which the body of an evidently murdered man was found near Lacombe, in Alberta. There was no clue to the murderer, but Superintendent Constantine, himself a keen detective, put Sergeant Hetherington on the trail. Hetherington proved to be a persistent sleuth. All he had to start on was a buckle on the vest of the victim, indicating Kalamazoo as its place of origin. It was a far cry from Michigan, but by process of investigation one James Smith from that State came and identified the body as that of his stepson, whose name was Leon Stainton. The young man, who had some money, had left Kalamazoo, in company with a more or less chance acquaintance, generally called "Bud" Bullock, though his right name was Charles B. Bullock. But Bullock had disappeared, leaving not a trace behind. He was known to be a miner, and Hetherington got on the track of mining areas. He first went to Kalamazoo and got a sample of Bullock's writing from an hotel register. Hetherington did not expect to find Bullock's name on hotel registers after the date of the murder, but the Sergeant studied handwriting and the formation of the letters in the name. Then he came back to Calgary and searched the hotel registers till he got a name where the same letters looked alike. Bullock had changed his name, but he could not get away from the alphabet. Then Hetherington haunted the mining districts all the way from Michigan to the mountains, and searched hotel registers and pay rolls for three long months. That took a lot of dogged determination, but though he was getting new names all along the way the Sergeant detected similarity in letters, and by mingling with the miners, found out where the man had gone from place to place. Then the handwriting would be compared in that new locality. Finally, in Montana, Hetherington found on a pay roll a new name where similar letters corresponded, and the man was at work there. The Sergeant went amongst the miners, recognized Bullock, and putting his hand on his shoulder said, "Hello, Bullock." The man started and said, "My name is not Bullock." "Oh yes, it is," said the Mounted Policeman, "it is Charles B. Bullock, *alias* Bud Bullock, and I am here to arrest you for the murder of Leon Stainton, near Ponoka, in Alberta." Then the man caved in and said, "I always felt that the red-coats would get me, even if it took years." He owned up, and as it was useless to fight extradition he came back with Hetherington and after trial paid the penalty for his crime. But think of the endless patience and doggedness of Hetherington, who, with only a scrap of handwriting on a fragment of paper, searched for months, day and night, over half a continent for similar letter formations till he landed his man. It was the Mounted Police way.

INSPECTOR FITZGERALD.
Died on Yukon Patrol. Photo. Rossie, Regina.

SUPT. CHARLES CONSTANTINE.
Pioneer Policeman in the Yukon.
Photo. Steele & Co., Winnipeg.

INSPECTOR LA NAUZE.

With prisoners "Sinnisiak" and "Uluksak," at Bernhard Harbour. June, 1916.

In 1912 we find Commissioner Perry still battling to the end that the services of all ranks in his command should receive recognition in the form of higher remuneration for the good reasons that the cost of living was going up; that men in civil life were getting much more for less important and dangerous work, and that the enormously increasing population of the West made ever larger calls upon the efforts and the initiative powers of the officers and men. And the Commissioner, who is always intent on keeping the Force on a high level, said that if the increased pay was granted there would possibly be more applications than vacancies. In such a case he would aim at constantly improving the personnel of the corps by accepting recruits on probation only, by discharging those lacking in energy, intelligence and character, and by making dismissal the most severe punishment that could be handed out to any member of the Force. The Commissioner's far-sighted policy in this and other regards has always told favourably on the high prestige of the Corps.

That year 1912 witnessed an unusual number of changes in the Force. Chief amongst these changes was the loss sustained by the death, in California, of Superintendent Charles Constantine, who had served in the Force for twenty-six years, after having seen active duty in the suppression of the two Riel Rebellions. I have already made special reference to the work of this officer, with whom I served when he was Adjutant of the Winnipeg Light Infantry. He never advertised or pushed himself forward, but by sheer force of character his merits became known increasingly throughout the years. His death was widely mourned, not only by his comrades, but by the people of the vast country where he had done so much foundation work. At the time of his passing out, Commissioner Perry, who knew the Force so well, wrote: "Because of his strength of character, sound judgment and physical strength, he was selected for much of the pioneer work of the Force. He was the first to command in the Yukon Territory, and in the early days of the gold rush his tact and firmness established the reputation of that gold camp as the most orderly in the world. Subsequently he was employed in the far North, and in the strenuous work of the Peace-Yukon road-making, contracted the disease which eventually caused his death." Constantine had taken a large share in Western history, and his name will not be forgotten on the roll of the makers of the country.

In that same year also two prominent officers who, as this record shows, had done splendid service in very difficult places all over the frontiers, and who had served with distinction in the Boer War, Superintendents G. E. Sanders, D.S.O., and A. E. Snyder, retired to pension. Others in recognition of merit were moved up to fill vacancies, Inspectors T. A. Wroughton, F. J. A. Demers, F. J. Horrigan, all tried men, becoming Superintendents, and such well-known non-commissioned officers as F. A. Gordon, A. E. Acland, J. W. Spalding, T. Dann, and G. W. Currie being promoted to the rank of Inspectors. Dr. S. M. Fraser was raised to the full rank of Surgeon, and Drs. W. H. Mewburn and E. A. Braithwaite, all of whom had been prominent on the frontiers, were made honorary

Surgeons. Thus were men coming and going. That year, over 200 recruits were added to the Force, which even then was less than 700 to patrol a territory larger than half-a-dozen European kingdoms.

To illustrate how the Mounted Police always sprang in to help in emergencies we recall at that time that a disastrous cyclone hit the City of Regina, where the Mounted Police Headquarters were at that time. Cyclones are rare occurrences in Canada, but after one sultry day this black tempest arose on the prairie and tore through the city, leaving death and destruction in its wake. The whole resources of the Mounted Police were placed at the disposal of the city. Officers and men worked with a will, unresting in their efforts to rescue the injured and make the city safe for the living. Every night till the trouble was over they kept guard over life and property, always in danger at such times, and the following, in a letter from the Mayor of Regina to Commissioner Perry, is a fine testimony. Referring to the work of the various organizations that had been at work during that time of trial, Mayor McAra says: "We have had so much reason to be satisfied with the working of the various organizations that had in charge the different features of the work in connection with this storm that it is difficult to express oneself adequately as to the services rendered by these several organizations. We believe, however, that the services of the various organizations have only been made possible by the service rendered by your Force. I believe that perhaps more was done to establish a sane understanding of the situation by the officers and men of your patrol than in any other way and, appreciating this, it is difficult for me on behalf of the Committee in charge, to properly express the feeling of gratitude we have." Herein did Mayor McAra, who knew the Force well, express a truth that had application not only to the situation after the Regina cyclone, but to the history of the West, namely, that the presence of the Mounted Police made the country safe for those who desired to develop its resources in the ways of industrious peace.

As another piece of evidence for the truth of this general statement, let me instance several letters of thanks and appreciation from officials, engineers and contractors on the Hudson's Bay Railway in 1913 to Inspector French, who was in command of the Mounted Police in the district. Vice-President Boyd wrote: "The services of the R.N.W.M.P. have been most satisfactory, the conduct of the Force stationed here and along our works being a credit to the honoured institution of which they are members." Assistant Chief Engineer Garrow: "In my opinion the general good conduct of the men in our employ and the prevention of trouble usually caused by illicit whisky-peddling has been obtained by the systematic campaign that you waged on the opening of this construction. In my personal dealings with yourself, Sergeant Munday and staff I found all courteous, always willing to co-operate and to take prompt action in case of emergency." Mr. M. McMillan, the Chief Sub-contractor, wrote: "I wish to compliment you and the members of the Force under your command on the very efficient manner in which you and they have policed the line of construction of the Hudson's Bay railway. I have never had a gang of men on any contract where there was less friction and less whisky on the work than on this job, and I realize that it is to you and your Force that we owe this state of affairs. I trust we shall all be together on the Nelson end of the steel." This, we repeat, is another instance of the way in which the men in scarlet and gold provided an environment and an atmosphere in which the industrial development of the country could be carried on under conditions that made for success. While never taking part with either employer or employed, the firm, impartial and tactful Mounted Police Force often became a living windbreak against social tempests, which without it might, at times, have thrown both sides into confusion and have wrecked projects that were vital to the progress of the Dominion.

While going through old annual reports of the work of the Police one is struck by the frequency with which one comes across deeds of heroism, which were only noted formally in a few lines at the time, and which have lain buried out of sight ever since. But if they had been done on other fields they would have won wide publicity and many decorations.

There is not much of a thrill playing on the surface of a report given by Constable Wight, who was the whole detachment at a village in Alberta. But one cannot read it in a short paragraph without finding between the lines a lot of danger in small compass. A man named Winning, who perhaps presumed on his name, decided at 1 a.m. that he did not like the room the night clerk had given him at the hotel, and wanted it changed. Rooms were not plentiful in these small places, and there was no other to be had, on finding out which, Mr. Winning, after raising a general disturbance to the discomfort of the other guests, went away and came back shortly with several sticks of dynamite. He said he was going to blow up the hotel, and this declaration did not add to the peace of mind of the hotel clerk and the guests. The town constable was on hand, but the gentleman with the sticks of dynamite flourished them, and said he would blow the constable to fragments if he interfered. Mounted Police-Constable Wight, who was some distance away, was awakened and told of the situation. Meantime, Mr. Winning, who had not committed any overt act, had retired to a camp near by with his high explosives. But Constable Wight got an information sworn out against him for having an explosive in his possession with intent to endanger life, which was putting it mildly enough when he was in fact dealing with a man running amuck with dynamite playthings. However, this served the purpose of Constable Wight, who rode out to the camp and arrested the man, explosives and all. It was not a very pleasant undertaking, but that did not count for anything with a wearer of the scarlet tunic out on duty.

Several times in this book has come the necessity for expressing regret that there is no decoration for valour in time of peace corresponding to the Victoria Cross in times of war. Of the two we have good ground for thinking that a gallant deed done in peace time in cold blood and with a full sense of the danger, is at least as great as the same kind of deed done when the blood is hot with battle and the risk is unknown or unconsidered. Take, for instance, the case of Constable Moorehead, as related not by himself (the Mounted Policeman's eleventh commandment is not to talk), but in a letter to Superintendent Primrose from Dr. Nyblett, the coroner near Nanton, Alberta, where was a reducing plant of the Natural Gas Company. The letter says, "It was reported to Constable Moorehead that some men were suffocating in the high-pressure station and he immediately rode over." He had no orders to go except from his own conscience, but there was no hesitation, though he knew the supreme danger. The letter goes on. "There was a disconnected four-inch pipe, with a pressure of 125 pounds to the inch, in the building, and Constable Moorehead could see one of the bodies moving and he thought there was life." It was probably being moved by the terrific gas pressure. "Moorehead placed his hat over his mouth and went in; on getting near the bodies the jet of gas struck him and blew him to the other side of the building; there he groped for the door, but was too nearly unconscious to find it. Another man who had come up saw him and was able to reach in and pull Moorehead out. When Moorehead recovered consciousness he found a bar and prised off some of the corrugated iron near the bodies. He then crawled in through the hole with the other man holding his feet, and pulled out one of the bodies; he then went in again and got another. He was so weak and exhausted by this time that he had not strength to pull the third out, but crawled in and tied a rope to it, and after it was pulled out did the same with the fourth." "Unless one was actually there," says the coroner, "it would be very difficult to realize just how plucky this act was. The pressure of the escaping gas was so great that the caps of the men were held up against the roof of the building, and the poisoning by this gas in large quantities is instantaneous."

We have not read anywhere in the annals of war a finer tale of gallantry. Constable Moorehead got another stripe for "conspicuous bravery" and became Corporal, received a small grant from the fine fund, and at a full-dress parade of the Division was presented by Judge McNeill with the bronze medal of the Royal Canadian Humane Association. All this was very suitable, but I still think there is room for a peace-time decoration up to the level of the Victoria Cross.

During the year 1912 there was constant oversight exercised in the Hudson's Bay and Mackenzie River districts, as well as in the Yukon. All this involved much dangerous patrol work, but it was carried out without any untoward happening. Superintendent Demers, Inspectors Beyts and French were in the former districts with a small but excellent body of men; Superintendent Moodie and Inspector Acland were in the Yukon and White Horse districts. In the Yukon there was a serious case of dynamiting dredges which Sergeant Mapley handled with great ability. Patrols and general oversight by these non-commissioned officers and constables may, to the superficial onlooker or reader, seem of no great value, but these men, by tact and firm, friendly dealing with the natives and traders, really introduced a new code of ethics in the Northland. The questions at stake may not have been very large ones from our standpoint, but the ownership of a sled-dog or the fairness of values in exchange of furs, were as important to the children of the wild as the possession of a province might be to people in Europe. And in these local matters these patrolmen became recognized as fair and impartial adjudicators whose word was law. Thus were new ideals as to the rights of property and the sacredness of life being inculcated in the vast spaces of the Arctic.

And these sturdy, courageous Policemen became so greatly interested in their strenuous work that they were always ready for a larger venture. It is interesting to find Corporal C. D. LaNauze, after returning from a patrol of some fifty-two days and over 1,000 miles, writing: "I cannot speak too highly of my dogs. I would like to see how far I could go with this train." Well, he was to get his opportunity to find out shortly. Whether with that train of dogs or not we cannot say, but when the opportunity came he used it to the limit.

There were some lonely places. Sergeant Edgenton, a noted patrolman in the Arctic, writes as to Cape Fullerton on Hudson Bay: "Fullerton during the winter has been very lonely. Constable Conway and myself and two natives were the only persons there." And it is rather a striking instance of Police methods to find Edgenton putting in the usual detachment report and, under the head of discipline, speaking highly of Conway: "I have had to leave him alone during my patrols, and always found everything in good order on returning. He is a good man for duty in the North, and has made several patrols in very cold weather." Other men well known in that district were non-commissioned officers like Sergeants Handcock, Belcher, Currie, Mellor, LaNauze, Jones and several Constables. And, like the army of Sparta, which was the wall around that country, "every man was a brick."

* * * * *

CHAPTER XVII

THE GREAT WAR PERIOD

The year 1914 gave us in history the spectacle of world-wide sword play, the rattle of machine-guns, and the roar of heavy artillery, along with an unprecedented loss of human life. It saw the British Empire, taken unprepared save for the Grand Fleet, hurling itself against the most colossal war machinery the world had ever seen assembled by one nation. And it saw this because Britain, pledged by a "scrap of paper," ordinarily called a treaty, to preserve the undamaged neutrality of Belgium against Germany or any one else, counted no cost too great for the maintenance of her sacred honour. But that fateful year saw our men not only on the field of struggle, but witnessed our people, whom the necessities of the case forced to remain behind, steadily keeping the wheels of industry turning at the base of supply, preventing internal discord and maintaining the integrity of the country unbroken, despite hostile influences that were at work. It is a common expression that when the Empire is at war Canada is at war. That saying has been proven again and again till it has become an undisputed axiom. It had been demonstrated before 1914, and then demonstrated again, till it needs no further proof. It is part of the Empire's history that the far-flung colonies of Britain are at her side when danger threatens their mother. Hence, at the sound of the war trumpet, Canadians rushed to the Colours.

Amongst the first who desired to be sent to the Front after the general call had gone out were the Royal North-West Mounted Police, who hoped to go as a unit. The request was made at the outset, renewed in 1917 and 1918. But the Canadian Government, fully aware of certain conditions in the country, not only refused this request, but ordered that the Mounted Police should be reinforced by the enlistment of 500 more men for important duty in Canada.

What those duties were could easily be gathered from the general situation. At the beginning, the United States did not go into the war, and the authorities there, who have always worked in friendly co-operation with our Police, intimated that there was a good deal of pro-enemy activity amongst alien elements south of the line. The American authorities would not knowingly allow their country to become the base of hostile operations against us, but, as in the case of the Fenian raids into Canada, it was possible for enemies along a 3,000-mile border to elude them and cross over to make serious trouble for us. Hence it was necessary that an experienced body of men should patrol the boundary region, and the riders of the plains were the only men who could carry out that task.

Later on, when the United States entered the war, this work became unnecessary, but there was still special need for the vigilance of this famous corps, whose great record and prestige gave such unique authority to their presence in any locality that nothing more was necessary. There were 175,000 German and Austrian settlers in the prairie sections of Canada, a quite formidable army if mobilized. It was specially necessary that the Government of the country, backed by visible authority, should see that this large number of people was prevented from making any hostile demonstrations against the flag under whose shelter they had sought new homes. And it was equally desirable and British to see that these immigrants, as long as they observed and respected the laws and institutions of the country whose citizens they had become, should not be irritated or persecuted by perfervid and unthinking loyalists. An immigrant cannot help his racial origin, and if the country has thrown open its doors to his coming to help in its development, and if he becomes a law-abiding Canadian, he is entitled to protection. To the credit of all concerned, it is good to be able to say that there was no trouble worth noting. There were some tried and convicted for seditious utterances, but, generally speaking, they were not of alien race. Doubtless the German in the middle west of Canada was glad to be away from the cast-iron military system of his Fatherland, and the Austrian was pleased to be out of the "ramshackle Empire"; while at the same time, the

Canadians around, like true British men, were willing to let these immigrants make good in this land of the second chance. But both were helped in their good intentions by the tact and firmness of the riders in scarlet and gold.

Besides all that, the Government knew perfectly well that a time of war is fruitful in opportunity for the man who wishes to upset human society by revolutionary methods. Hosts of the cool-headed thinking men are away at such a time, and in the general confusion the faddist and the anarchist get a chance to put their theories into practice. But, as Thomas Carlyle said, "It costs too much to have a revolution strike on the horologe of time to tell the world what o'clock it is"; and so it was important that destructive movements should be held in check. And, accordingly, the Dominion authorities felt that the Mounted Police should be on the ground. Further, in order that the Mounted Police could have an oversight of conditions and situations which, though more pronounced at some points, were in reality nation-wide, the Dominion Government decided that absorbing the Dominion Police, the famous Royal North-West Mounted Police should have their jurisdiction extended over the whole of Canada, from the Yukon and the Arctic clear across to the Atlantic coast. This involved the moving of headquarters from Regina to the seat of Government at Ottawa, the placing of detachments all over Canada, and the substitution of the word "Canadian" for the words "North-West" in the title of the corps. This change in the title gave to the "old-timers" who had served in the Force, and to us who had known it under the old name, a sort of sentimental shock, and was the subject of several protests, but it soon became apparent that the change of name was the necessary accompaniment of the extension of jurisdiction. It would be manifestly improper to retain the limited territorial designation of "North-West" when the territory to be covered by the Force was from sea to sea. In fact, the changes as to title and jurisdiction now commend themselves to all who study the whole situation, and credit in this connection is due to the Hon. N. W. Rowell, who, as the governmental head of the Force and a great admirer of its work, brought these changes to pass.

There was some discussion in the House of Commons when the changes above mentioned were proposed. But in answer to questions as to the necessity for the change being made in extending the jurisdiction of the Mounted Police and placing detachments all over the country East as well as West, Mr. Rowell gave clear and cogent reasons. It was pointed out by him that there had been for years a Dominion Police Force, under Sir Percy Sherwood, and that, as this Dominion Force was now absorbed by the Mounted Police, there was no duplication of law administration agencies. Broadly speaking, the Mounted Police have to discharge most important duties all over Canada for all branches of the Federal Government in seeing the laws observed in which the Federal Government is particularly interested, because these laws relate to the public revenue or to special Departments of Dominion administration. Thus, for instance, the Mounted Police have to investigate all matters in which Federal property is lost or misappropriated; they have to assist the Customs Department in preventing the all-too-common crime of smuggling, and the Department of Inland Revenue in regard to illicit liquor traffic. They have to co-operate with the Department of Indian affairs, and the Department of Colonization and Immigration in regard to the admission of citizens who may or may not be desirable, and also look into all matters connected with the nationalization of aliens. And more than once of late the Dominion Department of Agriculture has asked the assistance of the Mounted Police in stamping out epidemics amongst stock.

And that the placing of the Mounted Police all over Canada was opportune is evidenced by the fact that, under the guise of legitimate strikes, movements were begun which led to a sort of reign of terror in some communities, and in connection with which the real motive of some who manipulated them was shown, by evidence convincing to Judges and Juries, to be nothing short of seditious conspiracy to overthrow the constitutional government of this country. Incriminating papers were found in many Canadian cities in the possession of many who were suspected of sedition. And a curious thing arose when these suspected men raised their voices in appeal to the very law of the land which they had been denouncing to protect them from prosecution. Or, as Commissioner Perry, who gave very special and serious study to the whole situation, says: "Appeal is made by these men to British fair play to protect them in their efforts to destroy British fair play."

Winnipeg was chosen by the agitators as the storm centre of their movement, and it began in the shape of a strike by the metal-workers, led by radicals of a pronounced type, who used the strike idea to further their revolutionary aims, and who devoted themselves to bringing about a general sympathetic strike in order to paralyse the business of the city and thus help their enterprise. The radicals succeeded in securing a general strike even to the post office staff and mail clerks, and this led to similar sympathetic movements in Brandon, Saskatoon, Edmonton, Calgary and Vancouver. No doubt a great many in the various organizations going on strike acted honestly with the idea in their minds that the Winnipeg movement was of a genuine type and for usual and legitimate purposes. But the leaders at that point showed their real aim plainly when they started to take the control of the city out of the hands of the Mayor and Council, and indicated by printed cards that the only industries that would be allowed to continue were those that would run "by permission of the Strike Committee." Winnipeg was about the last city that would stand dictation from any other than their own elected representatives, and so citizens organized themselves to withstand the methods of the radicals and to uphold properly constituted authority. It was a critical hour in the history of that city and the whole of Canada.

The Mounted Police that were in Winnipeg in pursuance of the policy of distribution over the whole Dominion were under the competent command of Superintendent Starnes, who, as we have seen, had done important work in the Yukon, Hudson's Bay and prairie districts, and was known as a man of experience and sound judgment in emergencies. The Mounted Police did not interfere in the "strike," except by taking steps to protect life and property, and to see that public services, such as the carrying and distribution of His Majesty's mails, were not hindered. But on the 21st of June, 1919, the Mayor, being unable to cope with the situation, called for the assistance of the Mounted Police to prevent a parade of thousands who were defying the city authorities. Thereupon fifty-four mounted men, under Inspectors Proby and Mead, with thirty-six men in trucks, under Sergt.-Major Griffin, were sent out from barracks, Commissioner Perry, as well as Superintendent Starnes, being present with the Attorney-General of Manitoba. A reserve was held in barracks, under Sergt.-Major Greenway, but it was not required.

It did not take the mounted men of the old corps long to get control of the situation, though they were only a handful. When they arrived on the scene near the City Hall, they were received with showers of stones, shots and other missiles. But they maintained their reputation for restraint, and it was not till two of the men were in danger, through their horses falling and through a charge from the mob, that the officer commanding the Mounted Force gave the order to draw their revolvers and use them. This had the desired effect of clearing the street and of dispersing the rioters. Some sixteen of the Mounted Police were wounded with missiles, while on the other side one foreigner was killed, one fatally wounded, and several others hurt. This shows that the Mounted Police preserved their reputation for refraining from taking the aggressive until there was no other course open. But from that day the "strike" lost its strength. Hundreds of the strikers began to see through the real aims of their radical leaders and returned to work. A few days later the "strike" was officially called "off," and the sympathetic movements in the other cities died at the same time, to the general relief of all concerned. Events of a somewhat similar kind were happening sporadically here and there during the war period, and they still appear occasionally. We may get to a stage where government is not required in an angelic state of human society. But so long as there remains a proportion of human beings who glory in disorder and revolt against lawful authority in a democratic country like ours, where people through their elected representatives really make their own laws, there will be need for the men in scarlet and gold to preserve the peace, to prevent wanton damage to necessary industries, to protect human life, and generally to prevent society from sliding into the abyss of chaos.

We have emphasized at several points in this story the efforts made by the Mounted Police to get into the war from the outset. And we have indicated the grounds on which the Government declined to allow them to go abroad, when the situation at home demanded their presence. Of course, many of the Police, probably not less than a thousand, in various ways, by resigning individually or buying discharge, or by virtue of their term of enlistment lapsing, had managed to get away to the war during the years before a unit from the Force was permitted to go overseas. These men served with great distinction on many fields of the colossal conflict. In the House of Commons, the Hon. N. W. Rowell, in speaking on the subject, said: "I wish I had time to tell the House of some of the deeds of those gallant men. I will only mention two. The famous Michael O'Leary, V.C., was one of the North-West Mounted Police, and he set a standard for courage and bravery during the early days of the war which many other gallant soldiers have since emulated. The other, a constable in the ranks for two years—Constable Parkes, a young man now twenty-seven years of age. In 1915 he purchased his discharge to go to the front; he rose to the command of the 116th Battalion, C.E.F., and won the V.C., the D.S.O., and La Croix de Guerre. He proved himself an officer of the highest efficiency, and has been selected by the Canadian Corps to attend the staff college. I might mention other members of the Force and the gallant service they have rendered, but time does not permit. I should also mention that ex-members of the Force—that is, men who had served on the Force—provided our Canadian Army overseas with two major-generals, four brigade-generals, and colonels, majors and captains by the score. It shows the type of men who are serving in our Royal North-West Mounted Police." And one thinks at once in this connection of such men as that old campaigner and ex-Policeman, the late Sir Samuel B. Steele, who went over in command of the Second Division, but whose health, undermined by an injury on the way, did not permit him to lead his men in the field; of that dashing and distinguished Cavalry Officer, Sir Archibald Macdonnell, now Commandant at Kingston, and of Brigadier-General Ketchen, who came up from the ranks, and of many others. And then Mr. Rowell went on to say: "All the sons, of military age, of the present and past officers have served overseas, and no less than ten officers' sons died on the battlefield. The son of the first man who joined the Force in 1873 is an honourable and gallant member of this House—Brigadier-General Griesbach (of Edmonton), who has rendered such distinguished service in this war. He is one of the many gallant officers, sons of members of the Force who have served overseas."

One would like to place special stress on the way in which the sons and even the daughters of the first generation of the Mounted Police kept up the great tradition of their fathers, who had instilled into them that devotion to duty and that desire to maintain the right which made the old Force so well known in every part of the world. The names of these gallant young men and women are found in practically every unit of service in the Great War as combatants, nurses and so on, all showing that blood tells, and that the theory of heredity can find in such cases a real and indisputable demonstration.

And, while touching upon this phase, let me also mention that another unique tribute to the way in which the Force got hold of the imagination and enlisted the devotion of those who served in its ranks, is the fact that ex-members all over Canada organized in evidence of their desire to support the parent body in any crisis that may arise. Several hundred of these men, experienced in every detail of the work and trained to the minute, left their occupations and put themselves at the disposal of the Commissioner during the war, when the Force was depleted by enlistments for the front. Any organization that can thus count on the assistance of its former members in the hour of need, must have had elements in it that appealed to the best qualities of real men. Hence we find that the war and the social unrest called into being Police Veterans' Associations, whose aim is to continue the traditions of the corps, and whose members hold themselves at the service of the Government of Canada whenever required. In other words, anyone who tries to play "rough house" where these veterans' associations exist will have to reckon with the "old boys," who once wore the unforgettable scarlet and gold. And what is here said of the men is equally true of the wives and mothers and sisters of the riders of the Western plains.

But one of the most conclusive pieces of evidence as to the real quality of the men of the Mounted Police was given when, in those dark and deadly-looking days near the close of the war, the British Government let it be known that another cavalry unit from Canada would be acceptable. A call was placed before the Mounted Police to provide reinforcements for the Canadian Cavalry Brigade, which had suffered serious losses, and also to furnish a squadron to add as a distinct Police unit to the Cavalry Corps. In one sense it was not a good time to appeal for recruits. The allied army was fighting with its back to the wall. Our cavalry brigade had been decimated and all along the line our men were falling—

> "Grimly dying, still unconquered
> With their faces to the foe."

But every man in the Mounted Police wanted to go and help hold that line. Five hundred men were desired, but there was a rush, and before word could be got out by wire to stop recruiting, over 700, including some ex-members, had enlisted and had to be accepted.

This contingent was divided into four squadrons, the whole coming, of course, under orders of the Militia Department as part of the C.E.F., and on May 19, 1918, the following order was issued from Militia Headquarters at Ottawa: "The following provisional appointments of Officers in the C.E.F. are authorized: To be Major, Inspector G. L. Jennings; to be Captain, Inspector H. M. Newson; to be Lieutenants, Inspectors A. B. Allard, A. E. Acland, Thomas Dann, S. T. Wood, J. McD. Tupper, W. C. Proby, C. H. King, Denis Ryan, C. D. La Nauze, H. Townsend, Sergts.-Major T. H. Irvine, F. J. Mead, R. H. L. MacDowell." These were all Officers and Sergts.-Major in the R.N.W.M. Police, and were recommended by the Commissioner for the positions named.

Inspectors Jennings, Allard and Newson have since been promoted Superintendents, and Sergts.-Major Irvine and Mead have been granted commissions in the Force. Putting the draft into regular military form as a provisional Regiment, it was composed of four Squadrons and Headquarters Staff as follows:—To command the overseas Cavalry Draft and special Squadron, Major G. L. Jennings; to be second in command, Captain H. M. Newson; to be Acting Adjutant, Lieutenant R. H. L. MacDowell; to be Acting Regimental Sergt.-Major, Sergt.-Major G. F. Griffin; to be Acting Regimental Quartermaster-Sergeant, Staff-Sergeant A. H. L. Mellor (since promoted Inspector).

Squadron Officers: "A" Squadron—Lieutenants A. B. Allard (in command), H. Townsend and F. J. Mead. "B" Squadron—Lieutenants T. Dann (in command), S. T. Wood and D. Ryan. "C" Squadron—Lieutenants W. C. Proby (in command), C. D. La Nauze, and J. McD. Tupper. "D" Squadron—Lieutenants C. H. King (in command), A. E. Acland and T. H. Irvine. Also to be Acting Sergts.-Major of the above Squadrons in order named, the following Mounted Police N.C.O.'s, viz.:—Sergts.-Major W. A.

Edgenton, C. R. Peters, C. F. Fletcher and F. E. Spriggs. The whole draft was taken on the strength of the Canadian Expeditionary Force, and all members who were actively connected with the Mounted Police were on leave of absence from their corps until they would be demobilized on return to Canada.

On reaching England the men of the contingent were pretty well scattered by being assigned for duty with various units, but, finally, the Mounted Police Squadron to be attached to the Canadian Light Horse was sent over to France, arriving, to their disappointment, too late to take part in the Battle of Cambrai, where cavalry played a conspicuous part. But Major Jennings was requested to detail some of his men for "Dispatch Riding" in the 2nd and 3rd Canadian Divisions. Lieutenant Dann with 2nd Troop was sent to the 2nd Canadian Division, and Lieutenant Wood with 3rd Troop was sent to the 3rd Canadian Division, and remained there till the Armistice was signed. This was dangerous and difficult front-line work, and was done to the entire satisfaction of the Division Commanders, as was to be expected when the riders of the plains were on duty. The Squadron also furnished every day N.C.O.'s and men to go to different points immediately back of the front line to collect prisoners of war, and escort them to the different camps. And one who knows the record of the Mounted Police needs not to be told that not one prisoner escaped from their custody in France, Belgium and Germany. On October 28, probably in recognition of the thoroughness with which these trained and disciplined men from the Canadian plains had carried out every duty that had been assigned them, orders were issued that the Mounted Police were to be detached from the Canadian Light Horse and become an independent unit, to be known as the Royal North-West Mounted Police Squadron. This was the situation up to the Armistice, when the dispatch-riding troops, under Lieutenants Dann and Wood, rejoined the Squadron. Instructions came to have a troop sent to Mons, to be there at the triumphal entry, but this was found impossible. The horses of the dispatch-riding troops were completely fagged out with their strenuous work, another troop was on prisoners-of-war service, while the horses of the fourth were unshod and could not make the 32 kilos. over the paved road to Mons. Later, Acland's troop went on duty to a point near Bonn, in Germany, and Lieutenants King and Allard were sent on special service into Belgium. Things were in much confusion, and the presence of the scarlet riders seemed to give the people satisfaction.

The whole Squadron was kept busy at various points till December, when the Canadian Government, realizing that conditions at home demanded the presence of these recognized champions of law and order, sent a cable recalling the Mounted Police to duty in Canada. There was much to be done in the way of detail arrangements, gathering up the scattered members out of other units, re-enlisting for service in Canada, but in due course, after having added another highly creditable page to the history of the corps, the Squadron reached Winnipeg.

It was rather a striking coincidence that at the very time when Winnipeg was boiling over with red radicalism, this Canadian Mounted Police unit, that had been on service at the Front, arrived in that city. Things being as they were at that point, the Commissioner had Jenning's command detrain there. For some days they were held in reserve in the barracks, and no doubt the presence of these seasoned and disciplined men had a reassuring influence on good citizens, and a very deterrent effect upon the lawless advocates of violence and sedition. Their active participation was not necessary, and so they continued out into the various detachments all over the West and North. It is interesting to know that at the time of this writing Major (Superintendent) Jennings, who knows the vast North-land and its perils well, is in command of the Mounted Police at Edmonton, the front gateway to the new oil-fields. These men will see that human life and property are as safe there as in any part of Canada. The "gunman" and the disorderly and the lewd exploiter of camps and frontiers will not get into the country at all, and the unfit and unprepared and unequipped, however respectable, will be saved from the reckless folly that would send them on a wild rush into a country whose perils they do not know.

In summing up his report of the Overseas Squadron, Major Jennings indicates that the fine reputation for good behaviour made by the Mounted Police when in the Old Land, at Coronation or Jubilee celebrations, was fully maintained amid the temptations incident to war. He says, "The moral conduct of the men was most satisfactory." In regard to matters of discipline he states: "To my knowledge there was not one member of the Overseas Cavalry

Draft brought before a Court Martial. The offences were few and of a minor character, mostly due to ignorance in new surroundings, but the principal reason for the small number of offences was without doubt due to the discipline enforced by the old N.C.O.'s of the Force." "Sergeant What's-his-name" has always been one of the mainstays of the Army. And the Major adds: "No charge was ever brought against an officer." A good record in war.

In noting men's services, Major Jennings says: "Where all ranks showed such a spirit of loyalty to the unit and to the Force and such determination to do their duty, it is difficult to single out individual cases." This is fine, but there are some always who have special opportunities for service come their way, and so the Major specially mentions Captain H. M. Newson, Lieutenants Acland, Allard, Dann, Wood and MacDowell; and amongst the N.C.O.'s, Mellor, Darling, Edgenton, Peters, Fletcher, Spriggs and Hogan. The Major recommends for decoration Sergeant C. A. James, a highly efficient man who, while on dispatch-riding duty, captured single-handed five of the enemy and brought them into camp. Also Constable A. Brooker, a dispatch rider, who took a pack horse with telephone wire through heavy shell and machine-gun fire to advance Headquarters, thus enabling them to send back valuable information. Finally, Major Jennings expresses his own obligation for having been given the command, but his heart is with the corps, and he says: "No officer would ask to command a finer body of men. The high standard of discipline inculcated through years in the Force was adhered to throughout."

It will be recalled that shortly before the Armistice date it was thought that Canada ought to be represented, as well as the Americans and the Japanese, up in that perplexing land of Russia. Accordingly, a squadron of cavalry, to be known as "B" Squadron R.N.W.P., Siberia, was authorized. The officers were all of well-known names in Mounted Police annals, being:

Major in Command: George Stanley Worsley.
Captain, Second in Command: Arthur William Duffus.
Lieutenants: Richard Young Douglas, Thomas Mulock Belcher (now Superintendent), Frank Henry French, Thomas Caulkin.

Of these French, of the famous Bathurst Inlet patrol, related in the next chapter, was prevented by illness from going, and was replaced by Sergt.-Major Wilcox. Caulkin, whom we met before in this story in the vast spaces of the Arctic, was awarded about this time the King's Police Medal for service in that white North-land.

This Siberian Squadron passed through some trying experience by reason of epidemics, and by reason also of the unsettled conditions in Vladivostok and other points where they were quartered. They passed through train wrecks at the hands of Bolshevists, and various other exciting experiences. And Constable Pilkington, who penetrated into the interior of the country, gives some vivid stories of Bolshevik exploits. The Squadron did its whole duty, and did it well, but in a few months the Canadian Government decided to withdraw from the Russian situation, and so recalled the Force to duty in the Dominion, after an absence of several months in the enigmatic land.

Thus, whether amid the puzzling problems of the war period in the homeland, or in the face of new situations abroad, did the riders of the plains, to the full extent of their opportunity, make their usual thorough-going contribution to Canada's part in the making of human history. East, West, North or South, they have always answered the call to duty. In a word, they have always been on active service.

* * * * *

CHAPTER XVIII

GREAT TRADITIONS UPHELD

In the foregoing chapter I have, in order to preserve the continuity of the Police story through the war period, gone a little ahead of the chronological order of general events in the history of the corps. But history was being made all the time by these remarkable men, whether they were serving at home or abroad. They were always and everywhere on active duty, and "peace hath her victories no less renowned than war." Riding with dispatches in France was not more active and dangerous service than patrolling over the immense areas of trackless snow and ice in the Arctic Circle or facing overwhelmingly superior numbers where mobs were surging restlessly and riotously in our own country. Here and there on the plains or in the mountains little detachments were without display or advertisement carrying out tasks that were onerous and disagreeable in the extreme.

For instance, we have the story of a great mine disaster at Hill Crest, Alberta, where by a terrific explosion 188 men out of the 237 who had entered the mine on a June morning in 1914 lost their lives. The Mounted Police as usual rushed to the scene to see what they could do to relieve the situation, Inspector Junget taking charge. Experienced miners were at work bringing out the bodies, it being evident from the first that none but the few men who had come up in an exhausted condition were alive. The detachment of Mounted Police only numbered six, but they took effective oversight at once, first closing the bar of the local hotel in order to head off the danger of drunkenness breaking out in the camp. Corporal Searle and Constable Kistruck, from Pincher Creek, and Constable Wilson, from MacLeod, were posted at the entrance to the two mines to keep the crowd back and preserve order generally, while Corporals Mead and Grant and Constable Hancock looked after the mutilated bodies as they were brought out of the mine. Mead and Grant kept the check numbers of the bodies where they could be found, kept an inventory of the money or other property found on each, then washed the bodies, and wrapped them in cotton sheets. Then these bodies were taken to the Mine-Union Hall, where Constable Hancock looked after them, placing them in rows upon the floor. Handling 188 mutilated and grimy bodies in the warmth of June weather was a gruesome, depressing and difficult task, but these men, assisted by relays of miners, did this work for four days and nights until funeral services were held over the mangled remains of these unfortunate victims of the disaster. Mead, Grant and Hancock especially had a terrible undertaking, and they won the praise not only of the citizens of Hill Crest, but that of the miners also, many of the latter, though extreme radical Socialists who resented the very existence of the Force, saying, "We have no use for the Police, but we cannot help respecting its members when we see them working under such trying conditions." Thus were these gallant men winning the applause of revolutionists who hated them because they stood for law and order in the country. And I think it well to say here, after knowing the Mounted Police throughout the years of their history, that the only enemies they have had have been the elements that resented the fearless and impartial enforcement of law. Sometimes these elements were found amongst the reckless promoters and denizens of the underworld. Sometimes amongst those who would fan the embers of social discontent into a blaze that would destroy society and not infrequently in the ranks of those who would not scruple to plunder the public treasury. It has always been annoying and disconcerting to such elements to find that they could neither cajole nor frighten nor bribe these inflexible men in the uniform of scarlet and gold who stood for the administration of British law in a British country. *Noblesse oblige.* If the recruits of to-day measure up as they have been doing to the established reputation of the Force, that reputation will become increasingly one of the saving assets of Canada and the Empire.

Up in the Arctic areas during those days of war when some were on duty in France and across our own plains and mountains, the Police were battling against hostile climatic conditions that the sacredness of human life might be impressed on the inhabitants of the most remote regions under the flag. And sometimes their equipment was not very ample. One laughs when he sees attacks made upon Mounted Police expenditure. A country vaster than several European Kingdoms cannot be kept in peace and quietness for a trifle. If the Mounted Police were withdrawn and lawlessness was allowed to run riot in the country, people would soon realize that it is not the proper administration of law, but the absence of it which bankrupts a country. As a matter of fact, as this story has shown again and again, these men of the Police were constantly practising economies in regard to the very necessaries of life in case they should be considered as asking for too much. Here, for instance, in that war year when millions were being poured out elsewhere, we find Superintendent Demers, who with his men had to patrol the dangerous northern coasts in the Hudson's Bay region where wrecks and drownings are frequent, asking apologetically for six life-belts, as "patrols by water have to be made without any precaution against possible accident." We hope he got them. These men were not playing on a mill-pond, but were fighting storms in the fields of ice and reefs with bull walrus thrown in as an extra peril to guard against.

War echoes are heard during that period, but for the most part alien enemies soon recognized the wisdom of pursuing their work quietly, and in such cases they were not molested. And amidst it all we find the record of quiet heroisms as these Mounted Policemen who were not allowed to go to the Front pursued the steady round of their duty at home. Here, for instance, in 1915 we find Superintendent West, who was in charge at Battleford on the Saskatchewan, telling us of a piece of work whose fine courageous quality those who know the country can especially appreciate. West says, "Typhoid fever broke out amongst the Indians on the Island Lake Reserve and Constable Rose was sent from here to see that quarantine was enforced." Typhoid is a serious business in the dry season, and the constable would have done his regular duty if he had just put the place under quarantine and kept anyone from going or coming. But that was not the police way, and so Rose went beyond his duty. West goes on, "One man, Patrice Dumont, a half-breed, living close to the reserve, fell ill, as did the members of his family. Dumont, who was the sole support of the family, died. The rest of the family became hysterical and Rose had to be there continually. He dressed the body of Dumont for burial and made a coffin fastened with wooden pegs in the absence of nails, and as the flies were bad he buried the body next day with the help of some Indians. The circumstances under which Constable Rose worked were most trying, as he had to sleep in the same room with the dead man, while Dumont's children kept crying and clinging round his neck all night." The children, half-crazed with grief and delirium, recognized that the big policeman was a friend and very human in his practical sympathy.

It is evident that the Dominion Government feared that at one time the whole Mounted Police Force, if allowed, would have enlisted for service overseas unless their attention was very specially called to the vital necessity for their presence at home. Accordingly, in 1916, when many of the Force were renewing the efforts to go overseas, the Premier of Canada, Hon. Sir Robert L. Borden, than whom there was no one who understood the world situation better, sent the following special communication to the Mounted Police Force, "The Prime Minister desires to express to officers, non-commissioned officers and constables his very deep appreciation of the patriotic and devoted service which they have rendered, and of the faithful and efficient manner in which they are performing their important duties.

"He fully realizes the great desire of the members of the Force to enlist for overseas service, and he is aware that practically the whole Force would offer their services at the Front if permission could be given. This patriotic spirit is entirely commendable; but all members of the Force must remember that the service they are now rendering to the Dominion and to the Empire is not less important than that which they would perform if serving at the Front. Further, it is a service which can only be efficiently performed by a force which has been trained in the discharge of the duties it is called upon to undertake. For these reasons the Prime Minister has found himself unable to consent to the retirement from the Force of many officers and men who have asked that permission for the purpose of enlistment." Sir Robert is especially wise when he mentions how only the trained men of the Mounted Police could do certain duties. Men with less tact, firmness, fairness and discipline would have had the whole country in a turmoil a dozen times over during these recent decades. For during this period the West has been seething with an inrushing tide of polyglot people who have been naturally disposed to consider that the liberty of a new land gave them unrestrained licence to do what they pleased. Under proper oversight they have found their feet without losing their heads.

That year, 1916, Commissioner Perry reported that the Mounted Police had subscribed $30,000 to the Canadian Patriotic Fund. This later reached $50,000.00. These men were serving on a small wage, but if they could not get away to the Front they were going to help the cause to the limit and when the opportunity would be given they would show their readiness to go themselves wherever needed.

That year also the Commissioner reported the death of Assistant Commissioner A. E. R. Cuthbert, to be followed a few years later by the sudden demise of one of his successors, Assistant Commissioner W. H. Routledge. Both had given splendid service. Cuthbert had been thirty-one years with the Force and had served with distinction in South Africa. Routledge had served in all parts of the West, including the Yukon. He was a master of detail and system, and did work of unique value in arranging the reports and working out orderly methods in the use of documents. In the same report the Commissioner expressed the regret of himself and the Force at the retirement of Mr. Lawrence Fortescue, who had joined the corps at the very beginning, had made the trek to the West and then was recalled to Ottawa to assist with the work of the Department there. At the time of his retirement he was Comptroller of the Force. The corps has been fortunate in its Comptrollers, the men who are official administrative heads and have the general oversight of expenditures. Lieut.-Colonel Frederick White, who for long and faithful service was given the C.M.G., was the first Comptroller—a man of great ability and indefatigable disposition. The present popular and able Comptroller is Mr. A. A. McLean, a sturdy Highland type from Prince Edward Island, who was a prominent lawyer and legislator for years. Much of the steady frictionless movement of the whole department depends on the administrative talent of the Comptroller.

When we have heard arm-chair critics attack police expenditure, we have thought not only of the practice of economy as already indicated in the case of reports from officers at many points, but of the amount saved to Canada by the devoted and self-sacrificing efforts of these men to head off lawless movements and to create in the remotest points of the country a wholesome respect for constituted authority.

There were many wonderful patrols in the Arctic circle, but those which had to do with the detection of crime or the unravelling of mysteries connected with the disappearance of explorers and traders or others naturally attracted most attention. There were not many of these particular patrols, for the Esquimaux were not by any means murderously inclined. The cases investigated showed that they had been moved by provocation.

One of these cases resulted in the famous Bathurst Inlet patrol. In 1911 two men, Mr. H. V. Radford, an American, and Mr. T. G. Street, a Canadian, went on an exploring and specimen collecting journey into the North. They reached Bathurst Inlet in 1912, having wintered at Schultz Lake. In May, 1913, that well-known northern patrol man, Sergeant W. G. Edgenton, of the Mounted Police, who was in command of the post at Fullerton, reported that a rumour had come to him through Eskimo that Radford and Street had been killed by the Eskimos in June, 1912. A few days later one of the Eskimos, by name Akulack, who had travelled part of the way with the explorers, came to Chesterfield Inlet and gave Mr. H. H. Hall, the Hudson's Bay Company officer there, an account of what he had heard. It appeared that the wife of one of the Eskimos who was travelling with the explorers had fallen on the ice and was seriously hurt. So the Eskimo refused quite properly to leave her in that condition, upon which Radford tried to enforce obedience by repeatedly striking the Eskimo till a general row started and the two explorers, or whatever they were, suffered death. It took three years or so to get at the facts, with the final decision that, the murder having been traced to the perpetrators, the whole evidence showed that it was a case where the Eskimo had acted in self-defence and that, while in imminent fear of being killed by the white men, they had taken the lives of the latter. But the Mounted Police had to travel many a long and dangerous mile through many a weary month before these facts were discovered. We give an outline of the process in the following pages.

Superintendents Starnes and Demers recommended that an expedition be equipped for two or three years and sent out to investigate, but the wrecks of schooners and other untoward incidents interfered. But in July, 1914, over two years from the date of the alleged crime, Inspector W. J. Beyts, an officer of much experience in the North, left on a Government schooner from Halifax with a sergeant and two constables. The weather was so bad that they did not reach the Hudson's Bay Coast till it was too late to establish a post at Baker Lake. The next year, after enormous difficulties, he succeeded in planting the post, but the winter of 1915-16 was such that two brave attempts to get to Bathurst Inlet failed. Game on which they had to rely for dog-feed was so scarce that supply could not be secured. Dogs died by the score also amongst the Eskimo that year, and Beyts reports one case where there were only six dogs amongst ten families, and another case where the sleigh was being pulled by one man, two women and a dog. In the summer of 1916 Beyts, by previous arrangement, returned to headquarters, and his place was taken by Inspector F. H. French, who arrived at Baker Lake in September. This was more than four years after the murder, but the Police never let go their hold once they started on a case.

Commissioner Perry's instructions to Inspector French were these: "It will be your duty to get in touch at the earliest possible moment with the tribes said to be responsible for the deaths. You will make inquiries and take such statutory declarations as may seem necessary in order to obtain a full and accurate account of the occurrence. From information received, it is assumed that there was provocation. If this is found to be the case, it is not the intention of the Government to proceed with prosecution. If, however, there was found to be no provocation, the Government will consider what further action is to be taken."

French was "to the manner born" in the Police service. He was a son of that gallant officer, Inspector "Jack" French, leader of "French's Scouts" in the second Rebellion, who was killed by a half-breed sniper after having driven Riel's men from their coverts in one section of the fight at Batoche. And he was also the nephew of Colonel Sir George French, the first Commissioner of Mounted

Police after their organization, although Colonel Osborne Smith, as already stated, was Commissioner for the purpose of swearing in the men.

And this younger French was evidently a "chip of the old block," because he does not contemplate failure. In January, 1917, he wrote: "I hope to make a successful trip, commencing in March next," but he knows it will be a fight against the elements and against want, for he adds: "my only difficulty will be the inevitable dog-feed question, which rises at every point where a man moves in this country." He will have to depend on game and game is always uncertain.

French was fortunate in his party having with him Sergt.-Major T. B. Caulkin (later Inspector), a most reliable and persevering man who knew the Eskimo country, and he had also police natives, Joe and "Bye and Bye," with two other natives to assist. They were absent from their base at Baker Lake about ten months of almost incessant travel amongst the Eskimo, to whom on all occasions of meeting French explained the law of the country in relation to human life and property. In that regard it was a kind of missionary tour and did lasting good.

Getting into contact with the Eskimo tribe at Bathurst Inlet, French secured many statutory declarations which established beyond all doubt that two Eskimos who were known to be quiet and inoffensive men, had been goaded by ill-treatment into turning on their tormentors and putting an end to them. French had fulfilled his mission and did not consider it necessary to arrest these men. But the patrol had impressed upon these "ends of the earth" the lessons desired.

French's return was attended by great hardship. Game was scarce and wild. So food for both men and dogs ran out again and again. Dogs were shot as they became exhausted and fed to the other dogs. Deerskins were chopped up and made into soup. Fuel oil became exhausted and sleds had to be burned. As one of the party, French himself said, "It looked like their last patrol," but they struck some deer and got food, which toned them and their dogs up so that "they made the grade." But it was a close call and every member of the party deserved the eulogy expressed by French in which all who know the history include as chief the Inspector himself. He had done good service throughout the years, but the Bathurst Inlet patrol will always remain as an outstanding mark to his credit.

Similarly will the Bear Lake patrol go to the credit of Inspector C. D. La Nauze, who also was fortunate in having splendid support from his men. The occasion of the Patrol was the disappearance of two priests, Fathers Rouvier and Le Roux, who in 1913 had left Fort Norman on the Mackenzie River for a two years' absence in establishing missions amongst the Eskimo of the far North. When the two years were well on and no news had been received from them, their friends began to get anxious, and of course appeal was made to the Mounted Police, who were expected to unravel all mysteries and solve all perplexing problems. And it is to their credit that they never turned a deaf ear to such appeals. It took nearly two years and a half to get the solution of the mystery. There were others in the patrol when it started, but Inspector La Nauze, Constable Wight, Special Native Constable Ilavinik and Corporal W. V. Bruce were those who were in at the end when two Eskimo men, Sinninsiak and Uluksak, were arrested by them at Coronation Gulf as the self-confessed murderers of the two priests. Leaving Great Bear Lake in April, 1916, La Nauze, Wight and Ilavinik reached Coronation Gulf a month later and here they met Corporal Bruce, who had been sent out by Inspector Phillips from Herschell Island to gather information that would help to locate the priests, if alive, and if they were not found to discover the cause of their disappearance. Bruce knew the whole region and knew many of the Eskimos personally. Without exciting their suspicion he had found amongst them and purchased several articles of priests' wear which strongly indicated that the priests had perished. Ilavinik proved a treasure. The party found two of the explorer Steffanson's men and they had heard of Ilavinik, so that the way became easier. Finally La Nauze and Ilavinik began to talk to the people in their igloos, and inquire if any white men had been that way at any time. They said Yes, and then La Nauze sat back and let Ilavinik do the talking. In a little while he turned, trembling with the excitement of it, to the Inspector and said, "I have got on the track. These men know who murdered the priests and they are very, very sorry that any of the Eskimos should have done it." This led very soon to the arrest of Sinnisiak, who was said to be the chief instigator of the crime, his companion being of a milder type. After examination of the prisoner and witnesses, the Inspector formally committed Sinnisiak for trial by a competent court. Then La Nauze left the prisoner in charge of Constable Bruce, while he, accompanied by Constable Wight and a bright young Eskimo "Patsy" who was attached to the Canadian Arctic Expedition, went to South Victoria Land and arrested Uluksak. He was of a gentler type. Sinnisiak had rather demurred to being arrested and had indicated his power to make medicine that would sink the white man's ship if they tried to take him away. But Uluksak came forward at once and gave himself up. La Nauze asked him if he knew what they had come for and the Eskimo said, "Yes, to kill me by striking me on the head as the other white men did." He was formally arrested by Wight and committed for trial by the Inspector. From the evidence it seemed clear that the priests in their eagerness to get ahead had attempted to force the two men to go along with them. Uluksak said one of them put his hand on the Eskimo's mouth and would not let him say anything. Generally speaking the priests showed their lack of understanding of the Eskimo nature and fell victims to their own impetuosity in dealing with them.

The prisoners were brought all the way to Edmonton and then to Calgary, where they were finally tried. They seemed to be as guileless and simple as children, and gave absolutely no trouble from the day they were arrested. They became much attached to their captors and cried when they had to leave them. But they had told their story with clearness, and the jury brought in a verdict of "Guilty with the strongest recommendation to mercy a jury can make." They were sentenced to be hanged, but this was commuted to imprisonment for life, and they were finally sent back amongst their own people in the far North. It was felt that justice had been vindicated and that their story to their own people would be of great value to prevent any such event occurring again. These two patrols of French and La Nauze, along with a recent arrest of an Eskimo in another part of the Arctic Circle by Sergeant Douglas, revealed again to the world that the long arm of the Mounted Police was unavoidable once anyone had transgressed laws in regard to human welfare. And thus are the men of this famous corps patrolling the vast white North in all directions at the time of this writing.

That such patrolling is excessively difficult and dangerous may be gathered from such a report as that sent in by Inspector J. W.

Phillips, who was in command of the Herschell Island detachment in 1918. He, with Constables Cornelius and Doak, was wrecked 8 miles off Herschell Island, when their whale boat was crushed to pieces in the ice. They had to jump on the floating ice. The cakes were small and were churning round and up-ending. At times the piece on which one would be standing would up-end and then it was a case of jumping or being crushed to death. Finally they reached the shore ice. Then they started for Herschell Island, but found great cracks or leads in the ice too wide to cross. They changed their course and made for the nearest land. They found the leads narrower. By joining their belts and suspenders together a line was made. One of them would swim the lead and then assist the others over by this life-line. They crossed over more than a score of leads in this way before reaching the nearest land. We read this over and then think of men in comfortable armchairs finding fault with police expenditure.

But the remaining part of the report in this connection is still more amazing. Let me quote it. "The time spent by us from the wrecking of the boat on the ice to our reaching the land was ten hours. A gale from the north-east had been blowing all the time and in our soaking wet condition we suffered severely from the cold." One would imagine they would when he reads on. Phillips says, "The only clothing we wore at this time was our under garments, trousers and muckluks. Our Artiggies we threw away, as we found they hampered us too much when getting across the leads. Herschell Island post was still 12 miles away. We started to walk it. After travelling about a mile I noticed that Constable Doak was delirious. Constable Cornelius and I helped him to walk, but owing to cramps in the legs we could not manage. Constable Cornelius at this stage offered to go to Herschell Island for assistance, food and matches, and I permitted him to go. After he left I built a windbreak of driftwood. Constable Doak and I crawled into it. Here we remained till 11 p.m. the following day. Then we were rescued by a whale boat and taken to Herschell Island. We kept a sharp look out for Constable Cornelius, but saw nothing of him, and on arrival found he had not reached the post. I at once started out Constable Brockie and two natives with a whale boat, and found him on a sand-spit 10 miles away. He was brought in safely. I am sorry to say that at the present time (the day after the event) the two constables and myself are laid up with swollen feet and legs due to exposure." They must have had tremendous endurance to get through at all. And one gathers that the Inspector is not thinking of his own and the Constable's personal losses and exposure, but is rather concerned that some government property had to be noted as missing in the wreck. For he adds: "I must say that I am exceedingly sorry to have to give you a report of this nature, but I think you will agree that this occurred under circumstances over which I had no control. I am happy to be able to report no loss of life. As soon as I am able to send a patrol to the vicinity of the wreck I will do so, with the idea that there may be some government stores blown up on the coast." But most of us are willing to declare our readiness to let government stores go so long as men of this stamp are saved to continue their contribution to the great traditions of a corps that has done so much for Canada and the Empire.

Commissioner Perry's report for 1920 has just come to hand and is specially notable because it is the first presented under the new name of the Royal Canadian Mounted Police, and therefore the first since the jurisdiction of the Force was extended to all parts of Canada. It relates the change of name, the absorption of the Dominion Police by the Mounted Police Force, and removal of headquarters from Regina to Ottawa, all of which changes were made in pursuance of the policy adopted by the Government to have one Federal Force controlled by a single head and exercising authority in every part of Canada. A section of the amendment of the Mounted Police Act may be quoted here. It says, "Every member of the Force shall be a constable in every part of Canada for the purpose of carrying out the criminal and other laws of Canada and in the North-West Territories, and the Yukon Territory for carrying out any laws and ordinances in force therein." This legislation, as already intimated, involved the absorption of the Dominion Police, which in various forms had existed in older Canada from as far back as 1839. Its duties were mainly concerned with the protection of public buildings, though also with the general preservation of law and order. This Dominion Police Force came into more special prominence under the Commissionership of Colonel Sir Percy Sherwood, who was knighted for his services and under whom the Force grew to the number of some 150 men, who were scattered over Canada singly or in small groups guarding buildings, Navy yards and enforcing specific laws, as well as engaging in effective secret service work in relation to enemy aliens in war-time. After a long and highly creditable career in this service, Sir Percy Sherwood retired on account of ill-health in 1919.

The absorption of the Dominion Police into the Mounted Police was not free from difficulty, as the organizations differed fundamentally, the former being on the lines of a civil municipal force, while the latter was on military lines and engagement was for a fixed term. However, conditions of engagement were offered to the members of the Dominion Police and practically all of them enlisted in the Mounted Police, their service already given in their own Force to count towards pension under Mounted Police regulations.

The Royal Canadian Mounted Police is now the sole federal Force, and is under Commissioner Perry, subject of course to the Minister of the Dominion Government in whose department it comes, that minister at present being the Hon. James A. Calder, President of the Council. The duties of the Force may be summarized as follows:

(A) The enforcement, or assistance in enforcement, of all laws where the Government of Canada is directly interested or responsible.
(B) The protection of public buildings of the Dominion.
(C) The protection of Navy yards.
(D) The Intelligence Service.
(E) The maintenance of law and order in all territories and Dominion parks.
(F) Maintenance of finger-print bureaus.
(G) Paroled prisoners' record.

The Commissioner says, "The Force is distributed in the way best suited to perform its many duties. It is found along the international boundary, where it aids in protecting the revenue and preventing the entrance into Canada of undesirables. It is located on or in the vicinity of Indian Reserves to maintain good order, and to aid in enforcement of the laws pertaining to our Indian population. It occupies many lonely posts in the North-West Territories and Yukon Territory, and along the Arctic and Hudson's Bay Coasts.

It is found in centres of population, and at points where industrial activities are vital to the welfare of the nation." New outposts were established in the far North: one at Port Burwell on the Hudson Straits, to act for the Department of Customs and collect duties on foreign vessels entering the waters of Hudson Bay, and the other at Tree River, on Coronation Gulf, for ordinary duty. The latter is the most remote outpost and the fact of its existence there indicates the far-flung character of the operations of this ubiquitous corps.

When the Commissioner says the force is found at centres of population he visualizes for us the fact that our modern social life has created vast cities which have eaten up the green fields and turned them into asphalt pavements. These cities become the hardest problem for the administrator of law. Into them drift the derelicts of human society, and even these are drawn down to deeper degradation by the undertow of vice and crime. More mean in their lawlessness and much less open than the dwellers in frontiers and camps, the vicious elements in cities require from the State the oversight of an adequate force of fearless men. The illegal traffic in narcotic drugs, for instance, is carried on by the most degraded and the lowest criminals of the underworld, aided and abetted too frequently by dishonourable members of honourable professions. The gambler and the "bootlegger" and the white slave dealer find their habitat in large centres of population. And no force can keep these lawless elements in check like a force free from local influences, especially when that force is the Mounted Corps which for nearly half a century has built up a reputation for a fair and fearless administration of law. The prestige of the corps that has been proof against all attempts at intimidation or bribery on the part of the lawless classes makes it a unique power for good in the cities as on the plains.

And when the Commissioner says that detachments of the Mounted Police are found at points "where industrial activities are vital to the welfare of the nation" he strikes a chord that will find grateful response from every industrious citizen, whether employer or employed, who understands that "trade is the calm health of nations." There is nothing in this world of material things more to be feared than the wanton destruction of industries that have been built up by laborious endeavour and the unstinted expenditure of energy in brain and hand. Such destruction leads to endless suffering amongst the innocent and to the business stagnation which brings calamity in its wake. To guard against these dread contingencies the Mounted Police are on hand. They have never interfered in a partisan way when strikes and lock outs are abroad, but they stand by to preserve law and order and to prevent any destruction of human life and property which might take place at the instigation of irresponsible extremists. In this difficult and ofttimes dangerous duty the men who stand for constitutional order in society will always have the support of decent intelligent citizens.

Not only in the centres of population but away up in the Arctic regions beyond the sky-line of civilization have the Mounted Police in 1920 as always been doing their duty in their usual unobtrusive but extremely effective way. Amongst the Eskimos there were several cases of murder of adults and of infanticide, every one of which was followed up by the closest investigation even though it took months of work and patrolling amidst the rigours of Polar weather to do it. In these cases of murder there seemed to be a complete absence of that malice aforethought which constitutes the essence of the crime in the eyes of the law. The cases were very few, but occasionally an infant was put out of the misery of starvation when there was no food in sight and a man who became a moral nuisance to the tribe and was therefore considered insane (a fairly good inference) was quietly removed by the unanimous vote of the community. But the Police taught a different code of ethics, followed and investigated every case until the Eskimos have begun to see things in a more humane light. It is of great interest to find that in these recent endeavours to get the Eskimos to see these matters aright the Mounted Police had the aid of the two Eskimos Sinnisiak and Uluksak who had been convicted of the murder of Fathers Le Roux and Rouvier, as already related, but who had been finally pardoned and sent back to tell their people of the sacredness of human life. In fact, Sinnisiak entered the service as a special constable and did useful work as a guide and hunter, thus showing, as Staff-Sergeant S. G. Clay said, that "his now rather long acquaintance with the Police has had its advantages." Two other Eskimos who had been tried and acquitted were also taken back by the Police to their own tribes to preach the gospel of the value of human life.

In connection with these recent Northern patrols Sergeant W. O. Douglas with Constable Eyre and two natives left Fullerton for Chesterfield to look into rumours of a murder near Baker Lake. After a difficult patrol and serious risk Douglas arrested the alleged murderer, On-aug-wak, and brought him back to the Pas in Northern Manitoba after several thousands of miles of patrol for trial. The Eskimo made a statement as to taking the lives of two men, but there were many elements to be considered, and as the prisoner is deemed entitled to all the protection that British law affords, the Police with the accused are leaving for Baker Lake by the Hudson's Bay Company steamship *Nascopie*. A court will be constituted at Chesterfield Inlet with a jury from the crew of the steamship and the dozen or more Eskimo witnesses will be on hand to tell their story. This shows how carefully the Police work is done with due regard to every one's rights, no matter what his race or colour. But whatever the outcome of the trial the moral effect on the natives will be highly beneficial.

Similarly Inspector J. W. Phillips and Sergeant A. H. Joy made a patrol from Haileybury in Northern Ontario to the Belcher Islands in the sub-Arctic, taking seventy-five days and covering nearly two thousand miles, arrested an Eskimo named Tukatauk for killing a man named Ketanshauk, but the coroner's jury were unanimous in saying that Ketanshauk was "killed for the common good and safety of the tribe." Phillips saw the force of this verdict as reasonable from the point of view of the Eskimos and was satisfied with the opportunity to give them some appropriate instruction in law and morals. One other case was followed up by Phillips at the same time with somewhat the same result.

In 1920 Staff-Sergeant S. G. Clay, Constable E. H. Cornelius and Constable J. Brockie left Herschell Island and established the most northerly outpost of the Force 65 miles east of the mouth of the Coppermine River. The isolation of this post may be judged by the fact that the nearest post office is at Fort Macpherson over 600 miles away as the crow flies and the nearest telegraph office is at Dawson, over 1,000 miles distant. Here the Union Jack flies in the Arctic breeze and here revenue is collected for the Dominion from traders and trappers who venture north in schooners to ply their occupation. Sergeant Clay and his men made constant patrols to the Coppermine, to Bernard Harbour and Victoria Land, to Bathurst

Inlet and Kent Peninsula with their dogs. The question of supplies of food for themselves and dogs was always pressing and at Fort Norman on the return journey there was such a shortage that the whole party had to go to Willow Lake for a month's fishing and hunting to lay in a safe supply. About 20 miles east of Cape Barrow this patrol found a tribe whom the police had not yet met. This gave the opportunity for more instruction, and Clay opines "that with the advent of the missionary and other aids to civilization" the wrongs done in ignorance by these people will cease.

I have already spoken of the oilfields in the Fort Norman district, to which at the time of this writing there is a rush of people who see in their own imaginations such roads to wealth that they miss seeing the dangers of the way through these remote regions. But the Mounted Police, under the general charge of Superintendent G. L. Jennings, an experienced northerner himself, have made stringent regulations as to entry into the district which will protect the foolhardy from their own folly.

And then, swinging away in our story to the old cities of the East, we find the Mounted Police at the ports of Montreal and Halifax, engaging the services of such experienced social-service workers as the Rev. John Chisholm and Mrs. Bessie Egan to meet unaccompanied women and girls who land in Canada, to see to their requirements and to attend them on board their trains, so that they may not be misled or enticed in wrong directions by the unscrupulous individuals who fatten on the wreckage of human lives. Social-service workers have always found difficulty in this work because of the brazenness and the threatening attitude of some of the evildoers, but when the stalwart men in scarlet and gold are at the call of these life-saving crews at the ports of entry to this country the harpies who prey on the innocent have to keep out of the way. A right royal task is this, also, for the old corps that has headed off more crime than any similar body in the world. And for all the work in Canada we have sketched, the total strength of the Force is about 1,700 of all ranks. There are some few people who so lack the power to sense nation-wide conditions that they gird at the expense of maintaining the corps. But men of vision know that the Mounted Police save Canada annually from moral and material losses that make expenditure upon this famous old law-and-order corps pale into insignificance by comparison.

In the past year there were many changes in the way of promotions. Amongst the names our readers who have followed the story of the Force will meet many of the men who gave such ample proof of their fitness that their moving up a step came as it has generally come in the Force, as a spontaneous recognition of merit. The promotions were as follows: Promoted Assistant Commissioners: Superintendents C. Starnes, T. A. Wroughton. Promoted Superintendents: Inspectors R. E. Tucker, J. Ritchie, A. B. Allard, T. S. Belcher, G. L. Jennings and H. M. Newson. Promoted Inspectors: Sergt.-Major Fletcher, A./Sergt.-Major Trundle, Staff-Sergeant Mellor, Staff-Sergeant Forde, Staff-Sergeant Reames, Sergeants Bruce, Thomas, Moorhead, Kemp, Frere, Eames and Fraser. And these men, who had won their spurs, are with their comrades carrying on in a way worthy of the great traditions to which they are heirs.

Thus has the story of the famous Mounted Police of Canada been brought down to date. An encyclopedia might be compiled on the subject by writing minute records and dry details, but an encyclopedia was not desired. It would be prohibitive in cost to the people in general and would be lacking in the personal element and the personal human touch so characteristic of the history of the corps. The aim was to bring the records of nearly fifty years into a single volume without squeezing the life out of them. Incidents and names could not all be included, but nothing has been omitted intentionally that bore upon the general trend of Western Canadian history with which the work of the Mounted Police is inseparably connected.

Two years ago the Dominion Government, as already intimated, extended the jurisdiction of the Force to the whole of Canada, so that in towns and cities as well as on the frontiers of the far North and West the influence of the Force will henceforth be felt, backed by its great prestige. Referring to this the Duke of Devonshire, who as Governor-General of Canada was so close a student of its history and affairs, said recently, "The Force is now taking over a wider jurisdiction and increased duties. It will carry with it a great tradition and a great name, and we who appreciate and value its work can be assured that its record will be as successful in the future as in the past."

And our gallant Prince of Wales, who captivated all Canada during his recent tour across the Dominion, graciously expressed his approval and appreciation of the Force by speaking at Regina Headquarters after inspection in the following words:

> "It is not only a real pleasure, but a great privilege to me to inspect you on parade this morning, and to visit the depôt of the Royal North-West Mounted Police, though this is by no means my first introduction to the Force, which I have seen a great deal of throughout my travels in the West, and I have been very impressed by it, particularly by the mounted escorts and guards that it has furnished for me in all the big cities.
>
> "I am interested in the history of the Force, how it was organized forty-six years ago, at a time when treaties were being made with the Indians, whereby the lands of the North-West were made available for settlement by the white people. So well has it administered justice between all parties that it has won for itself respect and the confidence of both white people and Indians, and no new country has ever been opened up with less crime and violence than this North-West Territory.
>
> "Up in the Klondike, when wild and lawless men thronged the Yukon gold diggings, life and property were as safe in the care of the Royal North-West Mounted Police as in any other part of the Dominion, and the splendid police work which they have done and continue to do in the frozen wastes of the North, under the most trying conditions of hardship and privation, is recognized and appreciated everywhere to-day.
>
> "I know that at the declaration of war, the whole Force wanted to join up, though that was naturally impossible. The first to be allowed to go were many Imperial reservists, who have always constituted a large percentage of its members. Then, by degrees, men could he spared, and served in the Canadian cavalry, infantry and other units, and I know many of the last joined men are war veterans.
>
> "I was with Sir Arthur Currie, Canadian Corps Commander, when he inspected the Royal North-West Mounted Police squadron when they arrived in France a year ago, so that the war records of the Force have been of the same high standard as its records in the past.

> "The Royal North-West Mounted Police is a splendid Force with magnificent traditions, whose fame is as wide as that of the Dominion itself.
>
> "I know the men of the Force of to-day are proving themselves worthy of those traditions and will ever uphold them."

It was appropriate that the heir apparent to the British throne should thus address the Mounted Police of Canada, for their record is part of that British tradition and British sentiment which, delicate and intangible as gossamer, but strong as steel, bind our far-flung Empire into one triumphant unity.

And now, as a fitting climax to the history of the corps at the time when it was undergoing changes that meant larger opportunities and increased usefulness in the years ahead, there comes this note in Commissioner Perry's report for 1920 just off the press:

> "On March 8 last, Sir George Perley, High Commissioner for Canada, cabled as follows:
> 'With His Majesty's approval Prince of Wales has graciously consented accept position Honorary Commandant Royal Canadian Mounted Police and His Royal Highness asks me tell you how pleased he is to be associated with Force in this way.'
> "On May 3, an Order in Council was passed making the appointment.
> "The Force has been signally honoured by His Royal Highness, and it keenly appreciates the distinction conferred upon it."

This needs no comment beyond saying that the Prince of Wales knows Canada and knows the Mounted Police record in peace and in war. The Prince, who came to the overseas Dominions to represent our beloved King, has always shown his splendid capacity for thus appreciating the service of men who have stood and will continue to stand unconquered for the Flag

> "That may float or sink o'er a shot-torn wreck,
> But will never float over a slave."

BIBLIOBAZAAR

The essential book market!

Did you know that you can get any of our titles in large print?

Did you know that we have an ever-growing collection of books in many languages?

**Order online:
www.bibliobazaar.com**

Find all of your favorite classic books!

Stay up to date with the latest government reports!

At BiblioBazaar, we aim to make knowledge more accessible by making thousands of titles available to you- *quickly and affordably*.

Contact us:
BiblioBazaar
PO Box 21206
Charleston, SC 29413

LaVergne, TN USA
20 September 2010
197809LV00001B/13/P